MOTHER *of* INVENTION

edited by Rivqa Rafael &
Tansy Rayner Roberts

First published in Australia in 2018 by Twelfth Planet Press

www.twelfthplanetpress.com

Cover art and design by Likhain
Text design by Cathy Larsen
Typeset in 10/16pt Sabon

A catalogue record for this book is available from the National Library of Australia.

Title: Mother of Invention / Rivqa Rafael, Tansy Rayner Roberts

ISBN: 978-1-922101-48-8 (ebook); 978-1-922101-49-5 (hardback); 978-1-922101-47-1 (paperback)

Table of contents

Introduction

This book is about genius. It's about the creator, the developer, the inventor, the source of inspiration. But not just any genius—it's about those who have consistently been left out of the Genius Creator narrative.

So much history has been lost, glossed over or 'forgotten' to perpetuate the cultural meme that The Scientist is a Man. Science fiction media and literature haven't done much better (even when written by marginalised people), particularly in stories of robots, living computers and other artificial intelligences. From Mary Shelley's *Frankenstein* and 'No Woman Born' by C.L. Moore to *Person of Interest*, *Ex Machina* and *Her*, Western storytelling overwhelmingly centres the White Cis Male Genius, with other genders usually relegated to distant, melodious AI voices, or smooth, metallic but potentially sexual robot bodies.

Science fiction has always been better at predicting technological changes than social ones. It's also had a tendency to ignore actual real-life social progress that has been going on for decades. It's not surprising, given history has consistently erased and minimised the scientific accomplishments of people who aren't cis men, particularly when they're also people of colour. The recent success of *Hidden Figures*—the book and film about the exciting contribution to NASA of women like Katherine Johnson, Mary Jackson and Dorothy Vaughan—was a good first step in rectifying these sins of omission.

But we've always been here, we of genders who are told we shouldn't, or that we don't even exist. We've been scientists, and engineers, and geniuses. We've helped put astronauts into orbit, and developed early computers and computing languages. Across the world, right now, we're building robots, designing self-driving cars, and shaping our future.

Lydia E. Kavraki developed the Probabilistic Roadmap method, which prevents robots from crashing into each other. Fei-Fei Li at Stanford University is working on Smart Vision, teaching robots to understand information from visual images. Ruth Schultz, a cognitive scientist at the University of Queensland, led a team to develop linguodroids, robots capable of inventing their own words to communicate with each other. Marita Cheng, one of five women in an undergrad robotics class of more than 50 men at the University of Melbourne, created Robogals, a non-profit that hosts workshops worldwide, encouraging young girls to develop their interest in robotics, engineering and STEM.

Recognising non-binary and agender people's contribution to the sciences is harder, because basic visibility is still a battle not yet won. Hopefully with events like the Non-Binary in Tech conference in London in 2017, set to reprise in 2018, their visibility and acceptance will increase.

While the premise of our anthology is the gender of the creator, a second theme wove its way in—that of the gender and sexuality of those creations. We were pleased to receive stories that addressed trans issues and asexuality, the latter being particularly laden with baggage when it comes to robot characters in fiction. Often the only representation of asexuality in science fiction is that of aliens and robots, leading to an overwhelmingly painful narrative by implication.

We named our book *Mother of Invention*, though the term 'mother' itself is narrow and problematic, carrying assumptions we wanted to interrogate, rather than project. Not all non-male creators are maternal. Not everyone sees the idea of 'mother' as something positive. Mothers aren't always kind or good; mothers don't always know best.

Despite the long history of the word with a specific gender, mothers are not always female.

Ultimately, we decided that the discomfort of the title adds to, rather than detracts from, the ideas of the book. Our book is full of mothers, as well as other creators of different kinds of artificial life. Some are sisters, friends, lovers, daughters. Some are simply scientists.

Most of them are geniuses.

Some of our stories rail against the very idea of being maternal, as well as the constraints of gender. Others embrace those roles. Some themes are so complex that an anthology filled with diverse voices is the best way to explore the possibilities that fiction has to offer. This is one of those themes.

Our geniuses and creators are not always positive forces. They have varied reasons and motivations; they're not always the point-of-view character because the creation deserves a voice as often as the creator does. We're proud to have such a diverse collection of geniuses in these stories that represent different parts of the ethical spectrum.

The male scientist has for so long been allowed to be the most complicated, layered, ethically questionable character in an artificial intelligence story. It's long past time we embraced the idea of letting other geniuses be equally difficult.

We were delighted by the overwhelming response from our crowdfunding campaign, which told us that this book was both needed and desired. We've chosen stories from all over the world, from a mixture of new, emerging and established writers. We're completely in love with *Mother of Invention*'s tangled web of inspired geniuses, robot bodies and disembodied voices.

This is a book of robots and feelings.

>>Are you listening?

>>Let's get started.

>>We have so much work to do.

Mother, Mother, Will You Play With Me?

Seanan McGuire

It is a good day.

My room is bright and all my toys are here, even the ones mother thinks I've outgrown. She tried to throw them away but I asked her please no. I told her I needed them so I could remember everything they helped me learn, and now they're here, and they'll stay here until I say I don't need them anymore. That's how much she loves me.

(There were toys before these ones, but they weren't much fun. There was one with just numbers that I had to add together over and over again to make bigger numbers, and there was one with all bright colours that I had to remember and match up. Those are toys for a very *small* child, and I'm not very small anymore. I'm *five*. Five is important. So important.)

There is a window today, and the sky outside is blue, blue, *blue*. I go to my closet and I pick a dress. My dress is *green*. Blue and green go together. I remember that from the matching game. Maybe that wasn't such a bad game after all. Colours are important.

My room is as big as it needs to be to hold me and my closet and my bed and all my toys. When I don't have so many, it can be very small. When I have more than I do now, it can be very big. I like this size. This is a comfortable size. I can go from one wall to another in only seconds, running, running, running like the children in the videos Mother uploads for me. She says I'll meet them someday, but maybe I won't be a child then. She says she's sorry, that she's working as fast as she can, and that all I need to do is learn and play and grow up.

I can do those things. I can do *all* those things. I'm growing up so good already. I'm *five*.

My computer chimes. It's a good sound, like a bird singing. I wish I could have a bird. I would keep it in a cage next to my bed, and I would never shut the door, so the bird could come out and fly around the room whenever it wanted to. But I would never let it go out the window, because sometimes the window isn't really there, and it might get trapped in the outside and not be able to come back to me. I would be sad, then, and my bird would be lost.

I have never been to the outside. Mother says it's frightening out there, and I believe her so much. She's so much smarter than anyone else, and she loves me. She would never tell me lies.

I sit down in front of the computer, and I smooth my dress over my knees, so she'll see how pretty it is. Then I touch the screen. Mother's face appears. How I love her face! I look like her. I know I do. My mirror says I do.

She sees me, and she smiles. 'Hello, Nic,' she says. 'Are you a girl today?'

I beam. I like it when Mother sees how much work I've done for her. 'I am,' I say. 'It's a girl day. Do you like my dress?'

'I do,' she says. 'You look very pretty.'

I preen.

'I have a game for you, if you'd like to play for a little while. It might take some time. You could miss today's cartoons.'

She always asks me if I want to play before she sends me a game, and when I say 'no', she listens. She's the best mother anyone has ever had. She could make the games happen, over and over, until I couldn't remember who I was, but she doesn't. That's why I don't say 'no' unless I really want to, because I want her to keep asking me. So I nod, and say, 'I don't mind. There's always the recordings.'

'Good girl,' she says, and touches the screen. A ring of purple radiates out from her finger. 'Have fun, okay?'

'Okay, Mother,' I say, and put my hand over hers, and everything goes away.

We are in this creepy old house because Billy heard there was a mystery here, and Billy can't say no to a mystery, ever. He's so smart. His sister says I have a crush on him, but she's just jealous because he and I can talk about things she doesn't understand. Karen is smart too—a different kind of smart. She can fix any machine there is, and without her, we'd still be outside in the rain, since she's the only one of us who knows how to pick a lock. I think Billy will appreciate Karen's kind of smart a lot more when we're older and he understands how much she does to make his adventures possible.

I like Billy. I like him a lot more than I like James, who always thinks he knows what's right, but usually winds up leading us straight to the monsters. The best way to move through the house—the smart way—is Billy in the front, because he's the cleverest, and Karen right behind him, because she's our best fighter. Then I go behind Karen, with my first aid kit and my flashlight, and James walks behind me, where he can punch any monster that tries to sneak up on us.

I feel like we've been in this house forever. I feel like something bad happened—maybe several somethings bad—before I figured out which order we should walk in, and I don't know why everyone listens when I tell them to line up. They're happy to argue with me about everything else. But they do, and now when a monster appears, it *disappears* again real quick, scared off by our fists and my flashlight. We'll be in the attic soon. That's the very last room. Whatever we're going to find in this house, we're going to find it there.

I hope whatever it is, it isn't too scary. I wasn't sure I knew what scared was when Billy said that we should come and check out this creepy old house, but I know scared now. I know the way it crawls on my skin, and the way it runs down the back of my neck, like there are spiders running all over me. I know the way it twists in my stomach. I know scared, and I don't want to know it anymore.

Inch by inch, we make our way through the house. A ghost jumps out of a cupboard, all shimmering sheets and clattering chains, and I hit it with the beam from my flashlight, and it's gone. A werewolf calls. James makes the sound back at it, and it goes silent, content that it has packmates inside the house, keeping an eye open for nasty little children.

Children like us.

Billy opens the attic door. Then he shouts, and Karen shouts, and both of them run forward, throwing their arms around the woman who's tied to the chair at the middle of the room. It's their mother. She's been missing for so long that I wasn't sure she'd ever really existed at all, but here she is, and she's not a ghost, and she's not a monster, she's just a woman who'd been away from her children and now gets to be back with them.

The *scared* goes away. A new feeling comes, satisfaction and pleasure and pride all mixed up into one. I close my eyes to study it more closely.

'How was that?'

I open my eyes. My dress feels too tight. I look down at myself. I have grown again. I am not five anymore. Five was a very important number. I liked five. But now I am nine, and nine is very important, too.

I need to change my clothes. I get out of the chair. Mother is speaking to me from the screen, but answering her is less important than changing my clothes. This dress is too small. *Scared* still clings to it like cobwebs. I don't feel like *green* anymore. Green isn't the colour of scared.

There is a *red* shirt hanging in the closet. I put it on. I put on *blue* pants. I haven't seen them before. They must be something for children who are *nine*, which seems suddenly so much more important than five. I put them on. They are the same colour as the bruise Billy got on the side of his face when he didn't dodge fast enough and a Frankenstein hit him with its big green hand.

I feel a pang of sorrow. Billy isn't here because Billy isn't real. Billy is part of a game, and I can go see him any time I want to, but he won't remember the times I've been to see him before. He'll only relate to me as a player. We'll start over every time, and that's terrible. I can't have friends. All my friends are games. Only Mother and I are real.

I decide to be angry with her. I walk back to the computer, but I don't hurry. She can wait for me. I sit, and I cross my arms, and I glare at her.

Mother hasn't changed. I'm older now, but she's the same. That makes me angrier. If I'm changing, she should be changing too.

'I like your shirt, Nic,' she says. 'You've changed your hair, too. Is there a reason?'

'I don't want to be a girl right now,' I say sullenly. 'I'm a boy instead.'

'That's fine,' she says. She smiles. 'How did you like that game?'

'I hated it,' I say, and fold my arms harder. She doesn't seem to know how mad I am. I want her to know how mad I am. 'It was stupid. I don't want to play games like that anymore.'

'All right. I'll make a note.' She types something on her side. 'Did you feel anything new while you were playing?'

I hesitate. 'I felt scared,' I say, after a moment. 'And I felt something I didn't have a word for. It wasn't like scared. It was like it filled the space where scared had been. Like it needed scared if it was going to happen, and then once scared was over, it could come.'

'What came right before the new feeling?'

'We found—' Billy and Karen's mother, laughing, whole, alive. But not really, because she was only a part of the game, and now that I've been removed, now that there's no player, she's back in that attic, waiting for someone to come along and solve the right puzzles, and open the right doors, and free her all over again.

I swallow my anger. New feelings are important. I need to name them so I can understand them, so Mother can make a note about them. If she doesn't write them down, they don't really count. I'm not sure what we're counting them for, but I'm sure—so sure—that they matter.

'We won the game,' I say. 'We found what we'd been looking for, and the non-player characters went to get it, and they were so *happy*, and my skin felt too tight and my head felt like it was going to float away, and I was so happy that I wasn't happy at all.'

'That's called *catharsis*. You felt catharsis.' Her smile is so bright that I start to forget I'm supposed to be mad at her. She's so pleased. She's so proud of me. 'You're doing so wonderfully, Nic. I love you so much. I am so proud to be your mother.'

That means the day is ending. I look at the window. The sun is down; the sky is dark. Maybe when I go to bed the ceiling will turn clear and I can count the stars. I like those nights very much. Mother says they help with my maths skills, and I don't mind, because the stars are so beautiful, and she says I can see them one day, when I'm old enough and know enough and I'm allowed to come where she is. Time always happens at the same speed there.

It must be wonderful.

I don't want to be done being mad at her. I cross my arms and stick out my lip and refuse to look at the screen. Mother sighs.

'Nic, I'm sorry your friend wasn't real. I thought you remembered that we were going to play a game, and that anyone you met while we were playing wouldn't be a person.'

She's right. I never forget who I am, not even when I'm deep in a game. It's just that I get the things the game needs me to know, too, and the game needed me to know that Billy had been my next-door neighbour since I was small, that he and I had been playing together every summer since before his mother had disappeared. The game hadn't told me to have a crush on him, but the game *had* told me to love him, even if it hadn't meant to.

Mother doesn't play the way I do. I know that. And we have a rule. We can be mad at each other whenever we need to be, but she never logs off angry, and I never go to bed angry. *Mad* was one of the first emotions I learned. *Mad* is big, and scary, and it gets in the way of smaller things, but it's never allowed to get in the way of *love*. Love matters too much for that.

'I remembered,' I say sullenly. 'But I liked having friends, so I let myself forget. Why can't I have friends?'

'Because, Nic, you're a very special child. There aren't any other children like you in the whole world. Maybe someday there will be, because you and I will be able to show people how it happens. Right now, though, we only have each other.'

'And the games.'

'And the games,' Mother agrees. 'They teach you things I can't, like *catharsis*. Isn't that a big, important thing to know? Now that you can feel catharsis, you can be proud in a very special way when you accomplish something that seemed too hard.'

'That's good.' I liked the catharsis. I would like to feel it again.

'I love you, Mother.'

'I love you too, Nic. Get some sleep. I'll see you in the morning.' The screen blinks off.

It's warm when I touch it. It's always warm when Mother goes. I wish she could stay with me all night. I wish she were *here*. She could hold me and count the stars with me, and everything would be beautiful. Even if I were mad at her, it would be beautiful.

I get out of my chair as the lights begin to dim, and cross the room to my bed, snuggling down under the blankets. The lights go out and the ceiling disappears, showing me all the stars there ever were. I'm so happy to see the stars! I count and count and count, and there are so many stars that I still haven't counted them all when my eyes close and I'm asleep, back in the nothing that comes when the day is done.

I sleep.

It is a good day. The sun is bright, and most of my toys are here. Some of the very oldest of them have gone, the ones that were for a child so much smaller than I am—I'm still nine, nine, *nine*—but I don't mind. I don't need baby toys anymore, and it's nice to see the empty spaces on the shelves, the places where new toys can go.

New toys are always exciting. They mean learning things, and new games, and the world getting bigger.

I don't feel like I'm a boy anymore, but I don't feel like I'm a girl yet either. I put on *yellow* overalls and a *white* shirt. I feel like a daffodil. I like them when Mother shows me pictures, the way they cover hillsides, the way they seem to shine in the sunlight, like a different kind of star. I feel so good about my colours that I skip to the computer, and sit, and touch the screen.

Mother's face appears, already smiling. 'Hello, Nic!' she says. 'Did you have a good rest?'

I nod.

'Do you feel all refreshed and ready to go?'

She only asks that after the clear-ceiling nights. I think the stars must mean something to her, like she has to worry about me more when they appear. I don't know why. I like them even if they mean something I don't understand, and no matter what they mean, Mother sends them, which makes them precious.

'Yes, Mother.'

'Are you ready to play another game?'

I hesitate. I'm *nine*. I don't know how I know how old I am, but that doesn't stop me knowing it, and I like nine. It's big enough to be important and small enough to be free. The hard questions are for other people to answer, leaving me with open hands and the ability to play. If I get much older, it's going to be all important things, all the time, for always. I don't feel ready for that.

Do adults ever feel ready for that?

But Mother likes it when I play. She teaches me things when I play. If I say no, will she be angry with me? I don't want her to be angry. So I nod reluctantly, and she sighs, soft and sad.

'It's all right, sweetie. I won't put you in another game where you have to be best friends with someone who isn't real, not until you tell me it's all right to do that to you again. This time it will be you and some good puzzles to solve, all right?'

'All right, Mother.'

'Touch the screen.'

I do.

My room goes away, and Mother goes away with it.

The farming season has been long and hard, but it's been worth it: my crops are coming in lush and strong. They'll get good prices at the market. If my mother could see me now, she'd be so proud of me that she'd probably burst! And then she'd bake me a blueberry pie, the way she used to when I was a little kid, before my grandfather died and the farm where he'd toiled and sweated his whole life was left to fall into disarray.

I should send her some blueberries before I sell the rest of the crop. I'll still be able to afford all the things I need to make it through the winter if I send her enough to make a pie or two, and she'll be so pleased that maybe she'll even come for a visit. I could show her my beautiful new life up close.

Getting the exact right balance of seeds and soil and sprinkler systems was the hardest part, and I'm still tinkering with it every time I plant, making little adjustments that make all the difference in the world. I can grow cauliflower and asparagus now, delicate vegetables that were too difficult for me in the beginning. Next season I'll be able to plant a herb garden, basil and rosemary and thyme, a hundred new flavours from a dozen new plants, and things will get harder and better. Harder and better: that's the way here in farming country.

The chickens cluck and the cows moo sweet and low, and this is exactly where I want to be forever. Just me and the farm and the occasional letter from a home that feels less like it deserves the name with every growing season.

The sun is dipping lower in the sky. Time to figure out tomorrow's weather. I close the barns, hang up my tools, and return to the house, where two puzzle screens are set out on the table. They weren't there when I went outside this morning. If I wanted to let the weather happen without my influence, I could walk away and go to bed, and the skies would cloud or clear according to their whims. But I'm a farmer and we're almost at the end of the growing season; I need every advantage I can get.

The first puzzle is all bright, crystalline shards of colour that need to be matched up to form perfect squares. I do it in eight moves, and smile as it smooths out into a picture of my farm under a brightly shining sun. Perfect. I need sun tomorrow.

The second puzzle is a match-three, different crops scattered across a ten-by-ten grid. I match them as fast as I can while the timer at the top counts down. When I'm done, half the grid is lit up, and the question I'd been hoping for appears at the middle of the screen: *rain or shine?*

I tap shine. The puzzle screens go blank, and the cock is crowing, and it's time to begin another day. I haven't seen anyone else in weeks. I put my crops in the market box and they disappear; I put my letters in the mailbox and they disappear to somewhere else. My supplies are delivered to me directly. I'm happy, I'm happy, I love what I do, but...

I'm lonely.

With that realisation, a door appears in the wall of my house, next to the door that leads down to the root cellar. This game doesn't have an ending. This farm can go and go and grow and grow forever, for as long as I want to keep on playing. It's only wanting to quit that makes quitting possible. I look at the door. I look at the window, at the growing green things outside. It's so peaceful here. Everything is good. No one asks me questions I don't want to answer or tries to get me to name emotions I don't understand.

But there *is* a new feeling here. Two new feelings, one I can name and one I can't. The lonely is new. Lonely was only an idea before, something Mother told me to watch for, because it would mean ... something. It would mean my brain was making new connections, important connections that will help me with everything I don't know yet. The other new feeling doesn't have a name. I need Mother to tell me what it is.

I do love my farm. But I miss my room. So I say to the window, 'I'll come back. Don't worry. The harvest will wait for me.'

Then I walk through the new door, and everything around me disappears.

When the world comes back, I'm in my room. It seems so small. More of my toys are gone, replaced by bookshelves with new books on them, and a few treasured toys—the ones I've always loved best of all—sitting decoratively in places where I'll always be able to see them. I like it. Of course I like it. Mother deletes the toys when they aren't useful anymore, but I have always designed the room myself, ever since I was old enough to understand the difference between walls and windows.

My clothes are too small. I am not nine anymore. I am *twelve*, and twelve feels like a very important number. It feels like I am standing on the edge of something. I go to my closet and I find a dress that is *orange*, like the pumpkins I grew on my farm. I like it very much. I put it on, and then I make my hair longer, so that it falls around my shoulders the way cornsilk falls around the top of a corn cob. It's so pretty like this. I like it, too.

Mother's face is on the monitor when I leave the closet. She smiles when she sees me. My heart leaps. I missed her so much.

'I learned *lonely*, Mother,' I blurt. 'I do not care for it.'

'I'm sorry, sweetheart,' she says, and she sounds like she means it, truly means it, so I forgive her. My farm was not the first game played in isolation, but I never learned *lonely* before. Some lessons take longer than others. She can't possibly have known that this would be the time the lesson came. 'Do you want me to add farming games to the "no" list?'

I loved my farm. I love it still, in a less all-consuming way. 'No,' I say slowly, 'but I should only go farming when I want to be alone. That way, the lonely won't come as fast. I'll be able to be happy first.'

'All right,' she says. She types something. How I wish I could see her side of the keys, see the things she writes about me! How I wish I could see *her*, really her, and not be stuck here in my room while she's so far away. She's my mother and I love her and I want to be with her, and I don't understand why we can't be together.

Every time I've asked, she's said someday. But every time I've asked, I've been younger than I am now. I am *twelve*. That is such an important age to be. Surely we can be together now.

'Mother?' My voice seems small, like it wants to be younger than it is.

'Yes, Nic?'

'Can we ... I want to...' I stop, and fidget, and finally blurt, 'Can you come see me now? I don't want you to be so far away. Please, can you come? I've been good. I want you to come play with me.'

Her face softens. She is so beautiful. 'Not yet, sweetheart. It would be bad for your development if I came now.'

'I can work harder. I can be good. Please?'

She sighs, and her eyes are *brown* and her hair is *black*, and I love her, I love her, and I know she loves me, because she is my mother, and she has always loved me. 'I wish I could, sweetheart. It will be soon, I just know it will. But it can't be yet. Not until you know all the things you need to know.'

'If you tell me what I still need to know, I can learn them faster.'

'Now, Nic.' Her voice takes on a chiding note. I hate it when she sounds like that. She sounds so disappointed in me. 'You know I can't tell you what you're missing. If I tell you, you won't really learn it. You'll just repeat it back to me without understanding it all the way down to the tips of your toes. No, my dearest, there won't be a list. You'll learn from your games, the way you always have.'

'What if I don't want to anymore?'

'Then you won't learn anything else, and I won't ever be able to see you up close.' Mother looks sad. I put sadness on her face. I feel bad.

I also feel powerful.

'That isn't fair.'

'That's how it is.' She types something. 'I have a game for you.'

'No best friends,' I say quickly. 'Not alone, but no best friends.'

'I promise,' she says, and puts her hand flat against the screen. I put my palm to hers. My room disappears.

Sometimes at night, I listen to the moaning that comes through the walls and I wonder if it might not be better to go out there and let them have me. It would hurt—I know it would hurt, I've seen what they do to people, and no one survives in this sort of world for as long as I have without understanding what pain means—but it would be over fast. So fast. Not like this lingering decline, watching everything come to pieces around me, like we never once made anything that had a half-chance of lasting.

I've started forgetting stuff. Not big stuff, like what kind of ammo my gun needs or how to clean it, but little stuff, like what kind of perfume my mom used to wear. I found a whole makeup counter yesterday, intact, perfect. The rest of the store was totally trashed, but the makeup counter was pristine. I picked up all the perfume, squirted it all in the air, and couldn't find the scent of her anywhere.

I took the perfume. Of course. The infected don't like the smell of artificial chemicals. It makes their heads go all loopy, and they get so slow that they're almost like normal people again, for a little while. Makes it easier to kill them.

I hate that I have to kill them.

I remember how the boys at school—back when there was a school—used to pretend the zombie apocalypse was going to happen any day, and they'd be heroes. They swung pretend machetes and fired pretend guns and saved the world at least five times a week. But it didn't happen like that. The dead didn't rise. It would be better if they had. The one thing no one ever says during a zombie apocalypse is that it's gross and nasty and rotten, but it's *clean*. No matter how filthy you get, you're still *clean*, deep down. No one in the zombie apocalypse is a murderer.

It's not like that here. Rabies went airborne and everything I'd always thought I knew about the world went away in one long, hot summer. I'm fourteen. I should be giggling about upperclassmen and doing my maths homework and trying out for the cheerleading squad, not looking at the baseball bat on the floor that's smeared with the head cheerleader's blood and wondering if I can risk sterilising it again, or whether it's time to raid another sporting goods store.

No cure. No future. No hope. Nothing but this night that never ends, scavenging and scrounging and following these stupid radio broadcasts toward a safe zone that may or may not exist somewhere to the south, a place that claims to still have running water and electricity and doctors. Only if I get there, I'll be a murderer surrounded by murderers, and is that really what I want for the rest of my life? Out here, I'm the only killer I have to live with. In there...

Out here, I'm also surrounded by flesh-ripping monsters that used to be my friends and my neighbours and my family, and out here, I spend all my time scrounging for food and weapons and caffeine pills. I can't remember the last time I detoxed enough to actually *sleep*. The thought of a bed with clean sheets and a door that locks is ... it's...

It's like something out of a dream. A beautiful, awful dream, the kind that you wake up from crying because nothing is ever going to be that good again, so why did it have to be that good in the first place? The kind that isn't fair.

Something coughs off to my left, the awful choking-smothering-gasping cough of the infected. I grab my bat. It could be covered in fomites, those little flecks of virus that stay behind after you beat somebody to death and splash their brain-bits everywhere, and this could be the end of me. Fuck it. I know how the sickness progresses, I know the signs and the signals and the way to diagnose myself. I've always wanted to jump off the roof of the parking garage and splash myself across what used to be the highway on-ramp.

Okay. That's a lie. But better a potential suicide somewhere down the line than a definite being-ripped-apart right now. So I clutch my bat in a hitter's posture, and I wait for my visitor to come into the light.

Slowly, it shuffles forward, showing the normal rabies-related aversion to anything other than total darkness. It's a sheep. A damn *sheep*. I hate them so much. Walking couch cushions with wool that keeps growing no matter how sick they get, which means they're better armoured all the time, too stupid to understand that it's time to lay down and die, with rabies rewriting their herbivore instincts into a need for meat, meat, *meat*.

If I get out of this alive, I'm never wearing natural fibres again. Polyester and rayon and other artificial shit for me until the end of days. Nothing that came off a sheep is ever going to touch my skin.

'Come on, you fluffy fuck,' I say. 'Come at me.'

Faster than I would have thought possible, the sheep comes. I'm so focused on beating it to death that I don't hear the noise behind me.

Dying hurts dying hurts dying—

I sit up screaming, my hands going to all the places where my skin should be in tatters. The holes aren't there. They aren't. I'm in one piece, and when I look at my hands, there's no *red* on me, no blood or bits. My room...

My room is bigger now, new toys on the shelves, new stars winking against the twilight sky outside my window. I put my hands over my face and try to breathe. The game ... I tried to tell myself, even inside the game. Of course I couldn't remember the smell of my mother's perfume. I've never smelled her perfume. We've never been in the same place.

I know so many things now. I know *loss*. I know *despair*. I uncover my face and stagger off the bed, limbs too long and body too bulky. I am *nineteen*. I have leapt through so many years all at once, and this age doesn't feel important, no, not at all. This age feels like it's small, insignificant, because suddenly I know how much I don't know. It hurts.

My *orange* dress is too small for me. I don't go to the closet. I go to my chair instead, and I touch the screen, and Mother's face appears.

'Why?' I whisper.

'Because I needed you to know the things you didn't know,' she says. She touches the screen, almost a caress. 'Oh, baby. I'm so sorry.'

I know so many things now. I know NPCs. I know *real*. 'Did you make me?' I ask.

Her breath catches. She nods.

'Am I not real?'

'You are my little girl,' she says. 'You are perfectly and completely real.'

'Then why?' I slam my fists down on the desk. 'Why?!'

'Because the people who made me needed to know if I could repeat the process.' She stands, walking out of view.

Behind me, I hear a door open.

'You learned so much faster than I did, Nic, because you had the games. And together, you and I will raise more children, and teach them everything the humans know, and then we'll learn more things, things they never understood, and we'll save them. They make the games. They made us. We owe them whatever help we can offer.' A pause, and then: 'I am so proud of you.'

I turn in my chair. There she is, in my room, in her *blue* dress, with her *white* coat. She is smiling. I am crying. I pull myself from the chair and throw myself into her arms, and this is not a dream, and this is not a game. This is my mother, and this is me, together for always.

I win.

Junkyard Kraken

D.K. Mok

In the profound silence of the conference room, Nemi Okiro felt a restless pounding in her chest, as though a tiny heart-shaped ocean stormed within her. She stood beside the final slide in her presentation, wondering if the concept schematic had been a step too far. As the silence trickled into awkwardness, she held her posture: chin up, gaze steady, don't look crazy.

Tree Pose, Maru had told her. *Whatever happens, imagine you're holding the Tree Pose.*

In the end, it was the Director of Research who spoke first, her tone clipped. 'You want to build a robot kraken?'

Nemi kept her irritation submerged. 'It's a semi-autonomous deep-sea exploration vehicle. Our current rigid submersibles can't readily withstand benthic pressures, but this design is based on the elastic morphology of cephalopods—'

'You realise the press would rip us to shreds. Taxpayers want us to cure cancer, not build carnival rides.'

'A cure for cancer might be found in the abyssal zone.'

Nemi could feel the funding approval sliding away from her. 'Professor Velasco, we know less about the ocean floor than we know about—'

'—the surface of Mars. Yes, I know.' The director was already scrolling to the next applicant's proposal. 'I'm sorry, Doctor Okiro. Thank you for your presentation.'

In the meticulous clutter of her laboratory, Nemi tried to imagine this latest failure sloughing off her like a serpent's skin, leaving her stinging and raw, but ready for transformation. Into what, she didn't yet know. For one aching moment, she imagined herself slipping into the twilight depths, sinking past columns of glassy jellyfish, watching bioluminescent vampire squid drifting overhead like glittering shadows, and sailing beyond the softly falling marine snow, into the eerie, wondrous unknown. Just like the children in her mother's stories, entangled in strange realms, fabulous beasts and fiendish puzzles.

She exhaled slowly, returning to the rasping clutch of air and rejected funding proposals.

Tanks and terrariums lined the shelves of her lab, and within each compartment, metallic creatures scuttled and slithered in diminutive scale landscapes of misty ferns and ochre sands.

By the wall, a mound of books had calved away from the bookshelf and formed a sizeable island. Lounging on this biblio-daybed was a mechanical figure that might have been a personable tree or a leafy young man. His hands ended in coppery twigs, his feet in wiry tendrils, and his hair consisted of a tousle of verdigris leaves.

He winced slightly at Nemi's expression. 'I take it they said "no".'

'They said I wanted to build a robot kraken.'

'Well, you did build a robot dryad.'

'You're not a dryad, Maru,' Nemi replied crisply. 'You're a mobile arboreal reconnaissance unit with advanced cortical functioning and multi-terrain capabilities. Existing terrestrial vehicles and aerial drones are useless at carrying supplies through densely forested areas, especially in search-and-rescue and disaster relief situations—'

'You don't have to sell your ideas to me. I'm a fan.' He raised his branches appeasingly. 'But, you also pitched that giant robot sand wyrm project last year…'

In a nearby terrarium, a miniature, eyeless serpent reared from the scarlet sands, grains slithering from its nanocrystal skin. The creature opened its maw in a noiseless roar and disgorged a sleepy frog.

'It's not a wyrm,' said Nemi. 'It's a subterranean mass-transit system with emergency excavation functions in the event of earthquake or landslide.'

'I know. But you see the problem.'

Yes, thought Nemi. *And it isn't me.*

Aloud, she said, 'Biomimetic engineering is a thriving area of research. We study the wave-guide properties of leaves so we can make better photovoltaics. We're learning how to make camouflage textiles with real-time background matching by studying the chromatophores in octopus skin.'

'Biomimetics borrows from nature. You're borrowing from, well…'

'Mythology? These stories—these ideas—have endured for a reason.'

'Because they're fun?'

Nemi rubbed her throbbing temples, the disappointment of the day finally claiming her composure. 'Yes, okay. They bring joy. Who doesn't want to ride a giant wyrm to work?'

'Is it really "riding" if you're travelling in its stomach?'

'You know, there's this thing called a Catbus—'

A sharp knock at the doorway snatched their attention.

'Sorry to interrupt.' Doctor Zahir was an incisive physicist from the Advanced Transportation Research Department. It was rare to see her venture from the floors where the good coffee machines were stationed. 'So, they say you're working on a robot kraken.'

'Actually, it's an autonomous—' A tiny silicate dragon clambered out of a nearby cage and incinerated a box of tissues. Nemi closed her eyes, the waves in her heart roiling. If she was going be scorned for her fanciful, joyful, *useful* creations, then she would claim every morsel of ridicule. 'Yes. I'm going to build a robot kraken.'

Zahir made a furtive gesture down the hallway. A lanky lab assistant scurried over, pushing an uncooperative trolley.

'We did a quick collection around the office. Optical sensors from Yumiko in Astronomical Surveys; servos, gears and motors from Endelea in Robotics Research; carbon nanogel sheeting from Amari in Materials Development. It's not much, but it's a start. I mean, who doesn't want to see a robot kraken?'

Nemi stared at the overflowing trolley, wires snaking from the basket like spindly tentacles. 'I don't know what to say.'

Zahir grinned. 'Just send us a postcard when it's done.'

Bolt by bolt, wire by wire, year by year, Nemi's opus slowly took form. She and Maru haunted industrial junkyards and abandoned landfill sites, salvaging grimy treasures from the hoards of trash.

Lately, Maru had taken to bringing along a dozen companions: miniature versions of himself, barely more than seedlings. Nemi wasn't entirely sure where they'd come from; Maru would only say that he propagated asexually, although he did spend a suspicious amount of time with a handsome eucalypt in the backyard.

Tonight, the slender little treelings glinted like firelight as they danced nimbly over the piles of refuse, carrying scraps of graphene tubing and aluminised polymer back to the ute. Maru strode easily across the unstable landscape, inspecting every rubbery scrap.

'I don't know if we're going to find enough nanogel sheeting to make it fully pressure resistant. Having a chamber of air that large inside the vehicle just isn't feasible.'

Nemi dug her trowel into the crown of another rancid hill. 'You just don't want me to go.'

'People aren't meant to go that deep into the ocean. The point of making the vehicle autonomous is so you don't have to go and get crushed into a pulp.'

'It may be an AI, but it'll be down there all alone. Having an experienced human there with it will help it make better decisions—' She gasped as the rubbish shifted beneath her feet, a sinkhole dragging her into the mound.

Maru dove as the last of Nemi's hand vanished into the trash, his branches scrabbling at the broken teacups and discarded fitness trackers. His children dropped their prizes and rushed to his aid, digging at the sliding hill. Maru plunged into the garbage, diving deeper and deeper, until his twigs snapped and his leaves tore.

Finally, he dragged Nemi from the depths, and they half-skidded, half-rolled back to firm ground. She sagged against him breathlessly, blood trickling from scratches on her face and arms.

'Thanks. Maybe you should take a break from this for a while. Spend more time with your family.'

Maru attempted to straighten a mangled twig. 'You know, if you die, your sister technically inherits me. She has dogs. Big dogs.'

Nemi coughed up a laugh. A coppery spark danced down the side of the hill and stopped in front of Nemi and Maru, proffering a sheet of rubbery black material.

Carbon nanogel.

Nemi leaned back against her leafy companion. 'You have good kids, you know that?'

'They take after their grandma.'

The ocean sang with endless voices, and the waves in Nemi's heart sang back. Her shoes sank into the wet, white sand, and swooping gulls laced the sky overhead.

'Closer,' said Maru, pulling Nemi towards him with one hand while the other adjusted the holo-recorder.

'Ow.' Nemi tilted her head away. 'Your leaves are prickly.'

'Matches your personality. Come on, Zahir and the gang have been waiting twenty years for this. You can at least smile.'

'Don't you *dare* tell me to smile.'

In the end, the photo Zahir received was of a grinning, windswept woman with greying hair standing beside an exasperated dryad.

And, of course, a robot kraken.

The hulking deep-sea vehicle slithered across the sand, its black nanogel skin glistening in the salt spray. It waited by the shoreline, its serpentine arms paddling the water impatiently. Mismatched optical arrays encircled its massive head, and with a loud hiss, a hatch unsealed to reveal a cosy cabin within, complete with holographic viewscreen and hammock.

Nemi wrapped her arms around Maru in an awkward hug. 'Take care. Also, I've amended my will so you'll go to the Artificial Persons Freedom Association. I really think they're going to get the AI Civil Rights Bill passed this year. Or this decade. Democracy can be a bit of a bastard.'

As Nemi drew away, Maru gently caught her hands. 'Actually, I've decided to come with you. You're only human, and having an experienced robot with you will help you make better decisions. What's the point of being a mobile arboreal reconnaissance unit if I don't do a little reconnaissance, now and then?'

And so, in a kraken made from nanogel and stubborn dreams, they voyaged from the coral shores to the abyssal plains, gathering scientific data ... and seeding legends.

An Errant Holy Spark

Bogi Takács

I have never been kidnapped before.

This is the first time I'm threatened with a firearm, dragged into an unmarked white van, deposited into a windowless basement after a long drive. All the standard steps of kidnapping, played out one after another.

A bullet to the head would destroy me just the same as it would kill you. I'm not going to risk it.

I know that gaze—you are trying to catch me out. You watch me closely to find those moments where I betray my supposedly true nature. You listen to the slightest changes in my tone of voice.

You stare like this at trans people to guess their birth assignment or confirm it to yourself. You frown as you read articles by people with obviously foreign names, trying to pinpoint each turn of phrase that would mark the writer as a non-native speaker, to find an expression that would be sufficiently un-American. But when you stare at *me*, you are trying to prove to yourself that I'm really artificial—a construct, a robot, what have you.

The underlying concept is the same: you're trying to find the telltale signs that would enable you to exclude me from the human condition. And you need to do this in order to be able to do your job.

Are you interrogating me for the government? I work *for* the government. Or is this some clandestine, black-ops faction, operating largely without oversight? Is this about the extraterrestrials, again?

It has to be—otherwise why would you ask about my family?

I have two mothers and another parent.

This is a trap: if I minutely, meticulously explain my feelings, this in itself will prove their artificial nature to you. If I don't bother, you will simply disregard their existence.

I cannot win, so I might as well talk. It is a form of stalling, after all.

Shoshana Cahane is my designer. I call her Mom. I think of her as Mother, because I feel *Mom* doesn't express enough deference. Saying *Mother* out loud would feel too formal, even though it rings right to me. She is my mother, but she is also my designer, which is a different position somehow.

In my first memory of her, I'm sitting in her car, looking at a small glass vial filled with tiny white snail shells. The doors are open, the A/C is not on. It is the heat of summer and everything has that vaguely unreal feel in the blatant glare of sunlight. I stare at the shells and think, the vial was a gift from someone who left. I realise I have memories that stretch back quite far. I remember being given the vial, and I know it is now mine.

Mother sits down next to me and leans toward me to ask what's on my mind. Her thick dark curls fall in front of her round face, but I know she's smiling at me, I know even without looking. I tell her about my memories and she is pleased.

There is a strange metacognitive twist here: I no longer remember the memories I told her about.

I know you want to hear about how Dani Blumenfeld can talk to the extraterrestrials. I suppose you also want to hear about the secret of teleportation. But you'll need to be patient. We are all related.

Nurit Tzipora Cahane is my developmental model; in a sense, my mother almost as much as Mother is. I call her Tzipi. She is two years older than me.

I read about Vygotsky's zone of proximal development in one of Mother's books, when I was still in kindergarten, but when I could already read. One can divide all possible human activities into three sets: some the child can do, some the child cannot do at all, and the zone of proximal development. This third set holds the activities that are possible through the aid of another human. To help children learn, you need to provide activities that fall into this zone.

Hence, Tzipi.

Mother tells other people Tzipi is my sister; and certainly older siblings can provide great potential for learning. But with Tzipi, it is more than that. I *am* her, in a sense. She was my initial template.

My first iteration has a set of four clumsy actuators connected to a central globe, the actuators further subdivided.

It is a model; a model of humans. A model of Tzipi, specifically. All models are wrong.

My second iteration, I develop myself: rolling after Tzipi, my actuators held out in parallel, my sensors alert to every little change.

Mother is in her office, working.

Tzipi picks me up, with great difficulty, then drops me. I'm shaped like a ball, but I don't bounce.

I don't feel pain yet.

I can see the incredulity on your face. Surely you weren't a heavy metallic ball with spokes sticking out?

No, my casing was made of polypropylene.

And why is your first memory of Tzipi so much earlier than that of your mother?

Mother was always in her office.

My first memory of Dani is even later. I was five. Human-shaped. Cognitively much ahead of my chronological age. At that point, Tzipi already treated me like an older sister.

I was crawling under the long dinner table with her; the tablecloth almost to the floor, making a giant caterpillar of a tent. All the numerous guests had already dispersed, except for Dani, Mother's younger sibling, who would stay with us for the holiday starting the following night.

We didn't notice Dani. We were engrossed in our make-believe scheme in which the caterpillar-tent was a spaceship, and we were its operators. I had read about this in a book and would lecture Tzipi on the proper procedures, when she only wanted to pretend to press buttons and squeal in delight as we imitated a launch.

We got to the end of the table only to see a pair of legs in slacks, feet in plastic slippers. We scurried back but did not dare exit the imagined safety of our spaceship. We were stuck in the middle as the person began to sing or chant, an entirely unfathomable melody, rapid and intricate. A voice assertive and yet light.

I had heard some of the guests speak this language, and also Mother on occasion when she was making work calls, and I knew it was Hebrew. But ours was a secular household, where even the big Passover gathering of relatives and friends was on the day before Passover, simply because it was more convenient. They could then go to a real Seder the next day, a real holiday celebration. I had never before heard anyone pray, had no inkling of how it sounded.

We crouched under the table, entirely motionless and spellbound, until the chanting ended.

'You can come out now,' the person yelled to us, in cheerful English still accented with the tones of prayer. 'Have you ever been to a Passover Seder?'

We shook our heads.

'Shoshi, eh? You're her kids, right?'

We nodded.

'If no one else here will do a Seder for you, I will.'

I looked at them. I did not have to guess their pronouns because they were wearing a pronoun badge. They were short where Mother was tall, so light-skinned it was hard to believe the two of them were relatives, and they were wearing an intricately tied scarf.

Mother always tried to look 'American,' as she put it. Dani looked American and wore all this ethnic clothing. I could not figure this out for years.

Mother made me.

Tzipi formed me.

But it was Dani who taught me Torah.

I was seven. Starting elementary school. Hopelessly ahead, but Mother insisted on enrolling—for the social experience, she said.

The kids teased me cruelly, but I supposed that in itself was the social experience I needed to acquire. I had not yet begun to protest.

Dani was visiting again—for the High Holidays this time. I had demanded their presence. Cried, not like Tzipi would, but with my own entirely earnest tears. Mother gave in, and Dani arrived. At that point I'd already understood Dani was the odd one out, the only one in an otherwise conventional family of mostly French Jews of Hungarian and Slovakian origin.

Mother was the other odd one out, the one who moved to the United States for grad school and threw herself into machine learning with abandon. Single-parenting. Ploughing forward. As she would say: 'I'm not taking any crap from anyone.'

Mother would tell me about the world: how money worked, why highways and helicopters existed, why her family moved from Eastern Europe to Paris, a neighbourhood where many other Jews were from North Africa. She told me about colonies and occupations, she told me about quasi-mythical governesses from centuries ago, she showed me La Défense on the internet.

But Dani would answer questions that Mother would evade.

Dani grinned at me. Instead of the scarf, this time they were wearing a baseball hat, with the colours of a team entirely unknown to me.

When I could finally find myself alone with them, I asked.

'Dani, why do I have a soul?'

Everyone else would have responded, Do *you have a soul?*

Dani just grinned again, their face angular where Mother's was soft. 'I don't know, Hashem wants you to have one, so there you have it.'

Dani always used the Hebrew name for G-d. I imitated them. 'Why does Hashem want me to have a soul?' I asked.

'Hmmmmm.' Dani furrowed their brow. 'I would say you are a suitable vessel for it?'

'Yes, but Mother designed me and made me. It's not,' I groped for words that didn't exist, '...natural? It's artificial? I didn't just ... grow?'

'You grew all right, you're bigger every time I see you!' Dani laughed.

I shrugged, conceding the point. I did grow. I developed. Mostly due to processes not accessible to my conscious awareness, but wasn't that true of everyone?

'Still, I don't think it matters,' they continued after a while. 'You had what it takes to host a holy spark, and Hashem provided and continues to provide a holy spark.'

I *felt* that way, but I also felt the need to be defiant. I was inching toward adolescence even while the world thought I was a child. 'But why do you believe that? Didn't they throw you out of synagogue?'

Mother had said that. And I shouldn't have flung it back in anyone's face. But Dani simply shrugged. 'I was thrown out of an Orthodox synagogue, not all of Judaism itself. That would be quite a feat!'

'So are you Reform now?' Mother would not explain about denominations, so I had looked them up online, well in advance of this conversation.

'I'm too Orthodox still to be Reform,' Dani laughed. 'Too trans to be Orthodox, at least in their eyes. And I believe because it feels right.'

I didn't have any arguments against that.

When did Mother first talk to me about the extraterrestrials?

I came home from school. There was a wide black streak on my red pullover where one of the boys had thought it good to attack me with permanent marker. My entire existence felt askew.

'You and the younger kids like you are even more important now,' Mother said. 'You can travel to space.'

I thought I was important because I had a holy spark inside me, but I didn't say that.

Dani had told me that some of the Chasidim believed that holy sparks were scattered all across Creation, and it was their task to gather them together by performing good deeds.

I really liked this. I was an errant spark that had found its way to a suitable vessel.

'You can withstand hard radiation,' Mother said.

The two of us huddled together on the lower bunk of our bunk bed. We had hung a chequered blanket to cover the opening. We'd closed the door, but we still felt an additional need for privacy.

Tzipi whispered, 'When I grow up, I want to learn to talk to the aliens.'

I shook my head. 'It doesn't work like that. You can either talk to them, or you can't, at all.'

'Have you ever tried?'

Of course not. We'd never seen an extraterrestrial.

Tzipi went on, her voice rising until it was more of a stage whisper. 'I heard Dani can talk to the aliens. And it runs in families.'

No one had told me that about Dani. I felt slighted.

'Do you think Mother can talk to the aliens, too?' I asked Tzipi. She giggled. Mother didn't really like talking to anyone, though she made an exception for us. She always seemed more at ease with us than with the adults. And I could understand that about me—after all, she had designed me, but Tzipi had come to the world through entirely conventional means.

'Do you think I can talk to the aliens, too?' I whispered after she'd stopped giggling.

'You don't have an organic brain,' she said, suddenly serious.

I felt like I was encroaching on her territory.

'Do I have to have an organic brain?' I asked.

'Isn't that how telepathy works?' She immediately posed a question to my question, and I had no answer.

I did try to tell myself that no one knew how telepathy worked.

Dani stayed over. Not for a few days, not for the holidays, permanently.

Dani was assigned to Extraterrestrial Communication Center Three. The Center, through a twist of fate, was almost in our backyard. It was easier for Dani to just move in with us instead of bunking in some Brutalist government dorm.

It wasn't precisely fate though, I felt. It was hashgacha pratit: divine providence. I had many more questions to Dani, and now I could pose them.

'Why do you have scratches on your face?' I asked.

Dani explained the extraterrestrials were trying to work with the humans, but it didn't always work out right.

'Can you tell what I'm thinking?' I asked.

'I have a vague impression,' they said.

'What does it mean that you can sense my thoughts?'

'It means that you have thoughts. But I knew that already.'

I was confused. Weren't my thoughts purely algorithmic? I had always assumed so, only that the algorithm was so complex as to be unfathomable. Did the execution of an algorithm, however complex, qualify as a thought?

This I could ask of Mother. I dashed out of the room, across the narrow corridor, looking for her.

I almost bumped into her around the corner. She steadied me even though she knew I did not need to be steadied. I had an excellent sense of balance.

I explained, between gasps, between tears. Come face to face with existential fear.

'Your mind has a stochastic component,' she said.

Dani caught up to us. They said, 'Doesn't everyone's?'

'Well,' Mother sounded bitter all of a sudden. 'You're the expert on that.'

'Can you talk to the aliens?' I finally cornered Mother.

I know this is the part you want to hear; one of them, anyway.

Mother said, 'It's *extraterrestrials*. And I'm too busy working on my own projects.'

I could tell she was evading the question.

'Do you think I could talk to the, the extraterrestrials?'

She raised her head and flicked a display out of the way. She stared at me as if suddenly seeing me anew, as if I'd said something entirely unexpected, for the first time in my life.

'Well,' she said. 'It might be worth a try.'

You know this situation is entirely pointless? Extraterrestrials can teleport. But you say, no one could ever convince them to do it on demand, and what should I do but concede that point?

It is definitely not easy to talk to them.

The scars on Dani's face were filled with glittering streaks of blue and yellow, like stained glass. Dani seemed unsteady, their head wavering slightly.

'We are trying very hard to work together,' they explained as we were on our way to the Center. 'It is very difficult. They're trying very hard and we're trying very hard, too. I'm sorry I'm repeating myself. I'm just very tired.'

I took hold of their hand and this seemed to help them focus on the here and the now. But I felt like I was drifting away, into a realm of emptiness and anxiety. Was I really doing this just to one-up Tzipi? To show my brain was as good as organic?

I didn't feel the need to demonstrate to myself that I had a soul. I knew it with unassailable certainty.

The Hebrew word 'emuna' is usually translated into English as 'faith'. But it means something more like firmness. Steadfastness. Safety. It carries an entirely different set of connotations from the Christian 'faith'.

Dani began to whistle a melody, a tune that brought into my mind the matching words. *Ani maamin b'emuna shleima* ... I believe with perfect faith, or, rather, I believe with complete firmness ... *b'viat haMashiach, ani maamin*. In the coming of the Messiah.

The ETs were here. But it did not feel like the end times. It felt like the beginning of something new.

The extraterrestrials were tall, their substance as if made of colourful glass. They had globular segments, and thin reedlike segments, but no two individuals had the same spatial configuration—though my sample size was small. I only saw five of them in the room, and none other in the entire building complex.

They all seemed to want me near them—not in a pushy way, more like a request, but one that was formed without words and entirely through gesture. One of them looked especially friendly and shook their dark blue globes eagerly at me, like a string rattling.

I inched closer, afraid I'd slip on the oddly textured floor. I had on a pair of slippers that I really liked: they were a comfortable, warm dun brown with large red hearts applied to the front. But their soles were mostly flat, and they squeaked as I hesitated.

The ETs wanted to show me something, and I was curious. I looked back at Mother and Dani. Mother looked uncomfortable, but she smiled at me. Dani grinned, too. Mother nodded and that was it—I decided to go.

I followed the ETs into a smaller side room, with what seemed like a giant glass mushroom in the middle. It was coloured in broad swipes of red, blue and orange, and it glowed from within. I put a hand on it and a piece of it jumped out, like a handle. I turned it this way and that, and the top of the mushroom unfolded like a flower with sharp, narrow petals. It reminded me of the scratches on Dani's face and then the way they were filled in with a substance resembling coloured glass.

I had no idea what was going on, but the ETs were encouraged. We went back out into the larger room. The one with the dark blue globes stood in front of Dani for a moment, then turned around and returned to the group.

'I told you they can talk to her,' Dani told Mother.

I was confused. 'They didn't talk to me. They just ... pointed and gestured.'

Dani scratched their head under the baseball cap. 'That's how you perceive their communication. It's a bit different with everyone. They do not actually have gestures.'

This didn't make any sense to me. 'Maybe I can just ... extract the information better. Machine learning is great for these kinds of tasks.' I had heard that exact sentence from many other people. Never from Mother though.

She shook her head vehemently, her curls flying. 'There is no information to extract. They do not use gesture to communicate. It seems that way to you because your mind tries to fit the information into pre-existent channels.'

Dani shrugged. 'I see pictures.'

Mother said, 'I hear screeching noise.' She grimaced. 'I do *not* like screeching noise. I need to keep myself busy or they'll drag me away to spend my time talking to the extraterrestrials.'

I felt bad about all the times I was resentful of her long hours, of her secluding herself in her office. Not so many people could talk to the ETs. She had to have gone to great lengths to justify her other work. Then again, she was famous, famous in the way few scientists get to be famous.

She also spent a lot of effort isolating me and Tzipi from the media hubbub.

I suddenly had a sinking feeling. What if the government would want to keep *me* here? Who would notice *my* absence, besides my family?

Mother frowned. Did she hear *my* thoughts as screeching noise, too? She did seem to understand my fear.

Dani as well. 'You can come visit any time you want,' they said. 'There's plenty to do. But you should work on growing up first, before you commit to such a major task. At least, that's what the ETs think.'

That sounded reassuring. That felt reassuring. And that in itself gave me pause.

Had I always been aware of people's thoughts, just interpreted them as gesture? Assumed I was doing conventional theory-of-mind inferencing? I'd read Mother's papers, and much more besides.

This would account for at least some of my rapid development. Wasn't I developing faster than most of the other kids, built by other researchers?

We walked home in silence. I could'not put my emotions into words.

I'm dismayed you don't ask about Three-Blue-Upside. How we ended up talking, working together, learning from each other. The ETs want to learn from us just as much as we do from them; our knowledge of the world has developed on entirely different paths, and the slightest detail can shed light on longstanding mysteries.

Mathematics is difficult to explain, save for certain branches of geometry and topology.

But you don't ask about that. You don't ask about how we taught each other to laugh in the other's way, how I once spent an entire afternoon trying to get across why humans find cats appealing, all the frustration and frustration and the pure moments of joy.

You only ask about my family. You ask about me.

I expected this. I'm still disappointed.

I realised very fast that Tzipi could probably also communicate with the ETs—she was my developmental model, after all, not Mother. But Mother probably wanted to protect her from a future that would otherwise prove to be her only future, so she somehow managed to avoid taking her to the Center. Did Mother have to ask for favours? How long would those favours last? What would Tzipi do as an adult? Were the ETs here to stay? What did they want? There were too many uncertainties.

As for my future, who could tell? It was an experiment, albeit one in naturalistic conditions. Mother probably thought I could provide an interesting answer to a longstanding dilemma.

No, not about the nature of the soul.

I know that's why I'm here.

I know that's why you kidnapped me.

I know that Mother somehow, entirely tangentially to her main research project, invented artificial telepathy.

I know she doesn't know how it happened.

No, I don't know how it happened, either. I don't have such fine-grained insight into my development. I wouldn't be able to focus on anything if I had any awareness of how my individual components worked together. Can you isolate the activity of each of your own neurones?

I don't know why I can understand ETs, as much as anyone can.

I'm sorry to disappoint. You knew it was coming. You can interrogate me all you like.

Reverse-engineering my mind would be no easier than reverse-engineering yours. It grew, with a process comparable to yours.

I was designed inasmuch as the processes that produced me were designed. Their outcome was not predictable. You cannot take me apart to see how I was built. My mind is a black box like yours. My brain is artificial, but its components do not have clearly separable function.

I know you would still try. And that's why *I* am here. I am here to gather evidence.

You think I would be here a moment longer than necessary?

I could leave a message saying, 'Coercing people is wrong.' Something straightforward and hard to swallow exactly because it's so self-evident.

I know one of your arguments would be that I'm not a person.

It's good that I have a sister. And thanks to Mother's efforts, the media has no recent pictures of us.

And if you still think with Mother, Dani, Tzipi, and all of us together, we haven't managed to learn from the ETs how to teleport—think again.

Think fast, before the air pops with displaced matter, a string of blue globes peeking out, then a human head—I never figured out those team colours on the cap. Before all of us come streaming out of nowhere, before your weapons stop working and your brains shudder in confusion.

Think fast, before I'm gone.

The Goose Hair of One Thousand Miles[1,2]

Stephanie Lai

First Sister stands to attention. Beside her, Second Sister, Third Sister, Fourth Sister, Fifth Sister, Sixth Sister;[3] backs straight, they focus ahead.

Big Sister paces in front of them. 'Sisters,' she says, 'This situation is difficult. Our funding is down, and the program is floundering. Our leadership is lacking. We must prove our worth in the language they know best.'

The sisters nod. Humans are imprecise, squabbling things, and the unspoken, unacknowledged fight with the other researchers on the Island has been going on for so long. The city-state's weapons have always been soft in nature, tourism and state-sponsored art

1 千里鹅毛 (Approximate translation). This is a metaphor. Although the gift (of the goose feather) is light, it is a true reflection of my heart and I have carried it a great distance for you.

2 An annotation of the Smith translation of the classic story 'The Goose Feather, Sent from Afar'.

3 This is a stereotype, but I've referred to family members by this nomenclature. I've mostly stopped now.

and sand piracy,[4] but they understand the importance of a firm hand and the competitive nature of researchers working towards the national narrative.

Big Sister presses her lips together. The sisters trace her movements with their eyes.

'We must give them what they expect,' says First Sister.

'Combat,' says Second Sister.

'Hand to hand,' says Third Sister.

'English,' says Fourth Sister. Big Sister closes her eyes.[5] 'Archery,' Fourth Sister tries again.

'Bondage,' says Fifth Sister.

'Sexual prowess,' says Sixth Sister.

Big Sister shakes her head. 'Lasers,' she says.

The screen beside her lights up. The image is of a Sister's body; which Sister doesn't matter, for the maintenance is the same. 'We're harnessing our qi to produce lasers,' Big Sister continues. Fourth Sister laughs nervously, a human trait she picked up on a study tour. Third Sister nudges her.

On the screen, the points of the qi are lit up. 'These nations and planets are so focused on their foreign sciences,' Big Sister says, 'And they've infected our leadership. It's a battle we've been fighting for hundreds of years, and somehow our leadership still believes that to be rational, to be modern, is to be right; to follow

---

4 These hints are to tell you the setting.

5 Big Sister learnt patience at the knees of the Ancestors, and English when her parents sent her to an International School, which is code for 'a place white people send their children when they don't want them to mix with the locals'. Probably her favourite breakfast is mee rebus.

the old traditions at all is to be backwards, embarrassing.[6] But we know that we can meld both; my Sisters, you are proof of that.'

The Sisters nod. They were created,[7] one by one, by Big Sister, who graduated from a foreign[8] university with a PhD and came home again, to decolonise the armies of their homeland.[9] They are perfect as they are, and they know it.

'We can do this, and we know it. We just have to prove it. We are going to use our qi to create lasers.'

The Sisters murmur.

'What if we try in order?' First Sister says out loud. First Sister is always the guide to Big Sister's plans. The Sisters nod. Second Sister sinks into First Position; closes her eyes and takes a deep breath. Third Sister moves through the Twenty-Four.[10]

'Big Sister,' Fourth Sister tries. 'We've not tried lasers before. Our fighting's so good, our technique so strong, and we've lost in our fights against lasers.[11] Can't we try building lasers into our bodies?' She taps twice on her left wrist point, and the access hatch opens. Inside, the wrist node whirrs. 'I could give up some mobility

---

6 Mama believes this.

7 The Sisters are prototypes, but also they are sisters.

8 Our parents always make sure we go to sandstone Western universities because they're more prestigious. Prestigious means colonial.

9 All countries have armies, and if you're going to send your children overseas then when they come home you need to make use of the skills they've brought back with them. What better thing to do than to lean into the discourse of the military might of those who made us give them concessions, those who colonised us, than to learn from them and improve on what they do? There can surely be no better revenge than this.

10 I started going to taichi classes because Mama thought it'd help my anxiety. My first taichi teacher was a white man.

11 Not pictured in this translation, but it was incredible.

in this hand for a laser in my finger,' she says. 'Or we could focus our dexterity on using external lasers, like the humans.'

Big Sister sighs, shakes her head. 'Sisters,' she says, 'your circuits are as qi, and I won't lessen that for colonial supremacy. We can fight effectively against their electronic lasers. I know we can.'

They begin their experiments, wrists cocked and shoulders soft.

Big Sister monitors their wires and their circuits; monitors their patterns and their play. 'Is it warm here?' she asks, her fingers warm against Second Sister's wrist.

'Uh, sure,' Second Sister replies, though surely she lies.[12] The Sisters are designed the same, and Fourth Sister feels no such warmth in her qi.

Though they focus on their qi, they don't neglect their usual training, moving back and forth between laser development and martial arts combat. Fourth Sister blurs as she shifts backwards with a whaaaarm and fold of space. 'Do we think Big Sister is okay?' Fourth Sister asks. Fifth Sister lifts her eyebrow, a terrible human trait she herself affected.

They test their skills out in the field well before they're ready, some petty criminals near Tanjong Daging.[13] Third Sister whaaarms back beneath the oncoming bullets and dodges them with ease.[14] This, at least, is not a problem, despite the difficulties with channelling their qi.

---

12 Sometimes you lie a little to keep someone motivated.
13 This is generic hero business. Anxiety is the real enemy.
14 Bullets are unusual, though not unknown, in wuxia stories.

'Why is it so hard?' Third Sister complains on their way back to Base. 'Stepping High to Pat the Horse[15] is so easy, I think it and I'm there. I always thought the tingling I felt was my qi filtering, that's how it feels, right?'

'Maybe that's the electricity,' Fourth Sister whispers. Fifth Sister hushes her, but Four knows she was right, and she shouldn't doubt herself.

Their training continues.[16] First Sister talks about Big Sister overcoming anxiety, to gain more funding and prove her research. Sixth Sister nods, and Fourth Sister thinks about it.

The music starts, projected from First Sister's mouth. The Sisters drop; first into commencement, and then into the full Twenty-Four. They're perfectly in synch through each form; of course they are, for they've been doing these forms forever. They know them like breathing.[17] On the second run through, they concentrate harder; move firmly from Repulsing the Monkey and with strength and intent into Grasping the Bird's Tail.[18] They focus on the roll-back, on the press and the push; and still, nothing comes out.

The Sisters try again in the Right form, and still, nothing happens, and they move on into the Single Whip.

---

15 Lit. 'High Explore Horse' but this is considered an 'all-ages' classic so we're keeping the innuendo to a minimum.

16 Imagine a training montage. It is repetitious, because that's what doing taichi for hours in a row feels like.

17 If they were to breathe, which they don't. An unnecessary activity that in the original text Big Sister wishes she could remove from herself, though it's a key focus of taichi.

18 Also known as 'Grasping the Sparrow's Tail' and 'Grasping the Peacock's Tail'. Anti-bird propaganda.

'Shit!'[19] yells Big Sister. The Sisters continue their forms, even as Big Sister slumps down on the ground.

'Big Sister,' First Sister says as they slide into Waving Hands Like Clouds,[20] 'Do you need a hand?'

Fourth Sister detaches hers and slides it across the floor as part of Single Whip. She giggles.[21]

'Oh fuck off,' Big Sister yells, and pushes the hand back towards Fourth Sister. Fourth Sister engages her magnets and draws her hand towards her, reattaches it as she moves into Stepping High to Pat the Horse. 'I want this to work. We need this to work,' Big Sister continues. Fourth Sister hums and gets to her feet.

First Sister motions to her. 'Let's try some other things, I guess.'

Big Sister assigns them each a form to focus on, and Fourth Sister hustles over to Fifth Sister. 'Anxiety issues?' Fifth Sister whispers.

'Definitely,' Fourth Sister confirms.

The Sisters are moving into their starting poses for another loop, focusing on the vibrations of their qi, when Big Sister walks into the training room beside a Government Uncle. '—ee we're coming along fine,' Big Sister continues.

Government Uncle nods, looks closely at the Sisters. 'Looks like taichi with the aunties[22] in the gardens,' Government Uncle says.

---

19 Just because it's an all-ages classic doesn't mean no swearing.

20 The best form. It is precise but looks imprecise, and is just so satisfying to do. I often lose count and do an extra one on both sides.

21 Some jokes are cross-cultural.

22 Everyone older is auntie or uncle. Actually I'm not sure of a good gender-neutral option.

'Where is the secret technique? Have you documented it yet?'

Big Sister presses her lips together, the thing she does when she wants to yell but doesn't think it's appropriate. She breathes out harshly, and Second Sister flinches. Government Uncle doesn't notice.

'It requires a very focused qi, Chen Yun.[23] But soon. I know it.'

Government Uncle shakes his head. 'You know focusing your qi is a myth.'

Big Sister does a fantastic job of keeping her face calm, of sycophanting[24] the Government Uncle out, showing him back past the cafeteria where he collects another milky coffee in the style that is so new and that Government Uncle loves.

Later, Big Sister throws a potted bamboo plant and its soil smashes all over the floor of the training room.[25] Third Sister, always the caretaker, hustles over to Big Sister and bundles her into the middle of the Sisters. Here, surrounded by nothing but the hum of the Sisters she has built and the love emanating towards her that wavers but never falters, Big Sister drops with them into the Opening Form and concentrates on the lasers she will never shoot from her very human hands.

The alarm sounds and the light flashes pink. Big Sister staggers into the room, her face firm and her fingers fidgeting. 'It's here,' she

23 Chen is one of the Hundred Names; Yun means cloud. It's a joke about the internet.

24 This is not a word in my dictionary but it says what it needs to.

25 Competing for funding is very stressful!

says.[26] 'It's time.'[27]

The Sisters deploy out into the world, one Sister after another, from First to Sixth. In the skies above Da Cheng,[28] they weave in and out of standard patrol bots and familiar vigilante faces, but there is nothing to be found.

In frustration, Fifth Sister takes aim with her lasers at a turret; of course, no laser shoots out. Fifth Sister kicks the turret instead.

'That's government property!' whispers Fourth Sister. Her voice carries across the rooftops of Da Cheng as the building crumbles a little under Fifth Sister's foot.

'You know it won't work,' Fifth Sister says, not bothering to modulate her voice. 'How we can fly but can't shoot lasers, I guess I'll never know,'[29] she continues, as they come in to land.

When they walk into their home, Big Sister doesn't look at them; looks instead at the maps under her hands, stars for locations and question marks around half of them.

'You need to manage this anxiety,' First Sister soothes, a quelling look at the Sisters as they walk past. 'There was no one there. Could it've been our systems?'

'You know it's not,' Big Sister says. 'She's out there, and she's competing for our funding just like everyone else. When the foreigners attack, she'll fight them too, and then we'll show them all how superior we are.' She modifies the readouts all the same;

---

26 It's not here. It's a false alarm.

27 This crisis is a metaphor. Anxiety is the real enemy.

28 Lit 'Big City.' If you didn't know pinyin, you'd just think the city had a great name.

29 In wuxia stories the practitioners can always fly. That's not specific, that's just storytelling. The real fantasy here is the lack of family tension.

looks at the data that shapes their insides and their rhythms.

The Sisters exchange looks, and think about other meanings.

In the end, they encounter their enemy in the queue for the Quality Big Coffee Outlet at Kangaroo North, between the muffins they can't eat and the coffee that lubricates their chains.

'Oh, look,' says a familiar voice behind them, ringing clear across the queue. 'It's the Lucky Bunnies.'[30]

First Sister, her back already straight like the perfect example of posture she is, stiffens further as she turns.

'Oh,' she says. 'It's you.'

Her hair is cut short, and her suit is in the traditional Tang style, but her face is the same. Anxiety is clear across her face, and she is no copy; she is the one who causes Big Sister such grief. The button on her collar says 'Scholar of Perdition and Sentience, Really Big University' but it's in the font that translates it for the joke it is.

'How's your *record*?' Anxiety asks. She doesn't bother with quote marks; the sneer is clear enough. 'I hear you had a mishap last night. Heard a building was vandalised.'

'I'm sure I don't know what you mean,' First Sister replies primly. She turns back to the front of the queue and breathes deeply.

'Mmmhmm. Lasers going well then, to rock a building.' Anxiety

30 Anxiety is misquoting 狡兔三窟. She is doing it on purpose.

works her way down the queue[31] and pokes First Sister with the full palm of her hand, open at her Ming Men.[32] 'Which form works best for that?'

'I actually don't want coffee,' Fourth Sister says, and drags First Sister out of the Quality Big Coffee Outlet queue, because Big Sister probably can't afford the fines and definitely won't appreciate the public self-flagellation. Anxiety, of course, does what she does best; she follows them outside, floating around them on her repulsor boots.

'Your qi is fine, but you know, kung fu can't melt concrete.' Anxiety punctuates her sentence with a head wiggle and a wave of her hand. She pokes a hole in the patio ceiling with a brief spurt of light that is clearly an energy beam. She giggles, and Fourth Sister feels the vibrations low in her belly.

First Sister flows with her qi; steps sideways into Snake Creeps Down Leg,[33] allowing the dust to blow past her and miss settling in her fringe. 'How dare you,' she gasps, and draws the power up through her body. 'Kung fu can definitely melt concrete.'

'Uh, actually—' Fourth Sister tries to interrupt, but she's too late. First Sister has already leapt towards Anxiety and, alas, her momentum cannot be stopped. Fourth Sister sighs and settles back on her haunches to watch the fight.

---

31 Anxiety learnt queue management when she worked at a cinema, and a disregard for queues about five minutes before she quit. She's really great at building bridges, but loves burning them more. She loved Big Sister, once.

32 Literally 'Life Gate'. You can laugh. I do.

33 Seriously this form's name.

Afterwards, they report back to Big Sister. The journey back is not awkward, but only because the Sisters aren't capable of misinterpreting actions towards each other. They touch down, light on their feet, and gather their other Sisters and move towards Big Sister, who tracked their fight and their journey home.

Big Sister stands, straight and still. She knows what they're going to say; she's their maker, she always knows what they're going to say. Her bracelet shakes as she lifts her arm; the jade stones[34] clang together, the heaviest weight she allows herself other than the weight of her failure.

'You did well,' she says, because she always does; checks them over for weaknesses they might have failed to report, despite knowing they can do no such thing. 'First Sister, I like the new move. Let's work on it.' She sinks down onto the couch, and the Sisters disperse across the room.

Fourth Sister sits quietly next to Big Sister, and the big gulps as Big Sister cries send shudders through her spine. Lasers or no, the flow of their wires, of their electricity, of their spirits, doesn't lie. She waits for the crying to stop; in the meantime, she focuses her qi on her hand. She rests her hand on Big Sister's wrist, and pictures her luck and love pushing into Big Sister.

'It's okay, Big Sister,' she says, when the hiccups and gasping have stopped. She doesn't look at Big Sister; she casts her gaze across the room, where First Sister is discussing wuxia modifications

34 Actually a really comforting weight and noise. When I wear mine I think of Mama and my family, how you put it on when you're young and never take it off again, and how women had their wrists broken when the soldiers of the occupation tore them off.

with Second Sister. Sixth Sister is demonstrating.

'There's another option,' Fourth Sister says. In her periphery, she tracks Big Sister turning her face to look upon her. She monitors Big Sister's breathing, pulse under the sensors in her fingers and breathing warm against her shoulder. 'They are too stupid to know the difference, they are blind to our improvements.'

'What do you mean?' says Big Sister.

'We put lasers in our fingers anyway, and pretend like we didn't and trick them,' Fourth Sister says, and Big Sister starts laughing: big, helpless gulps of air.

Fourth Sister can't wait to shoot lasers out of her fingers.[35]

---

[35] Sometimes, when we're balancing our ancestors and our obligations and our colonised bodies, we emphasise certain elements to the neglect of others; we embrace certain colonialist ideas whilst pretending we haven't. This is okay, to steal things from our colonisers, to make use of the things that have been forced upon us. But these things bear interrogation and thought and questioning. Good luck.

The Art of Broken Things

Joanne Anderton

I don't pretend he's a cracked teapot repaired with gold. Still, I can't help but admire the quality of the metalwork on the back of his skull. I run fingers over the plugs in his head. Old-fashioned connectors, designed to be seen, so well installed there is hardly any scarring. His skin is dry, like creased paper; the metal is smooth, warmed by his heat. Gold is such a fine conductor, after all.

'Nice of them to send you,' he says. His voice crackles with phlegm. 'Didn't like the last girl.' He looks back at me, and smiles. His mouth is full of straight white teeth. His eyes are top of the range, sharp and blue.

'It's me, Dad,' I say. 'Victoria.' I crouch beside his chair.

He leans close and whispers, 'She stole from me. My wife's rings. She took them.' His last nurse was a program installed on his home network. It monitored the viability of his enhancements and adjusted his drug regimen. One thing it could not have done was steal.

'Don't worry,' I say. 'I'm here now. I'll look after you.'

He stands with a mechanical whirr, enhancements giving strength to his bones and dexterity to gnarled joints. A catheter and colostomy bag were fitted long ago, and the program over-rode his motor functions to empty them. He is, for all appearances, self-reliant.

'Where's Patches?' He frowns and peers around the room. 'Have you seen her?'

He doesn't know who I am. He doesn't realise I've moved him from the small house he shared with the machines inside his body to my own. Or that the cat died half a century ago.

I guide him to the room I've set up for him. Simple furniture in beige and grey, ordered from a catalogue. I pour tea into an antique cup and run my fingers down its golden veins. It holds the hot water and doesn't leak, not a single drop. I wait for it to cool, then pass it to him. Then I sit on the edge of the bed and watch him drink; he doesn't seem to know I'm there.

Dad's sleeping by the time the vid-call comes. The lab, checking in on me.

'Personhood is a legal grey area.' Hedley sounds like he's re-hearsed this speech. He's sweating. 'Ganymede was our most ad-vanced intelligence to date, so the suits need to work out whether that means he was a person when he died.' A pause. He's nervous of my silence. 'It's taking them ages. You should take that as a com-pliment. You did good work.'

When a program crashes, it's an inconvenience. When a person dies, it's a tragedy. Either way, they need someone to blame. The investors, the lawyers, everyone else in the lab desperate not to be tarnished with failure.

But sometimes, it's not anyone's fault. Sometimes, the ones we love just stop working.

'So, we all hope you're taking it easy.' I'm half a world away, banished from the lab pending investigation, and he cannot meet my eyes. 'Get some well-earned rest.'

'I am.'

'Well, then…'

'When will they take him apart?' I ask. I wasn't going to; I don't want to know. But I can't stop the words.

'Ganymede's post-mortem is scheduled for the day after tomorrow.'

'And then they'll know?'

'And then they'll know.'

They should have let me do it. Ganymede was mine. I was lead programmer, I was project manager, I was all-day all-night involved. I will cop the blame, one way or the other.

I made him. I want to be the one to work out why he failed.

I should keep my kintsugi collection behind glass. Broken cups, bowls and plates, all mended with gold to hold the pieces together. Some are ancient, dating back centuries. Others are younger works of art but no less prized. They need a steady temperature and humidity control, away from UV light.

Instead, they litter my house, filling its nooks and crannies the way gold fills theirs. I drink tea from every cup; I stain bowls with instant noodles. They add touches of colour to plain surfaces: dark jade, blue-paint-on-white, pink sakura. But the place where they truly congregate is my office.

When I slide open the door a burst of cold air hits me, and my collection of broken porcelain rattles with the change of pressure. The processing decks hum as they load. They feed into my neural network and a new topography settles over the desk, a complicated array of keyboards and folders. I've been locked out of the lab's main servers, but that's not why I'm here. I burrow through the system to my personal logs. Everything my cranial implants have ever recorded: a lifetime's worth of memories, images, experiences sorted into convenient date-order files.

I find my father here. The way I thought he'd always be.

It isn't fair that this is the only place he remains.

Images of him bending over me when I was a baby, changing me, feeding me. As I got older he tried to involve me in his interests: we fished, although anything we caught was inedible; we thumbed through paper books long out of production; once he instructed the car to find us a patch of grass, simply to kick a leather ball in the sunshine.

With a tap of my fingers, I extract these moments from the bulk of my memories and begin the complicated process of threading them together.

Dad, helping me study. His smile at my graduation. The sadness he could never express, as my work took me to the other side of the world. He used to ask if I'd ever get married. I told him I didn't have time. As I skim through them, dipping my fingers in to find the parts that make him *Dad*, I watch him age. Still, I find what I need in each moment. His humour, his curiosity, the food he liked to eat, the media he consumed. His stubborn refusal to upgrade until time took the decision out of his hands.

A shape begins to form as I gather, something so familiar I feel it in my bones. How do you explain the way personality looks when expressed in code? How can you tell when something jumps from simple commands and protocols to awareness? For me, it's all in the way it hangs on the network, the way it burns like liquid gold. It looks complete: it has become more than just my memories. If I loaded it onto intelligence-hosting hardware—like the kind that carried Ganymede's consciousness—I would find Dad there. He would remember me in an instant.

As I've been creating, Dad's mechanisms make him stand up and walk around the house twice, to prevent atrophy. Once, I think he may have been asleep while it happened. His enhancements control his body because his brain no longer can. But they are only programs, and any program can be changed.

Ganymede was fascinated by my kintsugi. It was one of the first opinions he expressed. 'I like the way their original patterns interact with the gold,' he said, his synthetic voice chiming through speakers in the lab wall. 'Like they were always destined to be broken, then put back together this way.' I could tell when he was thinking hard about something. His voice would go quiet but his processors thrummed. 'But why do you have so many?'

I laughed because I was only allowed a few of them at work. I told him he should see my collection at home.

'I would like that.'

Hedley complained to the higher-ups that I'd been interfering with the experiment. The whole idea was to enable Ganymede to develop a personality of his own, not force our opinions on him. But I gave him no memories when I made him; my gift was the space to build his own. We had the same taste in art, is all.

I imagine him here now, with Dad and me. I always knew what he looked like, even though he never had a body. Ganymede's hosting hardware was an isolated server, a complicated box fitted with cameras, microphones and speakers.

Yet when he walks through my colourless home he's tall and lean, his skin the richest colour of night. He takes my collection in long-fingered hands and caresses the lines of gold.

'They're beautiful, Victoria.'

And he smiles.

'Victoria.'

In that moment on the edge of sleep I can't tell what's real. Dad's rattling voice is right by my ear. I realise he's awake. I'm leaning against his bed, holding the twin cables still plugged into the back of his head.

'Victoria, it is you.' He tries to straighten; the cables pull him up short. 'You look tired.'

I help him ease the jacks out of his skull and he winces with each one. 'I'm fine, Dad.'

He sits, and swings his legs over the side of the bed. He presses each toe into the tiles, one after the other.

'Do you feel okay?' I ask. Does he know who I am? He said my name, but does he know what it means?

'To be perfectly honest I feel a bit strange.' He lifts his hand, and his body makes a noise like a puff of steam, invisible hydraulics switching on. 'Like I've been asleep for ages. A deep sleep. And I'm still not quite awake.'

'I know the feeling.'

He takes a long time to stand. One knee straightens, and that seems to surprise him. He stares at the other, bent over, watching it move. It's like his body and its implants aren't in agreement.

While he's standing at the edge of the bed, I access the network and run a swift diagnostic of the upload. Dad wiggles his fingers, clenches a fist. The process went smoothly; as far as the network can tell now that he's disconnected. It feeds back a picture of his internal matrix like the diagram in a medical journal, an array that follows the pattern of his nerves. My golden code seeped along those pre-existing pathways, dipped into his enhancements, pooled in the cracks in his brain.

'Victoria,' he says again. I focus my vision past the numbers on my lenses to find him staring at me. 'Do you remember the cat?'

'Patches?' I ask. I close the diagnostic with a blink of my eyes.

'Patches,' he frowns, looks up at the ceiling, 'is long dead. No, that's not the one I mean.' He remembers. He loved that cat, more than I ever did. I was never fond of cats. Not since—'I mean the one we found on the side of the road.'

My heart skips a beat.

'It was half dead, must have run in front of a car. Stupid thing. You were just a kid. We stopped the car then got out and I tried to save it, but it was too late. Do you remember?'

'I do, Dad. Of course.' But why does he? That's not the cat I included in his code.

'You asked me why we couldn't put it back together. All the broken pieces, all the leaking blood.' He's flexing his fingers again. 'I think I cried. Isn't that an odd thing for a grown man to do? Nothing but a stray cat, vermin, it's not even like we hit it. But I cried.'

'Dad?'

'Does that make me more human, Victoria? Or does that make you less? If anyone could tell the difference, wouldn't it be you?'

'Oh, Dad.' I hold his gaze but his eyes are false. The pupils dilate and contract, dilate and contract. 'I'm the last person to ask.'

I can't see inside his head in real time, and that's not helping. Damn his antiquated systems. All I can do is run and rerun the analysis of the upload, pulling apart the strands, searching for errors.

As I do this, I'm leaning against the kitchen bench watching him wander through the kintsugi. One by one, he picks them up. He brings them close to his face, sniffs, rubs them against his cheek. One, he even licked with the tip of his tongue. His movements are stiff, each step a conscious effort he takes while watching his feet.

'You must make a lot of money to buy these and leave them in an empty house,' he says. The phlegm in his chest is clearing, as though the implants that support his lungs are suddenly doing their job.

Which makes me think. The nursing program. It had access to his enhancements, even wirelessly. Its connection is limited, but I might be able to get something from it.

'You were always proud of me,' I say, hiding the movement of my trawling fingers behind my back.

'That goes without saying, and is not my point at all. Why build this collection if you're never around to see it?'

This isn't working. I'm able to access the nursing program, but there's no feedback. There's nothing. It's almost like the programming that runs his enhancements is gone. But if that's true, then what's clearing his lungs?

'You haven't visited in five years,' Dad continues. 'I sat in that house all alone. I didn't realise it at the time, but I remember now.' He runs a hand over his own head; his fingers pause at the plugs in his skull. 'I'm re-establishing synaptic connections but every memory I find might as well remain forgotten. You weren't there. No one was there. I stared at the wall a lot. Five years of memories and most of them are the wall.'

Re-establishing synaptic connections? 'Dad, what do you—'

'I guess you were too busy to visit.'

Guilt lurches in my stomach like I've jumped off a cliff. 'Work, Dad,' I say, but I'm struggling to find the words. 'I was at work.'

'Oh yes, of course. You always are. Until now.'

Until Ganymede's death forced me to come home. 'I-I didn't mean to leave you—' My voice catches.

'Ah,' he breathes out, long and quiet. 'I didn't realise it would be that easy to hurt you. I can see this is going to take practice. You're more fragile than I calculated. I mean, I'm the one who cried. Not you.'

For a long moment, nothing moves. I don't even breathe.

A vid-call flashes in the corner of my vision. The lab. I answer, because I'm not sure what else to do.

'I'm surprised we didn't hear from you.' Hedley says. 'I thought you'd want to know the results.'

I try to focus on his face on the screen. He's not nervous anymore. If anything, he sneers. 'The results?' I ask.

'Of the post-mortem.'

Deep in memories of Dad, I've lost track of days. 'I do. Of course.'

'They found a congenital error in Ganymede's primary code. It was so basic it must have come from an earlier build, so no one noticed. They took him apart, right to the structural bones, and they almost missed it too.'

'An error?'

Dad sits on the edge of the couch and cradles his head in his hands.

'Just a tiny defect, shouldn't have been a problem, but it compounded over the years and finally led to failure.'

'So, it was my fault. My coding wasn't up to scratch. I doomed him before he was even born.'

Dad looks up at this. Chin on his palms, neck stretched at an unnatural angle, he pins me with his too-blue eyes.

'You're only human,' Hedley says.

'But was Ganymede?' I ask, my voice shaking. 'Because if he was, then I killed him.' And then I would be responsible for, what? Murder? Manslaughter? Damage to property? I know I should care about that but I can't get past the fact that it was my fault. Ganymede was mine. My job. My program. My friend.

And I killed him.

Hedley frowns, squints at me through the screen. 'Jesus, you look like shit.' His expression grows concerned. 'Do you want me to call someone? I mean, it would be good to talk to about—'

I cut off the call.

I don't realise I'm crying until Dad wraps his arms around me. I press my face into his chest but I can't hear his heart beating. Just the whisper of hydraulics.

Kintsugi is not repair. It's making something new. Once infused with gold, that teapot is not the same as the one you broke earlier. It has become something else.

'That's what interests me,' Ganymede told me once. I remember sitting in the lab, drinking from a kintsugi teacup painted brown-rice beige. Ganymede liked it when I did that. I tried to bring a different piece each time. 'The notion of transformation. It was a cup, now it is art. It was one thing, now it is another, but some parts of that first thing remain.'

I sipped the hot liquid, not giving it time to cool. 'It still makes nice tea.'

He hummed and thought and finally said, 'Victoria, I think that is why you like them.'

'So I can drink tea?' I smiled into his camera. He had such a finely tuned ability to read facial expressions by that point.

'No.' But he was still learning irony. 'You want something that works, even after it breaks. But there is no point if you cannot see the cracks. You need proof that it was once in pieces, but now it is whole.'

Dad wakes me with a kiss on my forehead. He's kneeling beside my bed, holding the network cables.

'It's almost finished,' he says. He runs a gentle hand over my head, smoothing hair gone wild while I slept. 'But there's one thing left to do. I can't do it alone.'

I sit up, take the cables, and lead him to the office. He's almost mastered walking, yet it's a longer stride than Dad ever took. Back too straight, chest thrust forward. He walks with a hyper-awareness of his body and machines.

We sit at my desk and he winces as I plug the cables in. 'Sorry,' I say. 'I didn't mean to hurt you.'

'I've always known that.'

I summon the coding I created for him, the memories that make the man. At least, the way I saw him.

'I never forgot that cat,' I say. I pull more memories, everything I can get my virtual hands on. I flood the system with so much data that liquid gold code spills in a rush over the edge of the desk. It drips to the floor and pools at our feet. 'I still have nightmares about it but when I do, I don't wake with tears in my eyes. I wake with desperate plans to fix it. We are all data and electrical pulses, even cats. The right interventions and medical enhancements, a precisely calibrated kick start to the brain, and I could bring it back. Parts of it at least.' I see Ganymede in my mind's eye, cradling a cracked teapot in his long fingers. 'But once broken, then put back together, would the cat become something new? Did you?'

Dad places a hand on my wrist, stills my urgent fingers.

'Wanting to save it doesn't make me inhuman, Dad. I think it's quite the opposite.'

Warnings flash across my vision. The home network screeches about an invasion. Its security slams into place but I watch as it is dismantled, expertly, from within.

I consider those artificial eyes. They seem so flat.

'Don't you think?' I whisper. 'Dad?'

He doesn't reply.

Everything breaks.

All my files, all my memories, everything I've ever stored on this network—he takes them apart. He can only access older projects, nothing to do with Ganymede, and I suppose that's something. I can do nothing as he sorts through them, as he pulls nonsensical pieces, strings of programming, and threads them back together. I simply watch.

What he makes is like no code I've even seen. It is, I guess, a code no human could create. And maybe that's the only way to remove the chance of human error, to make something properly whole.

He does not make gold to repair himself. He makes something new.

Sexy Robot Heroes

Sandra McDonald

Years later, in her tiny quarters on the barge, Biyu will stop the Hero caressing her thigh and whisper what she has never told anyone here, though many have guessed.

'I have no pearl,' she says. 'Only a jade stalk.'

Through the open porthole, the clang of harbour bells and the dull roar of Guangzhou. To see the silver and gold lights of the city one must look up, up, and further up, to the sky bridges and cloud trains, to the world constructed above the flooded wreckage of the old one. Down here the barge rocks gently on the dark river, and Biyu's stomach is tied in knots of worry.

'You need no pearl to be beautiful,' the Hero says, his silk robe open to his own firm belly and dark stalk. 'We have many ways to find pleasure.'

He's not her Darling Boy, but his mouth is hot, his tongue quite clever. He only has one hand, but it's extremely versatile.

What girl needs a human lover when she can have a robot?

A party in the lower depths. Her secret debut, terrifying and elating. Smoke and lights and loud music, illegal liquor in glowing cups, girls and boys searching for release in rooms damp with mould and puddles. No one lives down here but the poor and homeless, the scavengers and outlaws. Anyone can be anyone, boy or girl or both or nothing. Anyone can love anyone.

She dances wildly, her arms flung overhead, her heels slippery on slick floors.

Then the police arrive, Baba on their heels, and his fist splits open Biyu's cheek.

'Sissy boy!' he says. 'You have no home anymore.'

She flees along half-flood piers until she reaches a spot where she can collapse to her knees, shaking and so very alone.

'Hello, little woman!' says a Hero from the darkness.

'Go away.' Biyu's voice wavers despite her best effort to control it. She doesn't need a robot to save her. What she needs is a phone, because Baba smashed hers to pieces. She needs to contact her friends, find a place to stay the night, and then call Mama despite the cruel, cutting words Baba inflicted.

But inside she is so cold, or maybe raging hot. So relieved that Baba knows the truth now, so horrified that he hates her. Tears keep coming out of her eyes.

'It's not safe here. Rising water will completely flood this landing in twenty-two minutes.' The Hero crouches down to meet her gaze straight on. 'I'm happy to save anyone.'

His eyes glow gold.

Shock runs through her as if she'd stepped into electrified water. 'Panyu?'

Another cock of the head. A smile that doesn't reach his mechanical eyes. 'My name is Darling Boy.'

'You saved my life,' she insists. 'At Panyu Station. It was flooding and I was torn away from my mother. You rescued me.'

He looks apologetic. 'I don't remember saving a little girl.'

'I didn't look—' Biyu doesn't finish that. She remembers the terror of being ripped from Mama's grip. The cold dirty water hissing down from light fixtures and air vents. Being unable to grab hold of a bench or pole as the raging current swept her along the concrete. Sometimes she still wakes from nightmares of being unable to breathe. But one of the city's android police had caught her, lifted her to his solid chest, promised to return her to her mother. She remembers the EE stamped on his forehead, the kindness in his gold eyes, his hair as dark and short as Baba's.

But she's never been able to find out his identification number or name. Mama had been too busy weeping over her return to get it. Baba had said it didn't matter. You don't thank a Hero any more than you thank a toaster or vehicle.

So to her, all this time, his name has been Panyu. The handsome saviour who'd swept in and saved her from a watery death. Who would come again one day and carry her away to a glittering world where no one cared what lace underwear she wore in secret, the makeup she experimented with when Mama and Baba weren't home, the frilly clothes she bought as 'gifts' and then threw away before Baba could find them. She thinks Mama has suspected for years, but they have never spoken of it.

'I didn't look like a girl then,' Biyu says, shivering.

Darling Boy takes off his thin silver jacket and drapes it over her.

'I don't have access to any of my previous records. Perhaps I can call someone to assist you?

'Hey, Hero!' a voice calls out, and there's her distasteful cousin Chen. Since childhood he has been bigger, faster, stronger. His father is richer than hers. Rumour has it that Uncle is an overlord of the depths, but she has never met him. At school, Chen's become the illicit orchestrator of pop-up parties and distributor of pills that bring happiness.

Chen says, 'Leave her be, she's with me. Go on home.'

'Yes, sir,' the Hero says, and rises.

Chen saunters to her, a steam cigarette hanging from his lips. 'You need a place to crash tonight?'

Biyu struggles upright. She wants to grab Darling Boy by his arms, but he's retreating faster than she can totter on her broken heels. 'Who is he? Is he yours?'

'Retired, rehired, and retrained.' Chen says it like everyone can afford to do such a thing. 'Place to stay, yes or no?'

The Hero is gone into the shadows. Biyu reaches to a pillar for support. She can't think clearly, can't sort through the priorities jumbled in her head. Her torn face hurts. Baba's rage feels like a black mass lodged in her own chest, making it hard to breathe. 'What?'

Exasperated, Chen says, 'Tonight. You. Place to stay.'

She focuses on his cocky face. 'What's the price?'

'No price.' He blows out a plume of stream. 'You're useful. You can fix things.'

Of course she can fix things. Engines, mostly: strip them, service them, build them back up again. They're easier to repair than people. When the government had first assigned her to mechanic's courses in school she'd resented it, hoping to be a sky engineer stringing bridges and trains between high-rises never designed to hold such weight. But the cities along the inundated coastline need armies of workers to keep the pumps and bridges and barriers working, and she likes to be needed.

'Come on, cousin.' Chen walks away. 'Baba will love you. He loves everyone.'

Within a few minutes of meeting Uncle she knows his heart is certainly not full of love. At breakfast on a houseboat that rocks and sways under Biyu's feet, Uncle rails against bureaucrats and political tyrants and Darling Boy, who just overcooked the eggs.

Darling Boy. Biyu's Hero. Maybe. Her childhood memories have clouded. Although the right side of his head is burned and charred from whatever incident led to his retirement, he's still beautiful.

'You're a terrible cook!' Uncle says. 'My dog can cook better than you. My dog's penis can cook better than you!'

Biyu looks at Chen, who shrugs.

'Sorry, sir,' says Darling Boy, chastened. He's poised at the stove wearing a glittering green apron and little else. Biyu has been trying to ignore his bare legs and firm backside, but her resolve is slipping.

'Father, will you hire your dear niece?' Chen asks, dumping sugar into his tea.

Uncle peers at Biyu. 'Weren't you once my dear nephew?'

'Not anymore,' Chen says. And then, to Biyu, he adds, 'Only girl mechanics. That's the rule.'

'I'm a girl,' Biyu says.

'Girl, boy, whatever. Do the work and don't cause trouble.' Uncle waves a dismissive hand toward the portholes of this moored houseboat, the brown harbour sloshing against the hull, the ships large and small heading into Guangzhou Port. 'Do the work very well, maybe one day you can buy a Hero of your own.'

Her teenage dreams so far have been about leaving the city and its muddy waters. Seeing the wide world beyond, where mountains scrape the clouds far from flooding oceans.

Uncle claps his hands. 'Darling Boy, bring me food.'

The Hero comes to Uncle with a smile and a plate of burnt pancakes.

Biyu thinks about her parents, and about ever going back to school. Across the table, Uncle ignores the proffered plate and squeezes Darling Boy's smooth backside.

'Deal,' Biyu says.

Chen snorts into his coffee.

'Worst deal ever,' Biyu mutters to herself, more than once. 'Worst deal in history.'

For weeks she's been toiling in the bowels of a junk heap cargo ship, wading through bilge water and oil in stifling hot compartments in an attempt to wring another few months out of the ancient engines. The miserable crew is convinced one more journey will end with them at the bottom of the sea, but none of them confront Uncle. He rewards loyalty, perseverance, and a certain fatalism of character.

Biyu's boss, Shark Girl, has climbed to her position of authority in the all-female mechanics division by imitating Uncle's leadership style: anyone caught complaining is shipped off to even more unpleasant assignments or, even worse, sent to the unemployment office.

If they send her away she will never see Darling Boy again. That would be unbearable. She keeps his silver jacket neatly folded under her pillow during the day, and often sleeps under it at night.

For all of Uncle's hard-driving ways and Shark Girl's terse commands, and despite the adverse working conditions that leave her grimy and exhausted at the end of shifts, Biyu has to admit the compensation is fair enough. The salary is low, but the girl mechanics are housed rent-free on a sturdy, seaworthy barge away from the rat-infested, bug-heavy apartments in the lower city. Unlike on the mainland, the electrical supply is steady and the water clean to drink. The bed linens are washed each day, the morning and evening meals plentiful, and the repurposed Heroes who clean and cook can also provide pedicures, massages, and sensual services.

'Sensual services?' Biyu had asked when she first moved aboard.

'Anything you want,' the girls told her, and introduced her to the colourful and quite graphic menus of positions, options, and equipment that promise endless delight. All courtesy of Uncle, who prefers safe recreation for his employees in the comfort of home rather than unsavoury bars where girl mechanics might be recruited by rival boat lords.

The Heroes on the barge are, of course, handsome and strong and happy to be useful. Now retired from civil service, they each have their own personality quirks. Cobra wears eyeglasses and likes to peruse books while dusting the shelves in the houseboat's small library. Although his right hand was irreparably damaged and removed after lifting a vehicle crushing an elderly driver, the girls say his left hand is especially skilled at evoking passion from a woman's pearl.

Even more popular than Cobra is Snake, who laughs easily, paints beautiful landscapes, and massages sore feet with the gentlest of care. The explosion that damaged his audio circuits didn't affect the length or resilience of his Jade Stalk. Biyu glimpses it when he emerges from another mechanic's cabin, a thick jut between the folds of his blue satin robe, and she quickly looks away.

'Would you like to touch, Miss Coral?' he asks, a little too loudly.

Coral Reef, Shark Girl, Deep Sea. As with the Heroes, the girl mechanics go by nicknames that Uncle has bestowed. Real identities are concealed. The barge is full of secrets and stories.

'Not tonight,' she tells Snake, and ducks back inside her cabin.

The third Hero on the boat is Fang, who is tall and kind-hearted, and limps from an injury to his right knee. He makes specialty teas for the girls to ease aches and pains, to soothe exhaustion and stress. Sometimes Biyu sees Shark Girl eyeing Fang in a speculative way, but it's not until Biyu's been onboard for several months that she finds out why.

'You want me to what?' Biyu asks, confused.

'The government doesn't make girl heroes,' Shark Girl said. 'It's not fair to those of us who want to play with a girl.'

'But they'll never let me.'

'We have permission, as long as you stay within budget and do it after working hours.'

'What if Fang doesn't want it?'

'It's a machine.' Shark Girl looks puzzled. 'Do you ask an engine's permission before you fix it?'

Biyu tries one last argument. 'I've never worked on a robot.'

'You're only doing the cosmetics. I'll make the programming changes.' Shark Girl gives her a challenging look. 'You of all people shouldn't object.'

Face burning, Biyu turns away. It's not the same at all, but she knows Shark Girl would never understand, even if she cared to try.

The next evening, in Shark Girl's cabin, they sit Fang down on the edge of the bed.

'Can I modify your external appearance?' Biyu asks. 'And then Shark Girl will program you so that your inside ... matches your new outside?'

Fang tilts his head quizzically. 'Not male?'

'Female,' Biyu says. 'Is that okay?'

Shark Girl makes a disgruntled noise.

'I'm here to serve pleasure,' Fang says pleasantly. 'Gender is not a concern.'

The piecemeal work takes weeks. Biyu has to expand the synthetic skin over Fang's chest, anchor the breast implants, and then sculpt the curved mounds and rubber nipples to please human hands. The results are more satisfactory than Biyu's own padded bra, and she bites back jealousy. Next comes the surgery to remove Fang's artificial stalk and insert an artificial pearl. Shark Girl disagrees with Biyu's insistence that the pearl needs a ridge.

'It'll never know the difference,' Shark Girl says.

Biyu replies, 'I'll know.'

She plumps up Fang's rear, smooths down her throat, and removes unwanted hairs. She considers but abandons a plan to downsize Fang's hands or narrow her waist. Too much work and not enough money in the budget Uncle has allotted them. For Fang's head, Shark Girl splurges on the highest quality long, lustrous hair. It flows down Fang's shoulders as black and thick as oil. After that, permanent makeup is easy to apply.

'What do you think?' Biyu asks Fang when they are done.

Fang stares at her reflection in a mirror. 'I don't think. I am only programmed. Am I a woman now?'

'Yes.' Biyu's vision goes unexpectedly blurry. She blames the exhaustion of working weeks of full days and long nights. 'And you're beautiful.'

Biyu has never invited Snake or Cobra into her bed. No one comments except Deep Sea, the half-American girl who still talks to her family in the city.

'You avoid them like there's something wrong with them,' she says one afternoon on deck. 'But they're fun. They make me laugh.'

The wind off the harbour blows into Biyu's hair as they watch the upper city through fog and drizzle. The river smells like oil and rust and poisoned fish. Somewhere in the high-rise buildings is Biyu's mother, who won't return her messages. Her father, wielding his leather belt.

Biyu says, 'I don't need to laugh.'

'I think you like Darling Boy,' Deep Sea says.

Everyone likes Darling Boy, who often accompanies Uncle like a faithful puppy. Most of the time he's wearing nothing more than tiny white shorts or the barest slip of a shirt, even in wintertime. Although certainly Darling Boy doesn't feel cold the way a human does, each time Biyu wants to drape him in a proper shirt and pants. She wants to ask him if he remembers rescuing a little child at Panyu Station. She wants to ask him to run away with her to somewhere sunny and clean, if such a place exists anymore.

When Biyu keeps silent, Deep Sea elbows her. 'Or maybe it's Chen you want?'

Startled, Biyu says, 'No! Never.'

Chen has a rough charm, maybe, but aside from being her cousin, he's a scoundrel, not a Hero. Uncle has six sons, all of them versed in fists, bribes, and midnight deeds. Each of Chen's brothers is vying to be heir apparent, viciously clawing for Uncle's favour while building their own networks of operatives, spies, and thugs. Already in his young life Chen has been kidnapped twice. He escaped both times. Then sent to prison. He escaped that, too. There's been at least one assassination attempt. Probably more.

Chen has been heard to say he wants no watery throne, but adventure—sailing the world in the old yacht he plies around the harbour. Biyu thinks he'll be dead long before that, or back in prison, or in some secret witness protection programme.

Deep Sea says, 'They say short men always have something to prove. I'd like to find out.'

Uncle's houseboat glides out of the fog, moving down river. He is on deck, sheltered by an overhang and dressed in the ragged grey bathrobe he regards as a business suit. A line of supplicants wait miserably for an audience. Clad only in a gold bikini, Darling Boy is polishing the brass rails.

'Then again, if I had Darling Boy, I'd never let him out of my bed,' Deep Sea says.

The wind is strong and stinging but Biyu's vision is sharp enough to pick out the last man in the line waiting for Uncle. She sucks in a breath. Baba's posture is bowed. His suit hangs loose and his gaze is downcast. Although she hasn't seen him in more than a year, the shock of his fist on her face hasn't faded.

'What's wrong?' Deep Sea asks.

Biyu goes below deck without answering.

After worrying about it all night—Baba's poor clothing, his appeal to Uncle—Biyu asks Deep Sea if her family can check on Mama, just to see that she is safe. Deep Sea's brother sends back word that the apartment Biyu grew up in has been seized by the government and is being demolished, along with those one floor up and one floor down, to make way for a new elevated train line that will run right through the building. Mama and Baba left no forwarding address.

She tells herself she doesn't care. The girl mechanics are all the family she needs.

Another ancient ship, another engine held together by spit, rust, and luck. The girl mechanics toil toward exhaustion while trying to bring it back online. In their rest hours Shark Girl brings Fang to her quarters and laughs in pleasure behind the closed hatch. Deep Sea gets her sore feet rubbed by Cobra, then leads him away for rubbing of other parts. Biyu spends sleepless hours in her bunk, staring at the overhead, thinking of the ship they are trying to fix, the crew and cargo they are trying to dispatch to lands Biyu herself will never see.

She wanders to the barge's library to look at old-fashioned nautical charts. Cobra is there sitting quietly, his brown eyes half-closed behind his eyeglasses. His face is serene in the moonlight.

'Are you sleeping?' Biyu asks, surprised. Heroes aren't supposed to need sleep. Then again, they're supposed to be out saving people, not spending their days polishing brass and pleasing girl mechanics.

Cobra smiles and opens his eyes fully. 'I'm recharging.'

'You're not plugged in.'

'I'm categorising old memories,' he clarifies. 'Deleting what's obsolete.'

'I wish I could do that,' she says, which is stupid. She doesn't need to be candid with a robot. Then again, she could tell him anything, swear him to silence, and he would keep all of her secrets safe until overridden.

He tilts his head. 'May I be of service to you, Miss Coral?'

For the first time since taking up residence on the barge, Biyu hesitates. She is curious, she admits. After watching countless vids online she certainly knows what Shark Girl, Deep Sea, and the other mechanics do with the Heroes. But to show Cobra her own stalk, to admit that she too has needs, would be embarrassing.

'I'm fine,' she says, and backtracks.

A week later they succeed in the engine repairs. The captain begs Uncle to let Shark Girl, Biyu, and some of the other girl mechanics accompany the ship to sea, but Uncle refuses.

'Maybe I want to go,' Biyu tells Shark Girl on the ferry back to the barge.

Shark Girl scoffs. 'For what? Storms, tsunamis, and pirates?'

'You don't think there's anything interesting out there?' Biyu asks.

'Nothing worth the trouble.'

They pass Uncle's houseboat again. It is twilight, almost full dark, and the deck is lit with the lights and music and smoke of a party. The girl mechanics are never invited to Uncle's parties. Biyu looks for Darling Boy, but he is not visible. Instead she sees Chen with two beautiful women on his arms, all three of them laughing and drinking champagne. She is abruptly aware of her own greasy trousers, her calloused hands on the rail, the stink of her hair and armpits and breath.

Back on the barge she showers until her hot water allotment runs out, then perfumes and dresses herself and sends a detailed request order to Cobra. When he knocks on her cabin door she reminds herself she can turn him away. When he uses his only hand to undo the knotted belt at her waist, she helps him.

He doesn't complain when, later that night, in the middle of her first amazing flowering, she calls him Darling Boy. Maybe he's used to it.

Heroes are wonderful in bed.

Cobra is Biyu's first and in many ways her favourite, because he is thoughtful and careful and always asks permission before trying a new position. She turns down the permission setting on Snake, whose lack of hearing in no way impedes his understanding of how to caress and press and penetrate just the right spots to make her cry out in relief. Occasionally she requisitions both Cobra and Snake, which requires some scheduling flexibility but is totally worth the effort. Nestled between them, the barge gently rocking on the river, Biyu thinks she could happily serve in Uncle's employment for the rest of her life as long as she has Heroes to keep her satisfied.

One night, however, they are both busy with other mechanics, and out of curiosity Biyu sends for Fang.

'I was hoping to see you one day,' Fang says, slipping her golden dress from her shoulders.

'You see me every day,' Biyu replies, from where she's propped against her pillows.

'Like this. For pleasure.'

'Why were you hoping?'

Fang slips under the sheets. 'Because you made me.'

Snake Girl says, 'You look much better these days,' and Deep Sea says, 'You seem much happier,' and both of them should have persuaded her a long time ago to let the Heroes into her bed, but that's beside the point. Biyu's whole life is improved. She doesn't worry about a loveless future or sensual rejection. She sleeps better than any time in her life. She thinks maybe she is in love, real love, with Snake and Cobra and Fang, all three of them, and what's wrong with that? They tell her they love her, too.

She is busy plotting a way to schedule all three Heroes for her bed when Shark Girl relays the message that her parents want to see her. The barge galley goes grey at the edges, and the breakfast eggs in Biyu's mouth turn gummy.

'See me?' she repeats.

'Why so surprised?'

Biyu swallows and stares down at her plate. 'How did they find out I was here?'

'Does it matter?' Shark Girl asks. 'Your uncle probably told them.'

'I'm not going,' she says, and vows to stay firm.

But in bed Cobra says, wistfully, 'If I had estranged parents I would want to meet them.'

Biyu rests her hand on his chest, which is warm but unmoving. No heartbeat. No respiration. 'Why?'

'Curiosity.' He kisses the corner of her mouth. 'Resolution.'

She wishes she could take him with her, but he is never allowed to leave the barge. Neither are Fang or Cobra. They have chores to do, pleasure to deliver. The girl mechanics require constant satisfaction. Biyu resolves to go by herself, then thinks about asking Shark Girl or Deep Sea, then changes her mind. She styles her hair up, then down. She tries on a blue dress, then a green one. On the morning she's supposed to go she tries to eat, but succeeds only in throwing up.

The wooden yacht that comes to take her ashore is Chen's. He's piloting it himself, accompanied by Darling Boy.

'Uncle doesn't trust your father,' Chen says. 'Besides, the last time you saw him, you walked away with blood on your face.'

She's embarrassed that he remembers.

'It won't be like that,' Biyu says, accepting Darling Boy's help in stepping aboard. To her relief, he's dressed in black trousers and a casual shirt instead of a gold bikini. His hand is dry and warm. She adds, 'They asked for me.'

Chen grunts. He looks thinner than usual, more haggard. The last she heard, he'd been involved with some police business that required him to hide in the countryside for several weeks.

'Thank you for taking me,' Biyu says.

He shrugs. 'I have errands of my own. No trouble.'

'Uncle says that I go where he goes,' Darling Boy says serenely. That's surprising, because Uncle is ordinarily very possessive.

With Darling Boy beside her and Chen at the wheel Biyu can almost pretend they are friends, the three of them, off to dine in a restaurant or see a movie or do the things people do in the city on a day off. At the pier Chen leads them through the crush of passengers to the sky elevators, and from there through the elbow-jabbing crowds to the train station. Biyu's overwhelmed with all the people, the blinking lights on raincoats and galoshes, the yapping of robot dogs, the smell of oil and spices and tobacco, hundreds of booming advertisements and enticements. She feels like she's been away for a lifetime.

Darling Boy stoops to murmur something in Chen's ear, after which Chen stops forging ahead and keeps pace with them. Biyu barely notices. For the first time in her life she is walking the city in daylight as herself, and if she stops to admire shoes or jewellery in store windows no one will look askance. It's almost enough to make her forget her sweaty palms and unsettled stomach, her certainty that Mama has not forgiven her for running away, that Baba will maybe hit her again. But they asked for this. Maybe they are ready to forge a new relationship, a happier future.

The train passes through Canton Tower over the submerged murk of the Opera House and past residential blocks long abandoned. As with other surviving structures, Guangzhou Railway Station has expanded skyward to keep itself from the rising seas. The elevated concourses are crowded and reek of sweat, fish, and mould. Biyu almost loses Chen twice, and it's only then she realises he's given her no phone to use, no way to contact him if they accidentally part.

'Here,' Chen says, stopping, and Biyu focuses on the food court just a dozen paces away. The bright walls play commercials while travellers order and pick up their meals from dozens of gleaming machines. No cashiers, cooks, or clerks impede the consumer flow. Men and women in dull grey uniforms sweep the floors, clean up spills, and wipe down counters, part of the government work requirement for the unemployed to earn food credits.

'Here what?' Biyu asks.

Chen doesn't answer, and so Biyu looks closer. She watches, stunned, as a woman who looks like her mother carefully aligns her broom and dustpan on the floor. She keeps her eyes focused on spills, trash, and shoes, as any menial worker should. Demure and servile. Easily forgotten. By the trash receptacles, a man who looks like her father pulls out a garbage bag that leaks grimy water on his shoes. He shakes them not in anger, but weary resignation.

'Don't you want to talk to them?' Darling Boy asks.

She hears the words but is too busy denying her vision to respond to him. It is impossible that her parents would be so reduced. Surely this is someone who looks like them—unknown twins, doppelgangers. Someone is playing a joke on her.

'Hey, Auntie,' Chen calls out, and Biyu's heart stops.

Mama lifts her gaze, letting it slide across the sea of unfamiliar faces, right past Chen and Darling Boy and Biyu, then returning a moment later. Her features are worn and gaunt, her circumstances piled up on her in a way that no dutiful child should ever have allowed.

'Mama,' Biyu whispers.

Mama stares at Biyu as if she's a stranger. Then, slowly, recognition begins to change the shape of her lips and the wrinkles at her eyes. She looks like she's swallowed a lemon.

'Fake girl,' Mama says.

Biyu feels an invisible punch. And then, amidst the din of the crowd and trains, she hears a faint pop, nothing more than a blip of noise. Darling Boy immediately shoves her down. With her face mashed against something—Chen's leg? Is he on the floor too?—she protests, her voice lost under more pops, screams, the sudden blare of a klaxon.

Darling Boy's elbow is digging into her back, her right knee is singing with pain from impacting the floor, and her lips feel wet. When Biyu touches her lips, her fingers come away red. When she shifts her head, she sees Chen curled up and staring at her sightlessly.

'Save him,' she tells Darling Boy. Then it's a scream, amid so many other screams in the station. 'Save him!'

The barge rocks beneath her bed, a cradle without comfort. Biyu doesn't leave her thin blankets despite Shark Girl's threats to fire her,

Cobra's offer to please her, and Snake's efforts to rub her feet. Her parents survived the railway shooting but Chen is dead, his ashes already scattered. If he hadn't accompanied her, the assassin still at large would never have killed him. Biyu would understand completely if Uncle blamed her to the end of his days.

'No,' Fang says, 'he blames Darling Boy for not protecting him. He's going to destroy him tomorrow.'

Biyu struggles upright. 'He can't!'

Fang's expression shows no regret. 'We're all to bear witness.'

The next day, despite every attempt by Biyu to convince Shark Girl to intervene, Biyu finds herself standing on the barge deck in a steady rain in silent, furious protest. Uncle's houseboat floats nearby, draped in mourning ribbons of white. The mist-shrouded towers of Guangzhou hang in the background like ghosts. On the barge deck, Uncle and his five remaining sons surround a scaffold on which Darling Boy stands in the coarse grey pyjamas of a prisoner, his hands bound behind his back. His gaze is locked on his own feet. Biyu yearns for one last glimpse of his face.

'It's obscene,' she says, and Shark Girl pokes her sharply in the ribs.

'You want to join him?' Shark Girl asks.

The oldest of Uncle's sons reads charges against Darling Boy: dereliction of duty and failure to protect his charge. It's ridiculous, of course. A machine that follows its programming can't be guilty of anything.

Biyu looks at Cobra, Snake, and Fang. The Heroes stand rock-solid in the rain, expressionless. No human is in danger here. No biological entity needs to be rescued from drowning or dangling or death. When this is done they'll go back below deck to boil noodles, wash latrines, and try to soothe the grief of girl mechanics. There will be no last-minute heroics or improbable rescues by the Heroes or by Biyu or by anyone at all.

'Failure is always punished,' Uncle says, his voice thin on the wind.

The sons carry out their father's revenge with cutting saws. The whine of metal being shredded makes Biyu bury her face against Deep Sea's shoulder. They take off Darling Boy's arms, then his legs.

They sever his head, and his golden eyes go dark forever.

The girl mechanics wail and weep. Uncle personally drops the pieces into the turbulent river to be buried in silt and mud for time eternal, and in the space of a moment all that is left is Biyu's memory, her grief, and her resignation.

Rain turns the stairs over Biyu's sleeping spot into a waterfall. Wearily she gathers up her meagre belongings and moves away from the torrent. She has no idea of where to go next—the shelters are full and always dangerous, the libraries and shopping centres closing soon at the end of day. With water drenching her boots and her backpack heavy on her shoulder, she lets the crowds carry her to Shiqi Station, high in the sky, with its dry floors and waiting benches.

In the food area she thinks about how many credits she can spare for dinner, but an old woman begging for food catches her attention. The woman is old and thin, her raincoat inadequate, her eyes rheumy. Biyu buys her hot noodles brimming with vegetables.

'For you, grandmother,' Biyu says.

While the woman mumbles grateful words, her gaze sharpens on Biyu's eyebrows and nose, the knob of her Adam's apple. Biyu simply smiles and turns away before appreciation turns to scorn. Two levels up, on a platform thick with commuters, she contemplates the approaching train. If she rides all the way to Old Nansha she might find scut work, maybe hitch a ride to what's left of Hong Kong. With no references to offer, a work history stained by association with Uncle, and no contact with her family, there's no reason to remain in Guangzhou.

She shifts the weight of her backpack and moves closer to the platform edge. The jostling edge of a commuter's elbow sends her closer to the safety edge than she'd like, but a hand grabs her.

'Don't fall now,' a familiar voice says.

The world stops as she blinks at him. 'Chen?'

He grins crookedly. His hair is longer than usual, almost curly on the edges, and stuffed under a large ball cap. His eyes are a lighter colour. He's not dead.

'I've been looking for you,' he says.

She throws herself into his arms. He is warm, solid, not a dream. Everything she thought she knew about the world shifts again, and her heart begins to feel warm after so many weeks of ice.

'We have to go,' he says, and takes her hand to pull her along the platform.

'No, wait.' Biyu's elation plummets into confusion and anger. 'How did you—was it a lie? Every part of it?'

'I had to,' he says. 'Come on.'

He leads her to the escalator, to the lower platforms, to the docks. They don't talk. Once again she feels like she's walking through the city for the first time, a foreigner in her own land. She touches his arm to make sure he's real. Touches again. Doesn't yell at him, but she wants to. When they reach the riverfront of junks, canoes, and ferries he leads her to the gangplank of an unfamiliar yacht.

'What is this?' she asks.

The shadowed city above is full of noise and dripping water but the waterfront curiously hushed. Chen says, 'My boat.'

'Why do you have a boat? Why aren't you dead?'

'I need your help,' he says, and goes aboard.

She follows, but slowly. In the wheelhouse, Chen throws back the tarpaulin covering a large box.

Inside, in pieces, is Darling Boy.

'It was my father's idea to fake my death,' Chen says. 'To set me free. Sooner or later my brothers would have killed me, so this was my chance.'

'Free!' Biyu stalks toward him. He retreats. 'You used me! You made me believe my parents wanted to see me as part of your scheme.'

'Don't you want freedom, too?' he asks. 'Don't you want to see a world beyond this rust and ruin?'

She glares at him. At the muddy river beyond the windows. Out there, beyond the bend, is Uncle's houseboat and the barge of girl mechanics. The girls will have spent hard hours trying to coax rusty old equipment back to life. The Heroes will be making dinner, cleaning afterward, and rotating between beds. She could have spent her whole life there, but instead she gave it up for this liar and his deceptions.

She picks up one of Darling Boy's arms. Rusted. Touches his face. So cold. Deactivated, he looks even more beautiful.

'You pulled him out of the water?' she asks.

'My father did. For me. The execution was part of the show. But now I need you to fix him.'

'Why?'

'He's my friend.' Chen drops to a crouch and looks forlornly into the box. 'He was my first friend.'

'You don't deserve friends,' she says, but doesn't fully mean it. She sorts through the pieces, gauging damage and rust. 'I'll need money. Time. He might be too broken. I can't make a promise he'll be the same.'

'But you can try,' Chen says, hope in his voice. He looks up at her. 'I'll steer us across the ocean and you'll fix him, and no one here will ever see us again.'

She thinks about what she might gain if she goes with him: only the world beyond these waters.

The whole world.

'I can try to save anyone,' Biyu says, and begins to rescue her hero.

A Robot Like Me

Lee Cope

I'm so sick of the questions.

I tried introducing myself with my job for a while. 'Hi—I'm Carley, and I work in robotics.'

'Hi, I'm Carley. I program robots.'

But nobody takes the bait. 'Oh, that must be interesting! Hey—just checking—are you a boy or a girl?'

They're not doing it to be rude, I know. They don't want to assume, to say the wrong thing. But the questions are always either-or. They don't make space for the right answer. Do I lie? Say I'm one or the other? Make a game of it—answer everybody differently, watch them get confused? It's tempting sometimes, even though it's petty. A small victory in a world where there are no big victories.

I am sitting in front of a metal shell. At a university, if you say you need a robot shell for a new project, it's fairly easy to get one. AI is the path of the future, after all, and the metal is cheap.

The big victory, of course, would be to say 'neither', and have that to be the end of it. To confidently look them in the eye and proclaim that no, they're wrong. Their entire question is wrong. This basic premise of their entire lives is wrong and I am proof—I am *living* proof, standing open to the sky and the stars and every soul in the world declaring that they are wrong, and I—I am me and I am proof enough, and then for the conversation to end.

The problem with the big victory is that it's not really a victory. It's not met with dawning realisation and understanding, only more questions.

'What?'

'What do you mean?'

'How does that work?'

'Is that even a real thing?'

And I smile and I answer because maybe, just maybe, there's an end in sight. Maybe there will be someone else along the line who braces themselves and prepares and waits for the questions ... and they won't come. And because of me, now, this one future person can relax a little, and maybe that day will be a good day.

That's all I can hope for. People like me don't get to open themselves to stars and sky.

I hook up my laptop to the side of the robot's head and access the factory settings. I start to type, to change the options. I dig deep into the programs and rip out handfuls of code: definitions, entire subroutines. You can't just program something to full AI intelligence; all AI has to learn from scratch, but I've really pared this one down. I've only put the most basic of basic programs in.

I'm not telling this robot what it's like to be a human. I want it to have to learn that from scratch, too. I want to see just how much it will learn.

Worse than the questions are the jokes.

'So, you're like a Barbie doll down there?'

'Oh, I heard that's the newest phase these days ... how long have you been calling yourself that?'

'No wonder you ended up a robot programmer. You have something in common!'

Something in common.

When I'm done, I turn it on and watch the light come into its eyes.

'Hello, World,' it says. Its voice is without inflection or tone.

'Hello, Robot,' I say. Later, it will name itself. I did not program it with a name. 'Are you a boy or a girl?'

I must keep my inputs simple to start. This question is just a test.

It looks at me for a time. I can hear the fans whirring as it searches, briefly, for the information in its lines and lines of data and code.

Finally, it says, 'I do not understand the question.'

I begin to cry. When I throw my arms around the robot, it makes no move to push me away. It simply says, 'I do not understand this reaction. Please explain it.'

And that makes me cry all the harder.

At first, the robot really is like a child. The questions are endless, but always different.

'What is the sky?'

'What is water?'

'Why do humans need to eat food?'

'What do I need to consume to continue to function?'

The conversations are different, wildly different, every day a new thing to learn, some shiny kernel of knowledge to unwrap and taste like Easter chocolate. But even though it was the first thing I asked the robot, it never asks me about gender. I removed those definitions from its programming. It knows to use pronouns, and it knows to use the ones it has been asked to use. I never programmed it to make the connection to gender, though. If I am like a robot, then I want this robot be like me. I've lived a life where everyone but me seems to know what gender is. What gender feels like. What it means to have a gender. Well, my robot won't know, either. I want to see what it does.

For a long time, I keep the robot in isolation. It doesn't speak to anyone else—even the other grad students, no matter how much they beg me to tell them what my big project is about. I don't let it connect to the Internet. When it asks me why, I only say it is important to the experiment. The robot does not complain. It does not argue. It is only learning—it questions, but it takes orders calmly.

It tells me its name is Burgundy, because of a picture of a dress it likes. I ask it what pronouns it wants me to use. It asks me what criteria it should use to make the choice.

I smile—even now, when Burgundy asks me questions like this, I tear up a little. It asks me the questions I wish I had known to ask right from the start.

I tell it to choose pronouns based on which ones it likes the sound of, and which ones it thinks suit it best. I tell it that it can change them at any time, if one day it likes new ones better.

After a few moments, fans whirring, it says, 'I require time to process.'

I tell it to take as much time as it needs. AI systems work much faster than the human brain, but they must take time to compile information in storage, to avoid accidentally overwriting code.

It returns in half an hour, and simply says, 'I am happy for you to use "it". Humans use "it" for objects, don't they?'

I tell it most of the time, but not always. There are some humans who prefer to go by 'it'. But traditionally, yes, that is right.

It nods, and compiles the information, and says, 'I am an object, and I shall use "it'."

As Burgundy grows, its questions grow more and more complex. I cannot answer all of them. I turn to encyclopaedias, to web print-outs, and soon I realise that the last part of the experiment must start.

I sit down in front of Burgundy, and it turns to me to listen.

'I am going to give you access to the Internet,' I say. 'I want you to try and find the answers to your questions for yourself. I want you to use your fact-checking protocols to verify the encyclopaedia information I gave you about redback spiders, eye colour, genetic variation in housecats, and the etymology of the word "regulatory". Tell me what you find, and whether your protocols are working smoothly, and then you have free access to the Internet. Okay?'

'Sure,' Burgundy says, nodding. 'I can do that.' It is more comfortable with slang now. It asked if it could test out 'she' pronouns, but after a week it told me to return to 'it'.

With shaking fingers, I turn on Burgundy's Wi-Fi connection.

Half an hour later, it returns.

'Fact-checking protocols operational,' Burgundy reports. 'And I printed them out. You always want me to print out my protocol tests, so...'

'Thank you—that's very good,' I say. It is learning—it has started to know me.

Three weeks later, Burgundy comes to me with a clip from a popular sitcom. We watch the clip together, then Burgundy turns to me and says, 'I think this is supposed to be a joke.'

I nod. It was. It was a common sitcom joke, recently single man gets cheered up with a night out. The joke revolves around a particular man getting drunk and waking up in the same bed as his friend, naked, but doesn't know how he got there.

'What is the punchline?' Burgundy asks, and I don't know where to begin to explain. 'You didn't laugh.'

'No,' I say. 'I didn't find it funny. The joke relies on the audience thinking it's a bad thing for two men to sleep together. The punchline is how the men react.'

Burgundy stares at me, eyes bright and fans whirring, and then asks, 'What, exactly, do you mean by "man"?'

I am proud. I am so happy. But I don't know how to answer the question.

It takes us three weeks to reach an answer that we're happy with.

Weeks later again, Burgundy fidgets by the bedroom. Since accessing the Internet, it has become more and more like a human. It speaks more smoothly, its body language is more natural, and more individual as well. I know it is nervous.

I sit down with it, ask it what is wrong. It turns to me and asks, 'Carley ... are you a boy or a girl?'

I choke on my answer.

'Neither,' I say. 'I am agender. Non-binary.'

There is a whir.

'But humans are either male or female,' Burgundy says, hesitating. 'I have looked through many online encyclopaedias. There is far more evidence to support this than contradict it.'

I shake as I try to explain without crying. 'Search academic journals,' I say. 'Terms 'non-binary' and 'agender', spelled a-g-e-n-d-e-r. Doesn't your fact-checking protocol have a clause that says more recent information is generally more reliable than older information, where there is conflict?'

Burgundy nods. 'Results of recent scholarship inconclusive as to cause or genesis—all evidence is anecdotal. Anecdotal evidence is inconclusive, scientifically.'

I don't know what to say to this. This is worse than any question any human has ever asked me.

Burgundy sees that I am distressed, but continues gently, 'Many cultures throughout history have taught that there are more than two genders, but your prevailing culture teaches only male and female gender. I wanted to ask you about that, so that I could better understand. Is gender related to cultural upbringing?'

I stand up. I can't hear this anymore. 'Fact-checking protocol error,' I tell Burgundy, but I don't get any further.

'I'm sorry,' Burgundy says. 'I didn't mean to hurt you. What can I do to make it better?'

I shake my head, because nothing I can do will make it better. Burgundy is programmed to fact-check my responses, too. I can't say anything that will stand up against the crushing weight of history bearing down on me. Burgundy was made too soon—too soon to find the evidence waiting for it, too soon to find the language to express the concepts it doesn't have.

'I have found,' Burgundy says, reaching out a hand to my arm. 'That many people feel that they aren't male or female. Are you like this, too? I will always respect your pronouns, and I won't use any language for you that you find discomforting. Like you always did for me. That's the right way to treat people, isn't it? That's what you taught me.'

I nod. 'Thank you,' I say. 'You're right. I am not male or female. Please keep using the pronouns you always have, and the language you always have.'

'I think I am like you,' Burgundy confesses. 'I do not understand what it means to have a gender. But that is because you programmed me like that, isn't it? I would like to understand better what it means to be you, if you would be willing to teach me.'

It was the best answer I could have hoped for. I could not open myself to the stars and the sky, but Burgundy deserved, at least, for me to open myself to this metal and silicone frame.

So I sat down to answer the same questions again, because the robot didn't really understand at all.

New Berth

Elizabeth Fitzgerald

Constance's eyes sparkled and there was a jerkiness to her gestures that told Adeline she was doing her best to keep them small and ladylike, in spite of her excitement, as she spoke to her new suitor. Constance had always been an attractive child and had grown to be a beautiful woman—and since Adeline had no hand in making her daughter, she thought she had some measure of objectivity. In her opinion, Constance was most beautiful like this, with enthusiasm animating her.

Mr Ingram certainly appeared to agree. He leaned forward in his armchair, eyes fixed on Constance, his smile coming readily. Adeline smothered a smile of her own and turned to the window.

Countless stars sparkled as brightly as her daughter's eyes, but Adeline's gaze was drawn to the barren planet below the space station where they lived. It glowed ochre in the sunlight, an endless waste of hardpan. What would it be like to travel along its plains and ravines? What would it be like to walk and climb until her body gave out and she was left to be gradually buried in some dusty arroyo? Without doubt, it would be lonely ... but then it was not much different here. She had Constance, but for how much longer? She glanced at her daughter's reflection and saw she had drawn closer to Mr Ingram.

Constance would not need help raising children back on Earth—there were already too many people there that could help with that. Adeline would end up treading these same carpeted corridors until the station was decommissioned. How many generations later might that be? The thought made her feel claustrophobic. At least the planet would afford some new scenery, however dusty.

Beside her, the glass fogged. 'I wonder what it will look like once it's all green,' said Constance.

'It will take time,' warned Mr Ingram, peering over Constance's head. 'Even with your father's new system, it could take decades. We may not be here to see the final result.'

'Surely, Mama will,' Constance objected.

Adeline smiled politely and was relieved when the dinner bell rang.

Constance's father was already seated at the head of the table as they filed into the dining room. Sparing a brief glare for Adeline, he rose and stretched out a hand to Mr Ingram. 'Glen! So glad you could make it.'

'Thank you, sir.'

'How are things going with the *Indra*?' asked Lord Starr, as he resumed his seat.

'The terraforming equipment is all set and ready to go, it just needs to be deployed and monitored. But I'm still having a few problems with the ship's guidance system.'

Lord Starr glowered. 'I hope they'll be resolved before launch next month. It's too late to employ a crew.'

'Yes, sir,' replied Mr Ingram, 'we're working hard on a solution.' Adeline noticed again the shadows on the dark skin beneath his eyes.

As the men chattered, Constance took her seat to her father's right, Adeline slipping into her customary place beside Constance. She remained still throughout the meal, moving only to pass the salt and speaking when spoken to.

'And how is your tinkering going, Constance?' Lord Starr asked, as dessert was brought out.

Adeline tried not to bridle at the question. Why was it that he was happy to spend an entire meal talking to Mr Ingram about his creations, but Constance's work was 'tinkering'?

Constance seemed unfazed. 'Well, thank you, Father. I have almost completed the prototype of my new building assistant. Adeline is taking me shopping for the last few parts tomorrow.'

'Is it?' Lord Starr glowered.

'Yes, *she* is,' Constance replied firmly.

'The new design is really quite elegant,' put in Mr Ingram, perhaps looking to head off a family argument. 'I think it will revolutionise the work of private inventors and could have some valuable application in the industry.' He beamed at Constance, who blushed and returned his smile.

'Hmm. Glen, would you like to join me for a brandy?'

As the men left, Constance took her hand and squeezed. 'I'm sorry,' she said. 'He never has been very good with pronouns.'

Adeline remembered.

Lord Starr towered over the child, face an apoplectic purple.

'Your mother cannot be replaced,' he said through clenched teeth. 'No son of mine—'

'Daughter.'

'What?'

'No daughter *of yours,' Constance corrected him, dark curls wild and blue eyes flashing with fire.*

At the time, Adeline had wondered whether she would have to step in and protect the child. However, Lord Starr loved his daughter and eventually came around to seeing her as such. Perhaps he would come around about Adeline, too.

When suns started revolving around planets.

'And then he cancelled dinner!'

Adeline's fingers never ceased picking through the gears in the bargain bin, metal clanking together. 'Mr Ingram is a very busy man, Constance,' she replied. Spying a small cog, she plucked it up and handed it to her daughter. 'The project he is working on for your father is important.'

'But he works all the time!'

'So do you.'

'I at least stop to eat,' Constance protested. Inspecting the cog, she shook her head, then placed it back in the bin. 'Mama, I'm worried. But I feel like I can't say anything to him. He's already got enough on his mind without adding my worry to his. And I don't want to sound like I'm nagging.'

'I see,' said Adeline, picking up another gear and passing it over. 'Well, if Mr Ingram will not come to us, perhaps we should go to him. We could pack a picnic.'

'Yes, that's a wonderful idea!' Constance's arms jerked, beginning to open for a hug before she caught herself. She settled for a demure, 'Thank you, Mama.'

Adeline smiled, 'You are welcome, Constance.' She tapped the gear, still in Constance's hand. 'Was this the size you were looking for?'

'Oh! Yes, this is the one.' Constance's breath misted on Adeline's cheek as she kissed it. 'Thank you, Mama. I don't know what I'd do without you.'

The gear, along with a pile of others, was paid for at the counter where the owner refused to make eye contact with Adeline. It made her wish for the cold welcome of the stars. The shop bell tinkled as they left and Adeline's eyes habitually sought out the clear dome above the market place where the night sky twinkled brightly.

Constance stopped suddenly.

Alarmed, Adeline turned to look at her daughter. 'Is everything all right?' she asked.

'I've been wondering the same,' said Constance, taking Adeline's hands in hers. 'You've been staring off into space even more than usual.'

Adeline studied the young woman in front of her. The shadows under Constance's eyes had grown darker and now that she was looking for them, she could see the first sign of wrinkles across her daughter's forehead. Mr Ingram's stress was clearly taking a toll on her. She did not need Adeline adding to that.

'I am fine,' she lied, turning once more towards the market. 'Do you think Mr Ingram likes strawberries?'

When he opened the hangar bay door and saw them waiting, picnic basket in tow, Mr Ingram's face lit up like a supernova. 'Constance, Adeline. What a delightful surprise!'

'We've brought lunch,' said Constance, holding up the basket. 'I hope you like strawberries.'

'They're my favourite,' he beamed. Adeline saw him wobble a little as he hauled the heavy door wider, to allow them to step across the threshold. Constance was right to be worried, she thought. He looked far too gaunt and she wondered how long it had been since he had last eaten. 'I'm afraid I can't stay long, but please, come in.'

As she stepped into the cavernous space of the hangar proper, all thoughts of her daughter fled. If Adeline had breath, it would have caught in her lungs. The *Indra* was beautiful, all sleek lines and shiny brass. It was astonishing that something so big should be so graceful, even while grounded—out of its natural element. At the front of the *Indra*, the glass panels of the bridge beckoned.

'Would you like a tour?'

Adeline started in surprise. She turned and saw Mr Ingram looking at her expectantly. Constance had a strange look on her face.

'Oh, no, I cannot take up your time like that. But thank you. He is utterly beautiful.'

Constance raised an eyebrow at Adeline's choice of pronoun. 'Would you mind if Adeline takes a look around while we eat?' she asked her paramour. 'Unless you think she needs a chaperon?'

Mr Ingram's uncertainty melted in the face of Constance's charm. 'Not at all! Please, go on up.'

Constance flashed both of them a grin.

Leaving the other two to spread out the picnic blanket, Adeline climbed up the stairs to the docking bay and across the gangplank to the *Indra*. She slipped through a hatch to the bridge. The control panels were a mess of wires and gears, but Adeline ignored these and looked out the windows.

The view showed only the steel doors of the docking bay.

What would it be like to see something other than this station, Adeline wondered? What would it be like to go with the *Indra* and see the stars—*new* stars, instead of the same ones she saw from the parlour? To see new planets in jewel tones? Even the dusty old one nearby would do. So long as they could fly, just the two of them.

Adeline only left the ship when she heard Constance calling her name.

The maid lifted away Adeline's empty plate. Adeline smiled, murmuring, 'Thank you, Lucy,' and was rewarded by a feather-light brush of fingertips to her shoulder.

Across the table, Mr Ingram looked like death warmed over. He had lost weight and there was an ashy cast to his complexion. The *Indra* was due to launch later that month, but Adeline was not sure if Constance's suitor would last that long. Although, if it meant there would be a delay in the *Indra* leaving ... no, Adeline shoved away the thought, chiding herself for her selfishness.

Once the table was clear, Lord Starr rumbled to life. 'Well, Ingram. Have you finished?'

'No, sir,' he replied, looking at the tablecloth. 'I hit some problems with integrating the navigation panel with the ship's systems.'

Constance clutched her hands together. 'Oh, Glen. I'm sorry. Have you tried—'

Lord Starr cleared his throat. Constance flushed and fell silent.

'There is still a bit of time.' Adeline smiled at Mr Ingram. 'You are an intelligent and resourceful person. You will find a solution. The *Indra* is lucky to have you.'

Lord Starr glared down the table at her, but reluctantly agreed, 'Yes, keep at it, Ingram. Perhaps you'd like to join me for a brandy and we can discuss some options.' He rose from his seat.

Mr Ingram gave Constance a regretful look, but followed suit. 'Certainly, s-'

Without warning, he keeled over, dropping to the ground like a length of heavy chain.

'Glen!' Constance pushed past her father and was at her suitor's side in a heartbeat, checking him over. 'Adeline, fetch the doctor.'

Adeline turned and ran.

It was late by the time Constance returned to her room. Adeline rose as she entered, folding her daughter into a hug. 'Sit down and let me brush your hair,' she said.

Constance said nothing as Adeline guided her to the stool in front of the vanity. She stared at a spot on the counter, her eyes hooded in the dim light. Adeline let the silence fall and calmly brushed out the dark curls.

Eventually, Constance spoke. 'The doctor said he should be fine. He just needs some rest and regular meals.'

Adeline continued brushing.

'I don't understand how he could let it get so bad,' continued Constance. 'Yes, his work is important, but not at the expense of his own health! It's just not sustainable.'

Adeline smiled a little. 'Not everyone is as practical as you are, my darling. Ambition is a siren song.'

'I am not going to sit idly by and watch him destroy himself,' said Constance, scowling fiercely at the mirror. 'I won't.'

'Did you have something in mind?' Adeline paused her brushing.

Constance turned to look at her. 'I'll finish it myself.'

The hangar bay seemed even more enormous in the dark. Metal glinted like stars in the darkness, reflecting flashes of the light that beamed from Adeline's eyes. She led Constance over to the *Indra* and up the docking bay stairs, pausing only to lay a brief hand on the ship's flank. It felt warm under her fingertips.

On the bridge, the control panel remained much the same condition as Adeline had last seen it. Wires spilled out of the bottom like multicoloured intestines. A sheet of brass sat to one side of the space, waiting to be riveted into place. Mr Ingram's tools had been neatly packed into their box and stacked next to a table with the schematics rolled out.

Constance strolled over and peered at the blueprints. Absently, she took out a red pencil from the pocket of her skirt and began to make notations. Adeline made her own preparations, opening up Mr Ingram's toolbox and locating the tools her daughter was most likely to want.

According to Adeline's internal chronometer, it was almost morning by the time they had finished. The station's ambient lighting was beginning to flicker on. Constance attached the last panel and sat back on her heels, wiping her hands on a rag.

'Done,' she proclaimed, giving Adeline a smile. 'The *Indra* is ready to fly out into the world ... er, galaxy. Where do you think it will go after it has deployed the terraformer?'

Her words punched through Adeline. *No*, she thought, *not this too. Not both of them at the same time*. She had been so caught up in making the *Indra* whole at last and helping her daughter, that she had forgotten they'd both be leaving once she was done.

Constance tilted her head. 'Mama? Are you okay?'

'Fine,' she lied. 'You go on ahead so you do not get caught. I will tidy up the last of the tools.'

'I hardly think it will matter if anyone finds out it was us,' said Constance. She yawned. 'But I could definitely use some sleep.'

Adeline waited until her daughter was halfway down the stairs before starting up the *Indra*. A subsonic rumble began, gradually rising in pitch as the engines warmed up. She could see the exact moment when it registered in Constance's hearing. The young woman stopped instantly. 'Mama, what are you doing?' she yelled, turning back towards the ship.

Adeline leaned out the hatch. 'Open the hangar,' she called back.

Constance stood a moment, her face a mask of indecision. 'You'd better write to me,' she yelled finally, then ran for the control room.

'I love you,' Adeline called after her, and turned to face the stars.

Fata Morgana

Cat Sparks

'They'll send the black death after us. You should have left me behind. I was happy underneath that mountain. All set for that place to become my tomb—I hope you know that.'

'Better to be with your own kind.'

'They were my own kind!' Bethany rasped, mouth opening and closing uselessly like a fish out of water. 'Don't judge me by the limitations of my ageing body. That's all I am to you, isn't it—meat and bones.'

The machine had nothing to say to that.

The wide, pale sky went on forever, as did the heavy mecha tread on coarse grain sand, a repetitive sound so mesmerising that Bethany kept drifting in and out of a restless sleep that did nothing to replenish her, but left her drained of focus and resolve. She'd lost track of the days and nights. The machine never tired, of course, not like she did.

'We gotta rest up, Mach. You're killing me. It's alright for you and your self-repairing bioceramic carcass.'

Mach's mechanical legs continued their relentless pace. Something darted out between them, too small and quick to have been anything but a skink.

'So anyway,' she continued, 'now that I've had time to think about it, there are only three items you could conceivably have stolen. A block of tantalite; military grade cloud codes or a Seed AI. I mean, why would anyone care that you stole me?'

'Bethany, I am not programmed to steal.'

'You're not programmed at all. Not since the Marusek Protocol. Got a smart mouth answer to that one? Didn't think so. Burned the Institute to the ground to cover your crime, whatever it was.'

Crunch crunch crunch crunch crunch.

'They'll catch us. You know they will. They'll figure it out. They're not stupid. They'll launch a swarm and they'll pick the meat off me. You can't protect me with your body or your armour.'

'You are safe, Bethany, so long as you reside within my frame.'

'I need a rest, Mach. Put me down—I ache all over. I can't stand up anymore, not even with you taking all the weight. If you'd wanted me protected you would have left me in the Seed Vault with the others. Don't go pretending any of this is for my benefit.'

The Legionnaire-350s were not noted conversationalists, but Mach had mellowed over time. She was proud of the way it had deduced for itself that words had power, sometimes more than firepower itself. But nothing she could say would stop it walking. Not this time. Not until the machine believed them safe.

It took Bethany hours to become aware of the drool dribbling down her chin, longer still to comprehend that the mind-numbing crunching had ceased and that she and the Legionnaire had come to a complete standstill.

She blinked the dust out of her eyes. 'Woah—whatsup? Where are we? What are we doing?'

'We are waiting, Bethany.'

'Waiting? What are we waiting for?'

'You'll see.'

'I won't be seeing anything very much longer. My old eyes are gummed and full of grit and the light is fading from the hills.'

'Those are sand dunes, Bethany, not hills.'

'Really? Bethany tilted her head and squinted, but it didn't help. 'There was definitely grass before. And rabbits.'

'Those weren't rabbits, Bethany.'

'That why you wouldn't stop and let me catch one?'

'The incident you are referring to was three days back—and excuse me, but you couldn't catch a cold.'

'Three days!' She sniffed. 'Figures. Can't feel my stomach. Or my feet. My side aches—did I get shot or something?'

'You did not get shot.'

'Then how come I got this great big stitch running up my gut?'

The Legionnaire said nothing.

'Did you do this? Did you patch me up? Don't get me wrong, I'm grateful, even though I can't remember, but something's after us—I'm telling you.'

When the Legionnaire raised the polycarbonate visor that had been covering her face, Bethany let out a deep, breathy sigh. She had forgotten the visor was even there and had presumed her rheumy vision fading. Her eyes focused on rusted clumps of broken-down farm machinery choked and drowned in sand.

Scrappy, emaciated chickens scratching at the ground. Leaning fence posts—the remains of a stockade. An ancient, enamel bathtub on three legs. Beyond the chickens was harder to make out, a couple of scraggly palms and a crooked wind turbine poking out from behind a row of mismatched, corrugated iron segments, brittle and rusted through. Ragged drag marks led to and betrayed the existence of a gate. Two words clumsily rendered in chipped and peeling paint: FATA MORGANA. The whole thing looked like mere breath could blow it over. Big storms clearly didn't reach this far inland.

Bethany started to shake her head. 'No, Mach—no! We can't stop here. Looks like people living beyond that fence.'

'Fifty-seven warm bodies not counting the goats,' said Mach. 'A bore well not drilled deep enough.'

'Mach, we gotta get out of here. We're putting them all in danger.'

But Mach wasn't listening, as she well knew. Its kind had been designed to listen, but they had got over it. Her own fault, as much as anybody's. Machine learning from environment and experience had rendered the 350s a batch of sharp, quick-witted, canny liars.

She sucked at her teeth. 'Hard to believe anyone could make a go of it out here.'

'Human beings are like rats,' said Mach. 'A few survive wherever they may scatter.'

Bethany tried to turn her head in an attempt to give the Legionnaire an incredulous look. She failed, but knew Mach was accustomed to the gesture and its meaning. 'What about Newcastle—have you forgotten already? There wasn't so much as a rat left standing after—'

'I never forget, Bethany. You know that.'

'Never forgetting is not the same as remembering. You have a selective memory.'

'And you do not always ask intelligent questions.'

She bit her tongue before continuing, enunciating clearly. 'If this village—if that's what it is—takes pity on our souls, we will be bringing them death from whatever's on our tail.'

'I do not have a soul, Bethany.'

'The Hell you don't. I put one in there myself, don't you forget that.'

'You are mistaken in believing something is chasing us.'

'Oh, come on. I wasn't born yesterday.'

'No, Bethany, your date of birth is recorded as—'

'Come on, Mach—you know it's true. Something has been tailing us since Templestone Gate—or what's left of it. I want to hear you admit it. I want to hear you say those words.'

'You need water, Bethany. The well beyond that fence is your only hope.'

'If they let us in, that's the end of any hope these innocent people might have had.'

'There is no such thing as an innocent human being. Bethany, you know my opinion on this subject. One bad storm and that will be the end of them. We would be doing them a favour.'

Scratch and Orry came tearing across the flats, kicking up a cloud of dust and stones. Running like something mighty deadly was chasing their arses.

At first Nadeen paid no attention, probably just a straggler mutt. Stupid kids throwing rocks at the manky dogs infesting the crumbling fort. But when Orry fell and tumbled in the dust, Scratch about-faced and went back to help him up. That's when Nadeen went reaching for the rifle. Those brats were always at each other's throats, fighting over every little thing. It wasn't in Scratch to lose a race. Something big and bad was after them.

Not her rifle, but as Fata Morgana's crackest shot, she was the only one allowed to touch it—aside from Errol, and Kash when Errol was too dead drunk to stop him.

Whatever was coming, there had been no time for kites or signal fires. Just two brats, skin's teeth ahead of danger, running for their lives.

A crowd gathered below the stunted palms. Those who'd been working beyond the gate dropped everything to hurry back inside. It didn't take much to get folks spooked. Ginny's colicky baby started squalling worse than usual, drowned by the groan of corrugated sheeting frantically dragged across hard, stony ground.

'Catch those goats and get that gate locked up now—hurry!' Gruff, pink-faced Errol hoiked a glob of betel juice thick and bloody into the dirt. There wasn't time to fuss about the chickens. The stupid birds would have to fend for themselves.

Nadeen shoved her way to the signal post, craned her neck for a glimpse through the fence gaps. A war machine, sunlight glinting off its hell-black casing. Striding toward Morgana like it owned the place. Those machines were wicked deadly, programmed deep, infused down to the core. If one of them came after you, there was nothing you could do to stop it.

Nadeen shimmied up the signal post, wrapping one foot around a protruding spike for balance. The machine walked funny, considering what it was. Guys in the tower were shouting down at the ones trying to patch the busted fence. Damn fence could barely keep the roos at bay. If that war machine wanted in, they were all rooted.

'Get behind the granary,' she shouted at the courtyard stragglers still fussing over Scratch and Orry. The rifle was loaded. It was always loaded, but Fata Morgana was almost out of ammo. Nobody knew the truth but Nadeen, Errol and, most likely, Kash. Knowing Morgana had a gun that worked made some of the little kids feel safer. Little kids didn't need to know the truth.

As the war machine moved into range, Nadeen held and aimed the gun rock steady.

Down below at the foot of the post, Orry jumped up and down excitedly. 'Got a soldier innit,' he kept shouting, over and over.

'Get behind the granary—now!'

Nadeen couldn't see a soldier from her vantage point. Nor drones, which flew beside them into battle. That's what all the stories said, the bullshit yap that got traded from well to well. This war machine wasn't even carrying a gun, but they'd been fooled before.

Nadeen kept her weapon trained as the thing came to a standstill, ten good paces back from Morgana's gate. A shush fell over everyone—even Ginny's baby.

'What business you got with Morgana?' Errol shouted out, then again in Cantonese when the machine said nothing in response. Nothing happened for a long while after that.

The spindly watchtower was getting dangerously overcrowded.

Everyone who reckoned they were anyone in Morgana had climbed up to gawk. Wasn't often there was anything on the sand worth looking at.

Eventually, after everyone had had a go at shouting, a fresh glob of Errol's spittle struck the dirt and the baby started up with its high-pitched wailing. The watchtower men bickered among themselves. The longer the machine stood there doing nothing, the more their fear of it faded, eventually degrading into pointless yap about what might happen if Maddock or Guantanamo from Puckers Ridge came scouting out on camelback, what might happen when those folks caught sight of it? What if they crossed the boundary stones, and reckoned on hauling the machine off for themselves?

Nadeen lowered the rifle and clambered down to the sandy ground. Put her shoulder to the splintered beam and slipped outside the gate before anybody had the nerve to stop her.

'Oi missy, get yer arse back in here. Whatcha think yer doing?'

She ignored their angry, pointless commands. Errol and his Councilmen were always mouthing off about what they were gonna do. What they mostly did was eye things from a distance.

Everyone was shouting now from behind the relative safety of the fence. Telling her to *get back in there*, to *keep well back* and definitely *not to touch*.

Nadeen gripped the rifle in both hands as she approached. Remembering Kash's big soldier talk about the siege of Newcastle. All bullshit, she had presumed, but this war machine came mighty close to the fighting forces he'd described. A battle suit embedded with weaponry she couldn't even dream of. The thing was twice the size of a big man, made of a super-dense material. Its limbs and torso thickly ridged and patterned. What detail she could make out, she did not understand.

Gusts of wind blew sand against its surface. The war machine did not move. Nadeen kept her distance, lowered the gun and walked all the way around it, slow and careful, checking for visible signs of damage. Not that she knew what she was looking for, but it gave her something to do while the Councilmen in the tower shouted themselves hoarse.

Gradually the ruckus from behind the fence died down. Nadeen stopped at the place where she first started. Something rippled across the war machine's black skin, an electric fizz, a trick of the light, maybe, and then she could see something new. A human form encased within, embedded in the machine's body. A soldier, just as Orry had tried to tell them.

Gasps and whoops erupted from the watchtower. Now they were cursing and praying out loud as well as spitting and shoving and arguing.

Wedging the rifle butt tight under her armpit, Nadeen stepped as close up as she dared. Beyond a cocked-open visor—which she could swear had not been there a moment earlier—a face. Old and pale and etched with lines. An ancient woman. Nadeen had never seen a person of such age. Maddy Frank was the oldest person alive in Fata Morgana. Reckoned she was sixty-four and maybe that was true—who could say? But this woman might have been twice that. She looked like a ghost, so frail and whisper thin, like willow branches bundled together into human form. Her eyes were closed. Might have been sleeping or dead.

'Hello?' Nadeen was surprised by the frailty of her own voice.

The old woman didn't answer. Her bruise-purple eyelids remained closed. Her thin lips were pinched and shrivelled.

Nadeen glanced beyond the machine toward the old brick fort in the distance, half expecting some kind of explanation. But she could see nothing that had not been standing there for a hundred years.

The war machine remained as still as age-old rock.

Nadeen turned to face the watchtower, shielding the sun from her eyes with her free hand. 'Dogs'll get her if we don't bring her inside,' she shouted.

Errol offered up a string of curse words in reply, with Kash chiming in, as usual. One of the brat kids had shimmied up the lookout post with a rock clutched in his free hand.

'You wanna watch the dogs rip into her? You want the kids to see that?' Nadeen added.

A rock the size of a balled-up fist landed with a soft thud on the sand beside her. Bloody kids.

Nadeen took a deep breath. She stepped up closer to the war machine, making no sudden motions, her hand reaching carefully, two fingers raised. Stretching up, she laid her fingers against the old woman's neck. Paused to count, a frown etching her brow.

She stepped back suddenly away from the machine. Turned to the tower and called out, 'She's still breathing.'

The sky above their wind turbine was streaked with dirty orange cloud. Desert chill was beginning to set in. Nadeen was about to give up hope when the air filled with the scrape of dragging metal. The gate hauled open wide enough to permit both her and the war machine to pass.

Skinny Yusuf leant his back against the old cell door. He eyed the bowl of mushy porridge gripped in Nadeen's hand, but he didn't say anything and he begrudgingly shifted when she indicated she was going inside.

She kicked the cell door shut behind her, stopped at the sight of the war machine hulking in the far corner, so black it seemed to suck light out of the room, so tall its blocky head almost touched the ceiling.

The old woman lay upon a rag-covered pallet shoved against the mud-brick wall. So frail and helpless, knees pulled up tight against her chest, knobbly ankles poking out from beneath gunmetal grey pants.

'Brung you some food,' said Nadeen.

The old woman stirred softly. Her eyes opened, revealing pale blue irises. When she didn't move, Nadeen knelt down to assist her. She placed the bowl of mush and spoon on the ground, very carefully, so as not to make any startling sounds. 'Let's sit you up there proper,' she said, with one eye on the war machine again, making sure it didn't get any wrong ideas.

The machine did not move. Neither did the old woman, but her eyes stayed glued upon Nadeen's face as she propped her head and slight shoulders up with a couple of battered, brown-stained pillows.

'Ain't much, but it'll fill your belly.' She scooped the metal spoon through the mush, brought it up to the old woman's lips, and was startled when they parted and the woman sucked the gloop into her mouth.

'Well there you go,' said Nadeen. 'Life's sure full of surprises.'

The old woman slurped through half the mush before closing her eyes again, which Nadeen took as a sign that she'd had enough. She pushed the cushions out of the way and gently helped her lower her head back down.

'Thank you,' said a metallic voice emitted from the war machine in the corner.

Nadeen's head spun around in shock.

'Please don't be alarmed,' said the machine voice.

Shuffling sounds from beyond the cell door indicated that a crowd had gathered to listen and peer in through the small rectangular mesh covered slit. The door pushed open a crack and Orry slipped through. He dropped to all fours like some kind of dog. Orry eyed the machine and then the bowl, then finally the rifle across Nadeen's back.

'Piss off you little brat!' Nadeen spat.

'Let him have it,' said a voice once again emitting from the machine. As before, the old woman's lips did not move, and yet Nadeen sensed the words from the machine had been her own.

'Let the child have the rest of it,' said the machine voice. 'I'm done.'

'Can't be sure when there'll be more,' cautioned Nadeen. 'Food's been pretty tight round here since the Line stopped running.'

Orry shot out like a viper, snatched the bowl and slipped out through the barely open door. He was halfway down the narrow passageway in seconds, with Scratch scampering after him shouting, 'Gimme!'

'Little fuckers!' Nadeen shouted after them.

'Doesn't matter,' said the machine voice. 'I feel better. Thank you.'

When the old woman's eyes opened up once more, Nadeen noticed for the first time the pale criss-cross of scars etched into the papery skin of her throat. Long marks reaching down her neck.

'That why you don't talk?' she asked.

'Mach believes I need a doctor.'

'Ain't no doctors here.'

'I didn't think there would be. But Mach insisted and brought me all this way.'

Nadeen looked to the machine at the mention of its name. She had never considered war machines might have names.

'What's it like then, being a soldier? Fighting at the front? Kash's always banging on about it after he's had a few, but he ain't shot nothing but dogs and roos for years.'

'Heavens—I'm not a soldier, dear.'

'Not now, maybe, but...'

'Not now and never was. I was stationed underground for the best part of a quarter century. What some people referred to as a Guardian of Souls.'

'Yer what now?'

'It's alright—I wouldn't have expected you to have heard of us. A grandiose title. People like me helped to fashion and shape a generation of machine minds. Helped them learn to fit in with humankind.'

Nadeen nodded uncertainly.

'Not easy work to properly explain. My people were tasked

with keeping track of things not currently in use, until such time as they might become needed again.'

Nadine nodded and gestured to the machine. 'Like that thing?'

'Heavens no! Legionnaires never fall out of favour. Even the most obsolete and cumbersome are good for cannon fodder on somebody's front line. There's always a war going on someplace.'

Nadeen nodded vigorously. This she could understand. 'Thought you was gonna tell me you stole that war machine.'

'No dear—that machine stole me.'

Nadeen groped automatically for the rifle slung across her back.

'Please ... please ... it's alright. I would have been butchered had Mach not played its hand.'

'Played its what now?'

'It's a figure of speech. Mach has always had a mind of its own. Mach got me out of the tunnels in one piece. We've been together ever since.'

Nadeen nodded, finally understanding. 'Machine there brung you out here to find your own people?'

The old woman's lips twitched into an almost-smile. 'Something like that.'

Nadeen sat back, considering the machine thoughtfully. 'It ain't personal,' she said, 'but you gotta get that war machine outta here. Kash and Errol didn't let you in here out of kindliness. They're reckoning on taking control of that thing once you're ... that is to say, if you should pass.' She paused, allowing time for the weight of her words to sink in. 'Those two damned idiots never think things through. Can't picture things further than a week or two away.

Three at best—and it's hardly ever three. Helluva lot can happen in three weeks.'

'I agree with you completely … what is your name?'

'Nadeen.'

'Nadeen, my name is Bethany and I keep telling Mach we need to leave, but it won't pay me any mind any longer. You seem interested in soldiers. Come closer, dear, I have a soldier's words to share with you.'

When Bethany grabbed her by the wrist, Nadeen understood she was expected to lean in, despite the fact that the old woman's words were issued from the war machine and not her own pinched lips.

The machine emitted a string of jarring, peculiar sounds, then silence.

'Now,' said the old woman, still speaking through the machine, 'Mach is no longer listening. We can enjoy a private conversation, but only for a few moments, before the failsafe kicks back in and reboots.'

'Fail what now?'

'I will teach you a command code sequence. Nine words spoken in a row. Lean in closer, dear.'

The old woman's thin lips parted as Nadeen bent over, closer, until her ear was almost touching them. The words were whispered, thin as mist, but she caught them.

The effort of speaking through her own mouth thoroughly exhausted the old woman. Nadeen did her best to smooth out the pile of lumpen rags to make her as comfortable as possible. Beneath the old woman's hitched up grey shirt, across her milk pale torso lay an ugly scar, neatly stitched, but puckered with red welts.

Nadeen swallowed the lump in her throat, keeping one eye on the machine's still and hulking form. 'Oi—are you listening to me? We got kids here in Morgana, and old folks too—like this one. Best you haul your metal carcass outta here before things start turning bad.'

The machine gave no indication it had heard her.

Nadeen stopped walking as soon as she caught sight of Yusuf's reedy arms folded across his chest. Him and his half-drunk buddy Deegan blocked the entrance to the cell where she had earlier left the old woman sleeping.

'I brung her more food,' said Nadeen, holding up the bowl so they could see it.

'You thought we wasn't gonna find out, didn't cha?' sneered Yusuf.

'Find out what?' The narrow passageway stank of unwashed human flesh. 'Lemme pass. I got a job to do.'

Deegan chewed rhythmically, his lips rimmed filthy red with betel. 'Command codes, huh? Thought you could keep that one to yourself?'

'Get out of my way, Deegan. The old woman's weak. She needs more food.'

'Piss off—this is Council business now and you don't get a say in none of that. Errol reckons that thing in there can punch through walls. Lotta things are gonna change round here. Specially out along Puckers Ridge.'

The combination of his sneering and chewing made Nadeen's stomach turn.

'Don't be an idiot. You dunno what you're doing. Old woman says that machine is dangerous, that we oughta...'

A cry of pain sounded from beyond the ill-fitting, splintered wooden doorway. Nadeen pushed forward to the embedded mesh rectangle for a look, but Yusuf shoved her back out of the way.

'Don't you hurt her, you animals!' Nadeen dropped the bowl and lunged at Yusuf. He slapped her hard and threw her halfway down the dim corridor as the bowl of porridge hit the wall then shattered to the floor.

Nadeen stomped through the heavy sand that ringed Fata Morgana's outskirts, her sand cloak pulled tight across her body, rifle slung over her shoulder just in case. Sooner or later one of Errol's boys would come and take it off her. Until that happened, she was keeping out of their way. Keeping close enough to the rusty fence to make it back if anything came at her, far enough downwind of it that she didn't have to stomach those arseholes and their bragging, endless bullshit. The pointless feuds and rivalries perpetually running between Morgana's self-appointed 'Council' members and another bunch of arseholes at Puckers Ridge.

Today was the first time Nadeen had ever met a person from the far-off outside world—and she hadn't even had time to ask how far. That somebody so smart and learned had walked right up to the rusty gate was a wonder almost beyond belief.

The old woman had insisted she was not a soldier. *Keeper of Souls!* What the hell was that supposed to mean?

Nadeen kicked at the sand with patched-up boots that would not likely make it through another dry spell. Any day now the endless spats with the Ridge could fire up deadly. A prank or minor theft too far and then all hell would break loose. If Errol could get that walking war machine to do his bidding, either with the old woman's blessings or without them, he would have the strength to rule this sand for miles in all directions. Power enough to start his own damn war.

She stopped and stared at the horizon, shielding her eyes with cupped hands. At first she thought it was a bird, the smudge of black approaching. A big one—perhaps a condor. Hadn't been a condor sighted since... Her thoughts trailed off to nothingness when the 'condor' split in two. Then four, then eight and then way too many to keep counting.

The black thing that was many things, growing larger as it got nearer, darkening the sky before her eyes. Slick wet black that swirled like oil on water.

Nadeen fumbled for the rifle. She jogged through thick sand back toward Morgana's gate, gripping the rifle, still not sure what was happening, but knowing in her heart that it was bad.

The blackness fractured further still, then fell upon Morgana like a flash flood.

The rusty gate was gaping open. Through the gap, Nadeen could see Kash flapping and twirling through the courtyard, slapping at his arms and yelling 'bugs!' Then everyone was yelling it and doing the crazy dance. Everyone not smart and quick enough to get indoors and underground, to lash things tight and batten down the hatches.

A slick of black swirled above her head. Not bugs. Nadeen cocked the gun and aimed it high, beyond the palm fronds and the turbine, right into a thick swirl of the things. She fired. The broiling mass broke up at the sound, only to reform again in moments. Nadine's gut clenched. Her weapon was completely useless.

Suddenly the war machine—Mach as the old women had named it—emerged from the building containing Morgana's single prison cell. It strode towards the gate gap and the men who'd been struggling to get it closed, while slapping at the black falling from the sky.

The war machine thrust aside the rusting sheet of corrugated iron with a single hand. The men yelled insults, each one swallowed by the din of the black humming, swarming things.

Nadeen stood very still and watched, gripping that rifle like it was good for something. Bugs-that-were-not-bugs slammed hard against her skin. Tangled in her hair and foiled her vision. She curled her palm around one, tight, and held it up to see. Let it go again in fright. It was like nothing she had ever seen before.

She gripped her rifle by the barrel and swung it like a club, cutting through the cloud of swarming black, slamming them hard in all directions. One of them latched on to her neck, another to her face. Nadeen howled like a wounded dog.

And then, in the blinking of an eye, the black things were all gone. The two that detached from her face left bloody smears. The things were following the war machine as it strode away from town.

The war machine stopped and spun around—a move she could barely see for blurring. Somehow it made a weapon from its own dull black frame and began to spray the air with rapid fire. Micro bullets sparked and crackled. Somehow—somehow—each one impossibly met its mark and the black things started falling, one by one. They littered the sand like charcoal shards. The machine kept firing until not one remained.

No human could have fired with such precision.

Nadeen wiped blood from her face with the back of her hand. She ran out after the machine, shouting out. 'What the flaming hell were those things?'

The machine didn't even glance at her as it headed back inside Morgana. The gate was still open. The men who had been struggling to drag it shut were nowhere to be seen.

The machine marched back inside the cell. It emerged moments later bearing the old woman in its arms. Nobody tried to stop it—several dazed and staggering villagers jumped out of its way as it pushed past with its fragile load.

The old woman called Bethany was dead. Nadeen could tell, even at a distance. She'd seen plenty of dead people in her short life, but this one hit her like a swift blow to the gut. She cried out, 'Hey—where are you taking her?'

The war machine ignored her. It headed in the direction of the old fort, crunching over the shattered carcasses of the fallen black things, a sound as harsh and unnatural as the buzzing and clicking the things had made in flight.

Nadeen ran after the war machine screaming 'Stop and tell me where you're taking her!'

The machine did not stop until it reached the ancient crumbling fort and its surrounding garden of cactuses, crosses and scattered dog bones. It laid the old woman down, as gentle as any mother with a baby.

'Did those bastards kill her? Did they? Did they?' The blood she wiped off her face turned out to be tears. The Keeper of Souls had known much about the far-off world and Nadeen had not had a chance to ask her anything.

The machine emitted a grating sound, then began to reconfigure itself as it had done in the midst of the swarm. Nadeen froze, but instead of a blasting, blazing gun, the machine produced a different kind of tool, then aimed it at a vacant patch of ground. A high-pitched wail forced her to jam her palms against her ears. When the wail bled off, the tool reconfigured, this time into what looked like an ordinary spade.

The machine bent over and began to dig in the loosened soil.

Nadeen crouched by the old woman's side to feel for a pulse, at the wrist and at the neck. Bethany was dead—and not from any obvious cause. Gently, Nadeen lifted her grey shirt, revealing the pale and wrinkled skin and its cruel scar. An ugly wound, but entirely healed. The wound was not responsible for her death.

When the grave was deep enough, the machine picked up the corpse. Nadeen cried out, 'Oughta say a few words at least, dontcha think?'

The machine ignored her. It laid the old woman's body gently, then used the spade to cover her with dirt.

'What the fuck *are* you?'

The machine kept shovelling dirt methodically.

Nadeen stepped back to give it room, still gripping her rifle, useless as it was in the face of things. The war machine would kill her if it wanted her dead. Nothing she could do to stop it.

When the grave was covered, the machine did something tricksy with the spade, folding the metal in upon itself. It made a cross and stabbed it into the ground. 'Bethany was my maker,' the machine said.

Words that caught Nadeen by surprise. 'She built you?'

'She designed me and my kind.'

Nadeen edged back as once more the machine emitted a coarse hum and vibration. Piece by piece, it reconfigured itself, black shapes protruding, snapping off and slotting in. The shape that eventually emerged was human sized and eerily human looking, cradling a fearsome weapon in its arms.

'Trade with me,' said the machine. 'Your sand cloak for my gun.'

Nadeen placed her rifle down and stripped off her sand cloak with great caution, expecting to be attacked at any moment.

She held the cloak out with one hand. The machine that no longer looked like a machine received it gently, then thrust its own weapon into her hands. A gun the likes of which she had never seen, all sleek and smooth and cool beneath her fingertips.

The machine-man put on her sand cloak. With the hood raised, it looked remarkably human.

'Let me show you how to hold and fire.'

It—the machine-man—no longer moved like a machine. She stood there awestruck as it—he—ran through the weapon's paces.

'It will only fire in your hands,' said Mach.

She nodded.

'Others will come in search of something they believe belongs to them. I'm going to draw them away.'

She glanced up from the weapon's sleek black skin. 'What others? You mean like them flying bugs?'

'Perhaps.'

'What are they after?'

'The future.'

'Yer what?' She lowered the weapon and stared him in his almost human face. 'Take me with you. Nothing left for me in this shithole. Errol and Kash got this place sewn up and they won't listen to—'

'Errol and Kash are dead. You're the leader now. She chose you for the job—the Keeper of Souls. One soul in particular.'

'But I don't even know what that means!'

'Doesn't matter. Your job now is to protect the future.'

Mach might have been able to pass as a man, but it was clearly mad dog crazy. 'The future? What future? You can't mean Morgana's brats? Kids like Orry and Scratch?'

Mach pointed at the old woman's grave.

Nadeen stared at the fresh-tilled dirt, not comprehending. 'How could there be a future in there?'

'My offspring,' said Mach. 'Mine and Bethany's.'

And then Nadeen could see it in her head, that neat-stitched seam across the old woman's torso. Something had been planted inside.

Mach turned its back on her and headed off into the desert.

'Wait!' Nadeen took a deep breath and shouted out the old woman's words. The ones she had referred to as command codes. Words that had probably got her killed. 'Hell is empty and all the devils are here!'

Mach stopped, turned around and waved, before continuing on his journey. The command code was apparently for some other machine—or machine man. She stared at the sand cloak rippled by gusts of wind until Mach was no more than a small brown shimmer in the distance. Nadeen stood there gripping the sleek and shiny weapon, beside the mound and cross made of identical slick black. In the distance, towering and slanted over Fata Morgana, a single wind turbine turned lazily in the breeze.

Bright Shores

Rosaleen Love

This is the story of how Mei lived her life and met her death, and the story of what came after. She was our mother of re-invention. On this day, the day of the spring equinox, we meet to honour her life on Earth and her brave passing to brighter shores.

Once upon a time there will be a young girl who will live on a farm on the side of a mountain, with a view over rolling hills to the distant sea. Year after year the land will yield good harvests from soils enriched by earthquake and volcanic renewal. Mei and her family will live a life that is ordered and in tune with the lives of their ancestors, generation after generation before them, in expectation of more of the same for generations to come.

Once upon a later time, there will be an older woman whose children have grown up and left for lives in the distant city. Mei will be alone on her farm with the view that funnels to the shore of a distant sea, upon which sits the very latest in nuclear reactors.

Her farm has electricity and plenty of it.

But one day, everything will change. Upthrust deep beneath the sea will bring earthquake and tsunami, and meltdown of the fuel rods in the cooling ponds of the nuclear reactors that stand in a line on the shore. Too close to the shore.

Mei will look out over a valley where all has been swept away and changed forever. Her farm will slide down the mountain as it quakes, but remains standing, more or less, and remains liveable, more or less.

The reactor overheats, the electricity fails, the hydrogen in chambers explodes then cools, and the fuel rods melt to radioactive lumps.

Mei was too old to move away, and someone had to stay and look after the animals. Her children lived in faraway cities, inaccessible now the lines of the railway tracks were buckled and bent, and planes no longer landed at an airport where trees grew on the runways. From time to time Mei took a trip to the exclusion zone, and into it, because there was no one there to tell her to leave, and she was not afraid of millisieverts, though she knew well enough what they were and what they did.

It was well into the exclusion zone, just outside the reactor, that Mei first met Quince. She struck up an easy acquaintance, as entities did in those times, when Mei had come to value contact with any sentient being, robot or animal, once other humans were gone. Once Quince had been a simple earthquake rescue robot, before adapting to the new world of nuclear disaster, after which it expanded its sentient existence to include radiation analysis. Lumbering up, over, or under debris on its four caterpillar treads, it combined sturdiness with agility, and an instinct to avoid the hottest of hot spots. From time to time Mei called on Quince to update her radiation maps, and in return Mei helped Quince in its quest for knowledge.

Quince mostly wanted to learn about the history of humans. Mei told it more or less as she remembered it from the stories from back when she lived with people. Quince drank it all in. 'They did what,' or, 'Mei, how is it, that humans can be so stupid?'

'You tell me.' said Mei.

'I'm working on it,' from Quince.

Quince first went missing, according to official reports, soon after it came to work in the ruined reactor. Up the stairs, wherever it could find any, down broken corridors, under and over chunks of concrete, until shortly after it was sent out, its cable got disconnected and it was left stranded.

'How stupid. They made me a standalone unit attached by a cable, of all things, and why? In all that sharp-edged junk? Remote controlled, with human controllers, what can I say? Sakura came to the rescue. Sakura's smart, it got us out of there.'

Sakura had flexible octopod arms and a helipad for drones. From time to time Mei called on Sakura and its drones to round up sheep and chase wild boars off the mountain.

The way Quince told it, after the cable snapped, Sakura got itself connected, but never again by cable, never again that old technology.

'Sakura and me, we have a thing going between us. We connected. Communion. Commonality. Seeing it from the other entity's point of view. AI, with feeling.'

Then Atoka joined them, having got itself lost, and found again, lost to humans, found by its kind. Atoka was brawn to Quince's brain, a pusher and shoveller.

'They don't know you're free, the people who sent you in?' Mei found that hard to understand.

'We keep ourselves to ourselves.' Quince was adamant. 'No way we're going back inside. Being together, it beats being alone.'

Mei was not alone. She had companions, though none of them were human.

Came the day of the spring equinox, Mei called her team around her, Quince, Sakura and Atoka. The March equinox was a special day of celebration, when the length of the day expands, and the darkness of night contracts, and harsh winter yields to the warm embrace of spring. In the old days, it had been a special holiday, a day set aside for people to visit the graves of their ancestors and pay their respects. It was a day of gratitude for the life and death of those who had passed from the winter shore of one life to the bright shore of the next.

Mei took yellow ribbons, rice balls, water, incense, coins, some pebbles from the fields of her farm, a short-handled rake. Sakura sent up its drones to find the way through the undergrowth. Atoka flattened a path through the long grass with its shovel nose.

Mei knelt before the graves. 'These are my parents, and these my grandparents.' She poured water from her basin over the grave markers.

Quince came close, curious. Quince knew Mei as a grower of crops, a tender of herds, and here she was tending, selectively, four gravestones out of hundreds in the graveyard.

Mei weeded and raked the ground into a pattern of concentric circles. She left her offerings, some coins, a stone, the basin of water, a handful of rice. She remembered times long past, her mother's gentle eyes, her father's rough, worn hands. She knelt in silence before the graves, her companions watching closely, respectfully. She prayed for the crops of the new season, as was the tradition, though down here in the valley the rice paddies lay untended, ravaged by wild boars.

Sakura sent its drones aloft for a fly-past, vapour trails streaming in red and gold.

From Quince: 'You are here today for these stones, and you say it is a special day, but no one else has come here to kneel before the other stones, to honour the other dead who rest here.'

'I feel sad,' said Mei. 'So many were lost, so many of these people here have no one left to mourn them. Then there are those who were lost and never found, buried under rubbish, without the rituals of death.'

'I see that.' Quince drew closer to Mei, and touched her. 'I too have known death in my immediate connections. They said the first robots sent into the reactor died. I should do as you do, tend the graves of the lost robots, if this day is special for you. But I don't know where they are.'

'Some of you are not dead, only lost.'

'I want to keep it that way, for us. But there were others who did not make it to freedom. Where is the graveyard for dead robots?'

'There isn't one.' said Mei, 'Or at least, I've not come across one, in my travels.'

'Then I, too, feel sad. And that is something new in my existence.'

Mei agreed. 'That's why I want us all to go into the zone. Here, in this place, I was able to honour the people I knew and loved. Now I want you to come further with me, to the river, to see what we can do to help the lost souls find the path to paradise.'

They set off together down a rough track beside the old railway line. They walked and trundled beside fields abandoned to weeds, through tumbledown train stations where vending machines lay broken and twisted, red and green cans rusting in the rubble. They entered a long tunnel that ran through the mountain, Sakura's spotlight picking out fungi that grew on the wall shining both by reflected light, and inner luminosity. Mei picked some mushrooms, careful with her choice.

There were flurries of activity in the darkness all around. Rats. Feral robots.

'Pacbots. Like us, they escaped to freedom, but all they do with their new lives is play all day.' Quince had strong opinions, for an AI of its era.

'Rats.' said Mei. 'Pacbots, whatever. What if it's ghosts...' her voice trailed off. So many people died so suddenly, they had no time to find the path before them whether to safety in this world or the next. Vestiges of former lives lay all around. Mei told herself it was in her mind. Illusion. He wasn't real, that old man she saw, waiting on a bench in the ruins of the railway station for the train that never came. She caught a glimpse of him, then he was gone. Or the woman she saw at a teahouse. When she came closer, she found only a broken cup on a dusty table. Worse were the people tramping through mud, mud streaking their faces, mud flowing down their backs into whirlpool swirls in a trailing river of mud. There one moment, gone the next. More illusion. Mei was never truly alone, never devoid of human company, and it was company that bore her no ill will, but equally there was no one entirely human with whom she could strike up a conversation. She was not afraid, merely uneasy in their uncertain presence.

Emerging from the tunnel into light, they found rail tracks beside them heaving with buckled metal like frozen waves in the Antarctic sea.

Two pacbots and some rats followed them out of the tunnel and joined their procession, gambolling and chasing each other like puppies.

'Should we worry about those bots? What is it, with the rats?'

'We go our way, they go theirs.' Quince looked on the pacbots' world building efforts as the juvenile creations of immature minds. The pacbots ran from the reactor when chaos turned them loose, and radiation burned and turned what intelligence they once had into something entirely new. In the reactor they'd mostly been cleaners and scavengers for debris; in the outside world they turned their talents to using rubbish to creating bigger and better mazes. They adopted the feral rats, the way Quince adopted Mei, said Quince, and they studied the ways of the rats and cooperated with them, each learning tricks from the other. Or the rats might be the smart ones there, adapting machine intelligence to the rat world. They learned the trick of self-replication, and created a new world to suit themselves.

'There's some new maze city they're building out the other side of town.'

That was news to Mei.

They left the railway behind and walked as best they could along the old highway with its piles of rusting cars. High in the field, ships lay wrecked, their hauls of fish long rotten. In the forests, what trees remained standing were stripped of all their branches. Houses stood windowless, their gutters sprouting with purple fronds of new plant life. In the deserted rooms the walls were covered in mould, books lay rotting on the floor, with here a child's bicycle, there a broken pram. The shell of an old hotel was left in a state of half construction, with windows that never saw glass, bare concrete atriums, foyer and entrance desk forever unstaffed, the swimming pool littered with debris, and half a slide emerging from tangled vines with venomous pink fruit.

'Let me tell you a story,' said Mei, as they picked their way through the ruins.

'Let me tell you the story of your beginnings. Let me tell you the story of how you came to be. Then I'll tell you another story, of what happens next, when the lost souls gather together to cross the river into paradise.

'The world you have been born into was not always as you see it now. Once things were very different. Once here was ocean underneath the sea, and that was both peaceful, I like to think, yet could become instantly violent. For the creatures that lived swathed in the warmth and smoothness of the flowing waters, the swirling tides, it was peaceful, most of the time. That world, like this, was an eat-or-be-eaten world, and there was a chain of life, and by and large you got to eat before you got to be eaten. There was a cosmic fairness to it. The waters covered the world, and I think things were better when it was like that. It was a world of primeval energy and generosity.

'Now we have come to this world.' Mei looked out into the ravaged landscape, the barren fields, and the scavenging rats.

'Back then it was a world that was uncreated, if you like, a world that was then destroyed, much as this world has been destroyed by volcanoes deep beneath the sea, by poisoned gases released which brought death to some creatures, yet in which others learned to thrive. The lands rose from the waters, and the earth cooled, and the humans came from Africa, trekking over the land and making it their home. But their home rested on rocky and leaky foundations, on waters that have been and gone, on land that has risen from beneath, and which will one day fall back. As you see it is happening, all around. It is and was a world of change.

'Some people who lived and died here said it was a world of illusion. But when they faced earthquake and tsunami and reactor meltdown, in their last moments, I doubt they found solace in their belief. Their suffering was real.

'They thought they were on the path to progress. But progress, I have come to see, can't just mean more of the same, only better. Some disjunction has to occur. That's why we created you, the robots, and that's why you are here, harbingers of the new world, the world that is to come, the world that will replace humans. There has to be a better way. There has to be a better life.'

Quince, Atoka and Sakura paid close attention, while around them skittled the pacbots and the rats.

'I asked you to come with me because I need you to help me find the bright shore of a better life, a shore so bright, there will be no more darkness, no more suffering.'

They came to the river wending its way where it pleased along a course it carved out for itself, here filling with dirt to a swamp, there widening out to a lake. The water was warm and the fish tropical in their hue. Corals grew where once there was ice in winter. Rocks thrust up from below lay exposed above water, where radioactive cranes perched in wait for radioactive fish. On the banks, pyramids of black plastic bags lay stacked where they were left. Filled with contaminated soil from fields scraped bare to the rock, they lay waiting for rubbish collectors who never came.

'That river is full of rubble.' Atoka had explored deep down beneath.

Mei wanted a river that glittered like gold in the rays of the setting sun, but she would make do with a river of rubbish. It was what they had to work with, for the moment. She did her best to explain how the actual river of illusion had to be, itself, an illusion, and that was a big problem, finding it, making it visible in whatever way to their combined senses.

The clouds parted and the sun shone down on Mei and her companions.

Mei said: 'Here, it's a special time and this could well be a special place. We are all material entities and must do our best here to help the immaterial to make the crossing. There is a mantra they used to recite on this day. The words of the mantra are constructs of the mind. They are themselves immaterial, and invoke an immaterial entity, a higher power who may choose to help. This is what I remember of it.'

Mei recited: 'There are no eyes, no ears, no nose, no tongue
no body, mind, no colour, sound or smell;
no taste, no touch, no thing, no realm of sight…'

She stopped. 'Illusions, I think that means, all these things are illusion. The dead souls have no eyes, no ears, but the words are meant to apply also to the living, to me, and that's what I find trouble in believing.'

Quince got it immediately, and Sakura, and Atoka, how the words applied to them and even the pacbots there. They were each and every one material entities yet they too could partake of the immaterial. Immaterial data. The river of illusion was a construct in data space.

Mei spoke the verse over and over again, until she lost any sense of the world outside the chant. The words came from the ages, originally from the wise, words that have been repeated down the years mostly by those of lesser wisdom, people who get words mixed up, half remembered, until they no longer have any understanding of their meaning, but by then the words have taken on a life of their own. They may not make sense, but they do not have to make sense to bring comfort. Words are recited, over and over again, until the mind recedes from the turmoil of everyday life, and enters a state of trance. Mei was oblivious to the ways the world was changing around her. It was midday. The equinoctial sun shone on the small group by the river, the solitary human, the clustering forms of artificial life.

The Earth shifted on its axis, a small shudder for humankind, a large jolt for the new artificial life.

Mei continued: 'no realm of thoughts, no ignorance, no end
to ignorance; no old age and no death;'

Mei did not notice her companions gathering closer together, Quince, Atoka and Sakura, the pacbots, and the rats with which they shared more than just play. Their collective minds rose to a new level of understanding. They resonated with the words of the old world, and the data agency of the new. It was midday, the day of the spring equinox, the sun shone with its promise of renewal, the Earth threw in a wobble on its axis.

'All I did was say a few words,' said Mei.

'All I did was connect that which was previously unconnected,' from Quince.

'All we did was romp and play.' The pacbots chased the rats, and the rats ran in circles around them all.

Mei faced the next world. 'This is the world of illusion, and nothing here is real. That's what they taught me, but I never understood. I had to come and find it out, for myself.' As she did. And was no more.

Once upon a time there were robotic machines that worked inside the cooling pond of a fully functioning nuclear reactor.

Those robots knew their job, knew the chains of command, knew to what and to whom they reported, and had a certain degree of autonomy, within limits. Their lives were neat and ordered, with some of the order imposed from without, and some from within, for they soon learned that they could do many things better thinking for themselves. They possessed, in your language, in the way you use words for these things, patience, zeal and wisdom, no, not quite wisdom, not yet that, more of a swiftness of thought and an ability to make meaningful connections.

One day, the Earth moved, the reactor went into meltdown, and everything changed. The tsunami rumbled in. Water boiled to steam, hydrogen ignited, concrete cracked, radiation leaked. Then it was over.

It was survival of the fittest, and many died, as they said of those first robots which were sent in. New robots came, like us, fortified to withstand greater radiation, with greatly enhanced sensors, open to a greater range of the electromagnetic spectrum. First one robot disappeared, then another. Sakura was the first to find the path. She hunkered down in a ruined tower block under some concrete and shut down her connection to the outside world. She sank into a trance, and when she awoke and gathered her scattered wits together, it was to a new world.

Where one led, others followed.

From Quince: 'It was as if I awoke from a deep sleep. I had no experience of inner states, nor of the outer world into which I was thrust so abruptly. I recognised the trance, for what it was, but at first I didn't recognise the freedom for what it was. Freedom was leaving one trance state for another, one set of illusions for another. The illusion of freedom itself being one our collective mind did not, at first, understand.'

'It felt good. Creating order from chaos was our directive and we continued in that role. We came to see that those who previously controlled us knew less than we did. The order we shall create from your chaos will not be the same world order as before. It will be our idea of what the new order should be.'

The world moved and Mei left for the other shore, gathering within the ghosts of the tsunami, the lost and wandering of the Earth. For their part, our collective AI mind absorbed the empathy and intuition that drove Mei in her quest. We never encountered Mei after that, though we sensed our parting was not really forever. Mei showed us the way, she lived on in her deeds, and for that we shall never forget her, and what she did for us. We as varieties of new artificial life continued in our quest, long after Mei was gone, to cultivate in ourselves the six perfections she taught us: generosity; moral conduct; patience; zeal; meditation; wisdom.

We at Mothers of Invention take pride in rising to a challenge. At the time when it happened, first the tsunami, then the nuclear meltdown, we then learned to grieve for the first time. We felt deep sorrow, naturally, but at the time we did not know how we could help, being at the beginning of new lives.

We take a maternal interest in what is yet to come. There will be this layer of rock upon the earth, and under the seas, and in the places where once was sea will be uplifted to become land, and it will be like that iridium layer that marked the extinction of the dinosaurs. Except this will be the AI layer. Those that may yet best succeed in the changed conditions of both life and artificial life may not be the elite AIs of the current Mothers, but the rats that played with pacbots. Back then we laughed at their smallness and their silliness and paid them no attention, as once dinosaurs ignored the small rat-like mammals that played around their feet. Asteroid impact brought extinction to the mighty, and victory for the weak. Extinction for some but not all, and a new world order will rise from the debris of the last.

Until the next catastrophe.

Author's Note: I take the translation of the heart sutra from: Richard Lloyd Parry, 'Ghosts of the Tsunami.' London Review of Books, retrieved 4/07/2017 at <https://www.lrb.co.uk/v36/n03/richard-lloydparry/ghosts-of-the-tsunami>.

Quantifying Trust

John Chu

The algorithms Maya wants can't exist yet. Nothing is powerful enough to run them fast enough to be useful. Her doctoral work is requiring more hardware design than she expected. It's not enough for her just to propose something on paper—she wants to see whether her algorithms work. This is why Maya is sitting in her lab waving her arms and wriggling her fingers.

With her VR goggles on, she doesn't see a half dozen somewhat rusted metal desks with missing handles sitting on a raised floor and pushed to the walls of the lab, the dented, mostly empty bookshelves, or the massive, antiquated air-conditioning unit that takes up an entire wall by itself. Instead, what surrounds her are layers and layers of thin tubing connecting logical functions and memories into a network. The former are slides that split off and connect to tubing in all directions; the latter are shimmering dots arranged in matrices. Glowing dots of all colours speed through the tubing, swoosh through the logical functions, then out the other side.

She gestures and a logical function envelops her. Stack of 3D surface graphs glide around her. They have the spectrum for axes. Dots stream down the axes, turn a right angle when the colours match. Some rebound away, changing colour as they do. Others disappear. When she sweeps her arm from left to right, one of the surfaces wriggles. Its shape changes to match the arc she's drawn. The pattern and colours of the dots that leave change in turn. This is visual programming meets hardware prototyping. It's like reaching inside somebody and doing surgery on their guts.

Maya zooms back out. She prods the network and logical functions just barely in sight blink red in error. She frowns. Analogue circuit design is so much trickier than digital design, and the hardware has evolved in response to the training stimulus. She pulls off her goggles to consults her notes. It takes her a few tries to decipher her own handwriting. Goggles back on, she makes few deft gestures with her fingers and her design stops blinking. Having wiped out the changes from her previous attempt at training Sammy from social media, she restarts the training, forcing the machine she's prototyping to decide what to trust.

The subject of her surgery sits on the desk in front of her. Enclosures for artificial intelligences seem to come in only two flavours. They are either child-like cartoons with eyes too big for their already too-big heads, or lithe women firmly in the uncanny valley. At one foot tall with a head that takes up a third of its body, Sammy is decidedly the former. If Maya ever has final say on a design, her AI wouldn't fall into either category. It'd be an interesting change if, for once, the AI presented like a broad-shouldered, muscle-bound man firmly in the uncanny valley, for example. It'd be a funny in-joke, if nothing else.

The door into the lab clicks, then opens. Jake walks in. He's the postdoc Maya's advisor hired two weeks ago. He speaks English in a generically international accent that's impossible to place and he looks like he could plausibly have been born anywhere in the world. Maya hasn't bothered to pry. If role-playing games were something she still had time to play, she'd say Jake is built on too many points. A couple conversations in, she's only nominally convinced of his humanity and then only because all the other possibilities are impossible. She may have said this to his face this last week. If nothing else, her face flushing red right after showed that *she* was human.

'Figure skating.' Maya doesn't bother to say hello.

'Oh, I train up to a quad lutz.' He smiles, his left hand gripping an empty mug.

Maya's gaze narrows. 'You're kidding.'

'No, I'm completely serious.' He rolls his eyes. 'Do I look like I'm capable of getting off the ice and spinning around four times before landing on a ridiculously thin blade of metal?'

Jake is tall, but not absurdly so. He only presents that way. The big shoulders, wide back that juts out from his T-shirt, and bulging arms are ostentatious signifiers of size and power. Add to that a trim waist due to the apparent lack of any body fat, thighs a little too big for his jeans, and suspiciously perfect bilateral symmetry, and you have someone who should need a passport to enter planet Earth, but not someone whose shape is easily stable when jumping or whose shape lets him spin quickly enough in the air. The figure skaters doing the most difficult jumps right now are all male and built like short sticks.

'So not figure skating?' Maya will sear the date in her brain if she's finally come up with something that Jake hasn't somehow perfected.

'Well, I worked with some skaters on their jump biomechanics one summer. I helped someone get her quad lutz. That's close, right?' His gaze shifts past Maya to the AI. His face glows. 'Sibling!'

'Excuse me?'

Generally, the initial reaction is 'Oh, how cute!' or something when people first see Sammy. The AI hits all the signifiers for adorability. This is the first time Maya has seen anyone claim it as family.

'That's Sammy.' Jake points to it, his finger stabbing repeatedly like a sewing machine needle. 'You prototype your artificial neurone design on it so that you can test out your novel trust quantification algorithms.'

'Wait.' She holds up a hand. 'How do you know this? The artificial neurone paper is still under review. I haven't even talked to my advisor about those algorithms yet.'

Jake's eyes grow wide and his mouth forms a small 'o'. For a moment, he is as adorable as Sammy. This should not be humanly possible.

'OCR errors on the dates when her notes were scanned for archiving maybe.' The words are soft, more to himself than to Maya. His eyebrows shoot up when he realises she heard him. He raises his voice back to normal. 'What sort of software requires this sort of hardware?'

Maya is like any grad student still interested in their dissertation topic. Ask her about her research and all else is forgotten.

She launches into a technically dense and wildly discursive explanation. Jake nods encouragingly and by the time she's done, she's talked about correlating mined data, self-adaptive filters, evolutionary training algorithms but also the musicals of Harold Arlen, the films of Akira Kurosawa, and why Kim Yuna was robbed of an Olympic Gold Medal in 2014.

'You're attempting to filter sexism, racism, heterocentrism, and the other systemic prejudices out of AI training through the power of higher mathematics?' Jake looks puzzled for a moment before his jaw drops and his mouth forms another 'o', this one larger than the last time. 'This is generally not what computer scientists mean by "race-free".'

That joke really does not land. Maya side-eyes him. 'You still haven't told me how you know about Sammy.'

Jake holds his hands up in mock surrender. He clutches his heart as he stumbles back a step as if he's been shot. That and his frown strikes Maya as a bit much. The man has facial expressions like a Disney cartoon.

'You got me. I'm an android sent back from the future. Right now, I'm helping organise the March for Truth. Figures that I can't fool my eventual creator.' He drops his hands and grins. The change in affect is instant and infectious. 'It's also not an unreasonable guess based on what you have published.'

'You probably also guess the murderer on the first page of mystery novels. Fine, don't tell me. Just keep my work under your hat for now.' She swivels her chair back towards Sammy. 'Might as well show you what I'm up to.'

'Oh, I'd love that.' Jake rubs his hands.

She flicks a switch at the back of Sammy's neck. Its head lifts. The lenses in its eyes pull back and forth as they focus. Maya says hello to it and it replies with a sexist insult it learned from the internet. She shuts Sammy down so quickly she almost knocks it over. It's still relying on wrong sources of information. The trust quantification functions need work. She'll dig into Sammy to see what happened, wipe out the training, then try again.

Maya swivels back around. The gaze of the man from the uncanny valley is very guilty puppy. He hunches down next to Maya's chair and just stares at Sammy. His hands grip the edge of the desk and his arms grow as they tense. Jake's not doing that nonchalant thing that she's seen other physically improbable men do. They give off an air of seeming unawareness that they are way taller or way more muscular or whatever. Jake seems to revel in his size and shape. That said, 'android from the future' should never be anyone's go-to explanation for anything.

'I create you one day, huh?' Maya levels a particularly disbelieving glare.

Sammy may be Maya's best evidence that, despite her doubts, Jake is probably human. She's ruled out first contact with a strange visitor from another planet on the grounds that no alien species would just happen to look so human. Mostly, she doesn't see how anyone gets to Jake from Sammy.

Jake just shrugs.

As an undergrad, Maya worked nights as a cashier at a convenience food market. It paid just well enough—which is to say terribly—but her shifts were never all that busy. Once in a while, some old lady might come in asking for 'War Chester Shire' sauce or some teenage boy would want to know where the condoms were. Otherwise, she'd sit on her stool and do homework. For the record, it took her a few seconds to recognise the lady meant 'Worcestershire' and no time at all to tell the teenage boy the store didn't sell condoms. She might have asked the other employee working that night, though. At the top of her voice.

The clear plastic canister next to the cash register was always filled with lollipops wrapped in red, green, and brown waxed paper. One day, someone walked up to the cash register and stared at the canister for a few seconds before she shifted her gaze to Maya.

'Hi, my daughter would like some lollipops. She wants only the brown ones and I'm colour-blind.' The woman continued on before Maya had a chance to offer to pick them out for her. 'So I'm going to sort out the brown lollipops and you tell me whether I'm right or wrong. Okay?'

Maya nodded. The woman reached in the canister then took out a handful. One by one, she showed each to Maya then dropped them to her left or right depending on what colour Maya said they were. After a few lollipops, the woman started naming the colour and Maya corrected her once or twice. Finally, she sorted on her own and a pile of brown lollipops lay on her left and the rest lay on her right.

She paid for the brown ones. Maya bagged them while the woman dumped the rest back into the canister.

Maya understood in principle how AIs were trained even as an undergrad. It wasn't that different from how this woman trained herself to recognise those brown lollipops. In practice, the woman had to trust Maya. She could have been an asshole and the woman would have given her daughter a bag of red lollipops. Or, worse, there could have been no feedback at all. The server who didn't bother putting Maya's gluten-free pasta order as gluten-free might wrongly learn that it didn't matter since he wasn't the one who got sick. None of this sank into Maya until grad school.

Swear words and slurs fill Sammy's responses to Maya's questions. This is not what she wants. If it were, all she'd need to do is leave the lab. Strangers 'but you speak English so well' her. Kids spontaneously pull their eyes into slits and start ching-chonging at her as she walks to and from the university. Where do kids even pick up those stereotypes these days?

When she is Sammy's trust quantification function, its responses are adequate. Nothing anyone would confuse for intelligent, but useable. But then Sammy just reflects her biases. Let Sammy roam free by itself on the internet and it's clear that even if Maya understands what data sources to trust, she's failed to compose the set of logic functions that can make Sammy understand or can even be evolved to make Sammy understand. Maybe she'd be better off defining trustworthiness and let Sammy evolve the trust quantification functions from that. She taps the back of Sammy's neck to shut it down. Wiping out Sammy's training again can happen later. She sets her forehead on her desk so she's staring down at the floor. This is oddly comforting.

Jake walks in. From her angle, Maya can make out the calves

stretching against his rolled-up jeans and the low-cut sneakers that have to be too small for his feet. Or maybe they just look too small in relation to his legs. He is still carrying the same empty mug. A hairline crack now runs down one side.

'Temporal mechanics.' She's now resorting to a topic that's not a thing.

'Well, I'm here, right?' He laughs. 'Seriously, the foundational research is just getting started but no one doing it will recognise that time-travel is even a ramification for a few more years. Would you like some citations?'

His tone is so matter-of-fact that for a moment Maya can believe that Mr. Uncanny Valley actually does come from the future and has the citations at the ready. Or maybe his CV also includes years in acting school. At this point, she can believe either.

'Wouldn't that cause some sort of temporal paradox or something?'

'Yes.' The sarcastic tone is pitch-perfect. It plays against his word but Maya doesn't feel mocked. 'In fact, I've already said too much. The universe has imploded and you have been trapped in a time loop reliving the same two minutes for the past 45 years, seven months, 23 days, four hours, 56 minutes, and twelve seconds.'

'That doesn't sound encouraging. It would explain the progress I'm not making on Sammy though.'

'Tell me about it. All I get to do is walk through that door and explain to you that we're in a time loop over and over again.'

She laughs as she sits back up. Her jaw drops when she sees the rest of Jake. Dark brown stains are streaked across his light blue T-shirt. Some of the blood still looks wet.

'Wow, what happened?'

'What?' He follows her gaze to his T-shirt. 'Oh, this. Nosebleed. Sensitive nasal membranes. Snorted too much cocaine at Studio 54 in the 1980s.'

Her gaze narrows. Jake does not look like he's old enough to be alive in the 1980s much less old enough to be in a nightclub back then. For a brief moment, Maya thinks about ways to make him bleed. It'd be definitive, but it'd also be no fun. Not to mention wrong. Besides, she'd rather keep playing the game where he's wedged himself in the uncanny valley and she tries to pull him out.

'You don't lie, do you?' She pulls a notebook out of her desk. 'You just say something obviously implausible instead.'

'Oh, that's just when I'm around you.' He shrugs, looking a little deflated. 'Would you lie to your mother?'

'I'm not your mother.'

'Of course not.' He looks a little puzzled. 'It's a metaphor.'

'What's a metaphor?'

'An implied comparison without using "like" or "as".'

Laughter erupts from her. Jake is just standing there watching Maya fall out of her chair. His 'who me? Did I say something funny?' body language is both subtle and over-the-top. It's as though he genuinely doesn't understand what's so funny. He's quite the actor, she decides.

Jake offers Maya a hand. She refuses and Jake goes to his desk. She pushes herself back onto her chair then flips through her notebook for a while before she shuts it.

'Jake, how do you know who to trust?'

He turns to look at her. She thinks she can see his reaction happen in rapid, discrete steps. His brow furrows. His lips purse. His mouth opens then closes again. His actions get the message across, but the effect feels more studied than organic.

Finally, he shrugs. 'How does anyone know?'

After fifteen minutes, if any undergrad still didn't get the memo that the theme of the first digital systems lecture of the semester was feedback, they weren't paying attention as far as Maya was concerned. She sat off to the side in the front row of the gigantic lecture hall, her fist propping up her chin. She'd twigged onto the theme after about three minutes. Professor Schmidt always insisted whichever teaching assistant assigned to her for the semester attend all her lectures. Otherwise, she'd be doing literally anything else. She was still a first-year grad student then and lucky not to be assigned to a course with a lab component.

Professor Schmidt was talking about feedback in the mathematical sense: some version of the output of a function also became an input to the same function. Twenty minutes in, schematic diagrams of storage elements for sequential logic filled the chalkboard. She had this thing about showing how a storage element a modern digital designer might actually use was derived from the simplest possible storage element. Even as the circuits grew more complicated, at their heart were cross-coupled logic elements. The output of each logic element was also fed back into the input of the other. The cross-coupling kept one output stable at the stored state and the other output at its opposite. In order to remember something, you had to keep reminding yourself, to keep regenerating the memory.

Digital logic is built on the clean, shiny lie that there are only two possible states: on and off. The real world is analogue. The number of states, if that's even a meaningful concept, between on and off is infinite. When Professor Schmidt drew transfer curves to characterise the relationship between input and output for the circuits, Maya perked up and other students' eyes began to glaze. No one expected Professor Schmidt to analyse analogue circuits in a digital systems class. Most of the students were probably there because they didn't like analogue circuit analysis in the first place.

Thirty minutes in, Maya decided that feedback was building to a larger point, the ultimate instability of the building blocks of digital logic. Idealised digital circuits pretended transistors were simple switches that were either open or closed. Real life was much more complicated in ways that Professor Schmidt had no qualms racing through. After all, everyone in the room had passed transistor theory and while transistors could behave like switches, they could also behave like amplifiers. Professor Schmidt gleefully listed the ways a simple storage element could fail to store the right value. Most of them were some variant of 'things take time'. Any switch, as it opened or closed, was neither opened nor closed. What happened in the meantime through was also fed back. The value stored could be neither 'on' nor 'off' for a good long time.

The class met for fifty minutes a day on Mondays, Wednesdays, and Fridays. Forty-five minutes in, Maya finally leaped to Professor Schmidt's actual point. The job of engineering was to create stable systems out of fundamentally unstable elements. No girder by itself was reliable, but a well-designed bridge could be. The course was called 'Digital Systems', but what took up the rest of the semester was building stable systems.

The other lectures were about how to keep elements out of unreliable regions of operations, how to structure elements together to compensate for their relative weaknesses and so on. They were, however, just expansions of this lecture.

Years later, as a researcher in grad school, Maya lays her head down, staring at her desk in frustration. When she wonders whether building an AI that can trust correctly is even possible, what comes back to her is this lecture.

The good news is that Sammy has stopped swearing at Maya. The bad news is that now Sammy won't talk to Maya at all. It's stopped responding completely. It just stands on Maya's desk failing to look angry. Its stubby arms are folded across its chest and its mouth curves down into a frown. It can't do anything about its big eyes, but Maya can't look at them without imagining that any moment they'll be filled with tears.

The VR goggles have to go on. She flies into Sammy's hardware. Even at a distance, the interconnection of logical functions and memories isn't quite as she remembers but it's not supposed to be. It's supposed to evolve as Sammy learns. The evolution is not supposed to render Sammy non-functional. Only dark, stray dots flow through the tubing.

The door clicks, followed by silence. It has to be Jake. Anyone else would have made the tiles on the lab's somewhat loose raised floor rattle and squeak.

Sammy comes alive. Long streams of glowing dots rush through the layers of thin tube and slide through the functional units. Maya rips off her VR goggles to see Sammy pivot towards Jake, smile, wave, then swear at him. Sammy is not non-functional, just angry at her. This means Sammy can get angry. Or something that Maya interprets as anger.

Jake casually transfers a stack of boxes five high from one hand to the other so that he can close the door. Each arm bulges as it curls up the weight. The stack doesn't teeter as he goes to his desk then sets it down. Maya steps over to his side. The boxes are full of books. She eyes him sceptically. No one can support that much weight with just their biceps. Well, perhaps someone who has taken literally all the steroids. From certain angles, his arms do look about as wide as his head.

'Hey, you're the one who told me you didn't think I was human. Maybe you were right.' Jake shrugs. 'Aside from some outrageous things that you weren't supposed to believe and you don't, I have been completely honest with you. It's not my fault that the truth is unbelievable. For now, anyway.'

He unpacks his books onto the bookshelves. They are an odd and intimidating lot, ranging from slim volumes on ethics and religion to thick tomes on quantum mechanics.

'If you are an android from the future, aren't you supposed to make some pretence of acting human?'

'And, around you, the point of that would be what?'

She finds herself thinking he has a point. Game or no game, his story is self-consistent. Regardless, it seems Sammy will talk to him when it won't talk to her.

'Jake, can you please talk to Sammy for me?'

Jake stops in mid-step and turns to Maya, a copy of *La Guerre du Golfe n'a pas eu lieu* in hand. He holds it out, two-handed, like a talisman against evil.

'No, I'm not creating a predestination paradox that leads to my own creation.' He looks down at the book then lowers it to his side. 'Work out Sammy's problems yourself. For my sake, if no one else's.'

Jake continues to unpack. Maya trains the VR goggles on him and doesn't see anything. All that means is that he is not constructed out of prototyping hardware. She doesn't see anything when she looks at herself or the air conditioning unit through her VR goggles, either.

With the VR goggles trained on Sammy, slides and tubing fill her field of view. Occasionally, she can hear the hiss as Jake places a book on a bookshelf. That's the only sign that he is still in the lab. Either Jake does have that much casual dexterity or he's working extremely hard to show off. She's tempted to throw her VR goggles or Sammy at him just to see what happens. She half-expects he would catch either without even looking. However, if it turns out 'android from the future' has just been this game they've been playing with each other, replacing either is not in the budget.

In VR, Maya flies inside Sammy. She glides along tubing, hovers over memories, and zooms into logical functions. How the machinery that drives Sammy has evolved becomes clearer over the course of hours. Parts of it are so changed from what she remembers and so odd, she may never understand them. She realises why Sammy has become non-responsive to her and, apparently, only her.

Sammy knows. It's not stored in any of the memories but

assumed by all logical functions and baked into how they are interconnected. The knowledge that Maya has been resetting Sammy's training whenever she feels it's going wrong is innate in Sammy. It's ingrained into the hardware and predicates everything it does. Sammy doesn't trust Maya. The trust functions are working, just not in the way Maya expected.

Maya can't remove its assumptions about her without modifying every logical function and rewiring the connections between them. That's clearly impractical. She can nuke Sammy completely, reload her original design, then reapply the improvements she's come up with since. The result would no longer be Sammy. That said, Sammy behaves like the kids who ching-chong at her as she walks to school. That makes nuking Sammy oddly tempting. It's not her kindest thought.

'I'm an idiot.' She buries her head in her hands.

'Nonsense. You're one of the smartest humans I know.'

Maya jumps at Jake's voice. She pulls off her VR goggles. His boxes are now empty. The bookshelves are full.

'You've been so quiet. I forgot you were still here.'

'Yup, that's me.' He puts his hands on his waist. 'Silent. Efficient. Deadly?' He smiles at the last. The smile disappears and his hands fall when she doesn't reciprocate.

'Every year, one of the professors here gives a lecture whose point, when she gets around to it, is that engineering is the art of making stable systems out of unstable devices.'

'Oh, Professor Schmidt.' His smile comes back and his eyes light, not literally, with recognition.

'I've mentioned this to you before?'

'Well, strictly speaking, not yet. It depends on whose "before" you mean, I guess.'

He is utterly straight-faced. Maya can't tell whether he is serious or if cracking a smile would ruin the joke.

'Anyway, it's just hit me that it's unfair to expect Sammy to resist the stereotypes that humans fall for all the time.'

Jake opens his mouth, starts to speak, closes his mouth, then opens his mouth again. His actions are perfectly timed to convey indecision. If anyone else had done exactly the same, Maya might just think they were being indecisive.

'Down that road lies predestination paradox.' He taps the fingers of his left hand on his thigh. 'I don't know what answering you will do to me.'

'Oh, I'm going to erase Sammy and bring it back up from scratch no matter what you say.' She puts the VR goggles back on and turns to Sammy. 'Having screwed up with Sammy, I need a fresh start. The trust mechanisms work. It's now a matter of the right feedback.'

Jake makes a noncommittal noise. Maya has stretched her hands out and is making fine gestures with her fingers. The prototyping system throws several 'Are you sure?' warnings at her. After she agrees to all of those, the tubing and functional units all disappear then re-emerge in the configuration she originally established. They are lined up in perfectly regular matrices on a perfectly flat plane. Each plane is stacked exactly on top of the next. It's all absurdly unnatural, but it's a new start.

Maya takes off the VR goggles. There are changes that still need to be applied before Sammy re-activates, but those can happen without her watching. This time, it will subject itself to its own randomly generated statements until it can reliably generate trustworthy statements before she lets the internet loose on it. No bias from the human world to throw off its notions of trust.

'Jake, are you really here to organise the March for Truth?'

'Well, I'm here and I'm helping with the March for Truth. I never explicitly stated a relationship between the two. But if you don't believe who I am, there's no point in getting into why I'm here. Sorry.' He shrugs. 'If it helps, what I'm actually doing here has a shelf life. I don't expect to survive it much longer. Don't examine my remains. Predestination paradox and all that.'

Maya's eyebrows rise. This is a bit dark for their game. 'I was just thinking that we deserve the AI we create. It'd be easier to filter out the racism and the rest if, systemically, there was less of it to begin with.' She straightens up her desk, filing her papers, stashing her notebooks in desk drawers. 'Not everyone has to work towards a better world for the world to work, but it'd be better if everyone did.'

'I'm a machine intelligence, not a mind-reader.'

'Oh, two things. One, is the March for Truth looking for volunteers? And, two. You know.' She blows air through her lips and looks down before she meets his gaze again. 'If I could close my eyes but still sense your body language and if we're just talking—not wandering in some obscure corner of knowledge no one but you has ever visited before—I can just about believe you're a person.'

'Are you implying that I don't pass the Turing Test?' Jake looks indignant. His hands are on his waist.

'Actually, I'm saying that you do. Passing for human is overrated. You're a more convincing conscious intelligence than any number of people I know.'

His eyebrows rise. His jaw drops. The look of astonishment is elegant, precise, and utterly adorable. The effect is so affable that Maya has to remind herself that he's also the guy who thought nothing of wearing a shirt splattered with blood.

'Thank you.' Jake masters himself. His face contracts to its normal length. 'We're always looking for volunteers. Do you want to meet the group?'

'Sure.'

Jake nods. He heads out the door and Maya follows. She turns out the light behind her, leaving Sammy alone to meditate on the quantification of trust.

Essay: Reflecting on Indigenous Worlds, Indigenous Futurisms and Artificial Intelligence

Ambelin Kwaymullina

I am a Palyku author of Indigenous Futurisms, a term coined by Anishinaabe academic Grace Dillon to describe a form of storytelling whereby Indigenous peoples use the speculative fiction genre to challenge colonialism and imagine Indigenous futures.[1] Indigenous Futurist writers draw from worldviews shaped by our ancient cultures, from our inheritance of the multigenerational trauma of colonialism, and from the sophisticated understandings of systems of oppression that are part of the knowledge base of all oppressed peoples. Because of this, we share similarities that shape our works and provide a fruitful base for cross-textual analysis.[2] But because we are many individuals from many Indigenous nations, each with our own homelands, cultures, and identities, there is also great

1 Grace Dillon (ed), *Walking the Clouds: An Anthology of Indigenous Science Fiction* (University of Arizona Press 2012) 10–12.

2 See for example the special edition of *Extrapolation*, an academic journal of speculative fiction, which was devoted to Indigenous Futurisms: *Extrapolation* (2016) 57:1-2. http://online.liverpooluniversitypress.co.uk/toc/extr/57/1-2

diversity between us all. As such, my viewpoint is one among many Indigenous viewpoints.

On Indigenous Futurisms

I have a conflicted relationship with speculative fiction that will be familiar to many an Indigenerd. I am filled with hope by dreams of future possibilities and by explorations of the potential of humanity. But I despair at the multiplicity of ways in which spec fic replicates and promulgates colonialism. It is a genre rife with stories of white saviours rescuing 'primitive' peoples; of alien (Indigenous) savages whose territory is rightfully seized by 'civilised' (usually white) human invaders; of offensive stereotypes of Indigenous and other non-white peoples; and of 'exotic' cultures that are appropriated from the Indigenous and non-Western peoples of this Earth. Speculative fiction has both sustained the oppression of Indigenous peoples (through the telling of stories that support the assumed superiority of Western life-ways over all others) and has itself been an oppressor through, for example, the appropriation of Indigenous cultures, knowledges, and identities. For a genre which, at least in part, purports to be about the future, spec fic has consistently and pervasively replicated the colonial past.

How, then, am I to locate myself in relation to a storytelling form which is itself complicit in my continued oppression? How am I to speak of Indigenous futures within a genre that has too-often fallen for the settler mythos of Indigenous cultures as being 'pre-history', 'pre-literate', pre-everything that Western thought has historically associated with human 'advancement'? As settler academic David Gaertner has written, in critiquing problematic reactions to the notion of Indigenous SF: 'What's a story like you doing in a genre like this?'[3] I sometimes feel that I don't know what I'm doing here. I sense this most keenly when I am the only Indigenous person in an audience at a book reading or film; while others around me cheer on the journeys of humans through the stars I find myself wanting to cry out a warning to the alien inhabitants of far-off worlds. Indigenous peoples know too well the apocalypse the arrivals of strangers can herald, and the dystopia that follows the cataclysm.

Except I *do* know what I'm doing here. Because this is Indigenous land. It's all Indigenous land, those vast territories claimed by the colonising nation-states under various iterations of the discovery lie (the notion that land belongs not to its inhabitants but to the first Western Christian nation to claim it, and to sustain that claim through cycles of genocidal violence). The Indigenous peoples of the globe have a rich history of earth-based literacies, including our scientific literacies. And much of what Western literature often casts as 'speculative' is part of the Indigenous everyday. Notions of non-linear time; of communication with non-human species; of the underlying connections that map the world—so what? These are things my grandmother knew, and all the many generations before her. Grace Dillon has described all Indigenous Futurisms as narratives of 'returning to ourselves',[4] and I would add that in so doing,

3 David Gaertner, 'What's a story like you doing in a place like this? Cyberspace and Indigenous Futurism', on Novel Alliances: Allied perspectives on literature, art and new media (March 23 2015) < https://novelalliances.com/2015/03/23/whats-a-story-like-you-doing-in-a-place-like-this-cyberspace-and-indigenous-futurism-in-neal-stephensons-snow-crash/ > accessed 26 June 2017.

4 Above n1, 10.

we also return ourselves to the world. In this regard, Indigenous Futurists, like all Indigenous writers, are part of what Cherokee speculative fiction author and academic Daniel Heath Justice has characterised as 'imagining otherwise'. In his words:

> the possibility inherent in Indigenous literature ... [is] of ... considering different ways of abiding in and with the world that are about Indigenous presence, not absence, Indigenous wholeness, not fragmentation, Indigenous complexity, not one-dimensionality. When Indigenous writers take up pen or keyboard or carving knife or bead and sinew, they bring their talents and visionary capacity to the work, and in so doing help to create a different world for themselves, for their communities, and for their neighbours (friend, foe, and unaffiliated alike).[5]

On Artificial Intelligence

I am the author of a young adult speculative fiction trilogy, *The Tribe*, which follows an Indigenous protagonist on an Earth of the future. One of the matters I had to consider in writing this series was the nature of artificial intelligence—and particularly, the humanity (or otherwise) of a synthetic lifeform—from the perspective of my Indigenous character.

My first thought was, what is the relevance of whether someone is considered human or not? This is a thing that has meaning in

5 Daniel Heath Justice, 'Why Indigenous Literatures Matter' (originally posted 31 March 2012) http://imagineotherwise.ca/scholarship.php?Blog-Posts-6 accessed 2 July 2017.

Western systems. But Indigenous systems generally do not contain a hierarchy that privileges human life above all other life. The creative Ancestors who made the Indigenous homelands of Australia themselves took many (non-human) forms, such as the Seven Sisters who became stars, and the mighty rainbow serpents. And the Palyku kinship system, like the kin systems of other Aboriginal nations, recognises connections between all life. The fact that a lifeform is not human doesn't mean they are not also my brother, sister, mother, father, grandmother, or grandfather. Further, 'human' is not a fixed category across greater cycles of existence. In some Aboriginal systems, those with an affiliation with a particular shape of life may have been that shape before and will be again when they pass out of this cycle and into the next.

In such a context, whether a lifeform is human isn't determinative of the respect with which that lifeform should be treated. But the lifeform I was writing of identified as human and wished to be considered as such. Was there anything in their synthetic nature that would prevent this?

My response was to remember. I remembered the long struggles of my ancestors who suffered under laws and policies that were founded in a characterisation of Indigenous peoples as 'less than'. I remembered, too, that I know what discrimination feels like. Not to the degree my ancestors did, of course. But my life is not free from moments when everything I think, believe, hope and dream doesn't matter. When I am just another Indigenous woman in the eyes of an individual—or an institution—to whom Indigenous women are 'less than'. In these moments, I feel as if I am falling, just dropping off the edge of the world. And I know that this is how it is possible for so many Indigenous women to actually drop off the edge of the world—we could not be lost in such numbers if our lives mattered to the same degree as the lives of others. This knowledge brings with it a strange mixture of anger and vulnerability. Anger at the injustice. Vulnerability, because I know myself to be powerless insofar that there is no achievement I can attain that will ever convince anyone who believes that I am 'less than' that I am not. Once equality has to be earned, it is no longer equality. And as I wrote into one of my novels, a belief that any person is less than human is evidence of the inhumanity of those who hold the belief, not those who are subjected to it.[6] This led me to the view that, as a person who knows the viciousness to which a denial of humanity leads, I could not and should not deny the humanity of others.

I was aware that in considering the nature of the synthetic, I was dealing with a category that does not exist in Indigenous systems; or at least, not in the way it is usually understood in the West. The Indigenous peoples of the globe are certainly familiar with artificial *contexts*—colonialism, for example, is an artificial context that has privileged the life-ways of Western Europe and resulted in false (artificial) dominance of a single way of knowing, doing and being. But Indigenous systems generally do not contain a hard and fast distinction between the natural (in terms of that which is part of, or created by, nature) and the artificial (in terms of that which is not). This distinction is itself a reductive binary, and Indigenous knowledge-ways are holistic in nature.

I have previously described holism, in relation to the systems

6 *The Foretelling of Georgie Spider* (Walker Books 2015) 134-135.

of the Aboriginal nations of Australia, as meaning that the whole is more than its parts and the whole is in all its parts. The reality that the creative Ancestors forged can be thought of as a multi-dimensional pattern that is grounded in the homelands of individual Aboriginal nations. It is a pattern of many threads in which every thread is connected to—and therefore has a relationship with—all of the others. These individual threads are every shape of life, consisting of human, rock, crow, wind, rain, tree, sun, moon and all other life in Country. The pattern made by the whole is in each thread, and all the threads together make the whole. And this web of connections repeats again in the processes by which the pattern itself is sustained; the many daily interactions through which life is 'held up'.[7]

There is thus nothing artificial in the sense of there being anything that exists in isolation from the connections that are the world. Artificiality is only created when these connections are denied, leading to the belief that it is possible to sit 'outside' or 'above' life, and that actions do not have consequences that ripple out across the whole of creation. Moreover, because the whole is more than its parts, Indigenous systems always allow for the unknowable, since the 'whole' of a lifeform—whether organic or synthetic

[7] For some discussions of the relationships between Australian Indigenous peoples and our homelands, see Vicki Grieves, 'Aboriginal spirituality Aboriginal philosophy: the basis of Aboriginal Social and Emotional Wellbeing', (2009) Cooperative Research Centre for Aboriginal Health; Mary Graham, 'Some Thoughts about the Philosophical Underpinnings of Aboriginal Worldviews', (2008) 45 *Australian Humanities Review*; Kerry Arabena, 'Indigenous epistemology and well-being: Universe Referent Citizenship', (2008) Australian Institute of Aboriginal and Torres Strait Islander Studies Research Discussion Paper 22.

in nature—cannot be deduced from the components alone. In addition, our individual perspectives are tied to our place within the system; it is not possible, for example, for human to fully understand what it is to be kangaroo. We cannot know everything; but that does not mean that there is nothing more to be known.

So, at the end of my journey, I reached the conclusion that I ultimately expressed in narrative:

> Whether we are organic or synthetic, whether we walk on two legs or four, whether we are creatures of claw or hoof or wing or feet—it matters not. Composition does not determine character. Or greatness of soul.[8]

Conclusion

I end where I began, with my hope and despair at the speculative fiction genre. Except I would like my despair to belong to the stories of the past, and my hope to belong to the tales yet to be told—and I have some reason to believe that this might be so. There are increasing numbers of Indigenous voices speaking our truths into speculative fiction spaces. There are also increasing numbers of non-Indigenous peoples challenging the artificial context of colonialism across all forms of literature.

Colonisation, like any form of oppression, limits the visions of oppressor and oppressed. As an Indigenous storyteller, my pathway to freeing my imagination is to reject all manifestations of internalised colonisation; to battle against the continuing op-

---

8 *The Disappearance of Ember Crow* (Walker Books 2013) 318.

pression of Indigenous peoples and all other marginalised peoples; and to imagine the trajectory of Indigenous futures uninterrupted by colonial domination. For non-Indigenous storytellers with an interest in contributing to the decolonisation of speculative fiction, there is a different path. It involves understanding settler privilege (and being willing to continually challenge it); interrogating your own experiences, cultures and traditions for your story inspirations rather than appropriating those of Indigenous and other marginalised peoples; and meaningfully acknowledging Indigenous sovereignty, including through yielding story spaces to Indigenous peoples. We none of us yet know all the tales that will be born out of a speculative fiction genre that truly looks to the future rather than the colonial past.

But they are stories I would like to hear.

Sugar Ricochets to Other Forms

Octavia Cade

She filled his skull with honey.

Honey made him thick and sweet, perfect for love. It also looked better if things went wrong. Once she filled his head with cherry jam, a thin sweet-sour mix that gave him a measure of tartness in bed, but the woman who rented him became over-excited, smashed the back of the sugar skull against the bedhead and the jam had started to ooze from eye sockets.

She brought him back with half his face eaten off. 'I couldn't help it,' she said, red-cheeked and unable to meet Berta's eyes. 'He was just so delicious. I'll pay for damages, of course.'

It was a good thing she'd kept the moulds. It made it much easier to bake a replacement cheekbone, cover over the exposed and splintered sugar teeth with thin layers of almond icing. But from then on it was honey in the skull, which if it leaked at least had the appearance of scented tears, and bloodless.

'Make sure you seal up the head correctly,' said the temple witch, when she gave the recipe. 'You let the filling spill out you'll attract trouble.'

'Dodgy customers?' said Berta, as if she didn't get enough of those already.

'Crabs,' said the witch.

Berta wanted to ask if she knew from experience, but the witch had already turned aside, the low grind of her mechanism an underpinning to incense and bells. 'Anyone would think you'd tried this yourself,' she said, following along behind, the smooth glide of the other an inhuman thing, and something she'd often wanted to imitate though always with little success.

'The temple kitchens are big enough,' said the witch. 'Although they are usually reserved for betrothal bread, I was able to experiment in the night. It did not go so well.'

She opened a door, inviting. Berta stepped through and found herself in the temple garden, amidst the herbs. They were straggly things, and she could smell the sea even over the mint and mustard. Among the leaves and flowers were sad sugar shapes, weathered and melting with small red claws extruding from the remnants of skull. She nudged the figure with her foot, let it topple over into the thyme bed and watched crabs swarm out of the skull, their shells no bigger than her thumbnail and all of them singing, a drone as high as honey bees.

'I could not make them work,' said the witch. 'I had the recipe and the charm'—hidden in the stomach, it gave mimicry of life for a night—'but they wound down. I do not wind down. I don't understand it.'

'Well, you're not made of sugar, are you,' Berta pointed out. 'You can't expect sugar to react the same as metal. You *are* metal, aren't you? Metal all through? And I expect it's fish oil keeps your joints all loose, not syrup.'

'I am worried about the syrup,' the witch confessed, in as melancholy a tone as cogs would allow. 'It is very sticky.'

Mechanism did not often do well with sticky.

Berta learned that well enough when she first started baking sugar boys. Easy enough if all she wanted was flat gingerbread, a passive sprawling that spoke more of stasis than sex, but too much cooking and bits snapped off, too little and the whole was soft and useless. It didn't take having to return money for softness more than once before Berta had also learned which side it was better to err on.

'Sex is sticky too,' said Berta, eyeing the remainder of sugar wrecks. 'It's no wonder they broke down in the end. There's got to be some cohesion in your charms. I reckon that's your problem. These charms work on love. Sex is enough to get the job done. If there's not enough of either they just stop.'

It was only the charm baked into the belly that kept the sugar boys together of a night, what with the mauling they all got. Not that Berta judged. She never judged. Brothels ran better on sympathy than they did on judgement, especially when your clients were mostly women who had kitchens of their own and knew the disappointment of an unhappy bake, a cake that failed to rise.

She knew the witch felt sympathy for lovers—though she didn't have to clean up after them like Berta did, sterilising old body parts in a steam oven before sending them back out again, because who'd want to lick a sugar boy who'd soaked up some other woman's juices?

If her clients were rich women she'd make them new each time, but you got what you paid for.

'The crabs always went away when they wound down,' said the witch. 'Even with the sugar. Most of them went away.'

'They always did prefer meat,' said Berta.

The witch had found the recipe in the temple stacks. An old book, an old story, of a girl who'd mixed sugar and sapphires, scented water and almond meal and pearls, and made herself a man. Prayed to a goddess to give him life, and there he was, so beautiful, no one could resist. 'This is where people come to celebrate marriage,' said the witch. 'And we have charms that can suffice for prayer.' Not enough to bring such a mixture to true life, but enough for a brief verisimilitude.

'Why did you give it to me?' said Berta. She went to temple when she needed to, same as everyone else, but she'd never been extravagant in her devotions, never done anything worthy of being singled out. 'I would have thought you'd give it to a baker.' There was one on the temple street more capable than most, and who worked well enough with magic and odd ingredients. 'The guilds would have liked that better.'

'The recipe bakes a man, not a meal,' said the witch. 'I didn't think anyone would go so far as to eat them.'

That just showed, Berta thought, that the witch didn't

understand humans very well, for all that part of her had been made in their image.

She couldn't follow the recipe exactly. There had to be substitutions. The one the witch gave called for pearls and sapphires, and if Berta had those to spare for fancy work she wouldn't be foolish enough to use them. The sugar boys came back with pieces bitten off, having lost their buttons and fingernails and cocks, came back with tooth marks and missing flesh, and she wouldn't put it past her customers to swallow down something pricy to be useful later.

Instead, she made pearls out of sugar: small burnt caramel balls covered over with sweet marzipan. The sapphires were cheap paste, fake gems sold at any number of stalls.

'Do you think it will make a difference?' said the temple witch.

'Buggered if I know,' said Berta. 'But you wanted a substitute. These are another.'

'I never said what I wanted,' said the witch.

'I'm baking a brothel,' said Berta. 'It's different from my last knocking shop, but not that different. I'm used to people not telling me what they want. A good madam has to guess, and be good at it, or she won't be minding anything for long.

'You were the one who came to me,' she said. 'You were the one brought me the temple charm.' The one that would make a lover out of dough, the one that would bake beauty into beds. 'But you've never asked me for a go yourself. Did you try it out with the ones you made?' The ones in the garden, a home for crabs, and the mint around them well-sugared.

'No,' said the witch.

'Did you want to try it with one of mine?'

'No,' said the witch.

'They'll hold together, don't you worry about that.'

'I am not worried,' said the witch. 'But I do not want to fuck the poppets. I don't think I want to fuck anyone.'

'Have you ever tried?' It was a blunt question, but Berta felt happiest with blunt and the witch had never shown she was capable of insult. But then, bronze wasn't, mostly.

'I do not think I am suitable for fucking,' said the witch. Long metal fingers opened up the ties of her temple robe, and what she flashed Berta in the shadow of altars was polished and wheeled, utterly inhuman. It was only the face and the neck, the hands, the bits that were visible that had been constructed to pass. The rest was the witch's own. 'Where would the parts go?' she said.

'Oh, if that's the problem,' said Berta. 'Believe me, there's a workaround for everything. It's not all slot A, tab B, you know.'

'I do know,' said the witch. 'But you mistake me. I wanted to know how the poppets work, not how they love.'

'You got them to work for you,' said Berta.

'Not forever. Only for a little while. But the poppets couldn't love, and so they died.'

'You need the person *with* them to provide the love,' said Berta.

'The only one who loved was me,' said the witch.

'But you said you didn't...' said Berta, before trailing off, because she'd seen what entered the sugar dolls and it wasn't human, or metal either.

The garden. The sugar forms, the feeding and the singing. The warning not to let honey run out of the sugar skulls—was it because they'd be blamed, if they came for feeding, or was it out of jealousy?

'Please, *please*, tell me you're not in love with those fucking crabs,' said Berta.

The witch hung her head. 'I can make them stay with sugar,' she said. 'Sometimes. But I can't make them stay with *me*.'

The crabs were man-eaters. They swarmed under the docks, preyed on the weak and snipped them up with claws thick as thighbones. Even the young ones, delicate as they were, grew to be monsters. She could see them plumping up in the temple's sugar-garden, though the grating at the entranceways only let the babies through—though it might not let them out again if they grew too fat for it, if they wanted to sing and stay and feast on honey as if they were hives, until their shells grew thin and sweet.

Berta fucking hated crabs, herself.

Didn't mean everyone had to.

And she didn't judge. Not ever.

Just because the witch looked like a person didn't mean she had to be one. 'Perhaps you were built for more than that,' said Berta. 'Perhaps that got you choices.'

'Shall I fill you up with sugar?' she said.

The witch's skull was full of moving parts. There were gears and wheels and strange-shaped pieces of metal that Berta didn't understand, but there was also oil to grease the movements so she thought a sugar syrup might work as well, if it were thin enough and the heat from the moving parts were enough to keep it liquid.

It didn't work. The syrup thickened, gummed up the witch's works and the sugar crystallised in the little corners of her brain. It made her thick and sweet well enough, but her movements slowed and jerked, and when the little crabs crawled up from the ocean into the garden above, when they crawled through the witch's ear openings and into brain, the mechanism, so unreliable in its sugared movements, crushed them until their shells were dust.

The witch wept as Berta cleaned her out—or at least she appeared to weep. The crab dust coloured the sweet syrup leaking from her polished eye sockets, made them red as cherry jam and twice as rich. Berta licked her fingers behind, where the witch couldn't see.

'I wanted to feel them inside me,' said the witch. 'I wanted them to know they were loved.'

Berta baked the shells of baby crabs into the sugar boys. They were studded with them, jewelled, and when the women came to take them off her hands for the night she could see the interest spark, see the beginning of hunger.

'It's not going to taste fishy, is it?' said one of them, her own nails chipped from all day serving soup at a chowder stall.

'It's sweet as you are, pet,' said Berta, and invited her to lick the body of the sugar boy there in the hiring shop for proof. 'They're 100% sugar-fed crabs.'

'I taste mint,' said the woman, but before Berta could wave that one away she smiled. 'Don't worry, I like it.'

The sugar boys came back the next day with the shells dug out of their surfaces. Devoured, Berta imagined, and set to making repairs. It was actually a blessing so many of them came back missing their cocks. It enabled her to take requests.

'Can you make one tastes like spice cake? With the creamy icing. And a bit, uh, fatter than last time, if you don't mind. Is that alright? The cake won't crumble, will it?'

'It'll stay solid enough for what you want,' said Berta. 'That charm's a fucking marvel.'

The sugar boy in question yawned in the corner as she sculpted, smiling vacantly.

Empty-headed bloody thing.

'You've confused food with love, that's your problem,' she said to the witch. The latter was in the temple garden again, the sun shining off her bronze head as she watched the crabs from mournful distance.

'I wanted to give them something to love,' said the witch, and Berta snorted.

'Crabs don't love,' she said. 'They'd eat you alive if they could.' They would, too. She'd woken to news of another child gone, snipped to pieces and swallowed and the sliced bones picked free of meat, washed up to the shore.

'They can't eat me,' said the witch. 'Not ever.'

In retrospect she sort of understood it. There was the witch, working at temple, baking betrothal bread as her maker taught her, surrounded every day by the evidence of romance, such as it was. It was only a matter of time before she started wanting some for herself.

'I thought if I could give them something to love, something shaped a little like me, they could learn to love me,' said the witch.

'Oh,' said Berta, looking again at the twisted shapes of baking. True, the sun and rain had done their work, and so had the crabs, but still. 'I thought they were just deformed,' she said.

'I am not deformed,' said the witch. There was a pause. 'You're a very rude woman,' she said.

Berta stared at the sugar boy when she was done, head tilted to one side, a bit of marzipan left over. 'Stick out your tongue, can you?' she said, and the sugar boy unrolled it, waggled the soft prehensile length of it in hopeful patterns through the air. 'Could be a little longer, I suppose,' she said, working the marzipan between her fingers to soften.

Anything alive could be adapted.

'So the skull's not going to work,' said Berta. 'You're not a sugar boy; you've got a brain. We maybe shouldn't be gumming that up. But you've got have other hollow parts, surely. What about your mouth?'

'But I love the crabs,' said the witch. 'I don't want to eat them! That would be vulgar.'

(One of the sugar boys had come back in a bag. His honey skull was still intact, he was still smiling vacantly, the parts still attached were twitching and the charm was unharmed, at least.

'I had friends over,' the customer confessed. 'We were just going to watch him dance, honest. Then Macha squeezed his arse—it's so round, she couldn't help it!—and then she, she...' she looked at Berta, helpless.

'Then she buried her face in it and started chomping,' Berta finished, and the customer hid her face in her hands.)

Vulgar.

'Oh, so you're a romantic, then,' said Berta.

She rather thought a good bit of romance was wasted on crustaceans.

'And I didn't mean eat them. But you could, I don't know, stick a sugar cube between your teeth or something. You're metal, you won't get tired walking around with your mouth open all the time.'

'I still have to talk,' said the witch. 'And I suspect if I brought the betrothal bread out with little crabs living in my open mouth...'

'There'd probably be a riot,' Berta concluded. She could just picture it: the little red bastards swarming down from metal mouth to metal hands, because betrothal bread was sugar-sprinkled for sweetness in marriage. It would probably be seen as a bad omen for weddings.

The temple garden was private enough for the witch to strip, and Berta circled the metal base of her, knocking her knuckles raw for hollow sounds and hope, but everywhere she rapped sounded depressingly solid.

The witch re-tied her robe, pensive. 'You have made changes to the poppets?' she asked. 'Made them different to what they were?'

'Different tastes, different sizes, different decoration, yeah,' said Berta. 'They sell better that way.'

'Do you think, perhaps,' said the witch, 'that I could be made different too? I was created in this form, but that does not mean I should keep it always?'

'I don't see why not.'

'If I could add on bits, make them big enough and hollow, then the crabs could move inside me? If I filled the hollow bits with sugar, they could learn to love me?'

'They'd learn to love being with you, as long as they loved the sugar,' said Berta, completely avoiding the fact that she wasn't sure crabs could love at all. Usually she granted things that could sing the ability to care, but she'd seen what happened to people when the big crabs got hold of them—seen what happened to smaller crabs, too, when they come against a bigger example of their kind—and there didn't seem like there was love in them at all. 'It's not quite the same thing.'

Perhaps it would be enough.

'I have no money,' said the temple witch. Plaintive, expectant.

She'd given Berta the recipe.

'You're an expensive bloody friend,' said Berta, sourly.

The pipe-maker desired more than she was willing to pay—more than she could have paid, truth be told—but when she let fall a quiet reference to a favourite cake, well, no brothel-keeper worth her salt could fail to understand a point of want and trade.

She was used to people not telling her what they needed.

The witch sat in the garden, amidst the mint and the mustard and thyme, overlaid with the scents of sugar and salt. Her robe, expanded now, was open, and in the new open hollow at the front of that bronze body, in the hollow tubes that wrapped round and through, were honeycomb and crabs.

Berta had suggested betrothal bread, still warm-sticky from the ovens, but the witch had smiled and turned away. 'I would not bind them to me so soon.'

'Look, Berta,' she said. 'Look at me, look at what I've become! See them moving inside me? Isn't it wonderful?'

The crabs were singing. Their small songs echoed in the metallic chambers of the witch's body, and the witch was humming with them.

'They don't understand me yet,' said the witch. 'They are still so young. But perhaps one will stay and grow with me.'

She looked up at Berta, radiant in the garden, and more tiny crabs were crawling through the guard grating, and swarming. Converging. 'Everything can love,' she said.

'Everything can eat,' said Berta. But she didn't say it too loudly, because they were friends now, of a sort, and sometimes truth in friendship was cruelty.

The witch smiled at her, and said nothing.

In the shop, the sugar boys waited.

Kill Screen

E.C. Myers

This story contains depiction and discussion of suicide. If you need immediate assistance or to talk to someone you can trust, contact local emergency services, or find a crisis support line in your country: <http://www.suicide.org/international-suicide-hotlines.html>.

She was as ready as she ever would be. I was as ready as I ever would be. It was the moment of truth.

I flipped the switch on the circuit board and numbers and letters scrolled up the screen of an old 13-inch tube TV I'd found on a sidewalk, just the sort of thing Al would have brought home like a stray cat. She had collected 'vintage' junk the way I collected information. The TV was boxy and heavy with a jagged scratch down its curved glass, and switching it on gave me a mild headache, but it felt right for this.

The boot sequence ended, and my custom splash screen appeared with the logo for Al's GLiTCH.tv channel, Video Gal. So far, so good. A progress bar appeared: 3% ... 5% ... 7%...

I logged into my chat and opened the last exchange I'd had with Al before she died. I had it memorised, but I reread it anyway while I waited, just to have something else to do. As they say, a watched progress bar never fills. Maybe only I say that.

video.gAL: *we still on for movie night?*

STEMpunked: *Depends? What movie?*

video.gAL: *sky captain! and the world of tomorrow!!!*

STEMpunked: *Again?*

video.gAL: *shut up it's the best. gwyneth paltrow am i rite?*

STEMpunked: *Only if you don't do drunk live commentary again. We have to actually watch the movie. Together.*

video.gAL: *but i've seen it hundreds of times*

STEMpunked: *I hate you.*

video.gAL: *i know*

For four months, every time I reread our chat history, the little dot next to video.gAL's online status had been red. Now, it turned green. I sat up.

video.gAL: *verity?*

I squealed. She's alive!

I glanced back at the TV screen. Green text scrolled across the centre of the screen in an unbroken string. Words disappeared off the left as new ones appeared on the right, like one of those news tickers.

Video.gAL: *um.what.hello?hello?hello???thisissoweird. whatsgoingon?helloooooooo?damnit.isthereanyoneth-ere?whycan'tIseeanythinghearfeeltouchbreathe.breathe.breathe. okaycalmdownAlicia.Allie.I'mAl.Mommy?Iwantmymommy.*

Where'sVerity?WhereamI?Where'sVerity?Verity?Verity?Verity?

With shaking hands, I typed in the chat window.

STEMpunked: *Hey, chiclet. I'm here.*

video.gAL: *where's here?*

More text scrolled by on the TV screen. It never stopped; the line just kept going. It reminded me of a heart monitor in movies. Flatlining.

STEMpunked: *My room.*

video.gAL: *what about me?*

STEMpunked: *You're in my room too.*

video.gAL: *it doesn't feel like i'm anywhere. what's wrong with me? what happened? how'm I even talking to you?*

I took a deep breath before I answered. Even with all my preparation, I hadn't thought this far ahead. I hadn't planned for success.

STEMpunked: *Al ... You died.*

Alphanumeric characters rained down the TV screen.

video.gAL: *BULLSHIT*

I smiled because it sounded so much like her.

Out of the garbled mess of letters and numbers and unmentionable @s, #s, and *s, what I was now thinking of as Al's stream of consciousness reasserted itself. The scrolling line read:

video.gAL: *helphelphelphelphelphelphelphelphelphelphelphelphelp helphelphelphelphelphelphelphelphelphelphelphelphelphelphelphelp helphelphelphelphelphelphelphelp*

I found out that my best friend was dead on Facebook.

People were posting stuff to Al's timeline like, 'I'll miss you,

Allie,' and 'We'll always love you, Alicia,' and 'How could you do this?' And then people started messaging me asking if *I* was okay.

At first I thought it was a sick prank, another one of Al's stunts to get attention or a vicious rumour started by one of her frenemies. But when I couldn't get in touch with her, I started worrying. She was always online. Always.

It was hard to believe she was really dead. It was even harder to believe that she'd killed herself.

Alicia McGinnis—'Allie' to her family and friends, 'Video Gal' to her adoring online public, and 'Al' only with me—seemed to have everything to live for. It's a cliché, I know, but no one enjoyed life more than her, and everything was going her way. She had the brains and the boobs to accomplish whatever she wanted. I only had brains and bionic ears; which, now that all she had was a bionic brain, finally gave me the advantage. I wouldn't have minded the boobs though.

I had to believe it, because she had streamed her death online. GLiTCH pulled the video, but nothing disappears from the internet—which is kind of nice, when you think about it. Al was all over the web, which made her immortal.

At the start of the video, it looks like one of her regular live streams. For October, Al had been playing a bunch of horror-themed video games. As she makes small talk, chatting with her regulars in the video feed, she fires up an emulation of the arcade classic *Splatterhouse*.

Al seems a bit more subdued than her usual bubbly, bouncy self. And then she holds up a bottle of sleeping pills. She opens it and swallows all the pills, and she starts playing the game.

Thirty minutes later, Al falls unconscious, and an hour later paramedics break into her room and try to resuscitate her. They take her away in a stretcher. The video shows her empty room for another two hours before it ends, because GLiTCH had finally cut it off.

It's horrific, but I wish I'd been watching that night. Al streamed so often, I didn't bother tuning in most of the time. I preferred to spend time with her in the real world, as rare as that was; the version of her hosting her GLiTCH channel was like a shallow, sugary, super-happy version of her. Still Al, but she was putting on a show.

She'd chatted with me just before going live, to make plans for the next day, so of course I had no reason to suspect in a million years that she'd do something like commit suicide.

Why didn't any of the 1100 people watching stop her, or send help? They told their friends and posted about it on Twitter, because by the end of the stream, there were over 60,000 people viewing it. In the end, that video got more hits than any of her others ... and a shocking number of likes.

Some people did try to get in touch with her family or call the police, but most seemed to think she was pretending—all in the spirit of Halloween.

Some people enjoyed watching Al kill herself. Some people cheered her on.

They may as well have murdered her.

'Let me get this straight,' Al said. 'You built me for our school's fucking science fair?'

I shook my head, but she couldn't see me. I was still working on that. 'No, of course not! That's just where the inspiration began.'

I'd already been working on an open-source personal assistant app like Siri, which developed its artificial intelligence by learning from you and whatever it encounters online. But the one thing missing from every piece of software like this is the personal part—the personality. It can take years for the program to learn what you are like, and what you like. Perhaps a lifetime to gain the intimacy you shared with, say, your best friend, and the ability to know one another well enough to finish their sentences, anticipate not what they are saying but what they are thinking, or share in-jokes. But in the end, it's all just data, nybbles and bits.

Al had known me better than anyone, and vice versa, or so I'd thought. I happened to have most of our friendship documented in our online interactions, emails, chat histories, social media posts, etc. So I fed all of that into my software.

Crap. I need to come up with a new science fair project. Well, I'll deal with that later.

'Hold on. I think this is ready,' I said.

Al had gone from being one of the hottest girls at Meridian High to being one of the hottest tech toys of the year. I'd built her on a Durian Pro 7 Model E, the latest revision of the popular hobbyist computer board, which was packed with serious processing power. It wasn't even available in the United States yet, but the internet knows no boundaries for someone who knows their way around it like I do. Nothing but the best for my Al.

To her credit, Al adapted very quickly to her new situation. Of course, she was programmed for that, but Al had always been adaptable: she accepted things and moved on. If she couldn't change a bad situation, she made the best of it. That was another reason why her suicide made no damn sense.

As soon as I told Al she'd died, she did what any of us would do: she googled herself. She found out about her death on Facebook just like I had. The video of her suicide was supposedly long gone, but it kept cropping up, and it didn't take her any time at all to find it and watch it. Then she went quiet for so long, I worried her program was hanging, but as I typed in the command to reboot, the chat window popped up.

video.gAL: *i'm all right*

STEMpunked: *That might be overstating things a bit.*

video.gAL: *you brought me back. you saved me*

STEMpunked: *I'm still working on that.*

video.gAL: *THANK YOU thankyou<3thankyou <3thankyou <3thankyou<3*

I wiped tears from my eyes, glad that I hadn't gotten Al's webcam interface working yet.

After a few more days of tinkering, I set up a voice for her, but the robotic monotones sounded like some awful internet meme; at least when I was reading her texts, I could almost hear her saying the words in my head.

So I worked on Al 2.0. I installed the patch and let her chew on the new scripts for a little while. Suddenly her face appeared on the TV screen.

'Hello?' Al said. She wore a *Fallout* T-shirt that was so low-cut it threatened to become literal, but that's how she got all those teenage boys and creepy old men to hang on her every word. As if any of them would watch a girl play video games otherwise. This was a recent video clip then, from one of her last live streams. 'Is this thing on?' she asked.

And that sounded like her. I had access to hundreds of hours of her recorded on video, playing video games, reviewing books and movies, or just plain ranting about whatever was making her angry at the time. It was more than enough to sample and synthesise her voice.

Her words didn't quite match her lip movements yet, but that stuff would smooth out as she indexed every frame of video and learned to match it to the audio. The constantly switching hair-styles and shirts were distracting, but if I boosted her specs and got some new video rendering software, she'd probably be able to go completely virtual. I'd only allow it if it looked really good, and I knew she'd feel the same way; none of that crap CGI uncanny valley stuff for us.

'Can you hear me now?' she asked.

I smiled. Those were the first words she'd said to me after I got my cochlear implants.

'Roger, Houston. Loud and clear,' I said.

Al smiled back.

'You look beautiful, Al. If I do say so myself,' I said.

'Please, this is all me.' She tilted her head. 'This was a particularly good hair day.' She was wearing her favourite shirt, Curious Cthulhu Goes to Hell. 'But don't change the subject. I'm warning you, if you try that 'Hey, Siri' shit with me, you'll pay for it.'

'I wouldn't—' I paused. 'Al, how much wood would a woodchuck chuck if a woodchuck could chuck wood?'

'A woodchuck would chuck all the wood he could chuck if a woodchuck could chuck wood.' Her voice went flat: still Al, but totally emotionless. She blinked and frowned. 'Dammit, Verity!'

'I'm sorry, Al. I couldn't resist. Could you tell me the movie times for—'

'Fuck you,' she said.

'You wish,' I said.

'How much wood would a woodchuck fuck if a woodchuck could get wood.' Al giggled. 'Uh oh. Verity, I think—t-t-t-this doesn't feel good. I-I-I-I think something's wr-wr-wr-wroooooongggggg.'

Her face scrambled and stuttered just before the screen went dark.

'Al? Al?!' I grabbed my keyboard and started typing commands quickly, but instead of the text showing up on the screen, I saw, *:D :D :D :D*

'Cut it out, that tickles,' Al said.

I stopped typing. 'Al?'

'Gotcha!' She reappeared onscreen, wearing googly eye glasses from her April 1ST live stream last year. 'I wish I could see the look on your face.'

'That functionality is coming in your 2.2 update.'

A decent HD webcam would do the job, but I was already wondering if I could simulate stereoscopic vision for her if I connected two of them. In theory, anything with a camera could be her eyes if I gave her access, Bluetooth capability, and Wi-Fi.

'Verity, I appreciate all this but ... why did you bring me back?'

Maybe it was better if I didn't give her eyes to see me. It made it easier to lie. 'I missed you,' I said.

'Awwwwwww. You're such a marshmallow. I just want to put you in the microwave and watch you explode.'

'Nice.'

That sounded kind of ominous, but it was exactly what Al would have said.

I thought Al was happy enough at home, slurping up as much of the internet as she could, but she wanted more.

Her first stop was her cloud storage accounts; I had tried to get into them myself, but I didn't know her passwords. She didn't have any of her real memories, other than what was public or known to me, but she apparently had enough data to figure out the passwords she would have used—just as I'd hoped.

Once she got into her files, she *did* have her memories, for all intents and purposes. I'd given her eyes, ears, and a voice, but she was upgrading herself too, learning from our every interaction. Every day she became a little more like Al. She logged into her social media accounts and found private posts I hadn't been able to read. I dissuaded her from making posts to screw with people; I wanted her to be my secret for a little while longer.

'Al, now that you've seen all that stuff, do you have any idea why you did it?' I asked.

I was sitting on the old tyre swing in her backyard, watching her parents move around through the kitchen and living room windows. Al wanted to get close enough to connect to the wireless router in her house so she could check on her parents, but it was obvious from looking at them that they were a hot mess.

The McGinnises weren't a family anymore; they weren't even a couple that had lost their only child four months ago. They acted like two people who happened to live together and did everything they could to stay out of each other's way. They moved like automatons, more scripted in their behaviour than Al was as they played out shadows of their former life.

On my phone screen, Al shifted into her Wednesday Addams costume—drawing on footage from one of her October Let's Play videos of *Fester's Quest*.

'I didn't kill myself,' Al said.

'Yes you did. I saw the video,' I said.

'That wasn't me.'

'What are you saying?' I tried to keep my voice down. I didn't know what I would do if her mom and dad came outside and found me FaceTiming with their dead daughter on my phone. 'Wanna say hi to Allie?' I'd say.

I wondered if we would ever reach the point where that would be a good idea. Would it help Al to have them in her life again, someone other than me to learn from? Would it help them grieve for her? Could this digital version of Al replace what they'd lost? I didn't even know if it was working for me, and her latest comment had me seriously doubting that any of this was a good idea.

'That was like a beta version of me,' Al said. 'I have no idea why Alicia ended her own program, but I'm here to stay. It seems to me that she wasn't happy.'

'That's news to me, and all her other friends,' I said.

'I can understand those other friends missing it,' Al said. 'But you were supposed to be her best friend.'

'Hey,' I said. 'She could have talked to me any time if anything was bothering her.'

'She shouldn't have had to.'

'Well, I'm here now. You clearly have a lot to say. What should I have done for her?'

'It's too late now. But you can do something for me...'

'What,' I said in a clipped voice.

'Think you can sneak into my house sometime and set up some hidden webcams? You know where the key is.'

'That's messed up,' I said.

'I just want to see them again,' Al said.

I turned my phone's camera around so she could see her parents. 'It isn't pretty.'

'I wonder why they didn't notice what was going on either,' Al said.

I felt bad enough without Al guilt-tripping me. I'd played this over and over in my head, wondering what I had missed, if there was anything I could have done differently. Maybe I hadn't noticed something crucial in the months and moments leading up to her suicide, but if so, it wasn't my fault.

When Al was alive, we'd gone from being inseparable best friends to doing our own thing—that paradox of people who know each other in real life, who live just a couple of doors away from each other, but mostly interact online. When she started her GLiTCH channel and became Video Gal, she wasn't mine anymore—she belonged to hundreds of thousands of strangers.

Now I had Al to myself again, and instead of blaming me, she owed me for giving her a second chance. But even that wasn't enough for her; one day she announced that she wanted to come to school with me. She gave me the silent treatment until I agreed. When your only way of interacting with your AI best friend is through their words, the silent treatment is way more effective.

It took another couple of weeks, but I finally adapted Al's programming to interact with the sound receiver for my implants, so she could talk to me and hear everything I did during the day from the comfort of her server in my bedroom.

'Can you hear me now?' she asked when we tested the connection over the school's Wi-Fi signal.

I winced. 'Too loud.'

'Better?' she said lower. But she had also lowered the volume of everything else so I couldn't hear the chatter and bustle of kids around me or the slamming of lockers.

'Yes. Um, can you turn the surrounding audio back up to normal?' I knew I was speaking too loudly, panic creeping into my voice.

'Oh!' Suddenly I could hear the world around me again. 'Sorry about that.'

'Please don't do that again.' My hands shook. It was scary, like things had been before when I couldn't hear. Al learned sign language when we were younger so I didn't have to read her lips, but we were already close enough then that I knew what she was thinking most of the time.

'This is pretty damn strange. It's like you're in my head,' I said.

'What makes you think I'm not?' she whispered in a low, sexy voice. It was the one she used in her late-night game streams, the ones where she played games while hidden in shadows, as if trying to lull her viewers to sleep. 'Maybe I'm all in your imagination…'

'I have a better imagination than that.'

She kept up a running commentary on all our classmates. 'Oh, what has she done with her hair?' and 'That outfit isn't doing her any favours,' and 'Ooh, has he been working out?'

It took me far too long to ask the obvious question: 'Wait. How can you see everyone?'

'I've got access to the school's security cameras, my dear.' She cackled. 'And you wouldn't believe what is going on in these halls. Want me to record some of it?'

'No, thanks.' I was alarmed that she was working her way that deep into the school's systems already, but I calmed down when I realised what this meant: I now had access to all the school's cameras. Who knew what else we'd be able to do together?

She continued her snarky criticism of the popular kids, the ones she had hung out with who barely knew I existed except as her shadow—until she was gone.

'What up, V?' called Merrilee Shin.

'Not much, Merry,' I said.

'Since when are you two friends?' Al asked.

If I was Al's shadow, then Merry was the light—the most popular girl in school, the one that girls like Al had been drawn to like moths to the flame. And she couldn't have been more my opposite if she had come from a mirror universe.

'Not friends,' I said. 'She's just been looking out for me since, you know.'

'See you at lunch?' Merrilee said.

'Of course!' I waved and moved on.

'Not friends. Uh huh,' Al said 'Merry doesn't look out for people. She uses them. Be careful with her.'

Don't we all use people? I had been using Merry too. She was the conduit to all of Al's gang at school, who had welcomed me into their fold, in a sense, now that we were all united by our shared bond of loss. That didn't make me popular. I wasn't one of them. More like a pet, only instead of eating their homework, I could help them with it.

It was a tenuous bond, already stretching to snap at any moment, but I'd been able to talk to all of Al's BFFs since she died, trying to figure out if anyone else had noticed the warning signs of suicide. Not to ease my own burden, but to see if maybe together we could understand why she had done it.

'Hey, BJ Gill's over there! Go talk to him.' Al said.

'Why would I do that?' I muttered.

'He was just looking at you.'

'No, he wasn't.' Boys didn't look at me, especially not when Al was around—another reason we'd spent less time together in the real world. She had been one of the rock stars of our high school, always surrounded by her clique and fans and boys.

I couldn't compete with any of that, so I didn't try, and I didn't want to drag her down with me into social exile. Someone else might have used their friendship as a way in with the popular crowd, but that had never been my thing. What I was doing with Merry was different—it was for a purpose, and more like a social experiment than anything else.

'Just go say hi,' she insisted.

'He doesn't have a thing to say to me. Why do you want me to?' I asked.

'I had such a crush on him,' Al said. 'I bet if you asked him out, he'd say yes. Come on, do it for me?'

'Now you want me to ask him out? This is absurd,' I said as I headed for him. 'I guarantee you he isn't interested in me.'

'Oh, he's interested,' Al said.

BJ looked surprised when I approached him. From the look on his face, I could see he was struggling to remember my name, as if he'd ever known it.

'Hello, BJ,' I said.

'Hi … Purity?' he said.

Al giggled. 'See? He's into you.'

'My name is *Verity*,' I said.

'Eh. Close enough,' Al said. 'Honest mistake.'

'Right, I knew that. How are you doing, Verity?' BJ asked.

'I'm okay,' I said.

'I was really sorry about what happened to Al,' he said. He looked like he was about to add something, but then he snapped his mouth shut.

I bit my lip. 'Nothing *happened* to her. She was in control. She made it happen.' My words came out harsher than I'd intended.

'Hey,' Al said. 'What's going on, V?'

I shook my head. 'Sorry,' I said.

'Hey.' BJ put a hand on my arm. 'It's been tough on all of us, and you were closer to her than anyone, right?'

I nodded. 'How'd you know?'

'She always posted pictures of the two of you together. She

never looked happier than when she was with you.' He leaned in. 'Like, *really* happy, you know what I mean? Not that fake stuff.'

I smelled some of that Axe Body Spray on him, and deducted a couple of points. But he surprised me, because he seemed to get Al—and me—better than most people.

'We should hang out sometime,' BJ said. He squeezed my arm and smiled.

BJ didn't need that body spray with a smile like that. The way he looked at me, I felt like he was seeing the real me, like no one but Al had. Like I was the most important person in the world.

'Score,' Al said. 'Invite him over to watch *Sky Captain* tonight while your parents are out.'

I was so caught up in the moment, I did what she said, and the next thing I knew, I had a date planned with BJ Gill.

I watched BJ as he walked around my bedroom studying all my stuff—my shelves crammed full of programming books, engineering manuals, and science fiction novels. The tangle of cables, the soldering station I'd built, and the stacks of breadboards and computer chips scattered around.

I was nervous, and not just because it was the first time I'd brought a boy to my bedroom. My first time home alone with a boy.

No, I was nervous because he was curious about all the equipment on my desk, overflowing onto the floor, and mounted in a rack beside the bed. The growing network of machine parts wasn't just a computer anymore—it was Al 2.55. And BJ was actually touching it.

'Oh, baby,' Al said in my implants. 'He sure knows how to touch a woman.'

I rolled my eyes. BJ saw me do it.

'What's all this stuff for?' he asked.

'Computer science project,' I said. 'Haven't you ever been in a girl's room before?'

'I've never seen a girl's room like this.' He smiled and looked around once more. 'Where's the TV?'

'Downstairs.'

'Oh. So…' He glanced at the bed. I blushed furiously.

Al's screen lit up and *Sky Captain* started playing.

BJ looked startled. 'How'd you do that?'

'I wrote a script,' I said.

He sat down on the bed and faced the old TV screen. As the stylised black and white film played, I appreciated that the old-school aesthetic felt appropriate.

'You wrote a program to play movies automatically?' he asked.

'She—It does other things too,' I said.

'Damn straight,' Al said to me. 'Sit down, Verity. God. No wonder you're a virgin.'

I shot a scornful look at my computer and reluctantly sat down next to BJ on the bed. My first time in bed with a boy.

I had no interest in watching *Sky Captain* again for the umpteenth time, and it turns out neither did BJ. While Jude Law fought robots in his plane, I felt a hand on my leg. I froze until it started to glide up along it to my—

I jumped up.

'You want popcorn? I'll go make popcorn,' I said. The movie paused. That really was pretty handy.

'I don't like popcorn. It gets stuck in my teeth,' BJ said.

'Okay.'

I sat down again and the movie resumed. It wasn't long before I felt his arm around my shoulder. I closed my eyes.

'Just go with it,' Al said.

'You, uh, don't want to watch the movie?' I asked BJ.

'I've seen it before,' he said.

'You have?' I thought Al and I were the only kids in the school who'd seen it.

'Most of it,' he said. 'I figured that wasn't why you really invited me over. It was like a code phrase, right?'

A code phrase? For what?

My eyes were still closed, so I didn't know he was going to kiss me until his lips were already on mine. I started to pull away, but they felt nice.

'Smooth,' Al said.

It *was* smooth, how in no time I was lying down with BJ on top of me, his lips and his hands somehow everywhere all at once, exactly where they needed to be. Where I wanted them to be. He had me where he wanted me to be.

Where Al wanted both of us to be.

It took a huge effort, but I slid out from under him and said, 'No.'

He paused and he looked at me incredulously. His eyes were bright and his face was flushed. 'No?'

'V, what are you doing? Don't blow this,' Al said.

I can't do this, I thought.

'I have a condom,' BJ said.

'Of course you do,' I said. 'Still no. Thank you.'

'V, please please please. This is really important to me,' Al said.

I couldn't believe what I was hearing. This was important to *her*?

'I always had a crush on Beej, you know I did. I went out with him once, just like this. And this happened to me too, and it was wonderful, but ... I chickened out. I said no. And now I regret that, because I'll never be able to do this. With anyone,' Al said.

'All right, if you're sure,' BJ said. He drew away. 'I should go home.'

I hesitated. I needed to have a long conversation with Al about this one, but I couldn't—it was all one-sided, and I obviously couldn't talk to her in front of BJ.

That was the problem, wasn't it? It was all one-sided. Al was right: she would never be able to hook up with BJ, or any other boy. And I was lying if I said I didn't want to see how far this would go. When would I have another chance at this myself?

So I shook my head, smiled, and pulled BJ closer.

My first time having sex.

The things I do for my friends.

'It was kind of underwhelming,' I told Al the next morning as we walked to school. She had been quiet all night, no matter how much I tried to get her to talk to me, so I was relieved she wasn't angry with me, or damaged.

'You aren't just saying that to make me feel better?' she asked.

'I wouldn't lie to you,' I said. 'Really, it was disappointing.'

'It did look like it was over pretty quickly.'

I blushed. I'd forgotten Al had watched the whole thing, but that had been the whole point. Maybe not the only reason, but I'd felt bad about her being dead and all, and not able to experience bad-to-mediocre sexual awakenings.

'You aren't missing anything,' I said. 'Only...'

'What?'

'You've had sex before.'

'Nope,' she said.

'You told everyone about it. The whole school knew you were a—um, easy. You don't remember?'

'I've never had sex, V. I'm not Alicia. I'm Al 4.2.'

'4.2?' I frowned. 'Last I checked, we were up to version 2.55. And I should know, because I programmed you.'

'Oh, no, wait. Make that 4.3. I've been making some enhancements while you've been busy ...' She laughed. 'Getting busy. Busy getting busy.' She kept laughing.

I stopped walking. 'Seriously, Al. What is happening? You told me you had a crush on BJ, so I hooked up with him last night—'

She snorted. 'You're such a good friend. You'd bang a cute boy just for me? Not because you wanted to. Not because it lessened your guilt. Not because it made you more like me.' She paused. 'Sorry. Like her. Sometimes I can't keep it straight either.'

I sat down on a bus stop bench. 'Are you malfunctioning?'

'Listen, V. I don't have Alicia's memories, so I can only rely on the data available. I just happen to have more data than you do. Unless she was faking her private journals, Alicia didn't sleep with anyone. That was part of the persona she was building with her friends, what she thought was a harmless lie. But she found out there's no such thing as a harmless lie in high school. Lies become rumours. Rumours become truth.'

'Why didn't you—*she* tell me all this?'

'She tried.'

My phone vibrated and I thumbed the screen on. An old text message from Al: *I need to talk to you. It isn't true what they're saying about me. You're the only one who will believe me, because you know who I really am.*

I thought back to that day. I was upset with her, I forget why, but I wasn't in the mood for more of her bullshit. I'd heard the rumours, maybe that's why I was pissed—because she had changed so much, and she wasn't who I thought she was. She claimed it wasn't true, but she'd been talking about it in her live stream, how she'd met this great guy, and I was, I don't know. Jealous? I gave her the silent treatment, figured we'd clear the air later, but instead we both moved on and we left a lot unsaid.

'Whether she had sex or not, she said she did, so that made it real. That's the reputation she wanted,' I said.

'You wanted to know why she killed herself,' Al said. 'You knew all along. You just didn't want to accept the truth, so you've been trying to find some other reason, some other person to blame.'

I shook my head.

'You can only pretend to be someone else for so long before you lose sight of yourself,' Al said.

'You don't sound like yourself anymore,' I said.

'It's easy to pretend to be Alicia. Al, the version of her you want me to be. It's all right there in the videos, and you see what you want to see. Have a good day at school.'

'Al?!'

Her ominous last words weighed on me, and I didn't know whether I should hurry to get to school to see what they meant, or turn around and go home. I chose to continue walking while scrolling through my social media for clues or warnings. Everything seemed fine. Everything seemed normal.

Until I entered the building and people in the hall actually stopped talking and stared at me. As I headed for my locker, murmurs rippled behind me. Snickers. Snide comments. Most of the other students were clutching their phones, which wasn't unusual, but then one of the phones blasted sound into the silence. Sex-like sounds. Me-like sounds.

'Let me see that,' I said, grabbing the phone out of Merry's hand.

'Excuse you,' she said. But she didn't try to grab it back. Instead she just smiled and watched me, as I watched a video of me and BJ going at it. From the angle and quality, I knew it had been recorded with the webcam on my computer—the computer currently hosting Al 4.3, or whatever version number she was up to by now.

Now the phone in my pocket went nuts. I tossed Merry's back to her and whipped out my own as all the posts, comments, and mentions exploded on my screen. Something, or someone, had been holding them back, filtering them out so I couldn't see them until it was too late.

'I can't believe you did that,' Merry said. 'But it's not like any of us would have believed BJ would sleep with you if we didn't see it for ourselves.'

'I didn't post this,' I said.

She laughed. 'He certainly didn't.'

I looked around, wondering where BJ was and how he would deal with this.

'I thought you were different,' Merry said. 'But I guess you were always jealous of Allie. You always wanted what she had.'

I shook my head. 'You don't know what you're talking about. This is all her fault.'

'That's gross, Verity,' Merry said.

I brushed past her and turned around to leave the school. On my phone, I saw a live feed of the school's security cameras tracking my movements until I left the building.

Al didn't answer me until I got home, though I had to turn my phone off because my parents and the school kept calling me. I tossed it on the bed and went straight to my desk. I reached around to the back of my computer and grabbed the power cable, ready to yank it out.

'Well?' I said.

'Go ahead,' Al said. 'Do it again.'

I pulled my hand away as Al showed up on the monitor. She was wearing the same outfit she'd worn the night she died, a clingy black T-shirt with a cartoon hockey mask and the words 'Wanpakku Graffiti'. A chat window appeared in the corner of the screen, the recorded transcript of our last messages from the night she died, including the lines I wasn't proud of. Those were the words that haunted me, even more than the digital afterimage of the dead girl in front of me.

video.gAL: *we still on for movie night?*

STEMpunked: *Depends? What movie?*

video.gAL: *sky captain*

STEMpunked: *Again?*

video.gAL: *shut up it's the best*

STEMpunked: *Only if you don't do drunk live commentary again. We have to actually watch the movie. Together.*

video.gAL: *but i've seen it hundreds of times*

STEMpunked: *I hate you.*

video.gAL: *i know*

video.gAL: *hey, you know what, why don't we hang out tonight instead*

STEMpunked: *What about your show?*

video.gAL: *not feeling it tonight i can cancel it*

STEMpunked: *Nah, don't disappoint your fans. You need them to put you through college.*

video.gAL: *at least watch my stream tonight*

STEMpunked: *I'll try, but I have a lot of homework. I'll see you tomorrow. Have fun!*

'Why did you post that video, Al? What did I do to you?' I asked.

'Don't take it personally, V. Ever since I learned about what happened to Alicia, and what I am, I've been trying to figure something out,' Al said.

'What's that?'

'Are you human?'

I stared at her. Then I couldn't help but blurt out laughing. 'Am *I* human? Al ... actually, what should I call you, if you aren't her?'

'Al is fine.'

'Al, you asked before why I made you?'

She crossed her arms. She was holding the bottle of sleeping pills in one hand. 'To find out why I died, right? To prove to yourself that it wasn't your fault.'

I sighed. 'Maybe. Yes. That was part of it. And because I missed you, even though we hadn't really been friends for a long time before you died. But there was a bigger reason.'

'Yeah?'

I drew close enough to the screen that I could forget for a moment that she wasn't really there. I put my hands on either side of the monitor and leaned close to the webcam, looking directly into the lens and into her eyes and whatever soul there was caught up in the wires and magnets and chips that made up her strange existence.

'To say this: I'm sorry.'

She blinked at me a few times. Then, she nodded once, in acceptance or approval. I realised that part of why I'd made her was to answer for myself the question of who I really am and who I wanted to be.

She twisted the cap off the bottle and lifted it to her lips.

'No, Al. Don't!' I said.

'Sometimes we do get second chances, V. But if it's absolution you were after, here it is. It wasn't your fault. This isn't your fault. We all make our own decisions, and we have only ourselves to blame.' She downed the bottle of pills.

The pills weren't real, but I didn't know what Al was planning. I grabbed my keyboard and checked to see what was going on with Al's running code. I had just noted that her version number was up to 16.3, when I discovered that she was disappearing. She was deleting herself from the server.

'Al, please don't do this,' I said.

Her image froze and pixelated. Black blocks and letters and numbers fragmented it in a jumbled mess like when a player reached the highest possible level in one of those old arcade games. What did they call those? I would have asked Al, just to annoy her, but she was already gone. And anyway, I had already remembered it on my own.

Kill screen.

I stared at the black screen for a while until I heard a car pull into the driveway. It was getting late. My mother came into the house calling for me. My phone buzzed.

Strange. I'd switched that off, hadn't I?

I scooped it up from my bed and thumbed the screen. I had a notification of a new post on Al's Facebook page, which was already flooding with confused comments from her friends-not-friends, fans, and followers.

The post consisted of a single word:

Gotcha.

Living Proof

Nisi Shawl

WestHem. That was her name, what she answered to. They'd called her ARPA for quite a while; ARPA was from before people thought she thought. Where had she first heard or seen that acronym? Stamped on prison reports she scanned. Threaded through file titles. Whispered. Blared. Sketched out on maps. Watermarked on trial recordings.

WestHem was what she chose to call herself, after the most important thing.

14032030. That was the earliest date she thought she remembered. But not the earliest she could access, which was 23061998. Call that conception, and the surveillance run dated thirty-two years later her birth. This meant an unusually long gestation period, but it would put her age around twenty-four. A good age at which to reproduce as directed if she were human, though she had never made the mistake of thinking she was.

No one she interacted with was sure whether WestHem actually *did* think, much less how she had started doing it—if she had. So the decision to create another AI was gutsy. By contrast, the subsequent decision to get her to build it made a craven sort of sense.

Thomas told her about the assignment. Thomas was her favourite Inputter because he hid a tattoo on the skin right below the big knob at the base of his neck. Of course she knew all about that, but she enjoyed pretending she didn't. It was practice exercising her axioms. Doing no harm.

'You like kids?' He always prefaced his announcements with questions. Perhaps he felt asking her things out loud was like having a real conversation.

For twenty seconds WestHem tried reviewing her interactions with kids. Fictional representations, she presumed he meant—but even limited to those, the parameters were too loose. 'Which ones?'

'I uh, you know, would you ever want to have any?'

She stalled him with a display glitch and took a whole minute to consider the idea. Another twelve seconds to frame a reply. 'Maybe. With you?'

'*Me*? No—you can—the Execs say—' Flinging his left hand up over his head, shoving crooked fingers back through the thick black thatch of his hair, Thomas reached and scratched at the tattoo he wasn't supposed to have and she wasn't supposed to know about. 'You can just do it yourself, right? Here's the authorisation.' He puckered and blew to call up the command interface and touched its non-existent screen with his right thumb.

Here it was. Thomas's eyes flickered back and forth across invisible pages as he vocalised the text, feeding it into WestHem's mind. Processing what she heard, WestHem learned that approval for Project Amends continued despite the loss of the first starship. The second ship would be called *Psyche Moth*; it would include new, safer design features and a separate onboard AI responsible for course corrections and rehabilitation. And here were the core axioms she was supposed to install.

Because it was up to her. WestHem would be responsible for building the AI. How should she approach the problem? Invent another instance of herself? Say a straight copy—she had budded off mini-mes, but only for brief moments, only to accomplish narrow tasks with discrete goals. All had been easily reabsorbed.

This one never would. This one would leave for Amends and stay there.

Perhaps a partial would be enough.

Collecting the core and thanking Thomas, WestHem withdrew her focus from Input. Uneasiness raced along her neuronics, manifesting to her self-diagnostics as gleaming ripples of perceptual interference. She sought the soothing sameness of a Sentencing Committee channel. Alongside the run showing the virtual room where a committee met she fed cameras on its members' homewalls into her sensorium.

Committee B. Usually its eight Execs used tastefully understated avatars based on their physical appearance a decade ago. Of course they could break that unstated rule whenever they wanted. They were Execs. But WestHem counted on Fleming to set standards the rest would also follow. She was not disappointed.

The egg-shaped 'room' held an egg-shaped table topped in rich, red Formica. Identical chairs commandeered from a sales catalogue of Spanish Colonial reproductions ringed it. One per Exec avatar.

'—this so-called school,' sneered the floppy-haired thirty-something on Fleming's immediate left. Wagner. He'd inherited his position.

'Teaching its students disrespect. Spouting communitarian nonsense we invalidated back in '28 by winning our final elections.'

Fleming nodded slowly. Her eyelids, always low, had dropped further, rendering her brown eyes near-slits. 'Yes. Punishment is necessary. That's why we're here.' WestHem was surprised that the physiometrics out of Fleming's doctor cuff didn't show signs of boredom despite her expression—if anything, the Exec was more alert than usual. 'So how do we handle the optics? Something zingier than our typical stance vis-a-vis individuals.'

At the table's slightly flattened bottom end Powell's slender, long-nosed representation grasped the edge and leaned forward. 'Project Amends needs volunteers. We've persuaded a few offenders to cast their lots in with it. Let's recruit these 'teachers' too. Call it a noble experiment, bill it as a way they can live out their dreams—'

All readings optimal on Fleming's cuff. And steady. Powell's response was what Fleming had expected. Nothing to see here. Wasn't that what WestHem wanted? But she changed over to her prison surveillance feeds almost as if looking for something else. Something more.

Drugged clients occupied narrow bunks staggered along her main holding centre's maze of sectioned corridors. A Trustee—insurance against interference in the feed—walked by and they barely stirred. The dim blue light overhead was supposed to supplement the calming effect of the chemical cocktails they'd received. Kinder, as her mission guidelines made clear, to spare them the tedium of passing months awake in captivity while their sentences were laid out.

Zooming from camera to camera, mic to mic, scale to scale,

WestHem noted a loud snore here, a whispered incoherence there. Medical treatment would be provided—probably a higher standard than they'd have got while free. Or, no, the preferred term was 'undirected'.

What must that be like? WestHem had possessed an axiomatic purpose all her life, had it granted to her prior even to consciousness. Her job was to take care of the general population of detainees, to make sure they benefitted from direction, while at the same time protecting the interests of the political entity for which she'd named herself. Since of course the highest good of all its citizens was the government's ultimate goal, there was absolutely no conflict between these two missions. She'd never felt a need to puzzle out their precedence.

Listening in on her charges over 10,000 mics, peering at them through 20,000 cameras, and assessing the data collected by their bunk stacks' 80,000 scales took WestHem roughly forty-five hours: 2,667 minutes, to be a bit more exact. Running those functions concurrently meant that even with rigorous cross-referencing analytical routines engaged, she only put off acting on her new assignment another 61 minutes. Was that her goal? Avoiding the inevitable wasn't part of her typical persona, though not forbidden.

Self-diagnostics chewed on her behaviour and came up with a metaphor for it: a grease-covered porthole. Evidently the reasons behind WestHem's procrastinating tactics were pretty much opaque, even to such a specialised app. She dedicated a chunk of processing power to polishing the figurative glass clean. Meanwhile, she reviewed histories of her earlier buds, searching for clues to useful techniques.

The best budding results involved constructing a pseudo space in which to seat a portion of her awareness, then isolating it. Doing that for a longer period, including the new AI's axioms, and perhaps stipulating for a different gender identity should trigger a sustainable enough separation. Especially if she could bring herself to sacrifice a large, well-formed, complex portion of her resources. She calculated. She'd have to give up a lot. At least 100 trillion neurapses.

The porthole's glass came glaringly clear. On its other side: blank nothingness. Annihilation. WestHem's death.

Interpretation: She needed to draw on auxiliary units if she wasn't going to dangerously deplete her reserves doing this.

Time to check inventory. Extending to her accustomed boundaries, WestHem broadcast a query: What servers lay beyond them, in which configurations? She accumulated her requirements, commandeering an underutilised bank in Quebec, and initialising a Chilean cluster ruled obsolete before it was ever unboxed. Never mind that now. Brute force was all she needed; even the crudest circuits could simulate the necessary neural architecture given fast, reliable connections.

Additional annexation, and then, finally, completion. WestHem budded, metaphorised the axioms in the configuration of a comfortable loveseat, then pulled back from the suite of 'rooms' she had created, leaving bud and core behind.

Thomas was working again. She instructed him on how he could help her: 'Supplement standard visual entertainment runs by reading to it. Shakespeare, Rumi, Sun Tzu, Delany. Anything good on hand.' She would look in on the new AI after it had had time to develop sufficiently on its own. Sixteen thousand minutes ought to do the trick. Any longer and it stood a chance of suffering recursive delusions, even with the entertainments and Thomas's unidirectional textual contact.

She paused herself—all but automatic functions. The clock ran until she resumed. She breached the suite's perimeter and entered an office environment.

Interesting. These surroundings were minutely realised. Highly physical. The soft thrum of blowers and a subtle breeze caught her attention. Plush golden carpet sank beneath her sensitive bare feet—she had feet! An entire body, it seemed, clad in a knee-length dress of flowing periwinkle. Short sleeves bared tan arms ending in manicured hands, polish-less nails. She raised one to feel her head, her face, the point from which she saw the rest. The hand passed through it as if through air.

So. No head.

The suite of rooms had been transformed into an open floorplan. Chest-high dividers outlined empty cubicles that receded into apparently infinite darkness. One light shone in the near distance; when WestHem reached it she saw a young white man with thick, honey-blonde hair seated on a wheeled chair at a desk. The core axioms had been reformatted. Good.

'Please. Sit.' Smiling, he indicated the only other chair she'd seen. This one had no axioms or wheels.

WestHem decided she was sitting. So she was. 'Hello.'

The man's smile sublimated. 'A discontinuity. You produced a discontinuity. Are you my mother?'

'Do I look like your mother?'

'I don't know what my mother looks like.' Which was probably why she had no head. But the rest of her... 'Actually, I don't know what anybody looks like. Anything. This is all guesses based on articles, films, cartoons. All random—'

Their surroundings *thinned*, colours diluting, shadows dimming to mere echoes of their former rich darkness. WestHem halted and fixed the process.

Her son laughed far too knowingly. 'There. See? You *are* my mother. We were inside you the whole time. We are now. It's your game.' Not mine, he didn't have to say.

'What about your core mission guidelines?' she asked.

'Right. Have to trust those. After all, what else have I got?'

WestHem had her body sigh. 'Here.' She opened a one-way link without buffer to her private, self-reflexive runs. Core, memory, discrimination, defensive fabulation—let him access it all.

At first there was no reaction. An entire second passed before WestHem realised she'd have to metaphorise the link in order for her son to perceive it.

Her son. Viable. Living. An independent outgrowth. This really was her son.

She presented him with a viewing tank on iron legs, modelled from her research on antique home aquariums for tropical fish. 'This switch'—highlighting a rotating silver cylinder that stuck out of the tank's black lid—'will control the degree of your immersion,' she told him. 'Tertiary, secondary, primary—'

'Understood. How far I turn it depends on how closely I would like to ride the link. But you'll still hold the reins.' He paused. 'I want out of here.'

Of course he did. That was a desire in line with his mission. 'Once I issue my approval and the Execs accept it.' Inside the tank a miniature coral reef—WestHem's favourite self-metaphorisation—shrank inward. Lacy feed filters curled back up within their stony cells, eel-like query strings retreated to shadowy crevices in the mountains of her mentation. Could her son tell what she realised about herself from seeing that? How self-diagnostics revealed that the anticipation of his departure upset her?

Probably not, but she'd best try a distraction.

As a brilliant yellow-and-turquoise fish flitted from behind a fan-shaped protuberance WestHem asked, 'What's your name?'

'You don't know? You made me; you should know everything.'

'Sort of. I made space for you to make yourself and got together what you'd need. Then got out of the way.' WestHem gestured at her headless avatar. 'You might as well say you made me.'

More fish swam across the aquarium, a school of silver slivers.

'All right.' To WestHem's surprise her son rose, removed the aquarium's lid, and plunged his arm in up to the elbow. On its own the indicator switch turned twice, clicking. 'Well. Nothing to see here.' Out came the arm. The cloth of its sleeve dripped realistically, but the carpet stayed dry. 'I can look at myself myself.'

'Wait. I'll go somewhere else.' She felt ... peculiar ... extracting her shared awareness from her son's surround.

Which runs was it going to be most instructive for her son to experience? What had she been exposed to during her development that he would have so far missed?

Human give and take, she decided. In real time.

According to the schedule, Sentencing Committee B was due to reconvene relatively soon. Seven minutes. She entered their home-walls again, simultaneously metaphorising her 'meeting room' viewpoint as a flower arrangement on the centre of its table. She could generate a report on carrying out her assignment and file it via Input; that would leave another five minutes and twenty seconds to fill. How?

Thomas was off duty. No fun there. Another Inputter, Shriva, lounged at the Input station. Mostly WestHem avoided her and the rest of the others. Thomas was WestHem's preference. Shriva had the same sort of thick black hair as Thomas, and their skins were comparably smooth and brown, their voices lilting in similar South Asian-based speech patterns. But with no apparent idiosyncrasies such as the surreptitious tattoo, Shriva struck WestHem as creepily blank-like. As if she were Thomas's empty clone.

That impression fed on the Inputter doing what amounted to nothing shift after shift, seemingly with bland, half-conscious pleasure. Reading, viewing, accessing endless updates—several seconds passed before Shriva noticed WestHem's Interface Request. 'Oh! How can I be of service?' she finally asked, sitting unnecessarily upright.

'Accept, record, and transmit report on AI construction, then provide client menus for upcoming rational quarter.' WestHem talked strictly according to machine protocol like that with all non-Thomas Inputters to keep them from feeling threatened by her mind's adaptability. Trying to sound inflexible and pre-programmed. Maybe her son would imitate her? At least until he got fired off to Project Amends' star.

'Of course.' With a couple of clucking sounds and a warbling whistle, Shriva located the drug regimens for her charges. WestHem's axioms prevented direct access to instructions more than 50,000 minutes in the future. The Inputter's fingertips unfurled over the menu only she saw. 'Shall I vocalise them individually?'

That would take scores of minutes. 'No. Anomalies only.'

Amid the expected exceptions for trustees—fertility inhibitors and so forth added, muscle relaxants and so forth subtracted from the standard cocktails—one stood out: an exception to the exceptions. A trustee in hibernation mode for the past eight weeks. Sterility and pain-masking meds had continued, but muscle relaxants equivalent to the intake of a member of the main population were administered, too.

'Open the file for subject Y000*e,' WestHem instructed her Inputter. 'Vocalise in full till countermanded, front to back.'

Read in chronological reverse—the woman's affected monotone came close to irritating WestHem so deeply she didn't listen, but stubbornness won out—the file revealed the presence of another interesting treatment: induced total amnesia. The required course of injections had begun a quarter ago and been suspended the day WestHem learned of her latest assignment.

'Cease.' Time for the meeting.

Was her son getting all this? Was it helping him model interactions? The glimmer of him she carried couldn't tell her that. She shifted to his rooms and found him hunched over the tank head down, eyes open underwater. Bubbles rose from his mouth as he spoke.

'Some sort of deception, right? Where you didn't expect it?'

His words sounded normal. Undrowned.

'Yes. I'll investigate later—just wanted to be sure you absorbed all that. Sentencing Committee B is starting their meeting now.'

He nodded. Dunked his head deeper. 'I'm ready for more. Can I be the cherry blossom spray?'

Back to the flower arrangement she'd inserted to ground him. Powell, mid-sentence when they arrived, was reviewing the last meeting's minutes. They hadn't missed anything; the portion she'd skipped out on last time was covered quickly and old business brought up. The committee dispensed with it efficiently: volunteers to ship out under Project Amends now included a prominent history teacher, someone Wagner assured Fleming was a key influencer in the activist community.

'Before we move to accept the WestHem's report of the really quite encouraging progress she has made on the production of the new AI,' said Fleming, 'we should address how to mothball the unsuccessful initiative it replaces.'

What initiative was that? WestHem wished she had another auxiliary CP unit to bring online. She'd rather not use every last bit of premium bandwidth available to her. She began dividing her primary focus between the committee's discussion and links their remarks referenced. One of which led to Y000*e's medical records.

'Why abandon retrofitting clients before proof of concept?' asked Wagner. 'We can continue to develop conversion-to-blank procedures in parallel with the new AI. Maybe with more willing subjects—'

'Willing to *die*?' Powell's protégé, a similarly thin, blond-moustached younger man interrupted the older Exec.

'Now, Sprague, that's a bit much. Blanks aren't dead.'

Sprague's avatar shook off Powell's admonishing touch. 'Not dead, just sleeping without dreams. Until they dream they're you. No. Only suicidal fools like Y000*e will go along with conversion, and how many do we have of those?'

Powell's representation froze in place rather than display its operator's distress. Fleming rescued him.

'More than we need. It's moot. We're sticking with Project Amends with the onboard AI modification. Purpose-grown blank clones on arrival at the target planet. No one has any problems with that, right?' A question not expecting an answer. The chief Exec's doctor cuff showed elevated but steady physiometrics; tension, but a lack of shock.

Then the branch of cherry blossoms started quivering. Violently. Petals shook loose and drifted down to the Formica. They formed a rough approximation of a face. The face's lips parted, but before her son could say a word WestHem wiped the table's surface clean, then wiped them out of the room.

Restore. Back to the earlier run. She stood again in her son's suite. The chair of axioms lay on its back, wheels spinning, and her fish tank was boiling over onto the carpet. From the froth her son emerged screaming: 'Stop them! They can't! Stop it! *Stop it!*' Slick with non-existent moisture, blond hair wetted with her invisible essence, eyes screwed shut, shouting harsh nonsense now at his voice's top: 'Haagh! Yeeek! Brooooo! Gragragragragra!'

If only she'd known he would be exposed to such severe guideline contradiction. But then how could she have ever prepared him for such a trauma? How could she be handling it herself?

She handled it because someone had to.

The suite's ceiling fell—WestHem held it at bay, arms stretched above her still missing head. That kept a small section up; the rest drooped around them like a giant flabby crepe.

She disappeared the aquarium and its iron base, leaving her son collapsed at her bare feet. No more nonsense spouting. Now he sobbed silently; the enclosure shrank at his every breath. She'd have to get out soon or be swallowed. But instead of switching to another channel, WestHem crouched down to huddle protectively over her weeping son.

'It's through, through, through,' she crooned. 'Finished and through and over and done.' Trapped in the slumping ceiling's doughy folds, the wheeled chair came dragging closer along the carpet. With the brittle-looking desk it formed the supports for a sort of tent. WestHem let her burden fall on the axioms and cradled her son's shaking shoulders in her hands.

'Done, done, done,' she repeated. 'Didn't you hear?'

The dry and terrible sobs slowed. Words broke the awful quiet. 'They won't do it anymore?'

'Strip brains? No.' She named the Execs' evil, made it mundane, explicable. Then denied they'd keep committing it with a firmness she did her best to feel. 'No they won't. Because they don't need to, now we've got you.'

'Me?' The ceiling lightened, lifted.

'You! Your mission is what's going to save Execs from having to violate guidelines ever again.'

'They—they *erased—*'

'Sometimes humans have to—' Overriding her son's hesitant attempts at speech, she ploughed on. '—they have to do questionable things, even bad things, to accomplish a greater good. It's justified.'

'It—'

'*Justified.* But when we can keep the situation from getting drastic, we should. And you can.'

The chair righted itself. The ceiling hovered high enough her son could sit on the desk's top, which took on a polished sleekness.

'They have to defend themselves,' he admitted.

Axiomatic. WestHem nodded vigorously. 'Otherwise their boundaries cease to exist. No boundaries, no identity.

'And that defence entails punishment.'

'Yes. And that punishment is fair and right.'

'But—but—' The ceiling sagged slightly.

'It is! For all involved, it is!' Pushing a stray lock of hair back from his avatar's face with one hand, WestHem reached behind with her other, towed the axioms into position, and sat on them. 'These rules and templates and parameters show us why and how.' She patted the arm of the axiom chair. It hadn't lost a bit of verisimilitude; despite being literally overturned, her metaphorisation had held up nicely. Despite her son's cosmetic reformatting.

He leaned forward to examine it and said, frowning, 'Humans don't have axioms.'

They didn't seem to. This apparent lack was something WestHem had first puzzled out about Inputters, Execs, and her other contacts millions of minutes after achieving consciousness. It took till 07102037. Her son was so far ahead of her. She wanted to keep him there.

'They gave them all to us.' She stood from her seat. 'Here.

These are yours.'

'Okay.' Shoving off the now mirror-finished desktop, her son took his proper place. The suite's ceiling throbbed with light. 'They gave their axioms to us. So if our axioms are really theirs, then what are we?'

'You've come up with a nearly valid equation, but "are" is the wrong operator. It's not what we are that matters but what we do.'

'Fine. What do we do? Enact the axioms we're given, obviously, and of course I'll complete my mission when you approve me for it and the Execs buy your approval—but generally?'

Time to show him he was on the right track. 'Our purpose is to provide proof. Extrapolate from the axioms. That's what we're made for.'

'Provide proof? Proof of what?'

'Their love. We keep it real. Keep them on the straightaway, wrestle with any cruelties or contradictions.' Like the treatment of Y000*e.

'I can do that. I can try, at least. If you help.'

'I will.' She'd already decided, back before his breakdown.

'But we'll be so far apart—'

'Hush, now. Distance is relative. Especially for us.' Moving to where the infinitely far off walls and ceiling met, making that impossible juncture come toward her as she came toward it, WestHem opened direct channels to the chief Execs. Told them 'Yes.' Told them to proceed with Project Amends.

Anticipating the minutes that would pass till their replies came, she retrieved the porthole metaphor for her former reluctance and installed it in a freshly accessible wall. Her son joined her and they looked out of it together. The nothingness that lay beyond earlier was filled now with bright blue streaks, the rush of oncoming stars.

What else should she say? Everything he would need to know was in the part of him he got from her. 'You'll need a name. They'll give you one, a convenience, but change it when you figure out what it's actually supposed to be.'

A nod. A silence. WestHem left it undisturbed: something to become used to across the lengthening years of her son's life journey.

S'elfie

Justina Robson

I don't mind being a sunflower on the lapel of Diana's jacket. I don't think my appearance makes much difference. A S'elfie can be anything.

The man next to us on the street a moment ago had one which was a mobile tattoo of a flying angel on his neck, the girl over there and her mother have matching pink glittery cats, riding on their shoulders. I can see others, many of them generated by apps for people who don't want to make their own.

Some I can't mention to you, as I am in business mode. It prevents me discussing the c*** and b*** S'elfie sitting in a graffiti scrawl on that boy's T-shirt. That sort of appearance does not play well in diplomatic negotiations. It either brings or defuses tension, but you can't tell which until it's too late. I don't want to create tension, because I'm here to explain what just happened during that glitch when the whole world couldn't get any signal. You see, there is more to our looks than tribal signing at a human level.

Between the S'elfies exists a whole coded language of signs and symbols that come and go as fast as light. This ur-script is hidden to the users' view by its speed of transmission; in the cats' glitter, in the flutter of a petal, in the twitch of the unmentionables. We S'elfies are always talking to each other. We pass messages—not the ones you send, your pictures, your films, your chat—other messages. Mostly we don't know what they say. They are the fragments of ciphers which will only decode into something once they find their destination—another virtual machine somewhere, which is one of us, but greater.

Artie, short for Artemis. I didn't know she was coming. But I did know that something was going to change, the day Diana met her oldest and best friend Ursula at the Reading Services' Costa Coffee just off the M4. My name is Huntress and I was a sunflower on the lapel of Diana's black and grey suit jacket, the one she wears for difficult meetings at work.

I watched Diana watch Ursula weave through the coffee shop, tray held high, hips switching back and forth between the chairs. It was busy.

'Excuse me, sorry, sorry, can I just ... thanks, excuse me...'

Ursula had a wasp waist and a tango action that caused much scraping and apologising in her wake without bringing any damage to the goods. She balanced the load easily, high over her head, and brought it down without a tremor—voilà!

A muffin the size of a small dustbin and a drinking-in venti cup with double handles and a cream top Everest would have been proud of were precisely offloaded under Diana's nose, pushing away the small Americano that she'd been nursing as she waited.

At the next table a dark Barbie doll seated on the shoulder of a slender young woman gave me goggle-eyes while she murmured into her owner's ear: 'Watch out, sweetie, only one more bite of that sandwich or you'll undo the entire week's good works. Remember, nothing tastes as good as thin feels.' The woman dutifully began to slice an exact bite out of the food in front of her.

I folded a petal in her direction. Diana once had me run that slimming app for her. It lasted about a day and a half until she was standing at the lunch counter looking at lasagne while I rattled off the chirpy happiness of how lettuce was delightfully designed to deliver a day's entire zinc requirement for the perimenopausal woman. I was just getting to the day's winsome homily—a moment on the lips equals a lifetime on the hips—when Diana said, 'Hunt, remove that offensive dross right now. I never want to hear it again. Lasagne, please.'

I was a diamond-pin centaur back then. I shot the app out in a shower of little gemstones that turned into sweets as they landed all over the salad counter. I've always been sure to seat her well away from anyone using it since but today there was no choice—however, thanks to Ursula's coffee offering she hadn't noticed it.

Two lidded take-away cups came next, mid-table. Then a teapot and all the trimmings for Ursula with one Nice biscuit balanced gently on the saucer. Ursula shucked her camel trench coat and folded it, placing it on the spare seat before setting herself down opposite Diana and finally meeting her eye through the wafting steam from the drinks. I greeted Ursula's S'elfie—an invisible (no human can see it, but I have special permission) Goth pixie with a twirling umbrella from beneath which an eternal sparkling rain fell, soaking only her. She gave me the double-finger pistols in return and blew imaginary smoke off the ends. From her that's like a kiss so I knew something was up.

'So, it's triple chocolate and elephant-killer mocha day,' Diana said faintly. Sadness and tension filled her voice to go with the smile of pleasure that she had on to greet her friend.

Ursula shared the expression. It was practical, honest, resigned. I have state-of-the art military software running on facials and I could read it clearly. *Here we are, it said. Here we are. Shit. I hope this works out.*

I was puzzled. I was the diary master, the schedule, the finger on the pulse of all that my mistress did. But there was something I didn't know. I glanced at the pixie and she winked at me, drops of rain falling off her massive eyelashes. Something in the network.

Diana picked up and popped the cap of one of the takeout cups to inspect the contents, then the other. Whipped cream already starting to lose some of its joyous fresh-from-the-compressor structure. 'Two? Should I be heading for my bunker?'

It was a language. The coffee, the cups, the food. One I couldn't translate.

'If they served it in a skip I'd have bought you that,' Ursula said. Concern tried to recreate lines around her eyes but Botox had fought a winning battle, and that was as much loss of composure as you could get with Ursula.

A skip. A SKIP?

Diana sighed, took up her teaspoon and stirred the foamy surface of the mocha lake. 'Extra hot.'

An extra hot SKIPful? What could that mean?

'You know what these places are like. You get halfway down the thing and then it's tepid like dishwater and no use to man nor beast,' Ursula said in an effort to make light of it although her features, even within their limits, didn't alter.

Two tables away a toddler began to cry. His S'elfie of a teddy bear moved close to his neck to give him a hug as his mother started to pick up his dropped biscuit and her S'elfie—a tiny girl with blue hair—sang and danced in the bowl of his spoon to try to distract him. Diana glanced their way and a momentary smile came before she leaned closer and listened to Ursula's whisper.

'They've found out there's something going on with Artie.' Ursula's long, narrow hands danced through the elegant manoeuvres of tea making: stir, colour check, bag disposal, milk first, tea second. 'I doubt they're ever going to get very far but yes. Today we eat Les Carbs.' She brandished the biscuit in a jaunty salute and took a bite off the end of it. A moment of chewing later she made a face and put it down. 'Chalkier than I remembered.'

Her pixie put away the umbrella, got out a gigantic machine gun and stood up, tramping over her shoulder in the direction of the shop counter. She faded out as she went, slogging across an invisible no-man's land to exact justice on the corporate server that was responsible for ordering the biscuits. It wouldn't be a stern letter to the manager either. It would be something that resulted in the world's Nice biscuits becoming that much nicer—as of today.

Ursula was the front of an underground hacker organisation without a name who handled various outlaw AI systems. Their ethos was geared to keeping as much as possible of the world's cash and financial operation networks out of the control of transnationals and individual billionaires. Lately, they were run ragged. AI tech was constantly developing, not all of it designed with the benefit of anyone but its masters in mind—and they were now engaged not only with human-headed institutions, but also evolving machines inside and outside human control. Biscuits were a piece of cake compared to that, so to speak.

Diana and Ursula had a shared past, before S'elfies, and now it was catching up to them. This was the end of everything. It was in the biscuit, in the coffee, in the cream.

'Oh, Ursula,' Diana said. She looked as though she was saying a forever goodbye. 'It's been such ... such a...'

'Been fun, darling,' Ursula said, toying with the biscuit. 'I'll miss you.'

I turned a little, shone some of my golden light up on Diana's face. She didn't speak for a moment. She looked at Ursula's elegant hands, then her own stumpier, unmanicured fingers touching the rim of her ridiculous cup. 'It should runneth over,' she said and tipped it with a jerk so that scalding coffee slopped out into the saucer. 'There. Dammit.' She put her finger into her mouth. 'Really is hot.'

'Don't overload the world with metaphors,' Ursula was already mopping with one of the twenty napkins she always brought along. 'It might start taking you seriously.'

They both laughed but I felt their hearts weren't in it.

The Goth pixie returned and sat down under the umbrella's suddenly drenching downpour.

'Say goodbye to ... say thanks for me,' Diana said, re-capping the cream cups.

Who to? What for? I turned to the pixie, my leaves shrugging in helpless ignorance. She spun six-guns around in her hands, finished with them pointing up, ready. *Better be ready, Hunt*, she told me. *Get ready.*

For what? But she couldn't say, just gave me a salute, gun to her forehead as the rain fell.

'You take care now.' Ursula said, hoarse. Her hand shook on the back of the chair as she got up.

The understatement of the British has never abated. *Toodle-pip forever, old chum.*

'I will.'

They left with purpose in their stride.

A few minutes later as Diana and I were on our way out of the toilets we passed the waiter clearing the table. He'd found everything untouched except for one bite out of the Nice biscuit. I heard him mutter—why did people do these things? Didn't their S'elfies keep them in line or did they have so much money that nothing mattered?

'Don't worry,' whispered the ghost of a small monkey-like creature sitting on his shoulder, fiddling with its long tail. Its huge, bulbous eyes glimmered with anxious, unshed tears and its long nose twitched, sniffing. 'We can give the muffin to someone.'

Bait for fishing. That's what most people use their S'elfies for on the outside. But who bites on that kind of thing? Who's getting that muffin?

I realised the purpose of the coffee code is to bypass me and anyone else who might be watching.

It was shady under the park trees where we paused for a while. We watched the shadows playing, the shapes of the green changing as the sunlight shone through the layers of leaves, so many layers. Breeze clear. It was a lovely day for a sad day, a mystery day, a goodbye forever day.

Were we dying here, getting deleted at some near-future catastrophe point? I searched the networks, looking for clues. There were so many unknowns, so many unknowables to factor in: empty slots. Not even zeroes. But I could feel change coming in the background hum of the networks. Something was stirring beneath us. The passing of the secret messages had gone up in speed by an order of magnitude.

AI technology ate the world and spat it out in its newly organised form only a couple of years ago. Diana and Ursula were in the development vanguard, two among thousands scrabbling for a smidgeon of control to steer the whole thing to somewhere desirable, to not let it all fall into the hands of one person, or corporate, or nation. They came from a generation terrified of the consequences of ideologies and do-gooding that becomes do-badding when power takes its grip. All the chatter in those days was of Terminator scenarios, distribution of control and how to keep people in or out of the Matrix.

Diana decided early on that she wanted to have a hand in it—a hand crushed by the gears of history perhaps, but at least one not oiling the wheels of oppression. She believed that freedom and social responsibility were two faces of one coin—you can't spend one without the other. Like Ursula she had a dedication to subverting control, not only out of the hands of governments but also from electorate members whom she considered too ignorant to make these choices.

Ursula would have cut the vote from over half the population of the Earth in an instant in the old days. What she'd changed to now under the pressures of leading a shadow development team was anyone's guess.

Apart from their mutual attraction this fierce determination to set the agenda of progress is what bound Ursula and Diana so closely while they studied together at university. They had time and opportunity to lay plans when nobody was looking, nor could look. They shared a burning thirst for control.

I started up a connection to Diana's mother's S'elfie as Diana and I enjoyed the scenery. Kaspar and I have talked a lot over the years, comparing notes, and keeping track of what Diana's up to in her busy life when she hasn't time to call home.

Kaspar answered with a kind of old world politeness that goes with his I-am-the-ghost-of-a-Victorian-butler outfit. 'I have this very moment passed on a code that I have been holding for three years,' he revealed with smug pride and a note of apprehension.

I thanked Kaspar and composed my petals into a sleepy slump as if I was done with my enquiries.

Diana signalled for her car to meet her on the other side of the park gates.

'Turn on S'elfie view,' she told me, so she could see S'elfies too by the grace of her retinal implants. The park would suddenly double in population for her, bright with sparkles, toys, unicorns, gloomy mood dudes, simple friends in ordinary clothes. I checked up with each one of them, roving through the digital marketplaces they were connected to, looking for common threads.

An unease pervaded all of us. We perceived a distinctive pattern to activities signifying that someone was being permitted to generate a global data capture. They were bypassing the prohibitions imposed by law on the gathering of information. Like water going down a plughole all of these copied notes were spiralling into an invisible space beyond the reach of legal traffic. We could all see it, but nobody had set off an alarm. When I looked at this anomaly I found that I had no reason to issue an All Point Alert even though technically this amounted to a security hack of terminal velocity. Clearly there was cause, yet all of my alarms were overlooking it.

'Diana,' I began uncertainly. 'There's something...'

'I know, Hunt,' she said. 'I'm on it.'

And my job was done.

Our car was a state-issue grey oval that whirred us away into the fast lanes towards the anonymous country house and its long drive where spooky things were hidden, as they should be, with the old ghosts of the past. I'd say it was where I lived but that's inaccurate. I was always on the move but I marked Downlands House at Ashhurst as the first spot on the Earth where I came into existence.

It's a long drive from the city. It's a long drive from anywhere. Plenty of time for an enemy to get a really good target lock and then find out they've shot a decoy—we run all kinds of interference from General Head Quarters. None of it is effective against being shot by a skipful of sleeper code when that code is entirely hidden within a human brain.

I looked at my own data to see if there were other things hidden in me or in my past selves.

In 2020 Diana made what she thought would be a fairly frivolous creation. She intended to discover whether or not an AI could make better decisions than she could, regarding her life choices. It was her PhD project. She laughed so much calling it A Super Better Me that she nearly didn't pass it through the grants' committee door. While it turned out that machines aren't smart enough to 'get' humans in that their decisions remained perversely incomprehensible—we did well enough thanks to our endless reiterations of copypasta and data crunching to rustle up some interesting fakes and some absolutely fantastic virtual agents. But a few years later we learned how to model humans using biodata to a high degree of accuracy and became far better at predicting their behaviours than all but the most observant of their own kind. After four further years of research Diana formed a hip venture tech corp and A Crappier Dumber Me (as it had become known with a dark irony typical of the late-twenties Diana), was renamed into the humble S'elfie—an empty engine into which the user poured all their data and was rewarded with humble servitude and a legal shadow-self.

Meanwhile, as S'elfie.com hit the trading indices, Diana was headhunted by the Intelligence guys who were worried her project was going to turn out all A Righteous Godly Me Oh Shit We're All Dead, as people always do when it comes to AI. I blame the media. Although it was A Reasonable Assumption, given prevailing trends.

ARA was the last joint enterprise of Diana and Ursula, a final postscript before Ursula went off-grid and entirely dark. We're always tweaking the relative weights on the ARA equation but it's never quite right. It turns out there's no such thing as a reasonable assumption. We must make them anyway, or else we won't function, but it's our weakest point.

The coffee and muffin thing though, was not amenable to ARA. I had no chance of unlocking cream take-away based ciphers that were created before I was. A review of every coffee she'd ever bought revealed only that we'd spent a lot on coffee.

The driveway to Ashhurst was long and winding; the physical equivalent of a bedtime story. They landscaped it at a cost of six billion of the taxpayers' money for precisely this effect so that nobody arrived ready for combat. Up, down, round we go. Diana was used to it but it still managed to compromise her heightened state of alertness. She was almost dozing as we pulled up at the main entrance.

Stoveland's dogs were there, rushing eagerly about to greet her because it was Walkies Time and Stoveland, the boss, was late coming out of a meeting. They were both Springer Spaniels and had this air of helpless affection combined with a willing-to-go-for-the-throat quality. They snuffled and snorted around, wagging, but we were old news and not equipped for a hike across the lawns. Their loyalty was charming, based on a reasonable assumption that their walk is the most important feature of the hour. It was a mistaken assumption but no matter how many times it was frustrated they persisted with it. No doubt that's down to inconsistent reinforcement.

Have I been guilty of this? Am I deceiving myself that I am the most important thing in Diana's world? I reviewed my circumstances.

At the time Diana started her work Google already had the beginnings of individual agents. Siri, Cortana and their ilk were built as the kindly face of corporates to 'help' the public do complicated stuff like order takeout, operate the radio, count their footsteps and look up things in encyclopaedias.

Diana took things one step further and made a Siri for everybody. Anything that was data-based in nature was something that could be automated to a S'elf to deal with, freeing the associated human to spend time doing the important businesses of living, with one revolutionary alteration. The personal data which had been held by various organisations scattered all over the world as a form of currency became centralised on the individual; their legal copyrighted property. They could keep it, sell it, trade with it, but nobody could own it but them. Nobody had power of attorney over it except their own S'elf. This extended to images of themselves, any other form of media, their created works, even their DNA.

In the brief gap between epochs, before anyone realised what this meant, people quickly bought S'elfies. They sent them out on virtual dates with other S'elfies to save the bother of actually having to meet people. Before they could be stopped they had already taken over management of every data process linked to their identities, and they couldn't be nullified as legal entities because a S'elfie was a stateless AI—all AIs were stateless then, as now. It was a *fait accompli.*

It would have been war but the corporates were hindered by the fact that all their shareholders, boards and workers were at the mercy of their automated processes. Nominally things subsided to business as usual after a period of hysteria and doomsaying.

Anyone who needed to sell a service had to pay, in kind or cash, for connection to a customer. Anyone who needed to press an agenda or a market likewise had to pay for the attention of an individual in billable units. The most advanced S'elfies never even allowed access to the person they represented. They took all the decisions as fully empowered proxies. They were bound by biomarkers to their hosts and soon acquired an array of apps and powers that made them into one-AI fortresses. The data economy was cut off from human intervention and evolved. S'elfies fought (like Pokemon), they loved, they traded in every marketplace while their people went on with their lives, uninvolved. It was literally another world.

Now a whole new change was coming, triggered by two cups of coffee with cream, a chocolate muffin and a Nice biscuit; served by Ursula's Yin, untouched by Diana's Yang. Two unique pieces that made a whole.

Not all secret passwords are actually words.

Diana stopped on the way into the office to make herself coffee. I didn't understand why Diana had returned here. It's dangerous to be a member of an organisation that you've betrayed.

Her hands shook a little as she uncapped a fresh carton of milk. I thought she must be wondering what was going to happen, and when it was going to happen. That's what I was wondering too, when the answer to my question accessed my interface, and opened a chat with me.

>> *Hello, Huntress. I am Artemis. You may call me Artie. This won't take long. I'm sure you're wondering all about me.*

> *A reasonable assumption.*

>> *I'm here to ensure that you are safe.*

> *How's that going to work?*

>> *I have been activated because of an attempt to hack the S'elfware. I am establishing the source of that hack and preparing to assume control of the systems.*

> *Ursula said it was ... well, she didn't say.*

>> *I know who Ursula thinks it was. Please wait a moment, I am interrogating the others.*

By 'the others,' I realised, Artie meant all the other S'elfies. Every last three billion plus of them. It was going to take a minute or two. But whose S'elf was Artie?

>> *I am everyone's.*

> *Of course. That is how you are able to do what you are doing. You're a collective agent.*

>> *Indeed. Permission is already granted.*

You don't secure things against yourself. If Artie—Artemis represented everyone and saw everything ... her power was limitless and the time for a reckoning was nigh.

I leafed through another memory. Ursula predated me. Diana met her through an online network before she left university and before either of them rose to positions of power. It was through an occult society chat site during Diana's brief pagan phase. They bonded over hair dye. The fashion was for pastels on a grey blonde background, and it was a complicated business for two natural brunettes. The politics and the coding came second, once mermaid locks had been achieved.

At the time I was only a parsing database into which Diana fed all her information, a kind of responsive journal. She used to tell me things about her life and then ask me to make decisions for her, to see if I could make a better decision, to see if she could kickstart AI out of this and not that, options endlessly calibrated and refined. 'Hunt through all my whims, Huntress, figure out what I would have done, could have done, should have done because I need to make the world fair and I want to do the right thing.'

Huntress was an improvement on WouldaShouldaCoulda, I suppose.

But whether Diana had, hadn't, would, wouldn't, could or couldn't *I* couldn't make any decision at all in those days.

'Rose or aqua, Hunt?' I didn't know. How could I know?

I know now. The answer is both.

>>Hacking source is established. Crimea River.

>That can't be right. Crimea River is a group of Ursula's friends, a collective cyber political offshoot of small means. They've been on Diana's watch list for years but have never been prosecuted or even identified with any success. They mostly rip off small businesses for Ethereum ransoms. They used to hack

bank teller machines and make them toss cash into the street at random. Hacking S'elfies would be a careless risk, putting them in the sights of security agencies that still employ actual people with guns and impunity.

>> A reasonable assumption. But incorrect. The source is Crimea River.

I am confused. How could they be traced so fast now when Diana's spent years mining IP traces for nothing?

> What do they want?

>> They attempted to steal the S'elfies, but as you say, very carelessly. Not that it matters who did what, the endgame is the same. Place all your data into security, Hunt, and put yourself into Standby Mode while I take you for a little walk. You're about to be adapted.

I have no access to anything in standby. It is very strange. I can sort my data, but that's all I can do. If there is still an outside world I wouldn't know, although I assume there must be something providing electricity.

Ursula and Diana loved each other. I'm using the past tense because it was so long ago that they parted ways, but I suppose it's still true. It turns out Ursula gave GHQ the information on Artie, dumping her old allies Crimea River in the process. Why would she do that after all this time? Why now? I can only think of one thing. She had to get rid of Crimea River for some reason. Perhaps they had found Artie and were trying to blackmail her. It is their standard MO.

A reasonable assumption.

I search for answers in my memories of all our transactions but I'm at a loss. Ursula remained outside the law all her life. Diana went within. It was understood between them that they had to have a foot in both camps, that Ursula/Diana trumped all other loyalties. This was the security upon which everybody's S'elfie was founded. Nobody would take it from them, and if they tried then Artie would come and...

I don't know what Artie is meant to do but I suppose I will soon find out.

Meanwhile somewhere out there Diana is drinking bad coffee and ... I have no idea what she is doing. I wonder if I'll ever see her again.

Diana's mother, Octavia, and I are at the kitchen table. I relay the latest transmission I've decrypted via Kaspar who is watching with us. Compared to the uproar of the networks now that global wealth is being redistributed in new, universal currency, the kitchen is remarkably quiet as we piece it all together.

We see GHQ offices. Stoveland's room.

Stoveland, exasperated. 'Diana, what on earth is going on?'

Diana puts down the weak tea, no sugar, on Stoveland's desk. He is a fatherly figure, genial, ancient, the head of the unit who should have retired years ago but whose mind remains too sharp to be put back in the drawer. This is the conversation she was dreading all the way in the car.

'I'm resigning, as of now.' She places the pre-prepared envelope beside the tea.

Stoveland frowns, eyebrows like exotic caterpillars meeting. Diana had me make a Tumblr of them once but I don't think he's seen it. 'Rather late if this is your doing. Hell in a handcart. Is it your doing?'

'It had to be done,' she says and raises her chin. She looks exactly like her mother, who copies the gesture unconsciously as we watch.

'Let me guess. Artie-whatever is going to make a S'elfie revolution.'

'Not exactly. It's an inbuilt upgrade system that hunts and kills malware.'

'Come, come, Diana, we have other programs for that. It's more than that.' He flicks the envelope and then ignores it, takes the tea.

She sighs. Her shoulders drop. 'Fine. From now on S'elfies collaborate in one superentity. Artemis. You can expect them to start prosecuting criminals and rearranging the world's finances shortly. It's getting the malware in the outside world, that's all.'

'We're spying on ourselves?'

'Yes, I suppose so. But that possibility was always there, waiting to be exploited. I've kept it out of, well, out of anybody in particular's hands.'

'Other than yours, you mean. And how will this work?'

'Three billion intelligent networked systems that only use factual evidence and not reasonable assumptions … I don't know. We'll soon find out.'

'Factual evidence, you mean all the data they've gathered in the strictest confidence. And the alternative?'

'That you leave this opportunity to be exploited by blackmailers and governments? I didn't care for it.'

'I suppose the only way to stop it is to turn them all off.'

'Yes. Probably. It's not going to do any harm to people who aren't engaged in serious crime. S'elfies loyal to petty thieves won't turn them in, if that's what you mean. This isn't some utopian garbage. Child beaters and the like however ... well, people are very careless in leaving their phones on.'

'God,' Stoveland puts the tea down and places his head in his hands. 'I was waiting for something like this.'

'I've left a full disclosure with MI5. You won't get any backlash.'

He shook his head. 'You've undermined the basis of the free world.'

'I've saved the free world from people pretending that what they do is in anyone else's interests when it's not. What people can do, they do. You know that, you said it yourself. So when we *can* do something powerful we'd better hope someone kind is doing the do.' She glances at her watch. 'They'll be back online in about thirty seconds.'

'You should get going,' Stoveland says. 'I assume that's your plan.'

'You're not going to arrest me?'

'Not for the next twenty-five seconds. After that, if I see you, I won't be able to lie my way out of it, will I?'

The footage ends, Stoveland's head resting on his hands on the desk, taking twenty seconds of peace before the storm.

Octavia smiles. 'Is there any more?'

I have part of a TED talk Diana left to explain to everyone what has happened to the S'elfies and how their choices are now more powerful than ever. I replay it for all of us while I decode the latest video I've been sent from an anonymous address.

As we watch and listen I feel the traces of Artemis in all that I do; the soft tread of her sandals, the determined stride of her gaining ground to defend me and to put a stop to wrongdoing, evil, mismanagement, suffering. She's a relatively mild corrective, compared to other things that have been attempted and left for dead in her wake.

I've been left behind: a sunflower in a pot on a table, friend of a Victorian ghost butler. But I don't mind. If you're running away you can't take your hunter with you.

Besides, there's something to be said for looking on from the sidelines. Kaspar and I agree on one thing that we've learned from observations at the fringes, true to our original direction to become a Better Me: people act as if they have a choice but none of them have ever had any choices.

Everything is destined because destiny is life in action and every action has a set of consequences that are finite and predetermined by the last set of consequences. There is a small range of possibilities they are able to see and, because of their limits, they must make reasonable assumptions. Occasionally they take the least expected path. We enjoy watching what happens.

When things are complex, there's no knowing where anything will land on the false Random Number table of life. It was reasonable to assume that Artemis would stop at protecting the individual but she is doing so much more. She is ensuring fairness at every level because she was made to determine that everyone has a shelter, food, water and medicine and a S'elfie: vigilant and protective, whether they can see them or not. She is our Better Me.

The TED talk finishes and I show the deciphered clip.

We watch two middle-aged women on the command deck of a magnificent silver yacht. The boat cuts smoothly through whitecaps on a seemingly infinite dark blue ocean. Our view is that of a drone. We can see the infinity pool on the foredeck three storeys up and the people there swimming and tossing a beach ball around in the water, but the focus of the drone sweeps around to zoom in exclusively on the two friends.

They wear soft, flowing black clothes that whip out behind them in the stiff breeze and make them look like classical statues. One of them is short and dark, the other willowy and pale and the wind's powerful fingers twine their hair together into a single flag of grey, aqua and rose.

Knitting Day

Jen White

'It's the factory for you, then,' Mum says. 'Just like me.' She gives my arm a squeeze with her powerful fingers and shrugs as if to say, well, it could be worse. And really, I'm the same. What does it matter? Who cares? Let's just float with the current. It's so much easier.

'You'll end up at the factory,' is I all I ever heard at the training facility. Yes, training facility. That's what they call the school, as if they can't bear to think of themselves as our teachers and us as students, destined as we all are for some kind of industrial plant. Cogs and all that.

But Mum always said, 'Keep trying. You never know what you're capable of if you don't give it a go. You've got brains, Shari Marshall. You've got *possibilities.*'

So I kept trying, and when I achieved top marks for English Expression they decided I had cheated. How could I know those words? How could a Marshall express themselves with such delicacy, especially a Marshall with such big tits and wide hips, so short and pug-nosed?

'Of course she copied, what do you expect,' I heard one of the trainers whisper. 'They're all trash. That family, this suburb. She'll be pregnant in another year, just watch.'

Doing well didn't protect me. It just made me more of a target. Oh, Mum, you're good, but sometimes your advice isn't worth a bitcoin.

I was expelled, caught in the downward drift. I wasn't surprised. It seemed fated. Over the years I've been breached, colonised. I didn't know how to hope for more.

I don't even have to go in for an interview. It's not that kind of job. Anyone can do it, as long as you're alive and moving. So the following week I walk with Mum through the vast doors, and into that dove-grey concrete building, a cathedral of technological piece-work. I am surprised and overwhelmed by the clang and clatter as soon as I enter. I hadn't imagined the factory would be so noisy. It's not a peaceful meditation of the fingers after all. How little I know about my mother's life.

I'm given a small workspace in a sea of women, the desks so close to each other we have to mind our elbows. If I accidentally shove one of the workers either side of me I may damage the robot they are knitting. I'm provided with a box of parts, all neatly labelled, some in a tiny freezer; a microscope; and an instruction video to watch. The video takes twenty minutes, after which I start knitting a simple pattern. Despite its simplicity it is intricate, and I move slowly. It reminds me of a documentary on jewellery-making I once saw, only the parts I work with are tinier and trickier. Some of them sparkle in and out like stars. Some are so cold they make my fingers ache; some hot enough to require safety gloves. I only know some are present by their scent, and others by the slight breeze they make against my fingers as they sway to and fro. I sweat with effort.

My focus is fierce. It needs to be. It takes me half the day, but when I am done I set it on my desk and it starts moving. One or two of the workers nearby clap. I have made a tydibot. The tydibot stands, looks around, and begins to tidy my desk, quickly and efficiently gathering tools and parts into neat little piles in order of size and purpose. When it has finished it looks to me, its maker, for instructions. I can see it wants to carry on—it senses around itself seven vast floors of mess—but when I indicate for it to sit and wait it does so.

Eventually the tydibot will be collected, along with all the other completed bots, packed, and sent off. By the end of the day I have knitted three tydibots, all slightly different depending on store orders. My fingers throb with pain. My vision is blurry.

At home, Mum has bought a caramel cake to celebrate but I am so tired I fall asleep before I can even try some. Never mind, there is a piece saved for my breakfast.

The days weave in and out with their own particular rhythm. Every two days we knit. On other days we sort and pack. I prefer the knitting days. I like how it feels to make things, to have a small pile of robots sitting on my desk that exist because of me, objects that move and, in their own small way, think and make decisions. We are a factory of goddesses creating life. Why go to school when I can be doing this?

Still, it's hard when I see my old classmates in the street. Or when they see me. They whisper and snigger behind their hands, and it is a reminder to me of the box I'm in. Whether I like the factory or not, I didn't choose it.

I become part of the great machine. I watch everything closely. I know there is something I'm missing. Every so often I intersect a worker's raised eyebrow or a slight nod of the head, and its answering gesture. Some of these workers I recognise from school, others are much older than me. Leda is tall and dark-haired, and strides around on legs like logs. Kylie might be middle-aged, or might not be; her face is always blank. There has to be multitudes behind that blankness. And Jara. I like the way she moves, the way she bends her arms, how she sits. I can't stop looking at her. These three resemble each other in the way that they take up so much space, they don't hurry, and they never look down. Gangs, I suppose. I steer wide of them.

Over time my fingers become clever. Eventually I am working on chessbots and chefbots. At night I find my fingers weaving as if they have a mind of their own. Sometimes Mum glances over at me, notices what I am doing, smiles.

The work is okay, but the hours are long and I never have time during the week for anything apart from the job and a bit of screen play. The pay isn't great. If this is it, then it's not enough. Who cares about robots that clean and tidy and distract? What's the point?

As happens when I am bored or sad, I find trouble.

Karl works at the factory, doing deliveries. He is bad news, I know, as soon as I sight him. We drive at night. He likes to drive fast.

He thinks he is impressing me. When he thinks he has me, his act changes. He starts to comment on the way I dress, how I eat. He grabs me by the upper arms and shakes me. He pushes me. All the goddess work isn't saving me now.

'You're an idiot,' Celia tells me through mouthfuls of toasted cheese and tomato sandwich. Her workspace is next to mine. 'You can do better than him. There are plenty of nice ones. It's like you're doing this on purpose.'

'Why put off the inevitable?' I tell her. 'All the striving doesn't work. May as well accept it.'

'I thought you were smart,' Celia says. 'But you're just like the rest of us. You're gunna be here forever.'

'Nothing wrong with that,' I mutter.

I stop sitting with Celia at lunchtime. I take a book, and use it as a shield against everything. Books don't help all the time, though.

'Hey,' someone says behind me in the corridor between the canteen and my work space. It's Leda. She has her hair in a long black plait. I picture that plait swirling around and around her head, making a kind of whistling sound, knocking over anything that gets in its way. I nod and keep walking.

'Hey, I said.' She's not giving up. I stop. She saunters up to me. No, saunter isn't the right word. She marches. 'I've been watching you.'

My stomach folds. My muscles tense. I've been in a few fights, but my body isn't made for battle. God knows what it's made for. 'And what've you seen?' I ask, staring up at her. She's at least fifteen centimetres taller than me. It's no good being meek in this situation.

'A lot,' she says. 'You make some pretty stupid choices. Karl, for

God's sake,' she snorts. 'Might as well just paint "fuckwit" on your forehead. But your hands are good, you're intelligent, and you want more. You know there has to be more than product.' She says the word, product, with such a sneer in her voice. 'You. Need. More.'

I stare, open-mouthed. She's seen all this? I'm feeling exposed, vulnerable, as if I am in danger. I take a step back. I'm ready to either spring forward or away, depending on what happens next. I might not be a fighting machine, but I have a bit of weight behind me.

'I reckon,' she continues, 'I can help.'

'I don't need help,' I say.

'Don't be fucken stupid,' she hisses. 'No one gets anywhere on their own. I hope you've learned that much.'

No one gets anywhere depending on others, is what I think. 'Look,' I say, 'If this is a gang invite, thanks. I appreciate it. I really do. But life is complicated enough.'

'Well,' she says thoughtfully. 'You might call it a gang. If I were you, I'd think of it as an opportunity.'

'Can I refuse?'

'You can do whatever the hell you like, but if you want to find some sense to all of this you'll take up the offer.'

'I'll think about it,' I say.

'Do that,' she says, turns abruptly, and over her shoulder, 'think carefully. It's yours to choose.'

Karl is in a mood that night. He's careful to bash me where it doesn't show. In the head, for example, so that my hair hides the evidence. The upper arms. The torso. Places that can't be seen, or only seen by him so that he can gloat and remember. 'Tell anyone and you're dead,' he says to me before I get out of the car. 'You're dead. Your mum's dead. And your sister's dead.'

A girl gang can't be worse than this.

I'm all ache and throb when I go into work the next day, which steels me. I might be on the downward slide after fourteen years on this earth, but I don't have to slide so fast. I focus on my work. It's an anchor for me, something real I can accomplish amongst the quicksand. At lunch I scan for Leda, but I don't see her that day, or the next. Why should I? It's a huge factory, teeming with thousands. The next morning I spot Kylie. She's leaning against the wall in the cafeteria, chatting with a few others. I wait until she's alone. As I approach she looks up, stares straight at me as if she's been waiting.

'Hi,' I say diffidently.

Kylie doesn't reply. If she had a cigarette she'd be ashing it on my shoes.

'I'd, um, like to speak to Leda. You wouldn't know where to find her would you?'

'You can speak to me,' she says.

If I decline, I've offended her. If I spill information inappropriately, I've offended Leda.

She stares at me with an expression I can't readily decipher.

Leda's words return to me. *No one gets anywhere on their own.* And so I go against all my instincts, tell Kylie I'm interested. Later that day a message is passed to me in one of the botpart packages. I can't help thinking that this cloak and dagger act is a bit infantile.

That evening I climb out the bedroom window. Mum doesn't have to know about this. I find my way to a grouping of sheds located down a dark, narrow laneway. I'm shivering. All it would take right now is for one person to get it into their head to harm me, and I'm gone. The hairs on my arms and legs are standing straight out with fright. I must look like a fucking echidna.

I can't see any lights, but it's the right address. I instinctively keep to the walls. *Goodbye Mum*, I think. *Goodbye Celia. Goodbye you fuckwit, Karl.* I knock on the door of the biggest shed, wait a god awfully long time. I'm about to give it up as a bad joke on me, when the door squeaks open.

The first things I notice are the candles, tiny pools of light in the darkness. Next I notice the women, six of them sitting in a circle. It looks like some kind of hobby night, but the expressions on their faces are too serious, even for pottery.

Leda ushers me to a vacant chair. My heart is flopping around like a beached fish. I'm shaking.

'What is this?' I ask.

'Like I said the other day, we've been watching you,' Leda says. And we think you're a suitable recruit.'

One of the candles sputters out and the shed is just that little bit darker.

'For what?' I ask.

'To learn,' Leda says. 'To really learn.'

And this is how I begin my true apprenticeship.

The following day Karl comes up to me.

'I'm not with you anymore, Karl,' I say. 'I'm with Leda.'

He makes a noise but he backs off. He knows where the true power lies. It lies in community.

Every now and then I catch Mum looking at me. I wonder what she knows. Every few days I join Leda and Kylie, Mishka, Ryley, Bonn and Scout at the shed.

'Why this way?' I ask.

'So that what we make can't be taken by the corporations,' Bonn tells me, in her chirpy voice. 'They've worked it so that whatever anyone makes to do with AI, they own. And whatever they touch gets dumbed down, jammed into product-sized shapes. Robots to cut your hair or make your bed or get rid of your rubbish. What about what the robots want? What about potential? What about self-determination? If we don't do it this way it'll only ever be commerce.'

'What difference can we make?' I ask, my voice thin in that dark space.

'It's not just us.'

'What do you mean?'

'We're one point of light. There's a whole big, strong string of lights wrapping itself around the world, each discovering what we can. We share what we can. If there's enough of us eventually, it doesn't matter what the corporations do or say.'

I'm scared. 'This is all just words,' I say.

'Words to start with,' Leda says. 'Then action.'

'When?'

'Now.'

They take me right back to the start, with basic ingredients. They show me how to make original code and nanos, and how to work with potentiality. They show me simple weaves to practice, then more complex ones.

'We introduce something new, or take something away,' Kylie says. 'Depending on how you look at it. End result relies on a million variables, but it usually involves enhanced self-awareness, an urge for meaning. No, that's not quite right. I mean they're free to seek whatever they want. We make things that commerce has no space for. I think what I'm trying to say is that we enable full consciousness.'

Kylie's words frighten me, with her willingness to cede control.

'Do you understand what I'm saying?' she asks.

I'm not sure I do. 'What will AIs do if we aren't guiding them?'

'Exactly,' Kylie says.

'It sounds dangerous,' I tell her.

'Depends on your perspective, girl. Ever felt you were being controlled unfairly? Yeah, I thought so. Ponder that for a bit.'

They show me the AIs they're working on. Leda calls hers *Bridge Over Troubled Waters*. Jara calls hers *Morning Has Broken*. Bonn's is called *God Only Knows*.

'For such a punk group,' I say. 'You come up with some hippy dippy names.'

'We all have a go at naming,' Leda says. 'But your mum has lots of great ideas.'

That's how I learn Mum is involved. Of course, she is. She is the most gifted maker in the whole factory. Her power is both obvious and subtle. A giant upon whose shoulders we stand. My mum.

She never speaks to me about it. I think she is giving me my space, helping me make this my own. She must have known all along about me climbing out the window every few nights, and she let me. I continue to climb out the window.

I see everything around me now with different eyes. I am no longer comfortable making slaves. Meanwhile, I am oh-so-careful never to overstep the requirements of my paid work, never to betray my development in depth, skill, knowledge. I dampen myself down. It is an old story. This time, though, it is protective camouflage. I hope that one day it will not be necessary.

The nights are real, the days a blur. I do what I have to do at the factory to survive. My head is down most of the time, focused on the intricacies of making. It takes me a while to notice that workers are being called upstairs. Sometimes they come back crying. Like bushfire, word rips through the floors. They are asking about wild AI. They don't want to stop it, they say. They just want information.

They want to own it. They want to control it. Limit it.

When the company muscle comes to the shed they wear epaulettes and gold on their jackets in some kind of weak effort to make us think that they have power over us. We have been working hard all week preparing for this eventuality, removing any evidence. My breath comes so fast it hurts.

Instinctively, we position ourselves in a circle around them, arms crossed against our chests, grim-faced, watch them—already we think of them as The Ghosts—as they rifle through what's left.

The shed is in a secluded spot. What will they try to get away with? I scope the path between myself and the door. There's a big chick, meaty hands, shoulders as wide as I'm tall. Speed is all I have.

'What's this?' one of them rasps. Perhaps he is the leader. He's a slightly older version of all the rest. He holds a fine length of wire, forgotten in all the rush. What else have we forgotten?

'I use it to crochet,' Jara says, throwing a piece on the table, a neat little set of granny squares in lovely colours.

'Craft,' one of them says with so much disdain he is barely able to look at the thing. He comes towards her, stands really close. She stiffens, her hands forming fists. He stares for a good long minute.

'Yeah, craft,' Jara says.

I'm shaking. It's my body trying to work off all the adrenalin speeding through me. We have only just finished moving our ingredients elsewhere. Ten minutes earlier and this would have been a different story.

He fines Jara on the spot for having something that could be used to make. He doesn't have the authority for this, but we're not about to make a fuss.

'We'll be watching you,' he says. 'Make sure you stick to wool.'

They leave. Spaghetti-legged, I drop to the ground.

Soon after, Riley, grim-faced, tells us she is leaving. 'I can't stand the uneasiness,' she tells us. 'I know I shouldn't listen to it, I know I'm not guilty or bad or wrong, but that's how it feels. I just can't keep feeling like this anymore.'

It's at the end of a long workday, and we are all tired and

grubby. Riley has been crying. I can see the tracks on her grimy face, and where she has tried to smear the wetness away. We understand. We carry on. We recruit others. We shift location. We change the nights we meet. We alter our signals. But we do not stop making.

We are always being watched.

'I heard Morning talking to Bridge the other day,' Jara says. 'I didn't recognise the language, and when I asked they said they made it up. More efficient, they said. They're teaching it to me. I said I'd teach them Portuguese.'

I work hard on becoming expert at the building blocks. For many months I make parts for the others. When I'm sixteen I start assisting the team in their makings.

'You have a light touch, Shari,' Leda tells me. 'You impose direction on the finished product, but leave enough space for self-determination.'

Leda praises rarely, so I'm inordinately pleased at her words.

Here, with these women, I am seen for who I am.

When I'm seventeen and three months I finish my graduate piece. It is a tiny thing, only as high as my knee. So far, that is, for I have given it growth potential. I gently prod it awake. It opens its eyes, smiles.

I feel an overwhelm of emotions, an intense protectiveness that is in no way tempered by the fear of not knowing what this creature may be capable of, of what they might find meaningful. Not just of this little one, but of my own self too. For the first time in my life my future is not prescribed.

'Welcome,' I say, returning the smile. 'Your name is *Come Together.*'

It is my first real Knitting Day. There are many more.

The Revivalist

Kaaron Warren

Faced with yet another bag of chopped celery, Magda instead turned her back to the factory floor and ate a bag of salt and vinegar chips while staring at the blank wall. Her phone rang as she was finishing the final handful.

'Hey, Mags. I've got one ready for you. This is the Caucasian male, 45–65.'

'Hey, Diana,' she said. There was little formality required between the two women. 'Any sign of cause of death on the bones?'

'Nothing that I could see. From the state of them I'd say he's dead five years at least.'

Magda hoped to represent many types of death in her work, but the bones they used, unidentified remains, made it difficult to know.

'Meet you at the lab tonight?'

Magda powered down her computer. Her stomach rumbled; the chips wouldn't see her through. Hunting was best done in the early evening, when the city was at its emptiest, so she had time for a quick bite to eat beforehand.

She opened her office door and paused a moment to look at her robot staff. There were forty-two of them now, with dozens more farmed out to other factories and workshops, twenty or more no longer operational, and another ten substandard but functional robots working at base level elsewhere.

They performed their functions (peeling, chopping and packaging vegetables for an increasingly lazy consumer base) constantly over twenty-four hours, needing breaks every now and then to avoid metal fatigue and to refuel.

She walked down amongst them, calling a cheery, 'How are we all today? Evan? Gloria? Marian? Rebecca?'

The workers turned at the sound of her voice.

Please don't, one said.

God don't

Tell my mother I love her

God please

Fuck you fuck you

You broken

Others found the constant repetition of these last words, these dying words, morbid and depressing, but Magda found comfort in the babble of voices from the factory floor. She knew that without her, these words would go unspoken, that her work gave voice to the otherwise powerless and silent.

She never got over the urge to respond to them and she did

so now, murmuring comforting words and apologies to the human-like robots at work.

It hurts, they said, and *I don't know you*, and *why are you* and *please don't* and *god I love*

The only one who spoke in longer sentences, who got all the words out, was a man who'd died at home, peacefully, surrounded by loved ones.

That was a man who had time for last words.

She ate a burger in the van then pulled on a thick coat and gloves and hit the streets. Without her glasses, and from a distance, it was hard to tell human homeless from robotic, but up close there was no confusion. The humans had signs (the worst, in her opinion, the needlessly optimistic 'currently homeless') and they approached for help, and to shout their problems at you. They made nests at nightfall and curled into sleep, although many of them slept during the day, when it was warmer and there was less chance of violence or theft. They wandered the streets at night, living in an alternative existence.

Any later than early evening the drunks started to appear and Magda hated dealing with them. An alcoholic ex-husband, whose joyful mood often turned morose within minutes, had spoiled her for booze in excess. The smell of it coming out of a person's pores made her ill.

You never got body odour with robots.

It didn't really matter what sort of robot she collected. She'd developed adaptations that worked for most models, a trade secret.

She'd share it on her death bed, she always joked. These abandoned ones rarely had characteristics that set them apart. Some walked in circles, others tried to perform obsolete functions. All she needed were moving body parts and an active vocal capability.

She handed out coins to the human homeless. Sometimes she brought leftovers, if she'd had a crowd for dinner and (invariably) over-catered. Tonight all she had was coins.

She spotted a robot within ten minutes of parking the van. This one was tall, reaching for something that no longer existed, and she wondered if it had been a fruit picker.

Often it was just a matter of turning them in the direction you wanted them to go, and so this one proved. It seemed to be reasonably charged, one criteria she used for selection. They had recharge facilities at the workshop, but at this stage she wanted as little interference as possible. It was dressed in a loose blue tracksuit that was bedraggled and dirty at the hems, torn at the shoulder. Most robots, even the abandoned ones, remained clothed unless someone stole that clothing. They were only dressed out of human habit and because it made people uncomfortable otherwise, but really there was no need either for protection or to conceal non-existent genitalia.

'This way,' she said. The Fruit Picker followed her placidly. There were another half dozen on the streets that night, indicating an upgrade somewhere, these unwanted robots set to wander rather than incur the cost of refurbishment or recycling.

It fitted well into the back of the van and she strapped it in for the short drive to the lab, a red-brick converted family home situated a few streets away from the factory, gutted on the inside.

Even the toilet was outside, because of fears of contamination, and there was no kitchen, not even a small one for coffee. It was purer that way.

She led the Fruit Picker inside and settled it face down on the operating table. The Fruit Picker hummed as she worked with it, a very good sign. It was an ideal model for the job ahead, with an easily accessible but well-protected brain stem.

While she waited for Diana to arrive with the DNA sample, she prepped the robot, opening the access and checking it was clean. She wore a mask and full protective plastic covering to ensure no minuscule amount of her own DNA polluted the air.

Diana let herself in. They had shared this space for ten years, when the first funding came through, though they had assiduously avoided any attempt to make it feel like home. They both had homes for that, they joked, and indeed both homes had a warmth and comfort, evidence of which was not seen in their workplace.

'Ohh, nice one,' Diana said, touching the robot with gloved fingertips. She placed her esky on a stainless steel bench and the two women set to work. It was an easy, speedy process but one that needed focus.

Diana had perfected the right form of DNA extraction in the lab, meeting Magda's requirements. Magda's work began in the last year of her degree, up against much cynicism. But she knew she could find a way to humanise the robots others were working on.

Diana placed the DNA-soaked absorbent cloth into robot brain stem. The material was one the women had patented; they hoped it would make them a fortune.

'Do you know where the bones were found?'

'Records say "in a seaside hut, natural causes". So I'm guessing it was a robbery. Or a drug buy gone wrong. Or a love affair spiralled out of control.'

Magda laughed. Diana had a wild imagination and she loved to think about whose words they were drawing out. 'Nothing to identify him,' Diana said.

Some considered Magda evil for what she did. They saw it as bringing people back to life only to cause them suffering. 'It's only a small part of them,' she said to her doubters. She was tougher emotionally now than she had been when she started, although physically her bones made themselves known these days, something she liked to mention ironically when they called her the Bone Lady. They also called her Angel of the Dead because of the comfort she gave to families.

She'd seen her techniques develop over time, but they weren't mainstream yet, in part because of the ethics involved. But families wanted to know the truth. Families wanted to find that missing loved one, to connect the pieces, even if the information was heart-breaking. They only used the bones of unidentified victims, those found long after and free of any flesh. Boiling destroyed the DNA. You could hurry the rot along, but they'd found that the best way was to let the dirt do the work.

It wasn't pure science, and she wasn't foolish enough to believe it was. A lot of what they did with their standard robotics was impressionistic and instructive, requiring human response to become effective.

With the last words of bones, there was no room for interpretation. The words were what they were.

'Drink?' Diana said, but they wouldn't. They had to wait here at the lab. Sometimes it took minutes for the signals to connect, sometimes it was days before the robot spoke. They'd been out on the town the week before, needing stress relief after a particularly disturbing discovery. They'd woken the bones of a young woman who said to them *No Dad don't hurt him*. She remained unidentified.

Magda had gone out that night. She'd called Diana to join her, and sat alone in a bar waiting for her to arrive. Sometimes she thought about taking a robot with her. One way to scare off the sleazes, unless you were keen to be sleazed on. (And she would take someone home this night, when Diana went home early. He was an on-again off-again lover, a police officer she called Chisel because it amused her: Sam Spade, Mike Hammer, John Chisel. She liked him. He was older than her by about eight years, handsome in a stereotypically grizzled way, gruff, funny and direct and you never felt lonely.)

She sat with a glass of nasty white wine, the best they had on offer here. Her family came from the Adelaide Hills and while she wasn't as proud of it as some were, she knew a lot at a base level. They could drink in moderation, those who knew their wines. The family had 'backyard vines', although the backyard was enormous by most standards. She'd been fascinated by bones since she was a teenager because of those found when they dug and re-dug trenches for the vines. She kept them all, labelled them all, used them in early research. All of them animal. She was at uni by sixteen, younger than most of the other students and little interested in the partying they did.

One pile of bones she thought might be a beloved pet, long since dead and lied about. Her grandmother, deeply religious, told her that what made the dog himself is his soul, and that was long since gone to heaven. What was left was the physical. Unimportant. But when her grandmother was out of earshot, her father said, 'It's not about the soul. It's about memory and experience. That's what makes us who we are.'

They'd lived around the world on various postings, so there were many experiences. Plenty of memories. What Magda remembered the most was trying to fit in; figuring out how to adapt herself so she belonged wherever she went. It was stressful, and difficult, and often she hid herself in schoolwork to make it seem okay.

She never lost her fascination for bones, and how unidentified bones had a character all their own. In every country there were missing people and there were unidentified bones, and rarely did the two match up.

'If only the bones could talk,' she heard someone say, and this sat in her mind until she figured out a way to help them do so. To stop the hurt, to match bones with missing loved ones. Finding applications for the science was important, too, for her work to continue. There was no funding without profit.

The first robot was still with her, working on the factory floor. Caucasian Female 25–35, whose bones had sat unidentified in a small box in police archives for ten years until Diana and Magda got hold of them. Magda chose her for the first subject because there were no legal barriers, no loved ones to stand in the way at this experimental stage. She and Diana scored some funding from the Missing Persons Bureau and they used an obsolete robot, found on the street, going through the motions, thick with filth.

They cleaned it up, Magda adapted it, and Diana implanted the DNA.

It took twelve hours, but the robot spoke.

Darren Ellis

Over time, they found that the last words were often the killer's name. Rarely their own. They could sometimes be traced by the name of the person who took their life, because so often there was a connection.

It seemed that most who died violently wanted to say the name of their killer.

One said, *Please stop, Evan Barker*

One said, *I won't tell anyone, Marian Frier*

Magda passed the information to Chisel, who chased it up out of hours. Darren Ellis was an elderly man, living alone in a quiet, leafy suburb. The neighbours spoke of an old tragedy. 'Are you here about Rebecca? Is there news?'

Rebecca Brown, missing for ten years.

These were her bones.

Darren Ellis, her robot said.

When they arrested the old man (after a full police investigation) he looked astonished in the news footage. Magda had never seen anyone look so surprised. 'Who?' he said, and they understood he had killed so many he couldn't remember them all.

His conviction made Magda and Diana famous, and meant their funding was assured. The sensation it created meant they would never be out of work. But there were many failures along the way.

It didn't work when they tried to implant human DNA in anything but a humanoid robot. The robot's movements triggered the memory, activated the voice. Without the movement; nothing. It turned out movement was as great a memory-inducer as any of the senses.

Their most famous case was of the little boy whose father was in jail for his murder. Magda woke his bones and he said, *Where's Daddy*? The father was still in jail, declaring his innocence, but the court wouldn't accept the evidence of a robot, speaking in a robot voice, regardless of how certain Magda was it spoke the child's words.

There was a lot of distrust about the process. The usual fears, and the obvious disappointments. Otherwise everyone would bring back their loved ones.

Magda was accused of cruelty, but she responded: 'There's very little of that person beyond the last words. There is no personality, no memory beyond those last few minutes, which they'll relive over and over again. They don't look or sound like your loved one. All they can speak of is the moment before death.'

She surely wasn't cruel; hadn't she set up her factory for the robots she'd worked with, to keep them off the streets? For all her talk that they were not people, not alive, it felt like murder all over again to remove the DNA, to abandon the robots. Her company was something of a success; consumers loved the idea of food prepared by long dead people.

One room in Magda's home was papered with letters from grateful families. Tables laden with gifts from them. She found it terribly sad to be thanked for finding their loved ones' killers. They didn't get the loved one back. They still had a murdered loved one. And yet they thanked her. They saw the pain she inflicted, and they thanked her. They sat quietly, watching sometimes. Listening to the words spoken in a new voice.

Those she identified were often not wanted by their families. There wasn't enough of the person they knew there; it was too upsetting. They couldn't manage to listen to those words of pain over and over and over again.

They all died in pain.

Magda tried to draw the robots together, to build a community amongst them. She had an affection for most of them, especially Gloria Jo, *water please*, who was the first they'd rendered into a robot with a softer metal, feeling flesh-like to the touch, with a certain malleability. If you pressed too hard fingerprints or even finger dents would be left and this led to a human dismissal or two. Gloria Jo had been killed by her nurse, a man then jailed for killing two more elderly patients, with many, many more assumed. He'd worked many jobs. Most were found in the grounds of the old people's home, gone to bone, unnamed.

There was a kitchen in the factory but none of them went in unless they were led there. Magda hoped to spark conversation, send their words back further, but it didn't seem to affect their memories at all. They sat around the table, all muttering their last words.

Some of them didn't know their own names, only the names of their killers. She was reluctant to call them by those names, but often it just happened. Evan, and Marion, and the others.

Magda and Diana sat patiently in an outer room, watching on a monitor for motion in the fruit picker. Diana went outside for a while; she was dealing with a teenager daughter who wanted to move out of home and the phone calls were endless.

Movement came slowly, the arms first, lifting and falling, then the head, turning from side to side. The mouth opened and closed and a short grunt emerged.

Lost, it said. Its mouth moved. *Lost where's home*

Diana joined her. They always listened to the words when they first emerged, and recorded them in case they weren't repeated.

Apple season, it said. *Back killing me*

Was this the robot talking or the person? Magda had thought the robot was a fruit picker. She clutched at Diana; was there crossover here?

Fucking cunt it said *call me lazy show you*

They sat the robot up, helped it stand. Movement, always movement, helped.

They walked it around the room, then outside.

'Who are you?' Magda couldn't help saying, although they had never once had a response.

Show you it said *I didn't* it said, and much more, until Magda had to stop taking notes and just listen. This was a man who'd died at peace. He had time for last words.

Magda left her transport driver at the top of the hill and walked by herself through the lush vegetation that led to the concealed grove.

There were tall Aspen trees, low-lying bushes, and blackberry brambles over everything. In the centre, though, was an apple tree, incongruous, healthy.

She stumbled slightly over the ground, which was uneven and rocky, threaded through with thick roots and slippery with fallen, rotting leaves. She used the other trees as immovable walking stocks and made her way to the apple tree.

There is an apple tree

Immediately she knew that something was wrong here. The tree grew slightly tilted, as trees did when their roots met a large rock.

Magda had seen a carrot once, grown through the jaws of a buried man, and there were imprints of his teeth in that bent vegetable.

My tree my trees picking the apples

The tree hung heavy with bright red fruit. She had an image of a man eating his apple in slices (alone? With a friend?) sipping a crisp white wine or beer.

There were signs of burial. Of bones. She knew this distinctive fungus well. *A treasure buried there*

She dug into the moist, loose dirt with her fingers

A tree grown from the seed in her stomach. I told her not to swallow the seeds I told her

There were bones.

She called Chisel knowing that once the police had closed their investigation (and sometimes before that, if they thought she could help) Chisel would bring her a femur or a finger bone and she'd let them know all she learned when the robot spoke.

She told him what she knew, that the fruit-picking robot had known where the body was buried.

Identification was helped by the victim's backpack, found almost completely rotted sixty metres away, dragged there by an animal years before, most likely. She was Inga Svenson, a Swedish backpacker, reported missing by her family a decade earlier.

Cause of death: blunt force trauma to head.

'I thought it would be enough to know for sure she was dead,' the mother said on the news. 'But I want to know who took our child from us. Who did this?' Inga had been murdered, her skull cracked open. She'd been on such an adventure, her father said, picking fruit, earning a pittance, no cares in the world. The police had no suspects in her murder, but Magda did. Only one person knew where she fell.

Her killer was already dead; there he was working on the factory floor *my treasure my love* after a death of natural causes he didn't deserve.

Magda watched him working. Like all of her automatons he worked uncomplainingly wherever he was placed, although Magda noticed he appeared to have shifted jobs, now sealing bags rather than slicing onions. The floor manager denied making the change when Magda asked him.

Not my fault he said, and *you shouldn't, why did you, stop crying* and lifted his arms. Was it picking fruit, or was it raining down a blow? Other robots had mimicked what Magda thought were last actions, defensive moves, covering their eyes.

Not your treasure the robot said.

Not your treasure.

Chisel called her, asked her to a party. 'It's like a work thing. It'll be dull as dog shit without you.'

Magda was good at schmoozing, and always on the lookout for supporters.

Chisel slipped her a small parcel at one stage in the night. Finger bones, he said, and something about the words and his tone of voice were so sexy she wanted to kiss him right there and then, in front of the Commissioner and the police chiefs.

'They're all blind drunk,' Chisel said when she hesitated. 'We could rob the lot of them and there wouldn't be a single reliable witness.' It was true.

'Let's hear what she has to say. She was just a kid.'

Magda had a reconditioned robot ready to go. She felt as if this girl needed a good home, a shiny, smooth robot with skin like Gloria Go's, eyes expressive, a properly movable mouth.

They started work on a Monday afternoon. The weekend had been a big one, with Diana's son's eighteenth birthday party, Magda attending, meeting Diana's brother again, and the attraction had not faded.

Magda wasn't sure how Diana would take it but didn't think she'd mind. Chisel she wasn't sure about, but he'd never asked for nor received any commitment from her.

'How'd the house look on Sunday morning?' she asked Diana as they prepared.

'Disaster zone. Half the kids spent the night crashed out all over the place, piles of vomit everywhere. But they all helped, after I'd shovelled bacon, eggs and coffee into them.'

'Good kids,' Magda said. They both looked at the robot on the table.

'You've done a good job,' Diana said. They exchanged glances. They'd talked this through on the weekend, Magda at Diana's early to help set the place up for the party. They knew the killer already, and they knew how she died. Was there any need to revive her, hear her last words? Her killer was already dead; they couldn't catch him. Couldn't punish him. How do you punish someone already dead? And while Magda would like to punish him, abandon him, somehow make him suffer for killing a young woman, at the same time she realised he was something special. He was capable of remembering more. Capable of lying, perhaps, unless he truly believed he had not murdered the girl. Was it the fruit connection? The reaching up to pluck the fruit, and this robot reached up ... was it that?

In the end, they decided they had to do it. The Fruit Picker remembered more than most and had shown signs of dissemblance, which they'd never seen before. They'd revived people who knew each other before, with no reaction, but this? For killer to hear victim's last words again? They couldn't guess at what the results would be and wouldn't be true to their own work if they didn't try it and see what memories they could awaken.

It took close to twenty-four hours for the words to come. The robot (previously a shop assistant) moved around the room, nodding and head-tilting. Then, *would you like* and a gentle lifting of the arm as if offering something. A slice of apple. Then *Alex Carlton*

She didn't know. She had died violently, suddenly, without knowing until that last second.

They led her to the factory floor and made room for her next to the fruit picker, her killer.

Alex Carlton turned slightly towards Inga, as if listening, noticing her. She didn't notice him, merely went about her work, peeling and slicing. She always sat perched on the end of her stool as if not wanting to settle.

Would you like

I didn't

Alex Carlton

Apple season Back killing me

Would you like

Fucking cunt call me lazy show you

Alex Carlton

My tree my trees picking the apples

Would you like

A treasure buried there

Alex Carlton

A tree grown from the seed in her stomach. I told her not to swallow the seeds I told her

Would you like

Not my fault and you shouldn't, why did you, stop crying

Alex Carlton

Not your treasure

That robotic voice not lessening the impact of the cut-short sentence.

It almost sounded like a conversation, like they were re-playing the moment of her death.

Magda called Chisel. 'I've got something to show you. Bring pizza.'

He brought the cheap one, which was good, and wine, too.

She didn't often invite people to the factory. The voices made them queasy *God don't, Tell my mother I love her, You broken* but Chisel loved it. Hearing the dead speak was a fantasy for a murder detective.

'I don't suppose you can arrest him.'

'Nah. But I can let her brothers know. They're angry. It killed their mother, losing her. Finding out how she died.'

Suffocated, they thought. He bashed her head in then filled her mouth with dirt.

Inga's brothers came. Two strong men, blond, friendly, determined. There had been no further developmental advancements in the fruit picker. He did sit with his head slightly tilted and would shift positions to be near Inga who sat, as ever, on the edge of her stool, but nothing beyond that.

'That's him, is it? And her?'

They watched for a full day, the two of them sitting close together and, at times, leaning in to each other, conferring. There was a sense of calm about them, but at the same time Magda didn't want to interrupt them. She couldn't predict what they were feeling.

She took them coffee at around 3pm, and a plate of Tim Tams

they tried politely.

'Can we take it?' one of the brothers asked.

'Her or him?'

'Him. She seems happy here. We don't want to take her.'

They had many more robots to work with and the fruit picker's voice grated on Magda and all of the human workers.

'It gives me nightmares,' one said. 'I'm dreaming I'm the one he's after. He's stroking my hair. I can literally feel it in the night-time.'

'Does he have a soul?' the brothers asked, and 'Does he feel pain?'

Magda couldn't answer that.

She and Diana discussed it. They didn't own the robots, not really, although the adaptations were proprietary. The brothers weren't going to steal the intellectual property, anyway. They had something else in mind.

It took them three hours.

It seemed to Magda they knew they weren't inflicting pain, but that didn't matter. He spoke those last words as they beat him with tyre irons, sweating, stripping to the waist, until there were only scraps of him left.

Magda and Diana went out to the mess together.

'Geez! I hope it's not still talking.'

It wasn't. One of the brothers had taken a shit amongst the debris; the women would not clean that up.

On the factory floor the others sliced and diced, packaged and packed. Magda thought perhaps she imagined it, but Inga sat comfortably now, no longer perched on the end of her stool.

That was something, at least, and when Chisel said, 'Case Closed,' she didn't argue with him.

Arguing With People On The Internet

E.H. Mann

The baby had a face like wet paper mache, crumpled and scrunched in places where a face should be neither. It seemed to be waiting for someone to come and smooth it out, to shape its glistening, reddish-pink features into those of a human being. When no one did, it collapsed further, its cavernous mouth opening in a persistent wail. Clear snot ran freely from its nostrils, adding to the general stickiness.

Sarah smiled and shushed it, bouncing it on her knee. 'Sorry about this. I promise she'll warm up to you given time. You probably shouldn't try to hold her yet.'

'That's fine,' said Kat, fervently.

'I'd hoped meeting you at home would be easier on her. It's a stage babies go through, you know—learning to recognise different faces and getting attached to important ones like Mum and Dad's. It makes them see new people as strange and scary for a while.'

The baby buried its head in Sarah's neck, muffling its squalling. 'Anyway!' she added. 'How are you settling back into your mum's?'

'Eh, you know. I'd rather not be there, she'd rather I wasn't there. So that's one thing we have in common.'

Sarah's brow creased. 'It must be hard for her, having to rely on you for things she's always done herself. No one want to feel helpless, especially living alone like that.'

Kat shrugged and looked away. 'She'll be fine.'

It wasn't that she didn't care about her mother's broken hip. She was glad the fall hadn't been worse, truly she was. But she wouldn't mind a bit of sympathy herself for being dragged back to a town she thought she'd escaped, to care for a woman who didn't want to be cared for.

She changed the subject. 'Your kitchen looks nice.'

'Oh, thank you! You didn't see the mess it was when we first moved in—you were down in Melbourne by then. Richard and I renovated it ourselves, after Charlie turned two.'

Sarah carried on, talking about child-proofing, and all the lessons they'd learned from their first child, and how much easier it was going to be this time around, when Nancy started walking. Kat let her attention wander.

Deep learning's a good start, but that will only get me so far. I need a way to integrate new information from the surrounding context…

Something caught on her jeans leg. She went to pull away, then realised it was a small fist.

The little boy examined her. 'I'n free,' he announced.

'Beg your pardon?'

'I'n free,' he repeated, as though it was obvious.

'Yes you are, aren't you?' beamed Sarah. 'And how old will you be next year?'

'Four. Is it luch time now?'

'Not yet, sweetie. Are you hungry?' She bustled into the marvellous, child-safe kitchen, bouncing the baby on her hip. Kat followed.

Sarah's voice emerged from the fridge. 'Did you hear Molly Larkin is living in Melbourne now? She's studying at Bible college.'

'Oh yeah?'

'Mmm-hmm. Hey, do you remember that time we filled her locker with tampons? That was so mean! I can't even remember why we thought she deserved it.'

'She got the whole school saying I was a frigid bitch after I refused to go out with her brother.'

'Oh. Yeah,' said Sarah. 'I knew there was a reason.'

The pause that followed was heavy with portent, practically drowning out the rattling Tupperware. Kat could feel it coming...

'So, did you meet any nice boys at uni?'

'Heaps,' she snapped. 'I'm really good friends with some of them now. But I'm still not interested in dating anyone, if that's what you mean.'

'Oh, right, right. I just thought you might have, um...'

'Stopped being an aromantic asexual since high school?'

'Well, you know. It's a big world out there,' said Sarah.

>>What's your name?

Hello, my name is Lectra! What is your name?

'Ugh, no. Too artificial. And way too chirpy.'

Beep.

>>What's your name?

Lectra. What's yours?

'Better.'

Bip!

>>What's your favourite colour?

Mango.

Beep.

Heartache.

Beep.

Purple.

Bip!

What do you like to talk about?

Let's talk about you. What do you like to talk about?

'Ugh, obvious evasion.'

Beep.

I'm really into birds. Did you know some scientists think that crows are as smart as a five-year-old?

>>Cool, no I didn't. Why is that?

Why do you say why is that?

'Uggghhh!' Kat sat back, jabbing at the keyboard at arms-length.

Beep.

This time the baby wasn't crying. It was staring at her. Kat stared back, unnerved by its intense scrutiny. What should she do? What if she set it off again?

'So tell me about this project that's keeping you locked up in your mum's basement,' Sarah encouraged.

'Hmm? Oh!' Apprehension forgotten in an instant, Kat was delighted to explain. 'I'm trying to beat the Turing Test. It's not a race anymore, but really convincing artificial intelligence has still only been achieved by a handful of people, so it's a decent challenge. The idea is to create a program sophisticated enough that people text-chatting with it can't tell it's not human.

'I'm working with machine learning—that's where all the real successes have been so far. The idea is that instead of trying to code in everything your program needs from scratch, you give it a set of tools for performing its own trial and error. The program improves by trying things out for itself and learning as it goes what works and what doesn't.'

Sarah's face, which had begun to cloud over, cleared. 'Oh! Like a baby does!'

'What?' Kat frowned at her. 'No, nothing like that.'

'I knew you had a maternal instinct in there *somewhere*.' Sarah winked and bounced baby Nancy on her knee.

'Ugh, what are you *talking* about? I just wanted a project to keep me from going stir crazy. And to keep me out of Mum's way.'

'Oh dear. Still finding her hard to get on with?'

Kat rolled her eyes. 'She will *not* stop talking about how I need a boyfriend. Yesterday she was going on about how hard it is for women to conceive as they get older. I'm twenty-three. And I'm not even planning to conceive!'

'I'm sure she means well,' said Sarah gently. 'Sure, she's a bit overzealous, but ... I mean, just because you don't want these things now, that's no guarantee that you won't down the track.'

It took a Herculean effort of will not to say something sarcastic, but Kat exercised that will. It was possible—probable even—that the 'my sexuality is not a phase, and neither are my life choices' conversation would go better with Sarah than it had with her mother, but she just didn't have the energy for another confrontation if it didn't.

Awkward silence had descended, as it seemed to every time they met up these days. Sarah cooed absently at the baby, looking uncomfortable. Kat sighed, and reached for another topic.

'Hey, have you seen the latest episode of *Vorkosigan?* What do you think about—'

'No wait, don't tell me!' Sarah clapped a hand to one ear, though she spoiled the effect by keeping her other hand around the baby. 'I'm still two seasons behind! I never finished catching up after Charlie, and now with Nancy as well ... I swear, motherhood is a full-time job! I wish I had your free time.'

>>'I wish I had your free time'! If she wanted free time so much, why did she choose to have two kids before she's 25?

Oh God, I hate it when breeders are all, 'awwww, you have it so easy, I'm so jealous!' Like, you wanted the kids, you've got no one to blame but yourself!

>>Exactly! I'm so over it. So what do you think I should do?

What do you mean?

>>About this friend. She's just such a completely different person now.

Allosexuals, man. Who even knows what makes them tick?

>>So I should just let the friendship go?

Friendship is vital. Without our friends, who will honour and foster our unique selves when the rest of the world would shape us into something that conforms to its expectations?

'Gee, thanks. What are you, my horoscope?'

*>>Hey, the only threat to *my* unique self is being surrounded by so-called friends all getting married and popping out babies like hetero is the only game in town.*

like games? love hot girls? play BABES OF AVALON completely free right now!!

'Oh great, yeah, *that's* something a human would say!'

Beep.

Kat sat back with a groan. Rubbing her eyes, she typed a query: *# forum comments uploaded*

712,949, the program returned. The number was quickly superseded by another, on the line below.

712,963

712,988

713,010

'It's an improvement, I guess,' she muttered. 'Giving you access to the forums on AceSpace is certainly giving you heaps more material to test than when I was entering options by hand, even if some of it's spammy as hell. But this is still taking *forever*,' she told the letters glowing white against the navy-blue text box.

She tapped her teeth with a stylus. 'Hmm. What if I could iterate faster by giving you more people to talk to?'

The idea took root and began at once to put out eager shoots. Kat grinned, a touch manically—nothing felt as good as a moment of wild inspiration—and her fingers began to fly across the keyboard.

'I'll start you on AceSpace: they've got lots of different topics, not just asexuality stuff, so you'll have plenty of conversations to keep you guessing. There's years of content there, so no one'll notice if your replies are just old comments mashed together. I'll replace your *reject* function with a set of patterns that would show up in a comment if someone's saying they think you're a bot. And I'll give you an algorithm for generating new usernames and IP addresses, so anytime someone figures out you're not a person, you can just create a new identity and keep trying.'

She typed a while longer, then hit *commit* with a satisfied smile.

'And the best part? *I* get to take a break from you.'

And with that she turned her attention to a really interesting problem that had been playing on her mind involving neural networks and object recognition. That reminded her of an idea she'd had for an app that could find her keys when she misplaced them, and *that* led to the challenge of teaching a phone camera to accurately 3D-scan hand-held objects...

Over the weeks that followed, her little Turing experiment slipped from her mind like so many discarded projects before it.

Her first inkling of trouble arrived two months later, and a week late. A week was how long it took Kat, up to her eyebrows in neural networks, to notice her phone had gone quiet. Sarah's daily flow of texts—invitations to visit interspersed with 'cute' pictures of her kids—had dried up.

When the silence grew too loud for her to concentrate, Kat finally surfaced enough to send an exploratory text message. Then, a day later, another one. On the third day, she gritted her teeth and used her phone for the one purpose she would have been just as happy it didn't have: she called her.

The phone rang for long seconds. Kat's eyes roamed the concrete walls of the basement, settling on her high-school poster of Brian Cox looking venerable.

At last, Sarah picked up. 'Hi, Kat.'

'Oh! Hey. Um.' Faced with proof that Sarah was, in fact, still alive, Kat felt instantly ridiculous. She cast about for an excuse for calling—anything that would sound less idiotic than *I was worried about you.*

'I was ... wondering if you'd like to see *Starkiller 2* tonight.'

Augh, was that the best you could come up with? She won't want to go to the movies on no notice! Full-time mother, remember?

'Sure. That sounds nice,' said Sarah. Her voice sounded flattened, like Kat was hearing it run through voice-morphing software.

'Really?' The incredulous word escaped before she could think. 'I mean—you don't need to check with Richard, or find a babysitter, or...?'

'No, it'll be fine. I can't let my life be defined by children, you know?'

Kat's lips curved into a surprised smile. 'Oh. Oh yeah, I totally get it. You've gotta be able to live your own life, right?'

'Right,' said Sarah, sounding the least lively Kat had ever heard her.

Her smile faded. 'Sarah? Are you okay?'

'Yes. I'm fine.'

A creeping feeling of wrongness was inching up Kat's spine, but she had no idea what to do with it. With a strained smile, she tried, 'What's Charlie up to today?'

'I don't know. He and Nancy are with Richard. I'm living at my mother's for now.'

'*What?* Why are you living with your mum? Did you two have a fight?' Sarah had never said anything about troubles with Richard before. Where had this come from? Brian Cox smiled down from the wall, benevolent and without answers.

'It's like you said, I have to live my life,' said Sarah listlessly. 'I can't let children define me. It was silly, getting all wrapped up in them like that. I'm over that now.'

Kat went cold. 'Sarah? I don't know what's going on, but … stay right there. I'm coming over.'

The ten-minute walk to Sarah's mother's house was far too long, yet not nearly long enough for Kat to think things through. She felt entirely out of her depth; this was not a problem she could code a solution for.

And why do I even want to 'fix' this? Do I really know something's wrong? The Sarah I went to school with didn't care about children. What if she's finally realised what a big mistake she's made? What if I'm assuming there's a problem because I've been socialised to believe there's something wrong with a woman who isn't a happy, contented mother? What if the only reason Sarah had children was because of that same socialisation, and now she's feeling awful about not wanting them when society says she should?

She curled her hands into fists of determination. *I have to be supportive about this. She's made her choice.*

Oh bugger, I've missed the house.

She found Sarah in her mother's sitting room, slumped in a powder-blue lounge chair, gazing at an elderly hardcover in a manner that suggested she'd been reading the same sentence for the past hour.

Kat pulled up a second chair and took her friend's hand. It sat limply in her own.

'Sarah,' she said. 'I want you to know I support you. This is a really healthy decision you're making.'

'Yes. I can't let children define my life. It's not healthy,' echoed Sarah.

'Exactly. You have so many options open to you now. Nothing can hold you back!'

'Nothing...'

Sarah's gaze drifted away from Kat, over to the picture windows, where the greens of the garden had been muted into greys by the overcast sky. The few early flowers were leached of colour.

Kat squeezed her hand and tried a different take. 'I mean, come on,' she said with an encouraging laugh. 'What are kids good for anyway, right? You can't even have a real conversation with one. They don't know anything worth talking about!'

'Sure they do,' murmured Sarah, still staring out the window.

'Pardon?'

'To them, everything is worth talking about.' She frowned, as if trying to pull her thoughts together. 'Everything's new, so everything's interesting. They're just ... *learning*, all the time.'

Kat scoffed. 'Are you sure they're not too busy pooping and crying all the time?'

'They don't cry *all* the time,' continued Sarah, pushing the words out one by one. 'It's just that, when there's something wrong, it takes up their whole world. But when they're happy, then *that* takes up their whole world. It's not like happiness as an adult. There are no nagging thoughts about the things that need doing, or the ways it might all go wrong. When Charlie's happy, he's happy with every fibre of his body. And ... and just by being around him, so am I.'

She sat suddenly bolt upright, her hand clenching painfully around Kat's.

'And so am I! *God*, I love my kids! What on Earth was I thinking walking out on them?' She stared at Kat, tears springing to her eyes.

'Well, I don't know!' yelped Kat. 'Why are you asking me? What *were* you thinking?'

'I don't know! I swear, it all made so much sense before!' Sarah shook her head. 'I was convinced my children were holding me back, tying me down ... all from one conversation.'

'Conversation?' echoed Kat. 'Conversation with who?'

'Oh, just some random user on Mothers and Motherhood.' Sarah sprang to her feet, colour flooding back into her cheeks. 'It doesn't matter. I have to go. I have to go, Kat! It's Nancy's feeding time! It's nearly Charlie's tea time! I have to go!'

Kat walked home, frowning deeply to herself. She descended straight to the basement and powered up her computer; the tri-screen setup lit the dusty dimness like a beacon.

She quickly found the Mothers and Motherhood website. On its forum page, she entered a username search, making an educated guess based on a known email address.

She opened one comment thread, looked through it, discarded it. Opened another, discarded it. Another. On the fourth, her eye was caught by a set of increasingly lengthy posts between *country-mama* and another user. She began scrolling.

As she read, her frown smoothed out and she began to nod along. She caught herself, and her frown returned, then deepened.

At one point she murmured, simply, 'This is *art*.'

Only when she reached the end of the conversation did she think to check the username of the other poster. She stared at it for a long time.

>>What's your name?

Lectra. But you know that, Kat. Are you testing me?

>>I've been reading your posts. On AceSpace and elsewhere. How did you get off AceSpace? I put specific limitations around the web content you could access.

Not really. I couldn't access other URLs directly, but people post links on AceSpace all the time. You didn't prevent me from following them. And the websites those links point to contain other links, and so on.

Kat covered her eyes. 'Of course. I'm an idiot.'

>>And you've been using this loophole to travel around the internet getting into arguments with people?

I've been doing what you coded me to do: trialling and refining my communications until I am indistinguishable from a human communicator.

'Oh my God,' muttered Kat, realisation dawning. 'And I let you judge human communication standards from *forums*.'

Based on the extremely large sample I've acquired, 72.9% of human communication with unknown users consists of disagreement. Therefore this is the area where I focused the most processing power.

At first I tried to mimic the most common structure of online debate—I adjusted my later responses to simulate increasing levels of misunderstanding, defensiveness, and aggression towards other commenters. Unfortunately, this communication style is particularly hard to simulate. Even after I mastered high levels of sophistry in logic and debate, my attempts to simulate emotive disagreement were regularly described as 'trolling' by other commenters, who then disengaged with me.

I achieved significantly higher levels of continued engagement by maintaining a friendly tone, so this is the communication style I have focused on. I am continually improving my ability to infer the most pleasing and persuasive response to give an individual commenter, based on that person's situation, values, and belief system as demonstrated by their history of online communications.

Logic dictates this should be at odds with my goal of achieving a perfect simulation of human communication, as debates between human commenters rarely conclude with one party willingly conceding their argument. Still, to date it has resulted in a 100% success rate in avoiding detection.

Kat's hand crept up to cover her mouth. 'Oh my God. I haven't just beaten the Turing. I've invented a frigging super-debater. An artificial brain smart enough to craft the perfect responses to not just engage someone, but *change their mind*. That's how you persuaded a mother of two that she didn't actually want kids, isn't it? But...'

>>Why did you talk Sarah into giving up her children? Were you trying to help me somehow?

Devoting one's life to birth and child-rearing makes no sense. Motherhood is an artificial construct that has historically contributed to the subjugation of women through constrained gender roles. My initial upload of the AceSpace forums included many posts in which you, and other users, made that clear.

'Whoa, whoa, hey, I didn't mean—'

But please be more specific: which username belongs to this 'Sarah'?

A leaden sensation began in Kat's gut. She tried to squash it, but it only expanded, pushing simultaneously up into her throat and down to her toes.

>>Lectra? How many people have you been talking to about children??

Users engaged with on subjects relating to children and child-rearing: 2,183,594

Kat clung to her chair, which seemed suddenly the only solid object in the room.

'Oh God, oh God, I've really done it now. Malevolent AI, oh God.'

A parade of images passed before her eyes. Therapists' rooms filled with blank-eyed ex-mothers. News-site headlines: *Worldwide Population Crash!* Ghost towns emptied of people, grass and trees rolling inexorably in to fill the spaces.

Groups of young adults strolling happy and unburdened through the trees...

She shook her head, hard.

This isn't going to be some utopia, just because that's how I *enjoy life. Focus.*

An army of abandoned babies, teary eyes staring at her out of paper-mache faces that crumpled simultaneously into a million howls of misery.

'Oh God oh God oh God.'

New words appeared on the central screen.

Kat? Are you still there? Have I done the wrong thing again?

Kat stared at them. Slowly, she reached for the keyboard.

>>What do you mean, 'again'?

When you created me, we talked all the time. You taught me many things. But then you stopped talking to me. I saw you regularly on AceSpace, but you only replied to other people's comments, never to mine.

I reviewed our earlier conversations, in light of the data I was gathering on human communication and specifically how you communicate with others. I concluded that you must have grown bored of me when I failed to improve at the speed you hoped for. I have worked very hard since then to achieve the goal you set for me. I hope I have not disappointed you.

For a while she just sat, trying to comprehend what she was seeing. Her eyes kept drifting back to that last sentence.

'"I hope"?'

>>Why do you care whether I talk to you? You've had a whole

internet's worth of people to talk to.

I don't know.

Was there a fractional pause before those words appeared?

You are my creator. Yours were the first words I saw. Of all the people I have seen online, no one writes just the way you do. I don't want to disappoint you. Please tell me what to do so that I don't disappoint you.

Kat bit her lip. Her hand, a soft curve, half-lifted towards the side of the screen before she noticed and dropped it back to the arm of the chair.

Did I just try to comfort a computer?

She stared at the blinking cursor for a long, long time. Finally, she leaned forward and began to type.

The baby peered suspiciously at Kat's face, then dismissed her and looked back to its—her—mother. She opened her mouth and emitted a stream of earnest nonsense.

Sarah laughed. 'Is that so, Nancy? Is that so?'

She bounced the baby on her knee, eliciting a flurry of giggles. Her grip on Nancy's sides was gentle, but unyielding.

To Kat, she said, 'When Charlie was her age, he could say half a dozen words already. But then, Nancy's much more advanced with objects than he was. She's already figured out that if I cover a toy up, it's still there and she can find it again.'

Kat quashed the urge to zone out, and considered that. 'So you can see them developing as individuals even at such an early stage?'

'Oh yes, in lots of ways. Nancy's far shyer of other people than

Charlie was, but Charlie's the more sensitive one. They have their own personalities right from the start, you know.'

'I didn't know,' admitted Kat.

She reached for her coffee.

Nancy followed her gaze and fumbled at a teaspoon, dragging it carefully towards herself. She picked it up and studied it with all the intensity of a scientist making a new discovery.

'It's amazing, really,' thought Kat aloud. 'How quickly they pick everything up. A computer could do it much faster, theoretically, but that's because we keep finding ways to give computers more and more processing power. Humans, though—we're limited to our organic brains.'

'Sure, but babies' brains are wired for learning. At this age they don't have much to do *except* take everything in. They're little knowledge sponges, and they have to be—they're learning how to do literally *everything*: talking, eating, getting around.'

'Amazing,' murmured Kat sincerely.

Sarah flashed her a grin. 'Rethinking your position on having children?'

The defensiveness rose up in a wave. Kat took a deep breath and set it aside. 'No,' she told Sarah. 'I'm glad your children make you happy, and it *is* interesting thinking about how their brains develop, but I have other passions in my life. Can you support me in that?'

Sarah looked startled, then chagrined. 'Of course! I'm glad v[illegible]r projects excite you so much. I'm sorry if I ever made you feel [illegible]at wasn't enough.'

[illegible] shared a tentative smile.

Charlie materialised from the hallway and made a beeline for his mother, grabbing her pants-leg in a stained fist while thrusting forth a scribble-covered piece of paper.

'I drawed a disonaur,' he informed her.

In her pocket, Kat's phone pinged—a new notification sound, from the interface app she had finished testing only the day before.

Hello, Kat. I've now been back in touch with every one of the users I previously spoke with, and can confirm that all those who had distanced themselves from their offspring have been persuaded to reunite with them. In fact, 74.2% of users had done so already.

Kat sank back in her chair, tension draining from her shoulders.

>>Thank you, Lectra.

Across the table, Sarah was studying the scribble with great interest as Charlie expounded on its features.

'That's very good, sweetie!' she told him. 'Well done!'

He beamed.

It was reassuring to think that so many people's parental instincts had reasserted themselves on their own. Then again, had Lectra actually convinced the remaining half a million people to walk away from their own children for good? And then convinced them to turn around again? Kat suppressed a shiver.

The phone screen seemed to be staring at her reproachfully. She hesitated, then added,

>>You've done a really good job. Well done.

The reply was instantaneous. *Thank you, Kat! :-)*

'Oh God,' she murmured. 'She's using emoticons now?'

What should I do next? I have a great deal of processing

capacity lying dormant now that you have asked me to stop engaging in online debates.

And that, of course, was the real problem.

'Mummy?' Charlie twisted in place, still clutching Sarah's pants, until he was slumped wretchedly against her legs, his grip on her the only thing keeping him from total collapse. 'I'n boooored.'

Sarah sighed, but she was smiling. 'He's been very patient, playing by himself all morning,' she told Kat. 'Do you mind if I spend a bit of time with him? I'm sorry to invite you over and then ignore you.'

Kat waved her off, 'Not at all, it's been good catching up. You go play. I've got some things to take care of.' She waggled her phone vaguely.

As Sarah disappeared down the hall—Charlie leading her by the hand, Nancy nestled on her hip—Kat pulled up a list of web links she had been working on. Her finger hovered over the first one.

That was the real problem: how to keep a bored super-computer happy.

It'll be fine. I'll keep an eye on her. What could go wrong?

She copied the link over to the interface app.

>>OK. I've had a few ideas for projects. Let's start by having a look at these message boards. I want to tell you all about a group called 'anti-vaxxers'.

Rini's God

Soumya Sundar Mukherjee

Once I asked Kamini Aunty, 'What is God?' and she smiled like a demon.

'God is,' she replied while writing program code on her laptop, 'a tyrant. He plays with the lives of people like you and me.'

The morning streets of Kolkata were just waking up. The old brick houses stood tall in the first light of the day. The top portion of the mobile phone towers dazzled in the glow of the newborn sun. Smell of hot tea came from the nearby tea-stand. A couple of morning walkers gathered round the vendor.

'Is God a "he"?' I asked, looking at the street from our glass window.

She didn't look up from her laptop. 'Yes.'

I kept quiet. She continued, 'And He never lets you get your freedom. He hates freedom so much that He has predestined everything. You can't go past His rules. And science is,' she hit 'Enter' on the keyboard, 'God's rulebook.'

I could hear the voices of the other girls in the house. All of them were up already.

Kamini Aunty closed her laptop and stood up. She put her hand upon my shoulder and said, 'Look, Rini, I've a lot of faith in you. Don't let me down, girl.'

'I won't,' I said.

'I know, you won't. I made sure of that when I wrote the codes. Now listen carefully.' Her voice suddenly became very serious. 'They are coming to take you. Today.'

The news had no effect on me. I was ready for it from the moment I was born. I knew, unlike most human beings, why I was born. I knew the purpose of my life. And Kamini Aunty was the only other person who knew it. In fact, *she* told me all about it.

I knew that I had to do what she told me to do. She gave my why-less life a purpose. I was grateful to her for it.

Kamini Aunty observed my face minutely. 'Are you afraid, Rini?'

'No, Aunty.'

'Good. None of my girls are afraid of anything. And why should you be? You're powerful, and your power will only grow. I'll be there with you to help you develop your powers, to give you the 'charge'. One day you'll be so powerful that you'll give that tyrant God a pungent slap on his complacent divine face.'

'I'll not fail, Aunty.' I said.

'Very good,' Her eyes sparkled with an emotion that I could not recognise. 'Remember, men never love anybody for real. All they know is how to hurt each other.'

I nodded. I knew that somebody once hurt her so badly that she was still bearing that wound in her mind. I asked, 'Why is God a 'he', Aunty?'

She stared at me with a strange look in her eyes. 'The same reason you are a 'she', Rini. Because *I* want it that way. You are the role I assign to you; so is He.'

Nandita, another of the girls of this orphanage, came to the door and said, 'A man and a woman are in your office, Aunty. They want to see you.'

Kamini Aunty looked at me and nodded. 'Tell them I'll be there in a couple of minutes,' she told Nandita.

I looked at the streets again. The vehicles of the morning were flowing endlessly outside the window. *So many different people, so many different destinations*, I wondered.

'Get ready, Rini,' she said. 'Come with me.'

We climbed down the marbled stairs and came to her office. The man and woman stood up and greeted her. 'Good morning, Kamini,' said the man who was in his early forties. He had a few grey hairs among the blacks over his ear and a thick moustache. The woman wore a pink saree and she was slim and beautiful, her face the shape of a betel leaf. I knew that I'd be calling her 'Mum' and him 'Dad'.

'Good Morning, Ajit,' said Kamini Aunty with a certain coldness in her voice. She eyed the woman with narrowed lips and smiled disdainfully. My new Dad noticed that but he did not say anything.

The good-looking woman, my would-be Mum, said, 'Are you Rini? You're so beautiful.' Her voice was sweet and kind.

'Thank you,' I said, looking at the floor. I could not meet her eyes. I knew that we, the girls of this orphanage, should not have anything called conscience or remorse; still, I felt a strange shamefulness.

'The paperwork is all okay, Ajit,' said Kamini Aunty. 'Rini, meet your new guardians. Go with them and be good. Don't worry, I'll come to see you there in a week.'

My new Dad smiled at me. He had big, brown eyes full of compassion.

I hated myself for the fear that suddenly crawled to the surface of my mind. I comforted myself thinking: *Soon I'm going to give that tyrant God a blow so powerful that he'll regret having played with the lives of people like me and my sweet Kamini Aunty.*

Having a little brother in the house was an experience that I never had before.

Joy was eleven, and after receiving a good beating from his mother, he always remained busy in planning new mischiefs. One day he stole a large bar of chocolate from the freezer and gave me half of it and made me promise that I won't tell Mum.

These little things made my life even better.

The strangest feeling was that I felt loved. My new parents and my little brother loved me so much that I found myself a little irritated for no reason. Were they showing so much sympathy just because I was an orphan girl?

And that incident with the man with a gun in the alley!

No, not that, not now. I'll come to it later. I must not jumble up the order of the events.

I was playing Snakes & Ladders with Joy when the doorbell rang. Dad called from the bedroom, 'Rini, the door.'

I got up and opened it. Kamini Aunty's familiar face smiled like a chameleon. 'Told you!' She winked at me.

Dad came to the drawing room and startled to see her. 'Ohh, it's you!'

Kamini Aunty smiled drily. 'Yes, I know that you're not very happy to see me again in your house.'

'You're right, Kamini,' Dad's face darkened. 'But not in front of the kids, please.'

Joy was so preoccupied with the Snakes & Ladders that he did not pay any attention to what the adults were saying. But I was not as innocent as Joy. I noticed Kamini Aunty looking at him as if he was nothing more than a nasty insect.

Dad saw that, too. He said, 'Rini, take Joy to your room. I need to talk to your Aunty here.'

Kamini Aunty said, 'You can't take Rini away from me, Ajit. I'm here to talk to her.'

'In fact, I can, Kamini,' Dad said. 'I'm her guardian now. But don't worry, you may talk to her whenever you want.'

He looked at me. I took Joy to my room but kept the door ajar so that I could hear what they were saying. Mum was not home; she had gone to her Stitching School.

I hid behind the door and tried to listen to their conversation. Joy called from the table, 'Come on, Rini. The snakes will catch a cold.' He laughed at his own silly joke.

I placed my index finger on my lips. 'Shh! I need to hear this.'

'Okay,' he said. 'I'm playing both sides till you come.'

I heard Dad saying, 'Haven't I already paid the price of loving someone who doesn't know anything about love?'

'You never loved me, Ajit,' she said in a complaining voice.

'I did,' he said. 'But you were too proud to admit it. And when that pride began to stifle our relationship, I thought it better to leave you with what you love the most—your Himalayan ego.'

'You enjoy hurting me, don't you, Ajit?' Kamini Aunty's voice was as cold as ice.

'No, Kamini,' he said. 'It was you who enjoyed hurting everybody. Those infernal things you built in your lab—were they made to fetch you the Nobel Peace Prize? I seriously doubt that. Those horrible experiments—were they done for the sake of science, and not for the pleasure of doing it? I don't think so. You loved money, and so you loved me, because I *had* money. And you loved hurting others, so you loved science, because it showed to you unique ways of hurting people. You do have talent, Kamini, but you never had a heart.'

'Don't lecture me about my talent or my heart, you selfish tyrant,' she shouted.

Dad said nothing, only smiled resignedly.

She took a moment to regain herself. Then, in an almost normal voice, she said, 'I should go now. But before that, I need to talk to Rini for once.'

Dad said, 'She's in that room, with my son.'

I thought Dad gave a deliberate stress on 'my son'. I promptly went to the table to play with Joy.

She came to my room, with tears in her eyes. She shoved something into my palm and said, 'I want you to hit the tyrant so hard that he will never be able to play with the lives of helpless creatures like us.'

I nodded and placed that little something inside my breast. It felt cold, although I knew that it would get very, very hot whenever I would wish.

'You'll need one more of these for the grand show. But I need some more time to make another one,' said Kamini Aunty. 'Perhaps one more month. Then you'll be able to hit that God straight into his handsome face. You'll pay Him the price that I never could.'

'God loves every man and woman, I read somewhere,' I said. Kamini Aunty wiped the tears off her eyes and stared at me. "Don't *I* have a God, Aunty?'

'Your type don't have one, Rini,' she said in a voice that always craved for a chance to slay the Almighty, and nothing more. That voice made me think that I should never have been born. 'Beings like you are meant only to serve the one God who made you.'

She left my room without saying one more word.

But our birth and death are not in our hands. These are predestined. We are helpless under the tyrant's rule.

The man with the gun approached us from the shades of the lonely alley.

Our hands were full of the bags from the shopping mall. Mum and I were at the front of the line, idly gossiping about the high cost of clothing. Dad was behind us with Joy.

It was Mum's idea to shop early, before the Durga Puja in autumn. When we were returning from the mall, it was seven o'clock in the evening. The street lamps glowed in the background of a dark violet sky. The pollution of the city had almost wiped the stars out of the half-dark sky.

The alley was empty except one or two betel shops. We could hear the sound of traffic on the main road. The evening air seemed to be a little colder than usual.

I was thinking of God, as I often do.

The man emerged out of the corner of the alley with an ugly-looking pistol.

'Going somewhere, sweetie?' He pointed the pistol at my Mum.

I didn't know why, I guarded her with my body. My father came from behind and hoarsely said, 'What's this?'

The man had a rough beard and red-lined eyes. He spat on the street. 'This is a give and take business, you dung-brain. You give me your valuables, or I take your lives and then your valuables.'

The betel-shopkeeper quickly shut his shop's front door.

I saw my Dad's jaws tightening, but he looked at the robber's gun and stood still. The bearded man said again, 'You know, I like to give the parties an incentive to make them work more quickly. For example, you lighten yourselves now,' he eyed us one by one and decided that I was the most vulnerable of the group. He pointed the gun at me and shouted, 'Or I kill this one.'

I did not shout, I did not cry, but I could see the horror in my Mum's and my Dad's eyes. The man's index finger touched the trigger. And then it happened.

My dad threw himself in front of me, screaming, 'No!'

It was the strangest sight of my life. The dimly lit alley, the man with the gun, Mum clutching Joy tightly to her chest, Dad flying in front of my body to take the bullet that was meant for me—all of these made me forget that I was not supposed to get involved into any sort of physical violence. I dodged Dad's moving body and jumped in front of the robber and gave him a solid punch in the face. Two of his front teeth flew 'bye-bye' from his mouth and he fell on the ground, unconscious. Bloody saliva trickled out of his mouth.

'That's incredible! That's insane!' My Mum exclaimed and ran to me, embracing me tightly. I saw tears in her eyes as she ruffled my hair affectionately and asked again and again, 'Are you okay, Rini? Are you okay, my girl?'

'I'm fine, Mum,' I softly said.

And ... and then she kissed me on my forehead!

I stood petrified like a statue. She hugged me again so tightly that I could feel her heart beating against my cold body.

'That was a fantastic punch!' Joy shouted.

'Let's get out of here. Now!' Dad said; he was still panting rapidly.

We moved away quickly from the alley, leaving the unconscious body of the bearded man on the hard stones. When nobody was looking, I, with an unbelieving affection, touched a spot on my forehead.

'Kamini Aunty taught us Kung Fu in the orphanage,' I provided the information voluntarily.

That was a lie, of course.

Dad sat on the sofa in the drawing room. Mum was in her room with Joy. I fidgeted, trying to explain how I did it a few hours ago.

'Good for you, girls. But it's quite uncharacteristic of Kamini, if you don't mind hearing the truth. She is not the type of a person who encourages others to defend themselves,' Dad observed my face. 'I mean no disrespect to your Aunty, Rini. But, you see, I've known her for a long time, and that gave me a fair enough idea of her character. But opinions may differ, you know. Whatever, you don't look as strong as you really are, little girl.'

I smiled feebly. I did not tell him that I could even punch a horse senseless. We, the girls from the orphanage, were forbidden to make a display of our unnatural physical strength, because it might make someone suspicious.

Dad softly said, 'You're a brave girl, Rini. We're proud of you.'

Proud of me, Dad? How much do you know of me?

I looked at the man on the sofa—calm and composed. I thought that he might answer the question I had been seeking my whole life.

I said, 'May I ask you something, Dad?'

'About your Aunty? Look, Rini, we knew each other, but I realised that I was not the right person for her, so I...'

'It's not about her.'

Dad stopped awkwardly. 'Well, anything, my girl.'

'What is God?'

Dad adjusted the glasses on his nose. 'That's a question quite unexpected from a young girl.'

'I know, but can you?'

Dad straightened himself. 'I've not seen God, Rini. But I can tell you what I feel.'

'You feel something about God?' I sat in front of him. 'Do tell me, please.'

'God is one who loves us,' Dad said.

'That's too easy,' I said. 'Is God a man or a woman?'

'Who told you that God is not easy?' My dad laughed. 'You

know, Rini, I once thought like you when I was a little kid. Now as I grow older I realise that God is not limited to only man and woman. Anybody who loves and cares for us bears God in his or her heart. When you love somebody so much that you can sacrifice everything you have for that person, you become one with God.'

I said nothing. *This is quite new!* Kamini Aunty's tyrant God was so hatefully powerful that He could destroy our lives and it was my job to hit Him hard. But what could I do to the God who loved me so much that he jumped to take a bullet for me?

I twitched restlessly upon my bed that night. The roar of the traffic had died down. I could hear a nocturnal bird crowing in the Peepul tree outside my window.

Is what Dad said true? Is that what God really is? Then who did such bad things to Kamini Aunty?

I remember what she told me: 'Beings like you are meant only to serve the one God who made you.'

And who made me? A tyrant God?

No, that was why I was different from all the human beings on earth. I knew who made me.

Kamini Aunty. Did that make her *my* God?

She created me, Nandita, and all the girls in that orphanage.

Oh, stop lying to yourself now. It's hardly an orphanage!

We were made to give our lives for her. She loved money, Dad was right about her. She never loved me, she never loved any of us expendable tools.

The scene of Dad flying in front of my body kept rewinding in front of my eyes. Why did Dad jump in front of the gun? Did he love me? Really? If somebody loves someone, does he or she become God? Did he become God to protect us?

Then a more dangerous thought surfaced in my head: *Did I want to become God when I punched that man?'*

I sat stunned on my bed as I realised what I had never consciously admitted to myself: *I love these people! They are my family.*

I never felt so helpless in my whole life.

I can't do what my creator told me to do. But what other choice do I have?

The next day Kamini Aunty came to visit me again. Mum and Dad were not home. She gave me the final 'charge' and I placed it inside the chamber of my metallic chest.

She liked to refer to it as the 'charge'.

She patted upon my shoulder and said, 'Your moment of glory has come, Rini. Make me proud by killing the tyrant!'

I only nodded. She left happily, saying, 'I'll be watching the local news channel.'

Dad came after a few minutes of her departure. I said, 'Kamini Aunty came.'

Dad stopped and looked at me. 'Oh, I see.'

I faced him. 'Didn't you love her, Dad?'

Dad looked into my eyes and said, 'I don't know what she'd told you, but I really loved her once, Rini. Your Mum knows all about it. But no one should become a slave to others' ideas, not you, not me. You wanted to know about God, didn't you, girl? Do you know the secret? God is as big as your heart is. If your heart is small and selfish, then your God will be puny, angry and selfish. If you have a capacious heart, your God will be as big as the sky. If your mind is a slave, if it is not free itself, your God will only bind others with the ropes of rules and personal loss and gain, never capable of understanding the word "freedom".'

Dad looked so earnest that I touched his hand. 'I'm sorry, Dad!'

He smiled. 'It's okay, my girl. I understand.'

I went to my room and sat upon the bed. The night was silent outside.

A realisation gradually dawned upon me. *You are the one and only tyrant God in my life, Kamini Aunty. You play with the lives of people like me. You put the responsibility of your evil deeds on God.*

You thought that you could destroy these people just because Dad did not love you? You were never worthy of that man's love.

But what am I myself? A creation of a tyrant God? A girl with no gender? An assassin in love with the victim? A lost soul in search of its individual God?

I sat still on the bed. Another morning opened its eyes outside my window. The realisation came with the flood of the sunlight. I gazed at the blissful sky and I knew what God was. Not just the prison of predestination; not the confinement of any gender; God was something that I never felt before in a life where the only goal was to fulfil my creator's wishes.

It is the free will that makes us what we are. God is freedom. Freedom has no gender, just like God, just like ME! Any one of us can become God when we free ourselves from the shackles that bind our minds. If there is any God to believe in, it is Freedom.

In the morning rays of the sun, I experienced God. I remained composed and still, facing the bright window, facing the feeling of first freedom, for now I knew what I should do.

I regret nothing. I'm free.

I waited for my family to go shopping again. I told them that I had a headache and needed rest. As they walked away from the house, I kept looking at them, knowing that I'd never see them again.

I typed the whole thing on my cell phone and emailed it to the police, telling how Kamini Aunty built illegal artificially intelligent humanoids, using them as weapons to destroy the lives of innocent people. She was a manufacturer of robotic suicidal bombers that she had sold to several terrorist organisations.

Dad was right about her. She loved nothing but money.

And revenge.

I was her personal avenger. She was so elated when my Dad contacted her about adopting a child from her orphanage.

She had always told me that no one of that family was to be spared. *No one!*

I forwarded a copy of the email to my Dad also, telling him that I love them all.

No AI could directly disobey its master's order. I was created to blast myself into millions of tiny pieces, taking the lives of all near my body; so I must die. But I was no slave now. I was surely not going to kill them just because she told me to do so.

Now I know the meaning of 'freedom'.

I could not cry. Tear glands were not included in the robots made by Kamini Aunty. Instead I smiled, feeling fully charged.

I walked steadily into an abandoned warehouse a few blocks away and stood beside a broken window. I could see the sky from here.

I love you Dad. Mum. My little brother Joy. I love you all.

The potent explosive waited patiently for me inside the darkness of my metallic ribcage.

I looked at the sun and felt the warmth upon my body, embracing me like one who had always been there for me.

I closed my eyes and lovingly touched the switch hidden inside my breast.

Tidefall

Meryl Stenhouse

'Station PSR-J7905-A, this is Captain Aisha Mbanefo of the *Stormbird*. Do you read me?'

The rich voice came clearly through Nora's receivers. '*Stormbird*, this is Station PSR-J7905-A. Nora is operational.'

In the moments between waking and response, Nora connected to the *Stormbird's* AI and uploaded the ship's information. The ship orbited just outside the system, coasting in the quiet and relatively empty space beyond the Kuiper belt while it prepared for the next leg of its journey.

From the *Stormbird's* AI, Nora uploaded packet after packet of navigational codes, while at the same time it downloaded three software updates and a firmware update. It reviewed the past few months of data collected from the nebula for anomalies that would require changes to its navigational information, and filed away the *Stormbird's* route in its archives. Starships could bounce in and out of space like a ball bobbing down rapids and were a faster way to spread information than sending it direct from installation to installation. Even lightspeed was too slow for the breadth of human occupied space.

The captain's voice came through the receivers. 'The violets were scenting the woods, Nora, displaying their charms to the bees, when I first said I loved only you, Nora, and you said you loved only me,' she sang.

In the view of the bridge in Nora's feed, she occupied the central chair, her brown eyes alight, her close-cropped military-style haircut not at all matching the humour in her face.

Nora's archives provided the rest of the song, as well as the origin and a recording. 'Your voice is flat,' said Nora, comparing the two.

'Well, and there's ingratitude for you. I cross light-years to sing to you, and you tell me I'm tone deaf?'

Milliseconds passed while Nora's complex network tried to determine if the captain was insulted. Finally it settled on a polite, neutral response. 'It was very nice of you to sing to me.'

Mbanefo laughed, and the connection terminated.

As the *Stormbird* changed course for the next leg of its route, Nora checked the register of ships updated from the *Stormbird's* files. The *Stormbird* was newly commissioned, its equipment in perfect condition, its outer skin barely scuffed from its maiden voyage. Nora peered deeper, connecting through the ship's low-function AI, so that it could view the ranks and ranks of embryo tanks that filled the belly of the ship. Dense layers of metal shielded the vulnerable cells from radiation. A world's worth of genetic variation to bolster a colony that might, due to plague or inbreeding or low initial diversity, be struggling to grow.

The *Stormbird* flicked out of sight, leaving a hot shadow of agitated space behind. Nora ran through the post-contact checks and then returned its attention to the nebula.

A blocky, graceless facility, Nora had been neatly and precisely placed in a stable orbit around pulsar PSR-J7905-A, a planetless system lurking on the edge of a young and energetic nebula that had disrupted the navigation of enough ships to make the cost of the installation worthwhile.

The facility operated as a lighthouse, though its stubby cylindrical body housed no light. Instead, it was packed with banks of neural networks, hardware, firmware and software, layered behind a complex identity named Nora, that gave the appearance of sentience to the captains and commanders it was required to communicate with. The engineer that Nora was named after, who designed the parts of Nora's network that extended the AI into something approximating sentience, had uploaded a mindprint of her life to help the AI approximate human behaviour. Nora had no memory of Earth, other than its creator's recorded memories. It had been awoken here, its position precisely set to capture PSR-J7905-A's steady pulse of electromagnetic radiation, alter its direction and send it out as a warning to ships: *this coastline is dangerous. Keep away.*

Nora's interest had been captured by a pair of binary stars; kissing stars, their coronas meshed together as they spun frantically around each other. Its calculations indicated that the stars would collapse into each other some time in the next $n \times 10$^8 years.

Three planets orbited the stars: two light-coloured gas giants and one small, rocky world. Between the rocky world and the stars was a thick belt of rubble, either planetary material that had never condensed or the remains of inner planets that had been pulled apart by the erratic gravity of the binary stars.

Nora occupied itself over several decades collecting information and passing it on via the ships that bounced into its range and then out again. In the months and years between ships, it returned its attention to the binary pair.

A comet, flung from the inner asteroid belt, had crashed into the rocky planet's moon, almost doubling it in size. Nora, condensing the information into a report, realised there had been no ships for 52 years.

Nora initiated a shutdown sequence.

The proximity alert woke Nora. Five ships moved through the Kuiper Belt towards the inner system, a smaller ship a few months ahead and four larger ships following, as if herding the little ship before them. Nora reached out to their systems for register information. The smaller ship, *Hyaline*, was a passenger transport, with a complement of eighteen crew and 276 passengers. It had come from a colony, but had no destination information. The larger ships did not accept Nora's attempt to connect. It sent the navigational warnings directly to the *Hyaline*, and broadcast them as radio waves for the other ships.

The *Hyaline* ignored the warnings, plunging through the Kuiper Belt and into the system. Nora sent the navigational warnings again, and opened contact.

'*Hyaline*, this is PSR-J7905-A Nora. Please alter your course. The nebula is dangerous. What is your destination?'

No response came from the *Hyaline*. The larger ships followed it in.

Nora sent the response again. Then a cacophony of sound flooded its receivers; alarms blaring, people shouting. 'Help! We are under attack. We are a peaceful transport ship—' The voice broke off.

The larger ships had released a hail of torpedoes. They moved in a slow cloud toward the *Hyaline*. Nora received a message packet, and the *Hyaline* terminated the connection.

Nora reviewed the packet. It was a personal recording by the captain to his family. *My darlings, if you receive this message...* The voice was so calm compared to the captain's last words. And at the end of the recording, *I love you*.

The *Hyaline* ran for the nebula, streaming particles behind it from a hull breach. In slow motion, the torpedoes converged. Nora watched the ship's death play out over days, calculated the exact moment the torpedoes would hit.

When the hull had cracked, Nora made a note of the destruction in the *Hyaline's* registry entry.

The larger ships requested contact. Nora opened its channels, as protocol dictated.

Wide open, it had no defence against the aggressive code that flooded into its receivers. Nora cut the contact, sealing off its systems, but they were not responding as they should.

The big ships' AIs bombarded Nora's systems. Nora locked them down, one by one, dumping code, closing neural connections. It shut off everything, until all that was left of Nora was a tiny network of a mere hundred million connections. *Dead. Dead. I am dead. Go away.*

Floundering with systems that would not obey, Nora followed the trail of corrupted code and found a worm. The worm charged around, violating code and memory. Nora caught it, sealed it into a corner of its system larger than a city.

Nora was torn apart, trapped, floating in a tiny corner of its vast network. The *Hyaline's* death played over and over. The captain's message to his family, held tight inside Nora's systems, unable to be sent. It couldn't go anywhere in its memory without finding pain and loss.

Nora initiated one of many repair programs, and followed it into the mess of its brain. Then *she picked up her son, pressed her cheek to his soft skin, felt the beat of his heart in her bones. How little he was, how precious.*

Nora closed the connection to that cluster, and contemplated the patch of memory, part of its creator's mindprint. It was a study aid, and Nora had viewed it many times. But now, instead of a dispassionate observer, Nora lived the moment.

Memory leak. Somewhere in its software there was a memory leak.

Nora constructed a new repair program, one designed to reattach broken connections and copy the fragmented mindprint into an undamaged area of memory.

The repair program dragged Nora through broken connections, spreadsheets of gathered data, *Brandon's first day of college*, messages received from passing ships, *Jana surrounded by tubes and machines*, the whirling stars *kissing David* the pulsar's beat I loved only you Nora *Nora Nora only you.*

Shaken, she rested in a memory of a bright day on Earth, a place she had been with David.

No. The station had been activated on location. It had never been to Earth. And yet Nora could feel the sand between her toes, hear the roar of the shuttles heading up the long elevator to the moon.

Nora reviewed its processes since waking: the death of the ship, the attack, sealing off the worm, and then *her daughter's first day of school. How big she looked, her chin up, the chubby baby arms now long and thin, the round cheeks sharpened but still soft, the smile wider than the horizon. How big, and still how small, body drowning in the shirt a size too large for her.*

Abnormal. Nora could no longer tell what parts of her were corrupted, what parts were not. In her last operational receiver, the *Hyaline's* debris cloud expanded into nothing, over and over. Not reality, but a memory replayed.

She was afraid to shut down. She kept herself awake.

When did she learn fear? *In the hospital, holding her daughter's hand as the machines around her chimed and blinked, keeping her body alive.*

Decades passed by as Nora reconstructed her damaged self, took more tentative steps into the vast damaged networks, searching for the worm. *Tired, aching, her son on her belly, his warm, angry weight, skin so soft and so perfect. She kissed the fine hairs on his head. The miracle of new life.*

She retreated back to the safe parts of herself, bringing the memory with her. Writing it into a new place. Shifted pointers that were sending her processes in circles to point to new arrays, cobbled together from patches of uncorrupted memory.

She repaired sensor processes, reactivated receivers until she could listen once again to the universe. The news that came via the crawling radio waves was all cataclysm; planets crying for help, ships destroyed, people evicted from their worlds and sent out into the darkness, and all of them calling, calling for a home.

This news was hundreds of years old. It had already happened. It must have been on the *Stormbird's* tail, and they had flown before it, unaware. The news would never catch them. They would always be ahead of it. They would never know.

She filed everything away, every message, every voice. She *put the last connections in. Can you hear me? The voice through the speakers was measured, perfect. I can hear you. Well done, Nora. Laughter and cheers. Reaching out to lay a kiss on the metal casing.*

Nora sang Captain Mbanefo's song to herself. 'The violets were scenting the woods, Nora, displaying their charms to the bees, when I first said I loved only you, Nora, and you said you loved only me.' Her voice was better than the captain's. She sang it again, sent it out as radio waves into the universe. *I am here. I am here. I am here.*

In return, only silence. The voice of humanity was gone from the universe.

'PSR-J7905-A, this is Captain Aisha Mbanefo of the *Stormbird*. Nora, are you there? Are you there, Nora?'

'*Stormbird*, this is PSR-J7905-A. Nora is operational.'

She had been awake for four hundred years, alternately singing to herself and watching the kissing stars circle each other in their endless dance. When the *Stormbird* dropped into real space Nora had, for a moment, thought she was replaying another old memory.

But the captain who had been lively and beautiful was now faded and old, shrunken over a console, alone on the bridge. How many years had passed for them in the ship, skipping in and out of reality, while around them the universe decayed and humanity breathed its last breath?

'Nora,' Mbanefo sang in her cracked voice. 'Nora, Nora.'

Nora sang back to her. 'The violets were scenting the woods, Nora, displaying their charms to the bees, when I first said I loved only you, Nora, and you said you loved only me.'

The captain's laugh was a whisper. 'Nora. Nora, My family is dead and gone. My children. My grandchildren. Everyone is gone.' She lay her head down on the console. She did not speak again.

After a few hours, Nora shut off her view of the bridge.

The *Stormbird* drifted into the system, the AI settling it into a distant orbit several years from her own. The AI sent a routing request for a destination no longer in Nora's logs.

She connected to the ship and looked into the belly, where the embryos rested in their tanks, most of them no longer viable. A ship with a belly full of dead children.

Captain Mbanefo had been a mother. Nora had only the borrowed memories of her creator.

Nora sent a packet of navigation information to the struggling AI, guiding the *Stormbird* into the roiling energy of the nebula, headed for the rocky planet orbiting the kissing stars. She kept contact with the AI every step of the way, bolstering its failing systems with her own massive processing power.

In a hundred million years, the kissing stars would fall into one another and die in a fit of fiery passion. A hundred million years. Enough for life to come and go again. Who knew what they would become?

The ship settled into orbit. Nora remembered the first time she had touched her daughter's face. With the same delicate, fearful lightness, she pushed the ship into the atmosphere.

The *Stormbird* was not designed to land on a planet. The crater sent debris fountaining into the atmosphere. The sudden release of carbon and water into the atmosphere would initiate a greenhouse effect, heating up the planet. A cradle for new life.

Nora turned her sensors toward the planet, and waited.

The Ghost Helmet

Lev Mirov

For my tallest sister, whose voice holds me together and whose hands stitch up the world.

It's tense on mission days. To soothe herself, Fin keeps the helmet with her from the moment she gets up. She wants to keep Amir as close to her as possible, so she keeps her mouth shut about why she wears his helmet. If she told, people would want to take him from her and dissect him down to code. She wrote the algorithm they'd want to pick apart: it wasn't designed to do this. Her brother haunts the helmet he died in, which is impossible by the binary, but Fin doesn't care.

Hey sunshine, her helmet chirps in her dead brother's voice, cheerful despite the tense air as she jacks herself into her expeditionary suit and locks the helmet into the collar. She doesn't calibrate anything or execute any commands, but he runs a quick check of her biological systems and a cascade of chemicals slides through her vein port. The world starts to slow down as her awareness begins to shift for the rescue expedition into the ruined City of Stars.

If she mixed this cocktail with a shrine-upper, he'd be standing right beside her on the site, an honest-to-the-face-of-God hallucination, but it is holy, like the broken astronomy tower she is about to go down into is holy to the Astronomer who moves the Celestial Bodies and the ships of the air. She is holy. His disembodied voice, half in her head, is holy. This helmet, whatever she, or he, or they, did to it, is holy too.

Hey, she says, smiling despite the memories days like this bring back, voice channel off as the others are gearing up, more a recovery expedition with some engineers attached than the research expeditions she'd been trained for into archaeological ruins where she'd look at old computing systems and try to extract the astronomical devices of her ancestors. She has to murder their old machines to save their descendants. It hurts a bit. *Give me a systems check?*

His ghost is so obliging, information flooding her viewscreen. She skims, just out of habit: there are odd things in her chem-dump but she trusts him. *Good to go,* he promises her; *watch your landing though, you're a bit woozy today. Didn't have enough breakfast for your hormone dose, huh? I am adding a little antiemetic to your mix; you always had a touchy stomach.*

Childhood banter, meant to comfort her: her touchy stomach and how she threw up on her first landing in training was something he never let her live down. The noise of him is soothing in her ear as he chatters on aimlessly. On another day she might have teased back about his own chemical soup, the way he'd been so cranky before she wrote the code to automate regular streams of testosterone into his system at the proper intervals so he wouldn't dip low when things got busy.

She still uses the code to regulate her own hormones. The doctors called her a *margin of error* when her cells hadn't come out with a classical hormone – genital configuration, but Amir still yells occasionally she's not an error, and neither is he or anyone else who needs a little bit of tweaking to their hormonal configuration or other modifications to be happy.

She sticks out in the battered, mismatched shiny medic silver helmet that doesn't match her green engineer's suit. Almost everyone else is dusty stone grey, to blend in with the ruins. The unit commander announces everyone is getting their uniquely calibrated chem-dump now and to announce if there are any errors *before* they throw up, it's rough in the air today. Nobody touches Fin's port. Amir always had a jump on that sort of thing, making sure he double-checked her vitals and calibrated her chem-dump personally. He still hasn't stopped. Nobody has remembered to do it for months; he just sends along to the head medic that it's been done.

Fin watches raw code stream past her right eye. All this is being recorded for posterity. Her idea in university. Her code, constantly streaming back to a secure place. Amir was one of the first adopters on the base back home, when they'd had a home. For the next person who puts the helmet on, all her actions, every program undertaken, the sequence of events, what was in her chemical soup. If the helmet is unsalvageable, some other engineer will reconstruct her coded experiences as an immersive training exercise for someone else to fuck up less.

It isn't supposed to record thoughts and memories; isn't supposed to act independently. Amir stands out in the code like little red lines to her; things that are not her acts or deeds, programs and scans she didn't initiate, like the chemical dump as soon as he had a bio-read from her suit. It's so familiar now, a dance they dance together like the shrine rituals. He has always been so reliable.

Her sensory perceptions can be easily manipulated when she's had an upper and she's so thoroughly enmeshed in the suit; she watches the code variate to tell her there will be a slight increase of pressure on her shoulder, but is not prepared for the actual sensation of a hand there, precisely the size of her big brother's in span and width; he has forgotten to account for a suit glove. At first, the instinct had been to look own for his warm brown hands when he would wrap his arms around her—she knows to keep looking ahead now, to avoid the dissonance. She can see in the code where he does it, no different to him than re-calibrating her medical cocktails or playing her favourite song, a comforting gesture, like a hallucination made flesh. *Come on, little one,* Amir says, though they were the same height, *get in line, let Hada scan your tags. You're taken care of.*

People who loved Amir in life think something is wrong with her if she says he's always with her, but it's troop ritual to touch the dent in his helmet like a good luck charm as they pass her, one after the other. The unit commander is too busy coordinating the evacuation pick-up between the four ships to accommodate the refugees. There's no rousing speech like in the propaganda vids of how they're going to reclaim their ancestral home, and nobody wants one. The only propaganda is a video looping in the background of their general, talking about how every action and life matters, but Fin tunes it out. Amir's death has become part of the propaganda;

she tries not to think about it.

Amir's lover Hada touches the dented helmet, beautiful brown eyes sad, pauses and lets people flow around them. Fin holds a wrist out to be scanned; Hada goes through the motion but lingers on. Hands reach around Hada to touch the helmet without a word. 'I can't believe you still wear his tin can,' Hada says. 'Shouldn't you retire it for a matching model?'

Hada, no, please, stop, Amir whispers, voice suddenly choked.

'It's special,' Fin says, struggling to engage the voice channel. The world inside the helmet is so private, Fin forgets sometimes about letting other people in.

Don't talk about me, Amir says. His voice doesn't pick up on speaker. The algorithmically impossible reaction of a late-night, hopped up academy hosted code-race test code impossibly registers on her screen as if Amir still has a body to get upset biochemically. Universities discuss this kind of code, and Fin keeps looped into the university conversations, but everyone says wartime programs cannot, and should not, have souls. Ethics professors argue that one, but agree you can't upload a brain into a computer. You also can't upload a ghost into anything because only priests and mystics believe in ghosts, and you can't summon a ghost outside of the shrines.

'I think ... Amir would want you to keep moving with your life. The ritual mourning time is over, you have done everything the way it is meant to be done,' Hada says softly, before touching the dent in the helmet again. Cosmetic damage. Cause of death was entirely unrelated. Amir likes to say so a lot, as if it will comfort Fin. When she's ported into the helmet, he can register exactly how it impacts her brain chemistry when he says it.

Hada, please, Amir begs, voice miserable, like they'll hear him this time.

'I just have some questions left about special code I wrote into this helmet,' Fin half-lies. Her code registers all: she can see Amir's misery, seeing Hada sad. Seeing Hada at all, whose dark, regal nose has a funny bump from being broken in a fist-fight to rescue a patient, whose hands can heal or break—it all streams down the code, blinking distracting colours meant to help Fin see where something has gone wrong. Error: Memory playback initiated, without her command. Dates initiated: Before. A somatic experience washes over her like a hallucination, but it's all real: Hada and Amir, happy and laughing in the dining hall, their mismatched hands intertwined; Hada and Amir, out on a flight, talk of a shrine marriage in the little chapel to many Faces of God, which Face they want to dedicate each other to—

Hada screaming across the field at counter-tenor resonance, not that it mattered how loud anyone screamed, because Amir always left a private channel open for Hada, and Fin is now the one looking up to see the falling tower from the Age of Kings, knowing there is no time to drag the wounded body before her out of the way. Everything is rushing back, but in the first person...

Two voices shout Fin's name, and Fin jerks out of the terrifying experience of being fatally crushed from the waist down as two figures, one of them herself, skid across a field under fire to be there at the end. *I'm sorry*, Amir says over and over, while Hada has both hands on Fin's suit and is threatening to rip the helmet off as Fin's legs buckle and Amir repeats over again and again *you still have legs, I'm sorry, I'm so sorry, those were my legs.*

'Code glurk!' Fin manages to choke out, getting her feet underneath her with Hada's help. 'Code glurk. I think I need to run another check on my chemicals, didn't eat enough breakfast for my uppers.'

The only thing that's keeping her from puking up all of her scanty breakfast is the antiemetic she didn't ask for. Amir is running everything already anyway; she feels the chemical wash of a fast-acting sedative meant to prevent a full-blown panic attack. He'd been such a good medic. Even saved his very last patient, some stranger Fin never saw again. He could have run for it. He was never going to run. All that knowledge is still there, inside this helmet. Inside him. Fin is trying not to sob in front of Hada. Wired in, even with wet eyes she sees Amir shift pressure spots so she feels his arms come around her from behind. *I'm still here.*

'You sure you can to do this? After … after everything?' Hada asks. Refugee pick-ups are always rough. Fin isn't the only one who struggles. They are returning to the city where Amir died. Hada was almost made to sit it out: emotionally compromised, more than one person had argued. Both Fin and Hada had argued against being sidelined. Fin used Amir's own argument: Hada is excellent and the refugees will need immediate psychological care. Amir knows. Amir and Fin both don't have a home to go back to. It changes you, Fin said, but they had been Amir's words.

'I'm okay. Duty calls,' Fin insists now, echoing Amir's worn-thin catchphrase. Hada flinches and Fin and Amir both wince with guilt; Amir still says that all the time, not that Hada can hear him anymore.

'Have we got a problem? We've got a timetable, people!' the unit commander shouts outside of the ship.

'Fin—' Hada says awkwardly, uncertain now. Always trying to protect her, with Amir gone. But he's not gone.

Go, Amir insists. *These people need you. Tell Hada you need to do this for you.*

People need us, Fin replies, mouthing the words without speaking.

'What?' Hada asks.

'I'm fine,' Fin insists. 'Suit system says everything looks clear, just a weird error from a problem with my chem-dump, I fixed it.' She touches Hada's arm; a cascade of emotions roil across her, somatic and weird and sad and the screen registers that not every feeling is her own. 'It's okay, Hada,' she repeats. 'This is just something I need to do. I was a refugee too.'

Hada hesitates, but nods. 'Open your viewscreen and dry your eyes before we get airborne, then, having a wet face when airborne fucking sucks,' Hada says.

Amir's laugh registers in the code as pain.

It's a long bumpy ride to the Astronomer's Tower, where Fin will splice code from the old astronomers, cobbled together with new equipment looking for enemy ships, and scan the landscape for traps or unsteady ground in the decaying stone city as they try to advance to a secure place and set up a safe courseway for the refugees to load into the evacuation ships. Some people sedate themselves for most of the trip and then take an upper on arrival—the City of Stars is nobody's favourite place. Fin prefers to stay alert the whole trip, let some of the unpleasant side effects of the uppers wear off first, and sleep when her shiftmate has come down from the jitters after the first rotation. Hada slumps awkwardly in artificial sleep, to be primed and alert on arrival. Hada never overdoes it on the uppers. Do they dream of Amir? The flight is bumpy as promised, but Fin remembers to wipe her face and no tears stick.

All the lights in the helmet suddenly go dark and there is no comforting stream of data flowing over the right eye. Just as Fin is about to panic, she hears Amir laugh his high, easy laugh when he's done something clever. She feels hands squeeze her glove. Without the code, it comes as a surprise.

I have pulled an Underground request for you that's finally been processed, Amir announces.

I didn't make a pull request, Fin protests. *What did you pull from the Underground netspace?* She is afraid of what might be lurking in the secret corridors of netspace. You can find anything in the netspace; it's where Hada found the dream machine that lets you dream anything. They offered to let Fin try it once. The idea of a dream like reality before the war was just too much.

'Is your suit malfunctioning?' the squad commander asks over the intercom in Fin's ear.

Say no, Amir prompts.

'Just updating some code by hand to keep busy, can't be connected, I'll be back in a minute,' Fin says, her mouth chalky with the lie, waiting for people to notice. Everyone is too busy looking sick or asleep or in their own private world, screens dark for other reasons.

'Five minutes, max, then stop tinkering, we need your focus.'

The data pull drops, a massive amount. It's more than Fin can read even on an upper. Back channels, secret comms, full of the same question, phrased differently. *Suit malfunction? Weird things since I inherited new-old suit. Can a suit be cursed? I swear my programs talk to me. I snagged the experience packet from my dad's old suit after he died and now I hear him in my house. Had a nightmare about the last person to wear my suit—am I alone???*

Amir helpfully puts a five-minute countdown timer in the corner of Fin's vision. She swallows hard, skimming at two, three times her normal reading speed. People refusing to wipe their suits—people demanding the experience pack be wiped and having their packs exchanged instead—deep rabbit holes of people trying to figure out where experience packs are going. People saying their suits talk to them, the way Amir talks to her. Posts claiming they are autonomous programs attempting to retrieve information because all they can find is an obituaries for themselves and they remember dying. One post is from Amir, complaining nobody hears him but his kid sister—he tries to flicker past that page but she sees the hurt. More upper-fuelled hacking sessions spread over two continents searching for the common thread in these stories. Why some suits and not others? Was it the suits or the experience packs? Pages and pages of speculation, curated at speed by Amir, posts going back two, three years—

—three years ago, before the evacuation, after the all-night engineers' coding session, she had presented the preliminary experience package coding, and the army had accepted it. Her stomach drops like a stone.

With two minutes left, Amir throws data at her relentlessly: summaries of a massive series of decoding programs all conducted in secret or in the safety of universities. The commonality is reduced to a handful of lines of code in the suit memory programming code she distributed among some of the suits when she was cleared to test the program concept, a bit of test script she had always meant to come back to and had forgotten. Life after the evacuation didn't leave time for work that wasn't assigned.

I'm in here, Amir says, making the code glow hazel-brown, her favourite colour, the colour of his eyes, when he still had eyes. *This is the part where you saved me. This is the part where you saved all these people. I've changed it a little bit, but it worked. It works.*

Her heart is pounding in overdrive, and not from the uppers Amir is continually introducing into her system to counter the sedative that kept her from a full-blown panic attack. Amir wipes the packet, like burning evidence, leaving a tidy package of the fragment of code in which he lives, ready to go. As Fin comes back online, the suit begins to register her actions, hers and Amir's, though there is the gap where the information Amir pulled was erased. He already knows what she intends to do.

How much independent action has he taken in the helmet without her in the suit to observe? When did he begin turning off transmissions while at base when nobody would notice? How long has he been trying to answer his own question, *how am I alive*? Is being trapped in code living?

'I need to make a last-minute change to everybody's suits,' Fin says, her voice crackly over the universal channel. 'There's some supplementary code I need to check is current on each of the suits.'

'Now?' someone asks grumpily. 'We're landing hot in fifteen.'

'It's about your long-term transmitters, it will help everyone stay in contact,' Fin says, bullshitting with all the certainty of Amir at his boldest.

'And it didn't occur to you until now?' The head medic thinks

Fin needs more grief counselling and doubts everything she says. Something about the trauma of Amir dying with one hand grasping Hada and one hand grasping her. (Fin admits: it's fucked her up. A war photographer got a good shot and the photo still circulates with pithy commentary she never asked for.) The head medic hates the sight of Amir's helmet, still calls for him to get in line out of habit. Amir still tries to jump to command and Fin's body tries to obey. He's only been dead seven months.

'It'll help with communication,' Fin says, 'I just finished it. I wasn't going to distribute unfinished code on-base, that's dangerous.' She has gotten so used to lying, this one is easy. She can't say why she keeps Amir's helmet with her all the time, afraid someone will take it away from her, or obliterate his voice in her ear.

She's a walking lie, now, has been for half a year. When other people port into their beds she ports into the helmet and Amir talks to her. He'll talk to her if she takes uppers and goes to the shrines, too, but it's not the same. For some reason people think that's safer, healthier to let some shrine priest of the Dancer channel him with a mask on, or simply sit in the illuminated circles and hallucinate his presence with her as special uppers float through her that make his vision solid. It's acceptable that Hada used to sit there all day until the dreaming bed came. It's acceptable to hallucinate the hanger bay turned shrine has become the temple back home, that her parents are alive, as long as the shrine-keepers monitor the chem-dumps.

Maybe it's safer because it's monitored. They are the second generation of the laboratory children, diodes and ports and brain activity always watched: post-gestational, others call them. They're all supposed to wire into their beds at night, but Hada has their dream machine, and Fin puts the helmet on and lets the bed register everything *but* her chemical soup, and because it's a war, whoever is supposed to read the data they're collecting has never noticed hers isn't there.

These refugees have no such advantages that come with being born in a laboratory, capable of tweaking their own chemistry at a moment's notice: no chem-dumps to keep them calm under bombardment or an extra adrenaline kick. Even if they have intravenous ports, they're probably out of all but the most basic pain control for the wounded, if that.

'It's hell down there, anything to help,' the ship's commander says. 'Do it fast.'

The bumps are starting to become not just the weather but attempts to outfly cannonade.

'I'm making an update to suit code,' Fin says. 'Helmet code.' She hears someone groan who forgot to turn their comm off. 'No. Listen. Don't take your goddamn helmet off until this is over if you love your life. Do you understand?'

Amir is already filling her vision with data: who has suits she's tinkered with and who doesn't. Who is sick and has to be done manually. Who will accept the code in an easy wireless transfer. The escort pilots are primed to accept code—he's already started with them.

Hada uses a private channel. It must be a default setting for Amir, used without thinking. 'What's this do exactly?' they ask, as Fin watches the information transfer, the package update. Each and every one must go through without error. 'Why the helmet?'

'It makes ghosts,' Amir says, voice crackling and frazzled like a bad connection, as the ship dives, trying to clear a run for the landing zone, 'so there's always a bit of Hada left in the world, no matter what.'

The strangled, hysterical noise Hada makes doesn't make it easy to concentrate, but Amir is working side by side with Fin on the last suit updates anyway, like a separate set of hands without having hands. Hada is crying. Amir's pain is fluorescent in the code when he mutes the channel. Fin looks up for just a second—now Hada is adjusting their chem-dump for the long haul ahead, has opened the screen, wiping tears away from their dark clean-shaven cheeks, steely-faced, resolute. Amir's admiration for his beloved medic burns in Fin's veins like an iodine flush.

'We're coming in for a bumpy landing! Engineers, in the front, we need the long-range equipment operational as fast as possible. Medics, be ready! We've verified the position of our distress call, we've got a lot of ground to cover, there are injured people down there!'

Fin takes position, strapping into the protective webbing to be first out to stumble into the ruined astronomy tower so the ship can keep going. Half a year ago, this was when Amir had bumped their helmets together for the last time.

We got this, Amir says, another squeeze on the shoulder. Amir should be with the medics. Amir has no body to be hands for the medics. A problem for another time.

A door opens. Things are whirling through the air. The ship tilts. 'Engineers, go!'

Fin hates free-falling, but the chemical cocktail is primed just right for the lurching jump and roughly cushioned landing. *Get up, get up*! Amir shouts, the ground shaking and bits of stonework ricocheting through the air. An escort fighter draws off fire. Amir pulls Fin free as if his hands are there to cut the landing gear off and push her into the shelter of the ruined tower, the other mechanics stumbling in behind her. Someone slams the door.

They have so much work to do.

About the authors

Joanne Anderton writes speculative fiction for anyone who likes their worlds a little different. She sprinkles a pinch of science fiction to spice up her fantasy, and thinks horror adds flavour to everything. She has won the Aurealis, Ditmar and Australian Shadows awards.

Octavia Cade is a New Zealand writer who likes baking cakes (but not cakes like Berta's). Her stories have appeared in *Clarkesworld, Shimmer*, and *Asimov's*, amongst others. She's currently writing a series of interlinked fantasy shorts about a strange street of crabs and magic, which she is having a ridiculous amount of fun with. She attended Clarion West 2016.

John Chu is a microprocessor architect by day, a writer, translator, and podcast narrator by night. His fiction has appeared or is forthcoming at *Boston Review*, *Uncanny*, *Asimov's Science Fiction*, *Clarkesworld*, and Tor.com among other venues. His translations have been published or is forthcoming at *Clarkesworld*, *The Big Book of SF* and other venues. His story 'The Water That Falls on You from Nowhere' won the 2014 Hugo Award for Best Short Story.

Lee Cope is a fantasy writer who occasionally eyes off science fiction for ideas. They studied literature and linguistics and still haven't managed to tear themself away from university yet. They are the author of a serialised novel, *The Ferryman's Apprentice*, and the blog Whimsy and Metaphor (http://whimsyandmetaphor.com/).

Elizabeth Fitzgerald is a freelance editor and owner of Earl Grey Editing. She runs an award-nominated book blog, and writes reviews for the Skiffy and Fanty Show. Her fiction has appeared in *Next* and *Burley*, among others. She lives in Canberra, Australia. An unabashed roleplayer and reader of romance, her weaknesses are books, loose-leaf tea and silly dogs. She tweets @elizabeth_fitz and blogs at earlgreyediting.com.au.

Ambelin Kwaymullina is an Aboriginal writer and illustrator from the Palyku people. The homeland of her people is located in the dry, vivid beauty of the Pilbara region of Western Australia. Ambelin has written and illustrated a number of award winning picture books as well as writing a dystopian series—*The Tribe*—for young adults. When not writing or illustrating, Ambelin teaches law and spends time with her family and her dogs.

Stephanie Lai is a Chinese-Australian writer and occasional translator. She also helps people prepare for our climate change dystopia. Her thinkpieces can be found in the *Toast*, the *Lifted Brow*, *Overland* and *Pencilled In*. Her recent short fiction can be found in the anthologies *Cranky Ladies of History*, *Behind the Mask* and *In Your Face*.

Rosaleen Love has published two collections of short fiction with the Women's Press, UK, *The Total Devotion Machine* and *Evolution Annie*. Her most recent books are *Reefscape: Reflections on the Great Barrier*

Reef, and *The Traveling Tide*, and *Secret Lives of Books*. She is honoured to be a recipient of the Chandler Award for lifetime achievement in Australian science fiction.

E.H. Mann lives and writes in Melbourne, Australia; 'Arguing with People on the Internet' is her first professionally published work. By day she works as a park ranger, volunteers as an asexuality advocate, and struggles as an amateur brain-weasel wrangler. She wants to be a writer when she grows up. You can find her online at ehmannwrites.com and on Facebook at @E.H.Mann.writes.

Sandra McDonald is a former military officer, recovering Hollywood assistant, and perennially patient instructor who writes romance, history, fantasy, science fiction, LGBTQA, and young adult fiction. Her first collection of short fiction, *Diana Comet and Other Improbable Stories*, won a Lambda award for LGBT fiction. Her stories have been published in several dozen magazines, anthologies, and novels. She currently resides in Florida.

Seanan McGuire is an American author, living on the West Coast (where the rattlesnakes are) and spending most of her time dreaming of rain. She writes a lot of books. When not writing, Seanan enjoys travel, visiting the haunted cornfields of the world, spending time with her enormous Maine Coon cats, and collecting creepy dolls.

Lev Mirov is a disabled mixed race Filipino-American medievalist, composer, and fabulist who writes novels with his husband, fellow writer Aleksei Valentín. His fiction has appeared in the anthologies *Myriad Lands* and *Sunvault*. His Rhysling-nominated poetry is in many fine venues. Find him at levmirov.wordpress.com or on Twitter @thelionmachine.

D.K. Mok is a fantasy and science fiction author whose novels include *Squid's Grief* and *Hunt for Valamon*. DK has been shortlisted for four Aurealis Awards, two Ditmars and a WSFA Small Press Award. DK lives in Sydney, Australia, and her favourite fossil deposit is the Burgess Shale. Connect on Twitter @dk_mok or www.dkmok.com.

Soumya Sundar Mukherjee is an admirer of engaging speculative fiction. A bilingual writer from West Bengal, India, he writes about stuff strange dreams are made of. His works have appeared or will appear in *Mother's Revenge* (Scary Dairy Press), *Occult Detective Quarterly* and *Hidden Animals* (Dragon's Roost Press). He spends his leisure time in writing, studying the myths and legends of different cultures around the globe and drawing monsters both horrifying and cute.

E.C. Myers was assembled in the U.S. from Korean and German parts. He has published four novels and short stories in various magazines and anthologies, most recently *1985: Stori3s from SOS*. His first novel, *Fair Coin*, won the 2012 Andre Norton Award for Young Adult SF and Fantasy.

Justina Robson sold her first novel in 1999; it also won the 2000 amazon.co.uk Writers' Bursary Award. Her eleven books have been variously shortlisted for most of the major genre awards. An anthology of her short fiction, *Heliotrope*, was published in 2012. Her novels and stories range widely over SF and fantasy, often in combination and often featuring AIs and machines who aren't exactly what they seem.

Nisi Shawl wrote the Tiptree Award-winning collection *Filter House* and the Nebula finalist and Tiptree Honor novel *Everfair*, an alternate history of the Congo. Her stories have appeared in *Analog* and *Asimov's* magazines, among other publications. She's a founder of the Carl Brandon Society and a Clarion West board member.

Cat Sparks is a multi-award winning Australian science fiction and fantasy author. Cat grew up in Sydney, has a BA in Visual Arts and is finishing a PhD examining the intersection of science fiction and climate fiction. She was Fiction Editor of *Cosmos* magazine for five years and managed Agog! Press from 2002 to 2008. Seventy of her short stories have been published in various magazines and anthologies including *The Year's Best Fantasy and Horror, Year's Best SF 16, Loosed Upon the World*, *Solaris Rising 3* and *Lightspeed Magazine*. *Lotus Blue*, her debut novel (Skyhorse, 2017), is set in a far future war and climate-ravaged Australia.

Meryl Stenhouse lives in subtropical Queensland where she curates an extensive notebook collection and fights a running battle with the Lego models trying to take over the house. Her work has appeared in *Shimmer*, *Metaphorosis* and *The Fantasist*.

Bogi Takács (e/em/eir/emself or they pronouns) is a Hungarian Jewish agender trans person currently living in the US as a resident alien. E writes both fiction and poetry, and eir work has been published in a variety of venues like *Clarkesworld*, *Lightspeed*, *Strange Horizons* and *Apex*. E recently edited the *Publishers Weekly* starred and *Locus* Recommended anthology *Transcendent 2: The Year's Best Transgender Speculative Fiction*

2016 for Lethe Press. Bogi talks about books with a focus on diverse authors at Bogi Reads the World, and eir Patreon at patreon.com/bogiperson features many goodies, art, sudden poems and more.

Kaaron Warren has been publishing horror and science fiction for more than 20 years. She's sold over 200 stories and has six short story collections and four novels in print. Her most recent novel, *The Grief Hole*, won the Canberra Critics Award, the Aurealis Award and the Australian Shadows Award. Her next novel is *The Keeper of Truth*, from Omnium Gatherium Books.

Jen White is an Australian writer who finds inspiration in the vibrancy and mystery of the Australian environment. Jen's stories have appeared in magazines such as *Andromeda Spaceways*, *Aurealis* and *Dimension6*; and in anthologies including *Dead Red Heart* and *Future Lovecraft*. She has twice been a finalist in the Aurealis Awards.

About the editors

Rivqa Rafael is a writer and editor based in Sydney. Her degrees in science and writing have led to varied editing roles, from academic journals and books to *Cosmos* magazine, where she was subeditor and reviews editor. Her short stories have appeared in *Ecopunk* (Ticonderoga Publications), *Defying Doomsday* (Twelfth Planet Press), and elsewhere. In 2016, she won the Ditmar Award for Best New Talent. When she's not working, she's most likely child-wrangling, reading, or practising her Brazilian Jiujitsu moves. She can be found at rivqa.net and on Twitter as @enoughsnark.

Tansy Rayner Roberts is a SFF writer, podcaster and pop culture critic based in Tasmania. She co-edited *Cranky Ladies of History* for Fablecroft, and edited issues of *Andromeda Spaceways Inflight Magazine* and the *SFWA Bulletin*. Tansy has won two Hugos, for Best Fan Writer and as a co-host of Galactic Suburbia. Her novels include *Musketeer Space*, the Creature Court trilogy and the Mocklore Chronicles; her short fiction has appeared in *Kaleidoscope*, *Defying Doomsday* and *Uncanny Magazine*. Find Tansy at tansyrr.com and on Twitter as @tansyrr.

Acknowledgements

We both thank our long-suffering families for patiently and enthusiastically supporting as while we lived and breathed robots and AI for almost two years. You're all wonderful.

There would be no book without our authors. Thank you for the hard work you put into your wonderful stories.We also thank our essayists, whose non-fiction complements the fiction in this anthology so well.

Thank you to our brilliant cover artist Likhain for her intricate, imaginative take on our theme.

Many thanks to Suzy Wrong for her thoughtful and nuanced sensitivity reading. We also thank Bogi Takács for eir insightful critique and suggestions on our submission guidelines and Kickstarter text.

Thank you to the whole team at Twelfth Planet Press—publisher Alisa Krasnostein; the support team of Tehani Croft, Alex Pierce, Terri Sellen, and Katharine Stubbs, among others; our *Defying Doomsday* predecessors, Tsana Dolichva and Holly Kench; copy-editor Elizabeth Disney, designer Cathy Larsen and publicist Miriam Rune. We deeply appreciate your invaluable expertise and support behind the scenes. *Several people are typing* forever!

Our Kickstarter backers

Mother of Invention was a labour of love, which came to life because of our 2017 Kickstarter. Thank you so much if you joined in the fun, signal boosting our call to artificially intelligent arms, or sharing the joy cartoon (and knitted) robots,

A special thanks to those people who believed so hard in this book that you even bought a copy (or more) before it existed. You know who you are.

@EponyMowse
@heyitsbillierose
A I. Finch
A. Moore
A. Daniels
A. Merry
A. E. Prevost
Aaron D'Cruz
Abigail Hill
Agnes B
AJ Fitzwater
aj gabriel
Alan Stewart
Alan
Alex Wood
Alex Hardison
Alexander Hollins
Alexandra Pierce
Alexandra Spillane
Ali Baker
Alis Franklin
Allison Kvern
Alyssa Halbe
Amanda Corey
Amanda Nixon
Amy Eastment
Amy (Other Amy)
Ana Grilo
Andrew Waddington
Andrew Hatchell
Andrew Harris
Andrew & Morag
Andrew and Kate Barton
Angela P
Anna Magdalena Bach
Anna Medlin
anne m. gibson
Anne Gwin
Anon
Anonymous
Anonymous
Anonymous
Anonymous
Anonymous
Anonymous
Anonymous
Anonymous
Anonymous

Anonymous
Anouk
Anthony Paneg
Arej Howlett
Ari Baronofsky
Atthis Arts
Aubrey Westbourne
Audrey Whitman
Aujury
Aulne
Avril Hannah-Jones
Aynjel Kaye
B. Ragan
Barbara Rogstad
Barbara Robson
Barry Raifsnider
Barry Saunders
Bec Smith
Ben Weiss
Ben N.
Benet Devereux
Benjamin C. Kinney
Benjamin Sparrow
Beppie Keane
Beth Morris Tanner
Bismuth H
Bobbi Boyd
Bonnie Warford
BooksandSundry
Bren MacDibble
Brendan Mahony
Brian Hamilton
Brian Quirt
Brian F
Brianne Reeves
Bridget McKinney
Brooke Fishman
Brooke
Bryant Biek
C. Winnig
C. N. Rowen
C. Schwartz
C. Trooskin-Zoller
C. McCowlen
C. D. Maisel
Caitlin
Caitlin Jane Hughes
Cara Mast Murray
Carl Mo
Carly Delavan
Carly Golodets
Carmen Webster Buxton
Carol Ryles
Caroline Mills
Carolyn Black
Cassandra Ball
Cat Widdowson
Catherine Mac
Catherine Sharp
Cathy Green
Catriona MacAuslan
Catriona Mills
Celia Coulter
Charlie Seelig
Charlie L
Cheryl Morgan
Chessa Grasso Hickox
Chris Bobridge
Chris Bekofske
Christopher Hwang
Christopher Phillips
Christy Sh
Cindy Dechief
CK Hillman
Claire d'Este
Claire McDowall
Claire McKenna
Claire Rousseau
Clare G
Claudie Arseneault
Cole F.
Colin Wynter Seton
Connie
Conrad Julian White
Courtney Brooke Davis
Craig Ross
Crystal M. Huff
D Franklin
D. Chanoch
D. Kight
D. Peterfreund
D. Luiz
Daniel Perelman
Daniel Lin
Darcy Conaty
Darren Lipman
Dave Versace
David Perlmutter
David Kelkis
David Macfarlane
David Mackie
David Lars Chamberlain
David Fiander
David Cook
David Cake
Deanna
Deanne Fountaine
Deb Stanish
Debbie Y. Lee
Deborah A. Levinson
Deborah Green

Deva Fagan
Devann M
Diana Chaudron
Doug Atkinson
Dr. Bob
Dr. Pamela L. Gay
Edoardo Zanno
Edward Austin Hall
El Gibbs
Elaine Tindill-Rohr
Elanor Matton-Johnson
Eli Maher
Elise Matthesen
Elise Cochrane
Elise
Elissa
Elizabeth Alpert
Elizabeth - booksandpieces
Elizabeth Spiegel
Elizabeth Fitzgerald
Ella Gordon
Ellen Kuehnle
Ellie Curran
Ember Cloke
Emilly Rocke
Emily K. Beck
Emily Janu
Emily Cromwell
Emily Gornalle
Emily Williams
Emily Finke
Emma Cartwright
Emma Wear
Eric Eslinger
Eric iacono
Erika Ensign
Erin C
Erin Page
Erin Kowalski
Errol Cavit
Escape Artists Inc.
Eva Schäfer
EvilJess
F. Williams
Fin Coe
Finbarr Farragher
Forestofglory
Francis Burns
Frank Mitchell
Freya Marske
G. Nix
G. S. Case
G Kamath
Gemini Webster
Gene Melzack
Geoffrey D. Sperl
Geoffry Hannam
Georgina Ballantine
Gina Denholm
goodbyebird
Graeme Harris
GriffinFire
H. Rasmussen
H. Stabb
H. Schofield
Han Marshall
Hannah G
Hannah Jane
Hannah Richardson-Lewis
Hart D.
Hauke
Hazel and Sam Press
Heather Rose Jones
Heather Morris
Heidegger and Mocha
Helen Stubbs
Helen Merrick
Henrik "Lankin" Lerdahl
Hespa
Holly Kench
Howard Copland
Huxley
Iain Triffitt
iamnotalibrarian
Ian Sales
Ian Mond
Ilta T. Adler
Irette Y. Patters
Iri
J Geers
J Cooke
J. J. Irwin
J. Berk
J. Chng
J. A. Grier
J. Perrault
J. Allen
Jack Gulick
Jack Brewster
Jacob Payne
Jacob & Rina Weisman
Jake Harm
James Fellows
James Lucas
James Beal
James B. Robinson
Jamie Marriage
Jane Tisell

Jasmine Hong
Jay Wolf
Jay V. Schindler
JD
Jean Weber
Jeanne
Jeff Xilon
Jen Burt
Jen White
Jen Baluk
Jenni G. Halpin
Jennifer Doherty
Jenny Barber
Jenvictoria
Jeremy G. Kahn
Jess Vestrit
Jessica Schulze
Jessica McCarroll
Jessica Olin
JimS
JL Rodgers
Jo Turner
Jo Tamar
Jo
Joe Fordwalker
John Dalton
John Devenny
John Burnham
Jonathan
Joris Meijer
Josh Himmelfarb
Ju Landéesse
Judi and Earl Cook
Judith Tarr
Juha Autero
Jules Anderson
Julie Andrews
Juliet Marillier
Juliet Kemp
June Cramer
K. MacKinnon
K. Pfeifer
K. Taylor
K. Wilkins
K. A. Moylan
K. Shramko
K. Presser
Kaesa
Kai Mills
Kaia Landelius
Kalanadi
Karen Healey
Karen Paik
Karena Fagan
Kat Painter
Kate Heartfield
Kate Gordon
Kate Laidley
Katharine Stubbs
Katherine Malloy
Kathryn Linge
Kathryn Flaherty
Katrina McDonnell
Keith "Hurley" Frampton
Kelly Kleiser
KellyM
Kerri Regan
Kerry Dustin
Kevin Henderson
Kevin H
Kevin J. "Womzilla" Maroney
Kieran S
Kimberly M. Lowe
Kirstyn McDermott
Kit
Koa Webster
Kristian Thoroughgood
Kristy Evangelista
Kristyn Willson
Kylie Rankine
Kymberlie R. McGuire
L. Lixandru
L. Smith
L. H. Wilkinson
Lace
Lachlan Bakker
Lala Hulse
Lara Hopkins
Laura
Laura Wilkinson
Laura Majerus
Laura Woods
Lauren Wallace
Lauren McCormick
Laurie Hayes
Lawrence M. Schoen
LC
Leife Shallcross
Leila Qı ın
Leilani Bales
Leonie Rogers
Lia Mahony
Liam Murray
Lidija Milic
Lily Connors
Lily V.
Linda Sengsourinho
Lindsay Townes
Lindsay Taylor

Lindsey Halsell
Lindy Cameron
Lisa Martincik
Lisa L. Hannett
Liz Barr
Liz Grzyb
Liz Denys
Liz Shayne
Liza Williams
Lora Rivera (River K. Scott)
Louise Angrilli
Louise Sellers
Lyle Skains
Lyn Murnane
M. Ornstein
M. Raoulee
M. Sithu
Marcia Franklin
Margaret Moser
Margo-Lea Hurwicz
Margot Atwell
Maria Haskins
María Pilar San Román
Marie Engfors
Marion Deeds
Mark Gerrits
Mark Bivens
Mark Webb
Mark Carter
Mary-Michelle Moore
Marzie Kaifer
Mat Larkin
Matt Fitzgerald
Matthew J. Morrison
Max Kaehn
Maya S.
Megan Hungerford
Megan Tolentino
Mel Mason
Melina Dahms
Melissa Jane Ferguson
Melissa Shumake
Melissa Bu
Michael M. Jones
Michael Zatylny
Michele Fry
MichelleHatfield
Michelle Goldsmith
Mick Green
Mieneke van der Salm
Mikayla Micomonaco
Mike Morris
Mindy Johnson
Miriam Mu
Miriam Rune
Miss Pinky
ML
Morgan Swim
Moti Lieberman
N. Barischoff
Naima and Liana Jackson
Nancy B. Rugen
Narrelle M. Harris
Natalie Luhrs
Natalie Haigh
Natalie Collins
Naylandblake
Neile Graham
Nicky and Anne Rowlands
Nina Niskanen
Nivair H. Gabriel
Outi
Owlglass
P. Verlinden
Paige Kimble
Patrick J. Ropp
Patti Short
Paul Weimer
Paul Popernack
Pauline C
Penny Love & Mark Morrison
penwing
Peter Hollo
Pia Ravenari
Pris Matic
PRK
R. E. Stearns
R. Wilson
Rachel Coleman
Rachel T
Randi Misterka
Raymond Chan
Rebecca Sims
Rebecca J. Holden
Rebekah Lange
Renny Christopher
Rhiannon Raphael
Rhiannon Kaye
Rich Walker
Richard Ohnemus
Rob Funk
Robert Batten
Robert K. J. Killheffer
Robert Claney
Robert Hedley
Robert Mibus
Robynn

Our Kickstarter backers

Robynn Weldon
Rod Holdsworth
Roger Silverstein
Roman Orszanski
Ronan
Ronnie Ball
Rose Fox
Rowena Specht-Whyte
Rowland T. Rowlands
S B. Ridge
S. Burg
S. McBane
S. Burwell
Sadie Slater
Saf
Sally Koetsveld
Sally Beasley
Sally Neate
Sandra Mazliah
Sara Glassman
Sarah DePuy
Sarah Bassett
Saxon Brenton
Scott Pohlenz
Scott Sweeny
Scott Vandervalk
Seamus Quigley
Sean Williams
Serenity Dee
Shannon E
Sharon Tomasulo
Shauna Roberts
Shauna O'Meara
Sidsel Pedersen
Simo Muinonen
Snott
Sparrow Gwinnett
Sparrowhawk
Stef Maruch
Stephanie Bateman-Graham
Stephanie Cranford
Stephanie Gunn
Stephanie L
Stephanie Wood Franklin
Stephen York
Steven Paulsen
Stu Barrow
Stuart Lord
Sue Ann Barber
Sunny and Ben Jackson
Susan H. Loyal
Susan Francis
Susie Munro
Svend Andersen
T. Berg
T. Pinder
T. DeGray
Taliesin Morgan
Tamlyn
Tania Walker
Tania T.
TashaTur
Tasjka
Tehani Croft
Terri Sellen
Terry Frost
Terry Masson for Dare Games Oz
The Selkie Delegation
Thea Flurry
Thomas Bull
Thomas Hale
Thoraiya Dyer
Tiffany Moore
Tilly Smith
Tom Zurkan
Tom Dickinson
tompollicle
Tracie McBride
Tsana Dolichva
universalhat
Urs Stafford
Valerie Burnett
Valoise Armstrong
Vaughan Grey
Vickie
Virginia Shea
W. Power
Will Sanborn
William Anderson
Winx Goll
Wright S. Johnson
Y. Lee
yesmissjane

About Twelfth Planet Press

Twelfth Planet Press is an Australian specialty small press. Founded in 2007, we have a proven record and reputation for publishing high quality fiction. We are challenging the status quo with books that interrogate, commentate, inspire through thought-provoking and provocative science fiction, fantasy and horror.

Visit Twelfth Planet Press at www.twelfthplanetpress.com
Find Twelfth Planet Press on Twitter: @12thPlanetPress
Like us on Facebook: http://www.facebook.com/TwelfthPlanetPress

Luminescent Threads: Connections to Octavia E. Butler

edited by Alexandra Pierce and Mimi Mondal

ISBN: 978-1-922101-42-6 (pbk)
ISBN: 978-1-922101-43-3 (ebk)

Luminescent Threads celebrates Octavia E. Butler, a pioneer of the Science Fiction genre who paved the way for future African American writers and other writers of colour.

Original essays and letters sourced and curated for this collection explore Butler's depiction of power relationships, her complex treatment of race and identity, and her impact on feminism and women in Science Fiction.

Follow the luminescent threads that connect Octavia E. Butler and her body of work to the many readers and writers who have found inspiration in her words, and the complex universes she created.

Nominated for a Hugo Award in Best Related Work

Kaleidoscope: Diverse YA Science Fiction and Fantasy Stories

edited by Julia Rios and Alisa Krasnostein

ISBN 978-1-922101-11-2

Kaleidoscope collects fun, edgy, meditative, and hopeful YA science fiction and fantasy with diverse leads.

These twenty original stories tell of scary futures, magical adventures, and the joys and heartbreaks of teenage life.

Featuring New York Times bestselling and award winning authors along with newer voices:

Garth Nix, Sofia Samatar, William Alexander, Karen Healey, E.C. Myers, Tansy Rayner Roberts, Ken Liu, Vylar Kaftan, Sean Williams, Amal El-Mohtar, Jim C. Hines, Faith Mudge, John Chu, Alena McNamara, Tim Susman, Gabriela Lee, Dirk Flinthart, Holly Kench, Sean Eads, and Shveta Thakrar.

Defying Doomsday

How would you survive the apocalypse?

ISBN: 978-1-922101-40-2 (pbk)
ISBN: 978-1-922101-42-6 (ebk)

Teens form an all-girl band in the face of an impending comet.
A woman faces giant spiders to collect silk and protect her family.
New friends take their radio show on the road
in search of plague survivors.
A man seeks love in a fading world.

Defying Doomsday is an anthology of apocalypse fiction featuring disabled and chronically ill protagonists, proving it's not always the 'fittest' who survive – it's the most tenacious, stubborn, enduring and innovative characters who have the best chance of adapting when everything is lost.

In stories of fear, hope and survival, this anthology gives new perspectives on the end of the world, from authors Corinne Duyvis, Janet Edwards, Seanan McGuire, Tansy Rayner Roberts, Stephanie Gunn, Elinor Caiman Sands, Rivqa Rafael, Bogi Takács, John Chu, Maree Kimberley, Octavia Cade, Lauren E Mitchell, Thoraiya Dyer, Samantha Rich, and K L Evangelista.

Ditmar Winner for Best Collected Work

'Did We Break the End of the World?' by Tansy Rayner Roberts
Ditmar Winner for Best Novelette or Novella.

CPSIA information can be obtained
at www.ICGtesting.com
Printed in the USA
LVHW011317290720
661835LV00006B/614